Queen of the Spinners

By: Anthony Fredericks

Copyright © 2000, 2001 by David Plieth
All rights reserved.
No part of this book may be reproduced, stored in a retrieval system, or transmitted by any means, electronic, mechanical, photocopying, recording, or otherwise, without written permission from the author.

ISBN: 0-75961-266-8

This book is printed on acid free paper.

1stBooks – rev. 2/19/01

Dedication:
To my family for years of support, patience, and encouragement.

And two people who deserve to be credited for their contributions:
Cover Model: Reischa Feuerbacher
Edited by: Leilani Rector

Chapter 1

When the sun rises over the Varden Wastelands, the view is one to depress the heartiest of souls. Roanne had stood at the edge of the devastated land only once in her short life, musing over the vast power it must have required to cause such a catastrophe. The Varden Wastelands, according to legend, once comprised a thriving port city, for which the wastelands were named, and the sprawl of towns whose proximity to the port was designed to capitalize on the prosperity resulting from the trading centers of the city. Many believed the gods themselves had laid waste to the region in their anger over the petty squabbles in which men had involved them. Those educated few, however, knew differently. Five hundred years not being long enough to wipe away this tragic reminder of the length men would go to satisfy their greed for power. Depending on the source of your information some even held that "Varden" was not the name of the city, which could not be found on any maps at the College of Wizardry, but the name of the wizard who caused the devastation.

Roanne was looking over the notes her father had made on the subject, and picturing in her mind the one time she had watched the sun set over the sandy dunes. She remembered how the heat of the afternoon had reflected off the landscape in waves that played tricks on the eyes. Somewhere out there were her parents. The possibility they might still be alive after all these years was slim, if there were any at all. It had been eighteen years since her parents left her in the care of Mathia, her father's brother, and fellow wizard. Three years ago, her uncle had gone off to Esconda for three months, during which she had run off, with the aid of Salina and her friends, to get a look for herself at the land her father had intended to bring back to life after all these centuries.

Roanne was a spinner whose talents were challenging the acceptance standards of the College of Wizardry in Altea. Since women had always been denied entry into the stronghold that housed the college, it was a foregone conclusion that women simply did not possess the talent for such studies as the men undertook within those walls. As a result, those women with talent, or power as Roanne had come to think of it, were relegated to tending the day to day needs for magic, such as minor healing, love potions, and charm making. Those tasks not requiring the special training of the college, and beneath the dignity of its graduates. "Spinners" was the term used to refer to them, or to insult a man who practiced the arts.

Uncle Mathia was once one of the strongest members of the Council of Wizards. So, Roanne lived in an environment where magic was in constant use, where the wizards from the college often gathered to debate issues and applications concerning their skills. The older men were too enwrapped in their discussions to notice the comings and goings of the young Roanne, and most of the younger students who often came to visit were enwrapped in the beauty of the young maiden for any to notice her deep interest in their activities. By listening and watching to what went on around her, and by taking full advantage of the vast libraries in the house, the one collected by her uncle, or the more extensive library left behind by her father, Roanne was able to educate herself beyond the level of most second year students at the college. At twenty years of age, though, she was far behind the men of similar age, and not likely to advance her knowledge much further. She had always been able to count on the help of other spinners, older and wiser, to get this far. Since the death of Salina two years ago, Roanne had noticed her progress was not as rapid as it once was. She had no one, now, to go to when she did not understand something. Early in her attempts to teach herself, she had learned her uncle had no patience for her questions. She was only a spinner, after all.

Though Uncle Mathia would never admit it, Roanne was sure there were others who would not dismiss her so casually. Pavlin for example, who had been her father's mentor, often asked how her studies were going when he used to visit. He was getting older these days, though, and rarely made the trip from Esconda, where he served as an advisor to King Sallas.

Roanne put her father's notebook away, it was past time she began preparing for the day ahead. It was the first day of the spring festival, which was a big affair in her uncle's household. It had become customary for Mathia to invite some of the more advanced students from the college to spend the festival at his estate, some fifty miles from Altea, home of the college. Also invited were the members of the Council of Wizards and other adepts, who brought with them their best apprentices.

That particular year, the festival also played host to a member of the royal family of Tularand, Prince Regus, to the surprise of Mathia, who held that the nobility of the kingdom deserved, for the most part, to be turned into toads, even if such a thing was not possible outside of fairytales. It seemed one of the nobility, Timond, son of Duke Bassel, had forsaken his inheritance, the powerful province, Bergian, on the border of the wasteland, to take up his education at the College of Wizardry. The nobility of the kingdom for the most part returned Mathia's feelings, and precedent held that while elevation to the noble class might accompany graduation from the college, no wizard was to be allowed to hold title in any of the provinces. Timond accepted this precedent, and left his inheritance to his younger brother, Andres. Normally, this might not have caused quite the stir this particular event did, but Timond's sister, Letitia, was betrothed to the crown prince, Regus, causing eyebrows to rise in suspision at such events so close to the crown.

Prince Regus' father, King Arantin Sallas, in the meantime, was getting along in years, and had decided part of the prince's education in matters of state should include learning to deal with the wizards who lived throughout the kingdom, in hopes of assuaging the anger of Bassel and a few other nobles over this situation. Leaving behind some of his apprentices for that year, Werdel, another member of the council, and a resident of the region of Bergian, brought Duke Bassel and Prince Regus to the festival so they might both learn a few things.

Roanne had no idea of the impending arrival of the prince on that day, but it was the arrival of one of the students at this festival that would change her life even more than her royal guests would. At the time, Calum was due to graduate at the end of the term, and had yet to accept an apprenticeship. Graduation from the college was only the first step in the struggle to reach the level of Adept. Afterward it was customary to serve up to five years as an apprentice to a current Adept, and then to distinguish oneself in private practice. Awarding the status of Adept was one of the many functions of the council, which also included complete governance over the practice of the arts, and jurisdiction over malpractice with the arts. Mathia was well respected among his twenty colleagues on the council, one for each of the nineteen provinces of the kingdom, and one for the king. A fact not lost on Calum, who also knew an apprenticeship with any member of the council was a near guarantee of eventual recognition as an Adept.

Needless to say the Spring Festival provided a perfect opportunity for promising apprentices to make a good impression on members of the council, and for students to impress potential advisors for their apprenticeship. As Roanne saw things, it was an opportunity for most of them to suck up to their betters, something those few with real talent did not need to do.

Second in his class, and obviously on the way up the ladder to success, Calum was one of those few. Everyone knew Calum was among the best, particularly Calum himself. With no need to suck up to anyone, his reasons for attending were far different from most students. Though brilliant of mind, Calum was seen very differently by people. Unfortunately, Mathia favored many of Calum's character traits, particularly those that would disgust Roanne most. What in Roanne's perspective was brash, conceited, overbearing, ruthless, and worst of all cruel, in Mathia's eyes became bold, confident, proud, ambitious, and demanding. Unlike Mathia, though, Roanne would learn first hand just how dangerous Calum could be when he wanted something, and since she was part of what he wanted, she was in danger. How much danger she had never realized until it was almost too late.

The first time Roanne heard Calum's name was while in the kitchens, checking on the plans for the welcoming dinner on the first day of the festival. Two of the serving girls were bragging of how they had caught the eye one of the students. Both girls were claiming to have been greeted with lusty pinches on the derriere, and then gifted with invitations to the young man's quarters after dinner that evening.

"My man's name is Calum," announced Shiva, a busty young girl, two years younger than Roanne, with fiery red hair that often caught the attention of visiting students. Her counterpart, Talia, froze in place as she was about to divulge the name of her pursuer, and lunged for Shiva, driving her to the floor. Talia was also well built for a young woman, but more muscular since she was often given heavier work to do around the estate, usually as punishment for every offense against the house one could think to commit, without giving grounds for dismissal.

"If I see you near that man the rest of the week," she threatened while securing Shiva to the floor by her neck, "I'll see to it that no man ever wants to lay eyes on you for the rest of your miserable life!"

It was more than obvious her lustful young suitor was the same man, and also obvious she had not realized Roanne was in the room. This was possibly the offense for which she could finally rid the household of Talia and her mischief. For now, though, there was too much to be done. Thema, the cook, managed to separate the two with the help of two other assistants, and Roanne sent Talia off to haul water for the baths their visitors would expect to remove the grime of the road before joining the festivities. Roanne also took the time to assign both girls additional work with the cleaning crews. Normally the staff worked at preparing for or cleaning up after festival dinners, not both. The punishment would insure neither of the two would be available to keep their rendezvous.

It was not until dinner was being served that Roanne usually met the guests, who had been arriving since midday, while Roanne was seeing to the preparations. It was her practice to work with the staff of the house for large occasions. She had done so almost all her life, and saw no reason to change when the running of the house had fallen into her hands after the death of Salina, the former stewardess of the estate, and Roanne's mentor. Her uncle had never married, so everyone just assumed she would take over. Because Roanne saw the staff as staff, not as servants, and left the day to day running of the house to them, she held the respect of even the older staff, even at her young age. It did not hurt, of course, that she was a spinner, and generous about using her talents to lighten the work of the staff whenever it was suitable.

After seeing everything was in order, Roanne was rushing to her rooms to change clothes for dinner when she ran into Calum, literally. The collision was only minor, but Calum's arrogance turned the mishap into a clash of wills that would eventually cost Roanne dearly.

"Ah, you stupid wench!" Calum screamed, looking down at the flour that had found its way from the fabric of Roanne's plain looking dress to his deep blue robe, the color symbolic of his coming graduation. "Look at this! See what you did to my robe?" He gripped her elbow painfully, twisting her around to look at him.

Roanne was set to apologize and offer to clean the garment, which would only have taken her a minute, when his words registered. During her long day, her hair, which was once carefully braided and packed away in a bulb at the base of her neck, had come partially undone, and her face, hands, and clothes obviously placed her in the kitchen. The dress was a plain drab brown thing she was not overly concerned might get ruined when she worked the way she had all day. "What did you call me?" she snapped back, jerking her elbow free of his grasp.

"Look at my robes, bitch!" Calum became even more insulting. "What are you going to do about this?"

"I apologize, good sir," Roanne feigned horror at the sight of his robes. "Here, let me look at that." She bent as if to inspect the damage. Taking the folds of the robe, Roanne used them to clean her hands.

A back handed slap drove Roanne back against the wall. "You dirty, filthy bitch! How dare you?" He waved a hand at Roanne, and she suddenly felt the air around her stiffen, holding her in place against the wall. "Do you understand who you are messing with? I can't believe your ignorance."

The pressure holding Roanne in place was so all encompassing she could not even speak to answer. Panic rose in her throat, the inability to speak would render even what magic she knew useless. She was defenseless.

Disdainfully, Calum took the moment needed to clean his robes using magic. He raised the powder and grease from the robe. Roanne had seen this little trick many times, and had even used it herself. The dirt swirled in the air in front of her face in ever tightening circles, until it made a small ball. Calum waved his hand again, and the pressure around Roanne disappeared. Caught off guard again, she slumped to the floor. Calum grabbed hold of her hair and pulled back hard. As Roanne opened her mouth to scream, the ball of kitchen filth flew in, stopping her. He held her a moment, waiting expectantly, until her eyes grew suddenly large. The ball in her mouth was getting bigger, and was soon causing her cheeks to bulge.

Calum walked away with a laugh. "That's more like it, silent and on her knees, like every good bitch should be."

It took Roanne several minutes to dig the obstruction from her mouth, using her fingernails to break it into smaller pieces. Shaken and crying, she made her way to her rooms, thankfully only a short distance from where her encounter took place.

It was not until her door was closed, and she was sitting weeping with her back against it, did it occur to Roanne to wonder what a student was doing in this area of the house. This wing of the building was almost exclusively set aside for her. Aside from her own rooms, there were rooms for three staff that were at her beck and call, and closer to the main dining hall and entrance were more "servants" quarters. Her wing also contained the rooms where her mother and father had lived, before their mysterious disappearance when she was still an infant. Uncle Mathia lived in the opposite wing, and the apprentices lived in rooms near his. There would be no reason for a student to be in this area. Guests were always housed in the third wing of Mathia's vast house.

Thinking more clearly by now, something else struck her as out of place. The student had used manipulations of air to entrap her, which was something she had never encountered before. On the table near her bed were a few books she had borrowed from her father's library, she could check them later to see what she could learn about his little tricks, so next time she saw him, she would not be so easily subdued.

There was no time, now. As it was, she would be late for dinner, which was not good at the best of times, but would really put her in bad light with her uncle this time. She had heard that afternoon there were royal guests in house for the festival. Being late was no way to leave a favorable impression.

When the arrival of Prince Regus was only a rumor in the kitchen, Roanne had considered whether she should change the dress she had planned to wear. Now that the prince was really there, she wanted desperately to make a switch. Laid out for her, though, was her original choice, and with the time such as it was, that would simply have to do.

She finally made her appearance as the guests were beginning to settle at their tables for dinner. Mathia spotted her at the door, and after excusing himself from his conversation with the prince, made his way through the crowd to her side.

"How dare you embarrass me like this? Where have you been?" he demanded.

"I'm sorry, Uncle," Roanne tried to think what to say. She was not about to raise the issue of her encounter with the student in public. There was no need to spoil the celebration for everyone. "There was a problem requiring my attention. I had heard the prince was in attendance, and I wanted to be sure everything went perfectly."

"Well it had better," Mathia did not seem mollified. "Now come along. I will introduce you to him. We also have the privilege to be host to his intended, Letitia, Bessal's daughter, and Bassel. Try not to embarrass me any further."

Roanne felt awkward in the presence of Letitia. The future queen was dressed in fine silk and satin, with intricate embroidery flattering her fine figure. Her hair was done up in an elaborate sculpture. Roanne was wearing simple linen, of fine quality, though slightly behind the latest styles from Esconda, and without the sophistication or elegance of her company. Her long dark hair, while as lustrous as any woman could hope for, fell freely down to the middle of her back, in the style of little girls it occurred to Roanne.

"I hope you can forgive her poor sense of time," Roanne heard Mathia finish her introduction.

"There is nothing to forgive," Prince Regus smiled. "I understand you are the one responsible for the fine reception we received, and this dinner. Actually, it is I who should apologize for the suddenness of my appearance, and the inconvenience it must have caused you."

"It's no inconvenience at all, Your Highness," Roanne curtsied as she was taught was proper.

"Please call me Regus, Roanne," he seemed genuinely friendly, and he took Roanne's hand and politely kissed the back of it. "And, this is Letitia Bessal, my betrothed, perhaps the two of you are already acquainted?"

"Unfortunately not," Letitia took Roanne's hand and held it. "Perhaps we can change that over the next week. I have heard nothing but praise for the way you manage the household, Roanne. Perhaps you might be able to pass along some tips on how you do it. My mother is usually in a complete panic whenever we host occasions such as this at Bergian, and something always seems to go wrong. Maybe, you can help me avoid such problems when it comes time to run the palace in Esconda."

"I'm sure any festival at Bergian requires much more work than I have with only the household and a small estate," Roanne was blushing slightly from the compliments, but greeted Letitia with as much grace as she had Regus. "It's hard for me to even imagine what would be involved in Esconda."

"Don't believe Letitia for a second," Duke Bassel stepped forward to be introduced by Mathia. "Your festivals here are heralded throughout the kingdom. I was thinking of possibly seeking your help in organizing things for Letitia's wedding. Today I have seen everything they say about the festivals here is true."

"It's the staff that does most of it," Roanne greeted the duke. "I will always be grateful to Salina, my predecessor. It was she who set the standards."

"Only to be surpassed these past two years from what I've heard," the duke was insistent, bowing in return to Roanne's curtsy.

"Well, the real test is yet to be met," Roanne suggested, "I believe the staff is waiting for us to take our seats before they begin serving the meal."

Roanne was pleased with the way that went, even if her uncle was still giving her angry looks. The dinner was a great success. Their cook could do wonderful things with the fish they got from the villages on the coast not far from the estate. As Esconda was essentially landlocked in the center of the kingdom, the prince did not often have the opportunity to sample such delights.

Roanne and Letitia talked quietly of the things Roanne did, or more accurately did not do, in running the house. Letitia was delighted, it had not occurred to her to simply let the staff, as she began calling them in Roanne's manner, do the things they did best, with as little interference from her as possible. By the end of dinner the two were becoming friends, and looking forward to opportunities to enjoy themselves in the coming week.

Queen of the Spinners

After the dinner ended, the guests began to mingle, exchanging greetings with old friends and acquaintances. Letitia went with her father and the prince, who wanted to seek out Timond, who was also somewhere in the hall. "I don't see what all the bother is about," Letitia commented to Roanne before going. "Tim is just doing what he wants, and Andres will make a fine duke when the time comes. I think I'll go with them, Tim will appreciate a friendly face after they get through with him."

Mathia took possession of Roanne's elbow and began to guide her across the room. "There is one other I think you should meet," he informed her. They were headed to the table where the apprentices working under Mathia were seated. Roanne realized Mathia must have been accepting a new one, which he did not do very often. This would give him three apprentices, and Roanne could never remember a time when Mathia took on more than two.

Roanne could clearly see the two apprentices she already knew well. Tagart had been in the house for three years, with only two more to go if all went well. He was a likable man, who seemed to get along with everyone. From time to time, he would be around to help the staff. Geralt was a more reserved man. He had another three years to go, if he lasted that long. Early in his stay with them, he had made a couple of careless mistakes, and Mathia was not the forgiving sort. It could be that Mathia was considering dropping Geralt, if he were willing to consider taking on another apprentice at this time.

The third man sitting at the table had his back to Roanne and Mathia as they approached. He was wearing the robes of a student, which was not uncommon at the festival since several students were invited each year.

"Calum," Mathia called when they were within hearing distance of the table. It took only a moment for Roanne to recall where she had heard the name before. When the man turned toward them, in a flash she remembered that face.

Chapter 2

Calum wore the same face as the student she had the confrontation with just before dinner. The angular jaw line, made all the more so by his beard, accentuated the point of his chin. His slanted eyes were distinctly sinister, and the darkness of his hair, which was not well kept, and poorly combed, turned his light complexion pale. His was a face no one could ever forget, and it was a face her uncle intended to have around the house for about five years.

Roanne's first thought was to wonder what Shiva and Talia had seen in this man to brag about his attentions, then she remembered his soon to be granted noble standing, which would attract most of the girls at the estate. Her second thought was much more odious. He had insulted and degraded her as casually, and as easily as a common street whore from the cities. She had been helpless against this man, and he was going to be staying in the same house with her for the five years.

"Uncle, I think I need to speak with you," she tried to pull free of his grasp and stop their progress toward the table.

Roanne's elbow finally came free of her uncle's hand as she firmly planted her feet. "Uncle," she finally had his attention as he stopped to turn back to her. "This man is the reason I was late to dinner. He accosted me when I was going to my rooms to change clothes."

Mathia's face was turning red with anger, but not at what Roanne thought. "Knowing you," he said. "You probably did something to deserve it. Now, are you going to continue to embarrass me, again? I should think there might some semblance of civil behavior somewhere in your mind, why don't you try to show it for a change?"

Calum was already on his feet. "Calum," Mathia's expression changed as quickly as he had turned on his feet, showing Calum a welcome smile. "Allow me to present my niece, Roanne. She will be the one to provide for your comfort during your stay."

"I have already met her acquaintance," Calum was quick to try and salvage the situation, "and I must apologize, I mistook her for a servant."

"No apologies are necessary, Calum," Mathia clapped the young man on the back. "She all too often behaves like one."

Roanne could not believe her ears. When the two men turned to her, she could see they were expecting something from her. "I'll see to it rooms are made available," was all she could think to say under the circumstances.

Calum's expression went from wary, and guarded, to a smug, satisfied smile, but Mathia was expecting more than that. "I expect proper respect for my guests, Roanne," he was getting angry again.

"No problem," Calum made an effort to calm the mood. "We just got off on the wrong foot, I'm sure, now that we know who each other is, there will be no trouble in the future."

Roanne had a scathing reply waiting on the tip of her tongue when she noticed a small movement of Calum's hand. The air in her mouth seemed to thicken, and suddenly she was unable to say anything. Slowly she backed away from her uncle and Calum, eventually losing herself in the crowd, and making a break from the room. By the time she stopped running, out near the stables of the estate, the thickness that had held her tongue was gone. She screamed her frustration at the night air.

"Roanne?" came a voice in the night. "Are you all right?" Out from the shadows of the house came Letitia. "I saw part of what happened, and when you ran out of there I was concerned."

"Letitia," relief loosened the knot of tension that had developed in Roanne's stomach. "I'm sorry if I alarmed you. It's just I can't stomach that man, Calum. He and I had a disagreement earlier. Now, I find out he's going to apprentice here."

Letitia laughed. "I know what you mean. He came just after we did this afternoon. Frankly, just looking at him turns my stomach. Fortunately for me, he avoids Regus."

Roanne felt embarrassed. She should not be dumping her problems on her guests this way. All she had to do was find some way to deal with Calum. There had to be something in her father's books that would give her the means to counteract Calum's spells. In the meantime, she would simply have to do her best to avoid the man.

"Look," Letitia suggested, "At least for the next week, if you want to avoid the man, come over by me or Regus. I'll let him know. That will give you some time to figure out how you want to handle this."

Roanne gave Letitia a genuine smile of appreciation. Time, that was what she needed, and was just what Letitia had offered her. All she could do was hope it would be enough time, for the next week she was going to be very busy with the guests and the arrangements for the festival. In spite of the advice she had given Letitia about letting the staff take care of such things.

For that week at least, things did not go too badly. The strategy of staying close to Regus and Letitia worked marvelously, and Roanne found she even enjoyed much of the week. They rode together in the morning hunts, and usually ate together for most of the meals.

She was busier than she thought she would be with the staff. Two of the staff, Shiva and Talia, were not seen for most of the week, and everyone assumed the two of them had simply run off after their fight. Roanne would not miss Talia all that much, she had been more trouble than help most of the time, but Shiva was a good worker. She sent out polite inquiries to Shiva's family, which lived on a farm at the outskirts of the region around her uncle's estate. No word came back, though, so she made plans to go visit once the festival was over, and make sure Shiva knew she was welcome to return to the estate if she liked.

Roanne also found the time to make a few discreet inquiries about Calum. Through her sources, she was able to learn he was not from Tularand, but from a kingdom called Curiland, which she knew was to the north of Tularand. It seemed magic was outlawed there, so Calum had come here seeking training, once he discovered he had the talent for wizardry. The Curilanders usually held the people of Tularand in little regard, and their monarch was openly hostile toward King Sallas, which explained Calum's tendency to stay clear of Regus. There was very little interaction between the two kingdoms, and most of what was known, or thought of Curiland, came by way of rumor. The other students at the festival said Calum was very closed mouthed about his life before coming to Tularand. At the college, Calum proved to be one of the better students, which was often attributed to his older age than most of the other students. His maturity seemed to provide more patience, which made it easier for him to master some of the finer details of the gestures, and chants required to properly perform magic.

Nothing Roanne learned was particularly encouraging. None of the students knew anything about using air the way Calum seemed to do.

The morning after the last day of the festival, Roanne came down to see Regus and Letitia off on their way home. During their talks over the past week, Regus had begun to develop an interest in Calum as well. That he was performing magic none of the other students knew about was particularly worrisome to him. On the last morning he made a point of pulling Roanne to the side.

"I want you to keep me informed on what you can find out about this Calum," he requested. "You can write to me through Letitia, which will raise fewer questions than if you wrote to me directly. I'll do a little checking of my own, and let you know whatever I find out."

"Why don't you just confront him?" Roanne was curious.

"Well, as you know," Regus answered, "The political situation between the Council of Wizards and the throne is not very healthy at the moment. Particularly with the situation involving Timond."

"So, you don't want to openly start questioning the activities of the council?" Roanne provided.

"You're smarter than you give yourself credit for," he agreed.

"Timond knows of the problem, too," Letitia mentioned. "He'll be asking around at the college when he gets the chance. But the professors are leery of him, still. They think he might be there as a spy for the king. Tim worries about coming across the wrong way if he's caught asking awkward questions about Calum and his magic."

"I'll also send you some information on Curiland," Regus offered. "That might help you understand him, and maybe find a way to deal with him. They are culturally very different from us, as I understand. I've read a few things, but I would prefer to make sure of what I know before I pass along any advice, so I can sort out the facts and the rumors. It would hardly serve you if I provided the wrong advice."

Roanne hugged and thanked her two friends. "I'll do everything I can."

"If nothing else," Letitia gripped Roanne's hand, "If you need to get away from here, you're always welcome in Ecsonda. In fact I am going to press my father and Sallas to have you there for the wedding in six months. So, plan on doing at least some traveling."

It was a comfort for Roanne to know she had the support of her friends, if not her limited family. Having a place of refuge if the situation were to get out of hand eased most of her worries.

The news later that day was not so encouraging. "Calum will be taking up residence in your father's old rooms," Mathia informed Roanne at lunch. "His things should be arriving tomorrow, be sure the rooms are ready."

"My father's rooms?" Roanne was bewildered. "Uncle, you know I use those rooms from time to time. They were just used to house Prince Regus, where will we put him the next time he comes? Where will my parents stay if they should return?"

"The prince can stay in the stables for all I care," Mathia's attitude toward the nobility came out now that the prince was gone. "As for your parents, it's about time you accepted the fact they will not return. They knew the risks when they embarked on their journey. It's no great surprise they did not survive it. It's been eighteen years. One would think you would be a little more grateful that I took you in after they left. The matter is settled."

Mathia turned to leave then stopped. "By the way, don't think I haven't noticed you've been messing in your father's library. Make sure all is in order there, because I'm giving it to Calum."

"You can't do that!" Roanne objected. "Those books still belong to my father. We don't know if he's dead or not. If he is, then those books are all I have from him, and I won't give them up."

"Your parents went into the wasteland eighteen years ago, with no word since then, and you don't think they're dead." Mathia countered her argument. "That alone shows how naive you are, and how useless those books are in your hands. You're a spinner, and that's all you'll ever be. It's time you faced that fact, too. The books belong to Calum, now."

Mathia left the dining hall, leaving behind a stunned household that had witnessed the entire exchange. Roanne left also, by the opposite door, and went out beyond the stables, where the Golden River flowed past the estate on its way to the Serpent Ocean, only a few miles down river. She had a favorite spot there, where she would usually go at moments like these to sort things out.

Her parents had gone into the wasteland when she was just a child. Her father had apprenticed with Pavlin at the royal palace, and the task that he had set for himself was to discover a way to reclaim the land that had been destroyed so many years ago. Mathia was right in saying that her father, Kendal, had known the risks when he undertook his journey. So did her mother, Ariele, who insisted on going with him. They had spent the last year of preparation for the trip at Mathia's estate, leaving Roanne in the care of Salina, should anything go wrong. Kendal was almost twelve years younger than Mathia. The elder had always maintained the task his brother had set for himself was futile, and the trip into the wasteland was an unnecessarily dangerous one. Kendal had been convinced the secret of the wasteland lay at its center, where, theoretically, Varden would have been.

Roanne was just reaching the point in her self-education where she could begin to understand some of the theories her father had recorded about the wasteland. If she gave up the books, or his notes on the subject, she would never get the chance to figure out what might have gone wrong.

A hand descended on Roanne's shoulder, startling her so she nearly fell from the bank into the river. "Child," Thema grabbed hold of Roanne's arm to steady her. "I didn't mean to scare you." Thema was one of the cooks, and Salina's sister. She was one of the few in the house who knew of this place. The two of them had spent nearly an entire day out here shortly after Salina had died.

"Roanne," she said once the younger woman secured in her position, "What are you going to do?"

"I'm not sure, yet," Roanne began to gather her resolve. "All I know is Calum will not get his hands on my father's books, especially the old tomes that are very valuable, and the notes my father took over the years."

"Does Calum, or even Mathia, know which books your father has, or what their value is?" Thema asked. "Salina knew more than I do, being a spinner, and she always thought those books would secure your future. Their value would make you a fairly wealthy young lady, and you have noble standing since your father graduated from the college. Salina always thought the books would buy you a good marriage, and since you're a spinner, even a high ranking noble would look favorably on such an alliance."

"Well the books are gone now," Roanne was on the brink of tears. "Which pretty much leaves me with nothing."

"No, not nothing," Thema corrected her, "It leaves you with some pretty good friends, and powerful ones, too. It occurs to me, if nobody knows what books are in the library, how will anyone know if any are missing?"

"Thema, are you suggesting I steal the books?" Roanne was stunned.

"Steal?" Thema laughed. "Child, what Mathia and Calum are doing is stealing. You can't steal what already belongs to you." Thema flashed that knowing smile she had always used when she caught Roanne up to some childhood prank, but did nothing to stop her.

"My father took some books with him," Roanne was beginning to get the idea, "Several crates of books in fact. I think I can pack up the most valuable ones left behind, but where would I hide them?"

"Oh, I think I might be of some assistance in that area," Thema eyes were alight with mischief. "My family comes from the farms out at the very edges of the estate. In fact Shiva is a distant cousin. I'm sure we can find some place out there for at least temporary storage. You'll at least buy yourself some time to figure out where to go from there, you, not just the books."

"Me?" Roanne was taken aback. "What do you mean me?"

"Calum has been asking around about you," Thema informed Roanne. "I can't be sure what he's up to, but I don't like him or it, whatever it is he's up to. You would be much better off as far from him as you can get."

"I'm not afraid of him," Roanne lied.

"You should be," Thema argued back. "At least give some thought to it. Decide where you would like to go."

"I'll keep it in mind," Roanne conceded, unwilling to share the offer of Letitia and Prince Regus for some reason.

That evening and night, Roanne spent most of her time packing up books and personal belongings from her parent's rooms and library. She had three trunks of books, and two with her father's notebooks. Thema was getting concerned all the empty shelves would make it obvious books were missing, but Roanne explained how that was perfectly explainable.

The few books she figured she needed to keep on hand, if she were to figure out how to counter Calum's magic, were set aside to consider what could be done to hide them. The problem was solved by the discovery of a few loose floorboards underneath the bed in her rooms.

As the sun began to peek over the horizon, the last of the trunks were taken down to the kitchen and loaded on a wagon. Sitting on top of the books in the last trunk was an envelope with a hastily scribbled note to Pavlin.

"Thema, I've been thinking about how dangerous you thought Calum might be," Roanne explained as the trunk was carried away. "If anything should happen to me, I want you to arrange to send these trunks to Pavlin in Esconda. All you have to do is write a letter to Letitia at the royal palace, and she'll make all the arrangements."

"I still don't see why you don't pack up yourself, and go now, with these crates, to Esconda," Thema was obviously worried.

"There are some things I have to do here, first," Roanne tried to reassure her friend. "I promised the prince I would do something for him. In four or five months I will be going to Esconda for the wedding, and I can go sooner if necessary. By that time I hope to know exactly what Calum is up to, and how dangerous he might be."

The following day was nearly as busy as the night had been. Mathia had not told Roanne Calum would be bringing all new furniture for the rooms. It was actually a relief to her, despite the hectic work it created after she had been up all night. The thought of Calum using the same bed her parent's had slept in had sent chills down her spine. She had all of her parent's furniture carefully placed in storage as it was removed from the rooms.

Chapter 3

Everything began to catch up to Roanne only two days after Calum had moved into her father's rooms. At breakfast that morning she was told Mathia wanted to see her in his study. Thema gave Roanne a conspiratorial glance, having a good idea of what it was all about.

"Where are the books?" Mathia demanded once Roanne had seated herself across the desk from her. Calum, the only other person in the room, was leaning against the shelves behind her uncle, looking her over suspiciously.

"What books?" Roanne innocently asked.

"You know damn well what books," her uncle was turning red. "Calum asked me up to your father's library this morning. There are an awful lot of empty shelves, and I want to know what you've done with those books."

"Why, uncle," Roanne seized upon his own words, "I'm so glad you are willing to concede the books belong to my father, not you, and certainly not to that toad standing behind you. So, I don't see what concern it is of yours where the books are. If you had been paying attention over the years, you might at least have an idea."

Over the past day, Roanne had decided she was not going to cower to either of the men she faced now. She had friends she could count on. The day before, she had sent a letter to Letitia explaining about the books, and asking a few favors to help cover herself. It was easy to explain away the necessity for all this. The information in several of the books she had taken could be dangerous in the hands of the Curilanders. Keeping such information out of Calum's hand until they knew better was simple common sense. That was one of the most puzzling things about this whole situation. Roanne could not figure out why the wizards did not see that, or if they did, how they justified it?

"Don't mince words with me, Roanne," Mathia was barely in control now. "Where are the books?"

"That depends on which books you mean," Roanne had carefully prepared her answer to this, making sure it was not an outright lie. She was not sure if her uncle would go as far as having a truth reading of her. "You were the one who told me my father took several books with him. I would think those are somewhere out in the wasteland now."

"He did not take that many books with him," Mathia was not going to buy that explanation, but Roanne had expected that.

"Over the years, several books have gone back to Pavlin in Esconda," she went to the rest of her explanation. "You passed along at least a few of the requests, so I know you were aware of that. I've also made gifts of several books to students and wizards I liked. If you would think a moment, you complimented me on the choice of 'Healing and the Art of Magic' as a gift for Herol after he graduated from the college. I can also think of several wizards, including members of the council, who have borrowed books. At one time I asked you to keep track of what your friends were taking so I could be sure to get them all back. Did you? Of course not, and I doubt any of those was ever returned."

Mathia was embarrassed now that she had layed at least part of the blame back on him. His expression showed he was trying to think, but Roanne knew he could not possibly be aware of how many books might be accounted for by those explanations. "I would never have allowed some of the more valuable editions to go out on loan," Mathia insisted to cover his embarrassment before Calum, "and you're even more useless than I thought, if you gave them away."

There was a long silence in the room, finally broken by Calum. "What about your father's notebooks?" Do you have any idea where those might be?"

"Those he didn't take with him are probably with Pavlin," Roanne suggested. "My father's work was, after all, under Pavlin's direction, since Pavlin was his mentor."

"I don't believe this," it was Calum's turn to get angry, and Roanne was just happy he had turned his anger more at Mathia.

"You told me everything I needed would be here, and now I find out you've let it all fritter away little by little. Perhaps I should seek out Pavlin, perhaps he'll have what I need."

"Wait, Calum," Mathia seemed scared, as the young wizard crossed the room to the door, slamming it behind him as he left. "I will deal with you later." Mathia threatened Roanne as he followed Calum.

Roanne found the exchange more interesting than she thought it would be. Something was out of place, most apprentices should be begging for the chance to work with her uncle. Mathia had looked as if he were prepared to do the begging when he had left.

Roanne thought a moment then followed the two men as far as the door, turning in the opposite direction in the hall, knowing they would be headed for her father's rooms in the opposite wing of the building. Rather than go that way, Roanne went off in search of Tagert, whom she was confident would have some honest answers for her.

Taze from the kitchen, a drink commonly used to help wake up in the morning, would serve as a sufficient bribe for the wizard, who often woke after all the taze was gone. He kept a supply in his room after the first year of his stay, at Roanne's suggestion, but this morning, Roanne would provide for him if he had the answers to her questions.

Tagert was traditionally a late riser, preferring to work late into the night and sleep in. His project was well suited to him, having something to do with star charts and moon cycles and their possible effects on the abilities of people to do magic. The college taught more than magic. There were also some science and other topics, though the college did make a token attempt to relate every subject to magic in some way. Tagert had wanted to do the project with Mathia mainly because of the location of the estate, which was free of the lights that hampered stargazing in the cities.

Anthony Fredericks

As Roanne expected, Tagert was still in bed, until she began to pound on his door. Shouts of, "Go away," and objects bouncing off the other side of the door failed to deter her.

"It's Roanne," she answered back, continuing to pound her fist against the wood of the door. "I brought you some taze."

"I have my own," a muffled voice replied.

"Tagert, I really need to talk with you," Roanne finally fell to pleading.

Finally, after several minutes, Roanne heard the distinct sound of the bolt being released from the other side of the door. It slid slightly ajar, but stayed there. Roanne pushed at it gently and it swung open. In the bathroom off to one side she heard water splashing, and a moment later Tagert emerged trying to flatten down his wild mop of hair.

"This had better be important," was all he had to say.

Roanne set the pitcher down on the only table in the room, after moving several papers aside, and began to pour for him. "I need to talk about Calum," she began a little nervously, "I just witnessed the strangest exchange between him and uncle, and I'm concerned."

Tagert straightened in his seat. "Oh, them," he took a quick sip from his mug. "I was wondering when you would begin to figure it out. You might not have noticed, but your uncle's influence with the council has been slipping the past few years, not that the council as a whole is doing particularly well. I suppose, if you really think about it, the problem first came up when your father disappeared."

"My father?" Roanne gave her complete attention to the wizard now.

"Mind you, I've never bragged that I was anything special, and my project is not going to turn the world on its ear when I'm done. I never said I was anything more than an average wizard. If I didn't need to do the star gazing, I could have done my apprenticeship almost anywhere. You never heard this from me, but your uncle was not in the top ten of wizards I would have chosen to work with otherwise."

"As for Geralt, well we both know he's a bit of a bungler. Your uncle hasn't mentored a real wizard in a long time, and it's starting to cost him in the eyes of the other council members."

"So, he really needs to bring in a top flight student, like Calum," Roanne concluded for him, "He might even be desperate for that kind of talent."

"It's not just Mathia, though," Tagert agreed. "That's what I meant about your father. Kendal is a legend at the college. He was the last graduate to really try anything of significance. Maybe people were scared by what happened to him, or the council got soft, afraid of losing more wizards. Your father was not the only one to be lost in those days. Anyway, the council is starting to panic over the situation. Roanne, you're a better wizard than half the students graduating from the college this year and you're self-trained. The council is looking for maybe three of the graduates to change things, and Calum is one of them."

"Do you know what his project is?" Roanne pressed, curious about why her father's library was so important.

"I don't know the specifics, but I heard him yelling last night at Mathia about missing books, so it must involve something similar to what your father was trying, might even be the same project, since no one," Tagert gave Roanne an apologetic look, "thinks your father will be coming back."

"Why not give this to one of the other students you mentioned?" Roanne was getting a much clearer picture of the situation.

"Maybe they refused," Tagert gave the obvious answer. "Remember, your father is a legend, and this was something he failed at."

Roanne glared at him, she had never accepted the idea her father was a failure, yet the wasteland was still there, and nobody knew what might have happened to him. "But Calum is a foreigner," she pushed for more information, "From a kingdom not on good terms with us. He has to learn something of the old arts that are banned here, because of the wasteland, to try and solve the riddle of it. How can the council let that kind of information into unfriendly hands?"

Tagert just shrugged. "Like I said before, they're panicking. The nobles, and the people in general, don't give the council the kind of respect they once did."

"Thanks, Tagert," Roanne began to gather up the things she had brought with her. "That explains a lot."

"Just remember," he said as she was leaving, "You didn't hear any of this from me."

Roanne had to keep herself from running as she left Tagert's room. She made her way to the kitchen, depositing the pitcher and cup in a sink. Thema, watching her from the corner of an eye, found some reason to cross the room in her direction.

"By the river this afternoon," Roanne whispered, "Do you think you could slip away for a while?"

Thema simply nodded and kept moving. Any casual observer would not have known there was any exchange between them.

Roanne moved on also, keeping as much as she could to her usual routine. Some of the minor diversions she allowed herself were to take care of things she would otherwise leave for the afternoon. Her uncle rarely paid attention to her comings and goings. To do what she was thinking, she would have to be sure nothing appeared out of the ordinary until it was too late.

That afternoon, she arrived at the riverside well ahead of Thema, giving herself time to organize her thoughts, and put together what she knew and what she suspected.

If the council was searching for a way to regain the respect of the nobility, this was certainly not the way to go about it. Their course of action could only lead to conflict between the two groups. The consequences of such a conflict would inevitably fall on the people, who in many areas of the kingdom were already overburdened by a ruling class that ignored the needs of the masses in favor of their own comforts. Apparently the crown was at least willing to entertain the idea of avoiding trouble between them and the council, at least it would seem so from Regus' recent visit.

Roanne had faith in Letitia, if not Regus. The more she thought about it, Regus was suspicious of the council, which is why he had asked her to spy for him. At least he was making a sincere attempt at patching up the relationship between them.

On the other hand, Roanne knew she could call on Pavlin for support. He was like a grandfather to her, sending her gifts each year for her birthday, and at each of the four season festivals. The situation might be beyond him, though, for surely he had objected to this plan, and it was proceeding in spite of anything he had said. It was possible the council was disregarding his advice. He was getting old, and Roanne could not even think who might be apprenticing with him, a sure sign his influence had slipped even more than Mathia's. Still, he was all she had, and perhaps he could be able to point her toward others who would rally behind her. They had to put an end to this as soon as possible. The longer Calum remained in an influential position, the greater the chance of his gaining knowledge that could be used against the kingdom. If there was anything Roanne could be certain of, it was that Calum represented a clear threat, and not just to her.

When Thema joined her, Roanne quickly related what she had learned. Thema knew enough about magic to be able to understand some of Roanne's reasoning on the situation. She needed no convincing that any clash between wizards and nobility was bad news for those caught between, the people, such as Roanne and her. Before Roanne could even suggest something had to be done to head off the impending collision, Thema was saying they had to do something.

"Is there anyone you can take this to, who might be able to keep things from getting out of hand?" Thema asked just as Roanne was getting to the plan she had.

"I think I can trust Regus and Letitia," Roanne nodded her approval of Thema's line of thought. "Hopefully Pavlin, or someone he knows, can take the other side for me."

"Then you have to get out of here," Thema jumped ahead. "They're all in Esconda, which is where you'll need to be. How soon do you want to leave?"

Roanne raised an eyebrow in surprise, then realized Thema had been pushing her to leave, this was simply a means to an end for her. "I was planning on leaving word that I'm going out riding in the morning, and was simply not going to come back. That's why I needed you, I want to send some things ahead to the outlying farms where I can stop and pick them up along the way, saddlebags with a couple of changes of clothes, and enough money to get me to Esconda. Once there I'll have access to the money my father left me."

"I'll have them pack you some food, also," Thema offered. "No sense in starving. We can also arrange for you to stay at farms between here and Esconda, it might be better if you avoided attention. There has been trouble in some areas, it will make your trip a lot simpler if you can avoid any of it."

"Thema? You sound as if there's some kind of underground network among the people," Roanne was surprised at this.

"Well, some of the nobles have been getting out of hand," Thema confessed. "So we've set up a kind of network to move around the people who get into too much trouble, before they get themselves flogged, or worse. In some areas it's gotten pretty bad. A few people have been killed for things the nobles used to laugh about."

"This is getting more and more serious by the minute, Thema," Roanne was suddenly unsure. "I wonder if I'm getting in over my head."

"You just remember who your parents were, and keep in mind all the things Salina taught you growing up, and you'll make out just fine," Thema tried to reassure her. "Your uncle should have taken you to the capital four years ago as a coming out. I wish I could be there to see the looks on all those ladies when they see who will be getting all the attention of the young men, at least until you decide which one you want."

Roanne laughed, and found it felt good. "I doubt any of them will be worried in the least if Letitia was any indication."

"Don't let them intimidate you. Letitia has nothing on you, and you have much more to offer than any of them. You're the Queen of the Spinners, child, and don't you forget that."

Thema gave Roanne the description of the farm where she would send the things Roanne would need the next day. There was a gnarled old oak in the front of the house, which would make the place easy to recognize. It was right on the road to Esconda, right on her way. The farmer's name was Ledin, and he would be expecting her.

Thema headed back while Roanne thought some more, trying to think if she were forgetting anything. Her books could go in her saddlebags along with the clothes, and she had to get them down to Thema just after dinner so Thema could send them out.

She considered what she was getting herself into. Thema might think she was the Queen of Spinners, but that meant nothing to the people she would be dealing with. Thinking of that now only served to bring out the frustration she had felt for years at being denied the chance to study at the college because she was a woman. Maybe, when this was all over, that would not be a problem for other women in the future. After all, if the lack of quality wizards was the main problem, the spinners could be the answer. She remembered stories told by Salina of things spinners had done that were more worthy of attention than some projects the apprentices were trying these days. There were also the things she had learned about her mother, who had accompanied her father not simply because she was his wife, but it was said because she was a good enough spinner that she might have been able to help him.

It was not very often a spinner and a wizard even got along with each other, much less married. Roanne could remember when she was a child, Pavlin would try and test her abilities whenever he visited Mathia, curious to see what kind of magic such a marriage might produce in the children. He never told her what conclusions he reached. Maybe it was time she found out.

She made her way slowly back toward the main house, being sure Thema would arrive well before she did. It was all she could do to keep up the appearance they were not meeting secretly behind her uncle's back. She did not see the pair of eyes casually following her progress through the pasture of stables, just as they had watched Thema not long before that.

Chapter 4

Roanne did not make it back to her rooms until after dinner. By that time, she knew exactly what she was planning to pack, and was confident it would only take a few minutes. After several years of retiring to her rooms early for the opportunity to read the very books her uncle was seeking to take from her, it seemed perfectly natural when she excused herself from dinner.

She entered her rooms and went straight to the closet where she kept an old set of saddlebags. Throwing them onto the bed, she next went to the dresser where she kept several pairs of breeches for riding, and for doing some of the work around the house. She did not have enough dresses to allow any of the good ones to get ruined that way.

As a last minute thought, she got out the dagger and short sword she had never taken the time to learn to use, and put them into the bags with the clothes. They were her father's. He had used them to protect himself before he had learned enough magic to make them redundant. Magic was a better and far less sloppy defense.

"Going somewhere?" an unexpected voice asked as she was stuffing the clothes into the bags. Whirling around, Roanne came face to face with Calum.

A lump rose in Roanne's throat for an instant, then her anger took over. "The door was locked, and you were not invited in," she stated the obvious. "Once my uncle hears of this you will find yourself tossed out of this house."

"Quite the contrary, Roanne," Calum did not show the slightest sign of agitation. "In fact, your uncle and I have reached an accommodation of sorts. Neither of us believes the accounting of the books you gave this morning. Now if you will come with me, I'll give you a glimpse of your future if those books are not within my grasp by morning."

Calum gestured for her to proceed him out toward the entrance to her rooms. When she made no response, he made a gesture, and it suddenly felt as though she was being pushed from behind. Losing her balance, Roanne stumbled the first few steps, then recovered enough to walk on her own. He came along right behind, with a real hand in the small of her back to guide her. Roanne turned her head to say something, and found her mouth stuffed with air again.

"All will be made clear in a moment," Calum continued to move her along the hall outside her rooms, toward the main house. The rooms Calum had taken from her father were on the main floor of this wing, actually below her own rooms. One of the reasons she had avoided even her rooms the entire day was the need to pass these rooms along the way. He opened the door to his rooms to let her in, then ushered her in the direction of the bedroom.

"I have acquired a couple of servants from the household to serve my personal needs," Calum explained as he placed his hand on the knob to open the door. "Of course, I prefer to call them what they really are, slaves." He pushed the door open as he said the last word. Putting an arm behind Roanne, he shoved her into the room.

In each of the far corners of the room was a small cage, the kind in which you would normally keep a large pet bird. Calum's pets were not birds. In the cages were Shiva and Talia. Calum went to the cage where Shiva was huddling and opened the door. Shiva had to crawl through the small opening, and once free of the bars, remained on her knees, cowering at Calum's feet. "Master?" she asked.

Calum laughed, reaching for Shiva's hair and pulling her erect on her knees. Roanne could see she had been beaten fairly severely. A whip of some kind had torn through the bodice of her dress, leaving welts on her back. Through the holes, Roanne could see where the fabric has stuck in the dried blood.

Roanne's stomach was turning over, and she knew she was on the verge of vomiting. Calum kicked a chamber pot, the kind used to allow bedridden injured or old people to go to the bathroom, toward Roanne, and gestured to dissolve the clot of air he had used to block her mouth until then. "In there, you stupid bitch," Calum ordered. For the next few minutes, Roanne deposited her dinner in the pot. The smell of the pot made it all worse. The pot had obviously been in use, and if Roanne had to guess, it was probably what he allowed his captives for relief when they had to go, so he wouldn't have to let them out of the cages.

Calum threw Shiva back toward the cage, using her hair. "Get back in your cage," he commanded, and Shiva crawled back through the door. Calum took a moment to wave his hands around the closed latch, which was probably how he kept the cage locked.

"I would say they are coming along just fine," Calum returned his attention to Roanne. He did some more gestures and, the gag was once more in place. "You're making progress as well. How did I put it to you the other day? Something about every good bitch should be silent and on her knees." Roanne had collapsed to the floor in the process of being sick. She stood up glaring at him in defiance.

Roanne shifted her view to Talia, who was sleeping contentedly in the bottom of her cage. Talia wore a revealing nightgown, and there was no sign of a mark on her. The thought she would be cooperating with Calum threatened to turn Roanne's stomach in a different way.

Calum moved to the foot of the bed where he pulled a sheet aside to reveal a third cage, which was shorter than the other two, but spanned the entire width of the bed. "This is for you, eventually," Calum informed Roanne. "Now we can make this easy, or we can do it the hard way. For now, I'm perfectly willing to be lenient, and let you remain in your own rooms until the wedding, by which time I expect you'll be well enough trained to be as cooperative as Talia, there."

Roanne could only look at him in confusion, surely her uncle had not agreed to such a wedding. He had to know she would never agree to such an arrangement. Roanne tried to back away from him toward the door of the room, but ran into a solid obstacle where there should not have been one. She turned first to the right, then left, only to find the same thing.

"I have a present for you, in honor of our engagement," Calum went to a table and picked something up, but Roanne could not see anything. The walls to each side of her seemed to close as he moved his hands together, pinning her arms at her sides. He came forward then, until he was standing right in front of her. "I believe it is the responsibility of all men to control their pets. While I'm willing to let you stay in your rooms I must be sure you behave yourself." His hands circled her throat, and when they came away, left something behind that held her neck tightly in its grasp. The walls around Roanne were suddenly gone. As Calum finished the movement of his hands that dispersed the walls he made a pulling motion, and Roanne was jerked from her feet by the thing he had place on her. He continued to pull, drawing her toward him. Roanne began to resist, but the thing that held her began to tighten, cutting off her breath. In order to get more air for her laboring lungs, she had to give in to the pull. Calum continued to pull, until Roanne was kneeling at his feet as he sat on the bed. "Good girl," Calum commented as he reached out and stroked her hair.

"Allow me to explain how I plan to train you," Calum made himself comfortable on the bed. "In order to control you, I have placed a collar around your throat, which comes complete with a leash. Every good pet should come with such an arrangement. The collar will choke you whenever you try to resist it. So, over the next weeks you will be conditioned to obey whatever I tell you. By the time we marry, you'll happily and enthusiastically come crawling to your new home." He patted the top of the cage.

Roanne's mind was in shock. Not one coherent thought would come to stand out above her fear and confusion. It was all madness. How could her uncle have agreed to this? She was trapped, with no way out. Given enough time, Calum could break anyone down. Maybe she should just kill herself.

"Now let's return you to your rooms," he laughed, "We wouldn't want anyone to think anything improper is happening between the two of us before we're married. I think the concept of a virgin bride is rather quaint, virgins fetch a very high price where I come from."

Calum pulled on the leash as he stood and turned toward the door. Roanne barely made it to her feet, and came stumbling after him. She wanted to scream, to call for help. Surely Thema would rally the rest of the staff to her aid. An overwhelming sense helplessness drained all hope of escape as she passively allowed herself to be led back to her rooms like a pet dog on a leash. She would give in, that would be the easiest thing to do, and the least painful. That must have been what Talia had done.

Back in Roanne's rooms, Calum took her to the bedroom. There he made a few gestures around the post holding up the canopy over her bed. "There should be enough slack in the leash to let you roam freely within the confines of your rooms, but you will not be allowed to leave. Talia has come along far enough I can trust her to come feed you, if I happen to remember."

He picked up the saddlebags Roanne had been packing. "You obviously will not be needing any of these things. I prefer to see you dressed in pretty gowns, so that is all you will be allowed from now on. I shall have a selection made for you that suits my tastes."

He turned away from her and began to leave. "By the way, all my reassurances are off if you do not tell where the books are first thing in the morning. In that case, you will be whipped until you wish you were dead. One way or the other, you will tell me." He blew a kiss at her, of all things, then turned and left.

Roanne tried to scream, but could not with her mouth full. She ran for the doors, only to be pulled up just short of them, her feet flying out from beneath her, landing her hard on her backside. Her anger took control, providing a focus for her thoughts. She would kill him, or escape. Something would come up to give her the chance. The books, they were still under the bed since she had not packed them. They might have a way to break the spell that held her. There was not time for that, though, it would take days to sort through the old tomes she had.

She moved slowly toward the door until she felt the tether grow taunt, then searched the air behind her until she felt the brush of a thin strand of tightly compacted air. It was easy for her to recognize it for what it was by comparing the feel to that around her throat. She pulled on it as hard as she could, hoping it would break, but knowing that was not likely. She had felt the crushing strength of the walls Calum had used to trap her.

Gathering the air leash as she went, she made her way back toward the bedroom, lighting the room with an almost negligent thought and gesture that brought the lamps to life. The dagger and sword were gone with her bags, but she had other things that were just as sharp, the scissors she used to trim the split ends from her hair, another dagger that was more ornamental, but still sharp. The strand of air might not break, but maybe it could be cut. It didn't work. In frustration she threw the dagger across the room.

Panic threatened to overwhelm her again, she could feel the tears coming, and she had the urge to curl up on the bed and simply cry. She concentrated on her anger, giving the tether a hard yank, then pulled again harder and longer.

It was hardly louder than a whisper, but in the silence of the night it caught the edge of her attention. Puzzled she looked around, then pulled again, and again heard the noise. Careful to gather the tether as she moved, she made her way over to the bed.

The bed, not the tether, was the weak link in Calum's trap. Following the feel of the tether, she found it was connected to the post right where the post was anchored to the foot of the bed. Roanne lay down, bracing her feet against the bed she pulled again, managing even more force with the help of her legs. The wood groaned as it resisted the force she applied to it. Again, and then again, she tried to pull. By the time she gave up, she was sweating from her efforts. Feeling around the base of the post, she tried to shift the tether up along the post, thinking it would be less sturdy more toward the center. Where it was, the baseboard provided added stability. Cursing the intricate design she herself had chosen, she found the tether was too tight to slide over the spindles decorating the surface of the wood. Her hands ached, and when she looked at them she noticed the thin strand had been cutting through the skin. She was bleeding enough to leave drops on the rug on the floor.

Roanne let go a hysterical laugh. "You're an idiot," she said to herself. "Almost every day you use magic so something like this won't happen to the staff, and you do it to yourself. Magic!"

Her head swung around to look at the lamps along the wall that she had lit so casually a moment ago, then turned back to the bedpost. It was so simple. She could burn the wood in the post. She concentrated a moment, wanting to be sure she controlled the spell, then made the appropriate gestures and rattled off the words in her mind. What she wanted was for the heat of the wood to rise slowly. She did not want to burn down the house after all. For a brief second she considered whether she did or not, but brushed that aside to concentrate on the spell. Suddenly, the base of the post exploded in flame. Roanne, who had been pulling to maintain the pressure on the tether, reeled backward releasing her grip on the tether in an effort to break her fall. The flame was racing along the tether now, and if she had been gripping it, her hands would have been seared as well as cut. She watched as the flame reached where she had placed the coil of air she had gathered, and blinked as flames spurted up, leaving the burned outline of a rope coil on the rug. The fire marched on along the length of the tether, and it dawned on Roanne it would reach her throat in next few seconds. Frantically, she extinguished the fire as easily as she had started it.

Roanne stared in wonderment at the charred remains of the bedpost, and coiled design burned into the rug. Seemingly out of nowhere, she recalled the basic lesson in the use of magic to make fire. Fire needed air to feed on. It would follow that if you compressed the air into a solid form, it might burn. Her hands went to the band, still tightly wrapped around her neck. She was going to have to be very careful around fires until she could rid herself of that.

A moment later she had her second awakening. She was free. Scrambling to the side of the bed, Roanne reached underneath, slid aside the loose boards and removed the books from their hiding place. She fetched a pillowcase to use as a satchel and packed the books inside. In her drawer were one last set of breeches, and a small man's shirt that would suffice as a riding blouse. Her dark cloak would help to hide her movements in the night. All she had to do was find her way to the stables, and she could still be well gone from here by the time the sun came up.

She headed for the door and stopped almost in mid step. To leave that way she would have to pass the rooms where Calum was no doubt sleeping by now, or tormenting Shiva and Talia. That was not a risk she cared to take, if she were caught, she had no doubt she would end up inside the little cage he had for her. Instead, she crossed to her bedroom window. Every kid had a secret way to slip in and out of his or her rooms, and she had been no exception.

Chapter 5

From her window, Roanne made it out onto the roof of the corridor that led from her wing of the house to the main house. Near the back of the house was a woodpile for supplying the kitchens, which she used to climb down to the ground. As she reached the ground, she thought of Thema. The least she could do was warn the woman, take her along even, to make sure she was safe. In fact, all the women should get out while they could. Then the thought of Shiva and Talia hit her. It agonized her to leave them behind, but that was simply not a risk she could take.

Thema's room was near the back door, and was easy to slip into. She was in bed, with the covers pulled up. Roanne almost pounced on her, covering her mouth to make sure she did not cry out. There was no reaction at all, though, and Thema felt cold.

Roanne pulled back, then tentatively reached out, rolling Thema over. Thema's eyes were wide open, as was her mouth. But there was no life in them.

Roanne heard footsteps and whispers in the hall. She moved into the closet to hide just in time, as two men entered the room.

"You killed her," came a voice as one of the men bent to examine the body. Roanne recognized the voice as Geralt's.

"Shut up, you idiot," Calum hissed. "Do you want to wake the others? Just help me wrap her in the sheets, and we'll go dump her in the river."

"But ..." Geralt hesitated.

"Look," Calum grabbed Geralt by the collar, "If you want any chance of becoming a real wizard you better help me. Otherwise, you can join her in the river. Do I make myself clear?"

Geralt had no response except to begin folding the bedding over the top of Thema's body. While the two men worked, Roanne realized it would take them some time to drag the body all the way to the river and back. Possibly, enough time for her to get Shiva and Talia, and warn the others.

When the men carried Thema out of the room, Roanne crept to the bedroom door, and listened for the back door of the house to shut. She peeked out first, then went out into the hall and peeked out the back door. Calum and Geralt had made it to the back gate of the courtyard.

Roanne broke into a run back through the house, it was not that far to Calum's rooms, but she ran smack into the barrier he had placed across the hall leading to them. It stunned her a moment, then her anger flared and she was almost ready to simply flame the thing before she remembered the collar she still wore. She retraced her footsteps to a turn in the corridor. From there she launched the spell, and ducked. Flames roared out from the corridor where the barrier had been. Even hiding behind the turn, it became so warm Roanne feared the collar might ignite. The blast lasted only seconds, though, as she fought to quench the blaze using the same magic that had started it. Perspiration beaded her forehead and she had to wipe it away from her eyes. She wasn't sure if it was the heat, or the effort to contain the heat, that caused the sweat. With the flames finally out, she ran for Calum's rooms, finding Shiva still in the cage. The lock flared out of existence even as she framed the thought. Talia, lying on the bed, came awake and sat up as it was all happening. Shiva still cowered in the cage, seemingly ignorant of the door swinging freely open. Roanne had to reach in and pull the girl out.

None of the three spoke a word, though Talia was making pulling motions. Perhaps she had not been all that cooperative if Calum saw fit to keep her gagged, Roanne thought, and reaching for Talia's hands, found the tether leading to the head of the bed. She burned it, letting the flames consume most of the tether as it led back to Talia, before stopping it.

Talia was off the bed and helping Shiva to her feet before Roanne was. Together the three of them made their way back to the other staff rooms. Talia picked out a door and began pounding on it, as Roanne went for one of the other cooks. They had each pulled their targets into the hall, frustrated at trying to mimic their respective needs. The noise they made woke others, which only added to the confusion. The back door swung open, but it was Tagert who came running in.

"I thought I saw a fire," he was breathing heavily. "Take me to it. I think I can contain it."

Roanne nearly jumped him, taking the paper and writing implements he used to record his notes. Hastily she wrote the bare minimum. "I need three horses now!! Get all women away from the house!!"

Tagert looked at the note, then back at her in confusion.

"Calum is slaver. Killed Thema. Must get women to safety." Roanne pointed at Shiva, whose condition was now obvious as lights flared in the room. As soon as everyone saw Shiva they froze. She had collapsed on the floor against the wall.

"Can't talk. Gagged with spell by Calum. Need to get away. Three horses." Roanne wrote when Tagert failed to move.

"Where's Calum?" he asked back.

"River. Hide Thema's body. Little time." Roanne scribbled getting frantic.

Finally Tagert seemed to get the point. He ordered the horses, then began to explain to all the women why they had to flee from the house.

"What is going on here?" came a yell from the other end of the hall. Roanne recognized Mathia's voice, though there was a crowd of people between him and her.

"I'll let Mathia know what's happened," Tagert tried to move past Roanne, who stopped him.

Pushing people aside, Roanne headed for Mathia. He was standing at the opposite entrance to the kitchen, now, arguing with someone from the staff, his back to her. She grabbed a cleaver along the way, and before he even saw her coming plunged it into his back, twisting it to cause as much pain as she could. He was a powerful wizard, and she did not want him to have the slightest chance to gather his wits and counter her attack with a spell. Pulling the knife free, she stabbed again, then again, and kept going. It was Talia who finally grabbed her wrists as Roanne reared back to strike again. Roanne glared at Talia before she realized what she was doing. She let her grip on the knife go slack, and watched it fall onto Mathia's still body. She was sitting on his lower back, covered with blood. Talia pulled her back to where Shiva sat, dazed. While Talia began to get Shiva on her feet, Roanne went and retrieved the pillowcase she had left in Thema's closet. The three of them made their way to the stables, Tagert trailing behind with a million questions Roanne had no way of answering.

The grooms were saddling all the horses. Men and women, sometimes two and three to an animal, were mounting up and heading for the woods out the front gates of the estate, in the opposite direction from the river, where Calum would hopefully be just arriving if Roanne's sense of time was at all accurate.

Thankfully someone had remembered them. The groom Talia had first waked was waiting with three horses. Seeing Shiva's condition, he mounted up, and had them pass the girl up to him. There was no way she was going to be able ride alone. Roanne winced as she watched Talia mount in her flimsy negligee. It was not going to be a comfortable ride for her, but the look in Talia's eyes said she accepted that. Roanne was mounted and they were headed out when she noticed Tagert mounting another horse and coming after them. Waving the others on, with a hand pointed toward the road to Esconda, Roanne wheeled her horse around to wait for Tagert, who was calling to her.

"There's not much point in my sticking around," Tagert said pulling up next to her. He held up the writing implements. "You need someone you can communicate with. I'll bet the groom can't read. Besides, I do know some legitimate magic. Maybe I could be of some help. That one girl is going to need a healer."

Roanne gave no sign of what she was thinking. She trusted Tagert, but right now, no wizard was on her list of favorite traveling companions. She realized he had a point about communicating, though, at least until she could figure a way to rid herself, and the others, of the blockage in their mouths. Turning toward the road again, she kicked hard to get her horse moving. Tagert followed right behind.

Talia and the groom were waiting just past the edge of the forest, where they could not be seen from the estate. As Roanne and Tagert passed, they fell in behind them, Talia eyeing Tagert with suspicion. Roanne slowed the pace for the horse that carried both the groom and Shiva. The last thing they needed was to run the horses right into the ground.

They made it to Shiva's home just as the sun poked over the horizon. Her mother became hysterical at the sight of her daughter. Her father and two brothers were ready to go to the estate for revenge.

Roanne was grateful for having Tagert along then. He explained as best he could what had happened. The family came up with clothes for Talia, along with some salve for the sores forming on her thighs from riding in the saddle, and an extra saddle pad when Tagert managed to get across to them why they couldn't stop there, but had to keep moving. Calum probably knew where Shiva lived they all realized when it was figured out he had somehow intercepted Roanne's messages to them after Shiva had first disappeared. They got clothes for Shiva, and bandages to wrap her in when they had time to take care of her properly. They were afraid to try and remove the tattered remains of what she had been wearing for fear of ripping open the wounds the material had stuck to. Roanne wrote instructions for Tagert, who got the family to go to Ledin's farm just down the road and help load the trunks of books into a wagon, covered with hay from the farm to hide them. The family would bring the books along to Esconda, while the three escapees, the groom, named Afton, and Tagert went on ahead, until they were sure they were beyond Calum's reach. Roanne promised they would wait for them then, and give Shiva the care she needed.

Shiva seemed to be more awake when they moved on, with a fourth horse for her from the farm. At least she was able to ride.

The party pressed on until they came to the next settlement, where Afton knew some members of the underground movement among the peasants. The town had a small inn, as travelers often made it a stopping place for the night, the next town being a full day's ride beyond it.

Four other fugitives from Mathia's estate had already made it this far, and more came straggling in as time went by. Some told of the estate being burned to the ground when Calum returned from the river, while all those remaining were trapped inside. Several of them knew who Calum was, but had seen no sign of him along the way, though they all had seen Shiva's family, and several more families forming a caravan.

Roanne decided they could probably take the time to care for Shiva now. She and Tagert began to inspect the damage Calum had inflicted on her, deciding they might be able to soak the fabric of her clothes away from the scabs on her back. From there, they did not see any problems. The problems were things they could not see, the damage to her mind. Feeling her way along, Roanne discovered Shiva, too, had a collar around her throat.

Tagert and she started to debate what to do about the magical entanglement of the tongues and throats. It was a limited debate, given Roanne's current inability to speak. Roanne explained about the effects of fire. When Tagert offered to burn away their restraints, Roanne's response was almost illegible, as she explained the danger of burning them severely.

Talia had been watching from over Roanne's shoulder as she wrote, and listening to Tagert's responses. She surprised them both when she took the pad from Roanne. When she gave it back, Roanne was even more surprised. "I trust you. Stopped leash from burning me. Can do this."

"You would have to keep a really tight control of the spell," Tagert read the words. "You might even be able to melt it away, if you found the right temperature, but it could be very close. I don't think I could do it."

Roanne took the pad, and handed it to Talia after writing a few words. "Me first. If goes bad, not want to hurt you."

Talia grabbed the pencil. "Me first. If you hurt, no second try. If I hurt, can still try again." She grabbed hold of Roanne's hand and pulled her over to a table. Talia lay on the table, indicating her mouth.

"Collar easier." Roanne wrote.

"Mouth first!!!" Talia demanded in return.

Roanne gathered her concentration, taking heart of the courage Talia was showing, and using it to feed her confidence, which needed all the help it could get. She moved around the table, closer to Talia's head. Talia was staring straight up at the ceiling. Checking quickly, Roanne noticed Talia's hands had a white-knuckle grip on the sides of the table. She turned Talia's head to the side, if she could melt the thing in Talia's mouth, she did not want her to drown or gag on the liquid. Cautiously she tried to stretch her senses. Feeling for the obstruction, trying to find the magic that held it together. There should be some sign of it. Most wizards or spinners could tell when someone else was working magic in the area. Over the years, Roanne had become nearly numb in that sense, with all the magic performed in her uncle's house. She found what she was seeking, the taste of magic in Talia's mouth. Roanne explored it, marking its dimensions, then slowly, concentrating on the area just below the surface, a little away from the tissue lining the mouth, she began to warm it. It was already at body temperature, having been held in place for who knew how long. She locked her concentration on the task at hand. Closing her eyes so she would not see the sweat on Talia's brow. Her hands held Talia on each cheek, making sure Talia remained absolutely still. Slowly she continued to raise the temperature. She felt Talia tense, and almost stopped, had begun to pull back, but Talia's hands came to hers, holding them in place, and she pressed on. Finally it happened. Roanne would never have noticed if not for her efforts to lock out the world around her, but there was loosening around the edges of the obstruction. She grasped at the temperature and held it. Sensing as the edges of the obstruction began to slip away, not as water, but straight back into the air. Still she held the temperature firm, not daring to go higher for fear of ignition. Her hands first registered the movement of Talia's jaw, showing that the object was shrinking. Roanne backed off a little, letting the temperature drop a slight amount, letting the momentum of the process keep itself going. She pulled back more, as Talia's movement increased, being sure to hold her in place. Soon she had pulled back enough to let Talia go, and the woman sat up and spat into her hand. The object was visible because of the dampness around it. Roanne took it from her, and going over to the fireplace, tossed it in. The flames flared bright as it hit. Behind her she heard Talia calling for water, and turned back to see how she was. She was gulping down liquid, then took a mouthful and let it soak the walls in her mouth for a minute, her head hanging down. After a long time, she tilted her head back, and swallowed. Turning to Roanne, she smiled. "I knew you could do it." She croaked in a voice little used in recent days.

Roanne was beat. The process had taken far longer than she thought it had. Tagert had finished cleaning up Shiva, who was now bandaged, and sleeping in a bed in one of the inn's rooms.

"There's no hurry," Tagert told her. "Rest and be sure of yourself. This morning someone reported seeing Calum, headed away from us, toward Altea."

Heading for the college, Roanne saw right away. He must have other allies there he thought could protect him if she made it to Esconda. With a sinking feeling in her gut, she thought he might be right. The council could not have been totally unaware of what he wanted, which she was still unclear about. She knew he wanted knowledge, but that was only a means, and there were no clues as to the ends he had hoped to accomplish with those means.

She made her way over to Talia, ready now to deal with the collar, which would be far less of a problem. All she needed to do was break the circle and free her. They could save the rest as evidence for Regus.

"Leave it," Talia croaked, "We'll need it as proof, to show what he was doing with his magic." She took another sip of broth a woman had made at Tagert's suggestion, in case there were burns in her mouth.

Tagert checked the damage. "The tissue is really red," he told Roanne, "And it may be a day or two before anything tastes right, but she should be all right."

"I gave Shiva a brew to make her sleep," he suggested. "If you do her now, you won't have to worry about her moving on you, and she probably won't even feel it."

Roanne agreed and went to find the sleeping girl. When she found Shiva, she made a decision. First she did the collar, giving an added boost to her growing confidence, and leaving behind a red spot at the back of Shiva's neck. It would not even blister. She applied some salve to it, to help cool it as she rested in preparation to remove the gag. As with almost anything, she was getting better as she went along. She turned Shiva's mouth downward, and held her jaws open so the blockage simply fell out when it had shrunk enough. This time did not take nearly as long as Talia's gag had. Someone came with a butter mix they spread inside Shiva's mouth to help the tissue cool.

After resting a moment in the room's only chair, Roanne leaned forward, planting her elbows on her knees and her jaws in the palms of her two hands and went to work again. The heat assailed her concentration, nearly forcing her to give up more than once. She took Talia's courage as inspiration, and drove herself onward. This did take longer because of the pain she had to endure along the way. When the gag finally slid from her lips, she pushed herself back into the chair and let herself collapse in exhaustion. Liquid was poured into her mouth as someone got her to drink something.

She woke some time later in a separate room, in bed by herself. Her mouth was still sore. As soon as she was aware enough, and had taken stock, she went in search of the room where she had left Shiva. Her senses were still so attuned to the magic she easily found the remains of her and Shiva's gags, and the collar she had taken from Shiva. She took them with her to the main room of the inn, where she tossed them after the gag she removed from Talia.

Talia and Tagert were both awake and talking at a table at the far end of the room. Roanne, after seeing the gags flare up in the fire, realized both she and Talia were in danger as long as the collars were on them. Evidence or not, they would have to come off, which meant more work for her.

She explained her thinking to Talia who after listening realized just how dangerous the thing was. Get too close to a cooking fire as they were traveling, and her head would be burned completely off her shoulders. After what she had already done, the removal of the two collars was easy. She did not destroy them, instead she gave them to Talia to hold on to, with the understanding they could not be placed anywhere near any heat source. Roanne could not put them in her own bags because if something were to set them off, her books, which included some of her father's notes, would be lost.

Shiva's family had caught up with them while Roanne had slept. They joined the three of them at the table to discuss plans, taking the opportunity to thank Roanne once again for helping their daughter.

Roanne suggested they keep Shiva with them, since they knew Calum was not coming after them. It was more than obvious Afton had a crush on Shiva. He wanted to stay with her to make sure she was all right. Shiva's brothers teased him about that, but Afton came through it with only a mild blush.

Talia, Tagert, and Roanne were going to push on ahead first thing in the morning. Tagert insisted on the delay, noting Roanne was still tired from all the magic she had been wielding. The family would bring the caravan along behind, assuring Roanne the cache of books would make it to Esconda, and be delivered to Pavlin at the palace.

Chapter 6

They were in the saddle and on their way with the first light of morning. Talia still struggled with the pain of their flight, the soreness in her thighs, and the burns resulting from Roanne's removal of her bonds. Remaining in the saddle was only going to make her situation worse, yet she gave not one word of complaint, nor asked for special favors or rests.

Roanne had spent a good part of the previous evening reassessing her view of Talia. The young woman had a lot of spirit, which frequently led her to trouble. While that often led to a headache for Roanne, she had to admit Talia had always been very careful about how far she went. Until that first day of the festival, she had never done anything particularly serious. She had also not given in to Calum, as Roanne had suspected. Merely letting the wizard think she had, as she waited her chance to escape. If she had not done that, Roanne had to admit, she would not have been able to carry either Shiva or Talia from Calum's lair, let alone both. Talia's willingness to sacrifice in the name of opportunity was, in its way as admirable as Shiva's attempts to defy Calum.

"You don't have to come," Roanne told the woman who had more than earned her respect.

Talia had already climbed her way into the saddle when Roanne had offered to leave her behind. Roanne was sure Shiva's family would be willing to look after her, as well. "You'll not be rid of me this easily, Roanne. I know you've never liked me."

"That's not very important, right now," Roanne replied defensively. "Maybe I've been wrong about you. You've certainly shown me more strength of character and courage in the past day than I would ever expect to want, or need to see in any person. I'm concerned you might simply aggravate your injuries. If they worsen, or get infected, it could kill you."

"I know of a spinner in the next village who is a true healer," Talia informed Roanne. "I've told Shiva's parents about her, also. She'll take care of me."

"Be that as it may," Roanne persisted, "There is no need for you to follow me. I want you to know I don't expect any more from you than you've already given, and I am not certain where I'm going is anywhere you want to go."

"You're going to Esconda," Talia answered, keeping her voice calm. "Eventually, I suspect you'll be going after Calum, wherever he flees to, and I want to be there to help you bring him down. Have no fear, I'll pull my own weight."

Roanne smiled at Talia's attitude. "Talia, that is the least of my worries."

At the edge of the small village another woman was waiting on a horse, with saddlebags, suggesting she was prepared for a long trip. "My name is Fenicia," she introduced herself. "I would accompany you where you go. I've also sent word on ahead to others who will be wanting to join you."

"I don't understand?" Roanne truly did not. "Why would you want to accompany me? What stake do you have in this?"

"My stake is my freedom," Felicia answered. "I heard what happened. If Calum and the wizards who support him have their way, all women could face what you did."

From out of the morning mist came ten more riders, men with swords, and bows. Some of them Roanne recognized from the estate. "Others will be organizing in all the villages," Zen, their spokesman, explained. "For us, making sure you make it to Esconda is our mission. We'll leave behind a network of messengers as we go along, and wherever you go, we'll be able to call upon a small army, of up to two hundred, that can meet us within a day, within a week that number would grow into the thousands."

"Why? Who?" Roanne turned to Talia, who shrugged, equally confused.

"They're friends of Thema, and others," Zen answered.

Queen of the Spinners

"The spinners," Felicia replied. "We don't have much faith the nobility will give you the help you need. If they do, it will be open war between the wizards and the nobility. In either case, you'll need all the support we can provide."

The men did not wait for Roanne's permission, but turned their horses, and started out in the direction of Esconda. Each of them was giving Tagert a wary look as they rode past him. Roanne's horse began to follow, and she let it, while she tried to figure out what was going on.

"Interesting," Talia said riding along side Roanne. "I had heard things, but I never suspected this. What was it Thema always called you, the Queen of the Spinners? Well, Your Majesty, it seems your subjects are coming out of the woodwork in droves."

"What have you heard?" Roanne asked, though talking was getting difficult as the pace picked up.

"Not much," Talia shrugged, "At least that I paid attention to. My mother sent me to the estate a couple of years ago. She knew of you, which until now didn't mean a whole lot to me."

"Who's your mother?"

"The healer, Lonora. She always had trouble with me, but couldn't bring herself to discipline me the way she thought I needed. She sent me to Thema, hoping she could change me."

"Your mother's a healer? That means you're a spinner."

"Potentially, remember, I had discipline trouble. My mother never managed to teach me a whole lot. I suppose I could be a healer, yet here I sit, willing to trade all the fun I ever had goofing off, right now, for the knowledge to heal myself."

Roanne laughed. "I know a little about healing, not that I would trust myself with your problem." She noted Talia had shortened her stirrups, and was making every effort to remain standing in the saddle. "What little I do know is healers can't really do much for themselves. Part of the process involves drawing the pain, and some of the damage, into yourself, away from the patient. Healers can't do that for themselves."

They made good enough time to reach the healer's village by mid afternoon. Lonora was an older woman, older than Thema had been. It took her only half an hour to deal with Talia's troubles, but then an odd request was tendered for payment for her services. Talia had told Lonora of Shiva, who would be arriving later that day. Lonora asked Roanne not move on until the next day, so Lonora could accompany her.

"Your training is not complete, far from it the last I heard from Thema," Lonora explained to Roanne. "Pavlin can help you some, but you will need me. There are things you must know before you face Calum and his allies again."

"Wait a minute," Roanne finally objected. She had been trying to make sense of Fenicia, the men, even Talia, and now this, and was only getting more confused. "I don't understand this. Everyone is acting like I'm leading troops off to battle. All I'm doing is running. I have some friends in Esconda who I hope can help, but once I inform them of what happened, I'm out of it."

"All the more reason to wait, and learn," Lonora said. "I will do my best to make everything clear, if you'll join me for dinner this evening."

Roanne's frustration was beginning to turn to anger. "Why don't you take your men and set up camp at the edge of the village?" Lonora suggested. "I'll make dinner, once I've taken care of this Shiva, and will bring it out to you. In the meantime, you can talk with your men, and learn what you can from them."

"They are not my men," Roanne wanted to scream it, but managed to hold her temper. Lonora was only making sense. Maybe she could talk them all out of this somehow.

"She is truly Ariele's daughter," Roanne heard Lonora say to another older woman as they walked away. The other woman laughed in agreement. Roanne chose to ignore that for now, but before the night was through, she was going to get some explanations.

"All right everyone, you heard the lady," Roanne turned her attention to the growing crowd waiting on her. "Let's set up camp. Then I want to talk with all of you. We've got some things we need to get straight here."

"You know," Shiva's father came into the camp several hours later, after dropping his daughter off with Lonora. "You keep running on ahead, and then we catch up. Wouldn't it be much easier on you to relax a bit, maybe slow down? You could ride in the wagon, it would be much more comfortable."

"Exactly, that is exactly my point," Roanne ran with the thought. She had just started to talk with the people who had gathered in her camp. "I could have been half way to Esconda by now, but I keep stopping for this, stopping for that. When I first planned this, I thought I might have been able to catch Prince Regus even before he reached Esconda, or at least been only a day behind him. At this rate I may never get there."

"As you originally planned this, I would still be trapped in a cage back at the estate," Talia picked at Roanne's premise, which she had just listened to for the last time if she had anything to say about it. "You'll not get any complaints from me about how things have gone."

"You know what I mean," Roanne tried again. "I'm not complaining about last night's stop, it was necessary, but I could have been half way to the next village by now. The worst thing is, I don't understand why I'm sitting here waiting for someone to explain what is going on here, when I feel I should already know."

"It's simple," Zen offered to try to explain for the fourth time. "There is in all likelihood going to be a battle. The problem has been heating up for years now, and you just boiled it over the top of the pot. Not that it was your fault, mind you. We all know where you stand, by the way you treat the people who work for you, and we are willing to stand behind you. When you get to Esconda, you may find the nobles won't back you, or, as we think, they will be split on the matter. Some of the nobles have been getting very abusive of their people in recent years, and we think they may side with the wizards in this dispute, essentially relegating all of us to the status of slaves."

"We, the spinners, believe," Fenicia picked it up form there, "if what we have heard is true, Regus will take your side in this, which might result in a division within the royal family, since we don't know how Sallas will go. Regardless of Sallas, we are with you. Regus, with or without his father, does not stand a chance against the wizards without some kind of magical ally, so he will need the spinners, and particularly, he'll need you."

"After all," Lonora's voice came from the back of the crowd. People moved aside to let her and Shiva through. "You are the daughter of Kendal and Ariele." Others had come with Lonora, and began passing out food to their guests.

"I don't see what that has to do with anything," Roanne was beginning to see what they were all talking about, except what part her parents had in all this. "And I don't see why Regus has to have me to fight this fight, I'm a nobody. Even with all the spinners, Regus would not be able to take down the wizards. He'll need to get what allies he can from the ranks of the wizards."

"He'll get most of the wizards, I would think," Tagert offered. "I'm certainly on your side, though my magic is admittedly not very strong. Several lower ranking wizards have disputed council rulings on a lot of things lately, more and more often, as the council's influence has dribbled away. How much we can contribute though, is somewhat of a question. It will depend on how the council itself breaks down. I would have thought the council would stand square against the likes of Calum, but someone put him in a position of high influence, and Mathia all but handed Roanne to him. I still like to think most of them have no stomach for this kind of thing. Pavlin should know how the council will break down."

"Possibly," Lonora looked Roanne over, openly appraising her. "You really don't know, do you? Thema didn't tell you?"

"Tell me what?" Roanne demanded.

"That you're the Queen of the Spinners," Lonora said nonchalantly.

Talia laughed. "She called Roanne that a lot, but everyone thought Thema was teasing her."

"Well, it's not like we have coronations, or anything like that," Lonora waved her daughter to silence. "All the spinners recognize the most powerful one among us as the queen, and you, Roanne, are it. Just as it was your mother, Ariele, before she went running off to the wasteland on that fool of a husband's project."

"I'll have you know my father ..." Roanne started to defend him.

Lonora stopped her by raising her hand. "Was a brilliant wizard, I know, but I will never forgive him for taking your mother from us. If she had been around, maybe we would never have come to this. She might have been able to put a stop to all this nonsense years ago when it all started. Instead, she left us to try and deal with it, and we weren't up to it. Until now."

"Why now?" Roanne challenged Lonora. "What has changed that makes you think you can deal with this now. Me?" She scoffed at the suggestion, which raised mutters around the fire that had been lit.

Lonora stared into the fire as if she could see the answers there. "Why now?" She repeated. "Because we no longer have a choice. We either deal with it now, or generations to come will suffer for our failure."

"Why me?" Roanne really needed to know.

"Magic is inherited, or rather the ability to use it is," Lonora stated the obvious. "That's why in magic the hierarchy is usually familial, unlike with nobles, whose nobility has nothing to do with their parents. The stronger the parent is in his or her magical skills, the stronger the offspring."

"And both my parents were very strong." Roanne finished. "My mother was the strongest spinner, which covers the female half of the population. Add to that my father's strength, which I gather, from what I've heard, was tremendous. He would be unchallenged on the council if he were here today."

"And what do you get from such a joining?" Lonora asked. "Nobody is really sure. The wizards have been watching you, and the spinners have been watching you. Even the nobles have been watching you. I don't think any of us really appreciates what you may be capable of. Regus might not need any wizards or spinners to win this if you stand with him. Nobody can be sure."

"Pavlin can be," Roanne corrected her. "He's been testing me all along."

Lonora's eyebrows raised, but then she shook her head. "I doubt even he knows. From what I've heard, your power is still growing. I'm just glad you and I are on the same side."

"Are you sure about that?" Roanne asked, and the crowd hushed.

Lonora just looked at her a moment, then laughed. "Yes, you are your mother's daughter." Everyone seemed to find that amusing except Roanne. "I'm sure." Lonora said after getting herself back under control.

"So," Lonora said picking up on that lighter note. "Just how strong do you think you are?"

Roanne thought for a few minutes. "I have no idea. There's never been anything I've tried that has failed for want of power. Education has held me back, but I had a pretty extensive library available to me. Between that and Salina, I could usually figure things out. Education is still a problem, I think I would be in maybe the second year at the college, judging from the things the students talked about when they visited my uncle."

"You're much better than second year," Tagert spoke up again. "Calum and Spence were the best of this year's class. I couldn't give you a complete comparison, but I just watched you rip Calum's work to shreds, and it was getting easier for you as you went along."

"Was that Calum's best work?" Roanne questioned. "Or did he simply underestimate me? He doesn't have a very high regard for women."

Tagert shrugged. "I couldn't say, but I can say this. There was something odd about the work you did last night. The control you had to use was beyond anything I've ever seen, even from the council members. Then there's the way everything seemed to get easier once you figured it out, like Calum's spells weren't even a challenge"

"There's more to it than that," Talia suddenly spoke out, "There was something even odder about it. How many spinners or wizards can work a spell without using hands or words?"

"What?" Everyone who knew anything about magic echoed, including Roanne.

Talia laughed, pointing at Roanne. "You didn't even notice it. I've been sitting here trying to figure out what was so different about your talent. Then it struck me. When you removed Calum's spell from my mouth, you were holding my head the whole time, with both hands. You couldn't have used them for the spell you were casting. I was listening for any little sounds in the room to try and distract my attention from the pain. At first I could hear and see Tagert moving around the room, but then he left. It was absolutely silent in the room then. You weren't chanting the way every other person I've seen work magic chants. That little bit of mumbling that goes with the magic, it wasn't there. Also, if you went through the same pain I felt when you removed the spells from yourself, I don't see how you could have done it."

"It was painful," Roanne shrugged, "But I was probably better at it by then. I did myself last."

"And the inside of your mouth was still scorched," Tagert observed. "Talia's right. I don't know anyone able to work even the simplest spell under those conditions, let alone what you did."

"Bring a fire brand over here," Lonora came to sit next to Roanne. "Hold it up so I can use it to see." She told Zen who picked a burning stick out of the fire. "Open your mouth Roanne. Why didn't you say anything earlier?"

Roanne tried to object, but Lonora clamped her jaws with her hands, and Roanne gave in. "You say she was scorched like Talia and Shiva were? I healed both of them today, their mouths were both pretty bad." She was standing over Roanne now, looking down into Roanne's mouth.

"Roanne was just as bad last night," Tagert confirmed.

Lonora let herself fall back into her seat, and sat scratching her head. "What?" Demanded Roanne after waiting in the silence of the crowd for a few minutes.

"I don't know how," Lonora seemed confused now, "But you must have healed yourself, and I'll bet you didn't even know it. Did you?"

"She told me healing doesn't work that way," Talia pointed out.

"It doesn't, usually," Lonora searched for some explanation.

"You mean to tell me there was no need for me to ride all the way here on those sores, she could have healed me?" Talia shrieked.

Roanne could not do anything but sit there shrugging, and blushing in embarrassment. "Are you sure about this?" she asked Lonora. "I should have been able to heal Shiva, too, shouldn't I?"

"Your mouth was burned last night," Tagert interjected, when he could control his laughter enough to speak. "There is no way it could have healed without magical help by now."

"Don't let Shiva worry you," her father reassured her. "You did fine by her just getting her out of there. She's all right physically, though it will take some time before the emotional scars will heel."

"My hands," Roanne suddenly remembered. "They were cut up on the night we fled the estate." There was no sign of damage on the palms she stretched out into the light of the fire.

"So all right now," Zen butted into the conversation, "What is the plan from here? We have to let the people in the network know what's up."

Everyone looked at Roanne, who was dumbfounded for a moment. "Well," she began simply to break the awkward silence. "I was headed to Esconda, to speak with Regus and Letitia. They're the ones I need to help me convince the king to get involved in this. Then I was going to have a talk with Pavlin, to see what I could learn about where the council stands in all of this."

"Sounds like a good plan to me," Zen shook his head in approval.

"You already know the peasants and spinners are behind you all the way," Lonora offered. "If it comes to push and shove, that's a lot of weight you have backing you, remember that."

Chapter 7

Roanne stayed with the wagons the next day, though she rode alongside, not in, them. Tagert was making it a habit to stay close to Roanne, now, though Roanne suspected it was not out of concern for her in any way. The people they were traveling with had shown an open and deep distrust toward wizards. Talia was also nearby at almost all times, and Lonora and Fenicia were never far away.

Roanne watched the movements of the people around her. For all their swords and bows, and even the green shirts all the men had donned, as if it were a uniform of some kind, they were not much of an army. There was no discipline about them. They just loosely arrayed themselves to each side of the wagons as they slowly made their way along. If this were all she had going into battle, they would all be slaughtered. She looked at each man, picturing him dead, and the import of what was happening fell on her. She located Zen, riding along on the opposite side of the wagons.

"Tagert, come with me," she said, and began picking her way around the nearest wagon. Once on the other side, she made straight for Zen.

"Zen, do any of the men with you have any military training at all? Do any of the men in your entire organization?" she asked.

"No, all we know is this fight is going to be over us, and whether or not we'll be free men at the end of it," Zen answered, "And we intend to have our say in the outcome."

"Tagert," Roanne turned to the wizard on her other side. "Don't they teach military tactics at the college?"

"Well, yes, but it's not a required course or anything like that," he was beginning to see where she was headed with this. "I didn't study anything like that."

"But you have seen the king's troops, right?" Roanne was planning, even as they were speaking.

"So have I," Zen offered.

"Good, I want the two of you to talk," Roanne liked this, it might help Tagert get more friendly with the people. "Think about what you saw the king's men doing, and compare that to what we're doing."

"And make the necessary changes," Tagert finished for her. "I don't know, these men aren't likely to take direction from me."

"No, but they'll take it from the two of us," Zen offered, catching on to Roanne's plan. "I can think of something right away, we need outriders to scout, make sure we don't run into something it would be better to avoid."

"We should also watch our back trail," Tagert picked up on the idea. "That's where Calum was last seen, near Altea. If there's any pursuit coming from behind, they might be able to catch us at this pace. It would be nice to have some warning."

Roanne left the two of them to work it all out. She knew little of military matters, and didn't think she would have much to contribute.

She rode up next to the wagon with Shiva and her books. From the side of the wagon, she watched Shiva, who was sitting in the back. Lonora had been correct in her assessment of Shiva the night before. There was emotional and psychological damage not so easily healed as the physical had been. Shiva had a look on her face that could only be described as vacant. There was no life in her eyes. She did not smile, or frown. All she did was stare straight ahead.

"Sad, isn't it," Roanne turned to see Fenicia had ridden up next to her.

"It's as if she wasn't there," Roanne commented, looking back at Shiva. "As if the only way to protect herself from the hurt was to leave, desert her body, and she hasn't come back. I wonder if she ever will."

"It must have been hard," Fenicia agreed with Roanne. "I was talking with Talia, to see if there was any possibility she could slip into the same state of mind. It can happen with women who've been raped, and what they went through was one long rape, two weeks of constantly being degraded and humiliated, as well as physically, and sexually abused."

Roanne shuddered, remembering Calum had planned something similar for her. She wondered if she would have been able to hold up as well as Talia had, or if she would have given it up, like Shiva apparently had. She remembered the jumbled thoughts that ran through her mind when she was afraid she would not get away. Several were akin to giving in, letting Calum have his way.

One of the families traveling with them stopped at the next village, where they had relatives. Like Lonora's village, they provided food for the rest of them while they camped. Throughout the kingdom there were specific settlements where travelers could stop for the night. Occasionally there were smaller gatherings of people in between these towns, where particularly good farm land, a rich mineral mines, or fish laden rivers might have made the secondary settlement worth the while of the people. These villages were not normally equipped to houseguests, particularly not small armies like the one following Roanne.

This village had a river nearby brimming with trout this time of year, and the local women had developed a number of marvelous recipes for preparing it. The guests were treated as well as Mathia had treated the visiting royalty in his home. While the villagers served them, the guests met with the village leaders, bringing them up to date on what was happening. The leaders passed along what rumors they had heard, which ranged from the near truth, that the wizards had tried to enslave a settlement, and the people had revolted, to stories that a renegade spinner was assassinating wizards, with the intent of taking over the command of magic in the kingdom, and enslaving the men.

Lonora worked at setting the leaders right, while a disgusted Roanne moved off from the group, in search of a little privacy in which to consider what she was doing. She replayed it all in her mind, trying to think if there was anything she might have done differently, that might have led toward a brighter view of the future than one with a war between the wizards and the people. She could think of a few things she could have changed, if she had it all to do over again, but in the end, she always came to a point where her only options were no better than her current situation, sometimes even worse. The one thing that might have made a difference was if she had killed Calum.

Roanne had never been a big believer in the gods that ruled the religions of the world, but at a time like this she was willing to seek aid from the most unlikely sources. Anything was better than war, she started to tell herself, then stopped. No, not anything, slavery was not an acceptable alternative.

"Roanne?" Tagert called out before he approached. "Something just happened I think you should know about."

"What is it now?" Roanne closed her eyes and hoped it was not another group of loyal fans wanting to come with her. The group was too large as it was.

"You know how wizards communicate," he said it as if he assumed she did. "Well there are a lot of communications flying around right now, and I picked up a couple." Communicating was a very specialized line of magic, not unlike healing was. The telepathy the wizards used had its limits. Several wizards could send general messages heard by any wizard, but only another communicator could answer them. Only a few could direct their messages to individual, and then only to an individual they knew well.

"They are using the general channels to summon all the wizards to Altea," Tagert explained. "The wizards are to recruit what men they can along the way, and kill any spinners they come across."

"They're to what?" Roanne could not believe what she had heard.

"That's not the worst of it," Tagert hurried on. "They put a reward out for you, a thousand pieces of gold. They say you are wanted for the murder of Mathia."

"A thousand gold?" This was bad. A thousand gold pieces were almost as much as the richest of the nobles had. Copper was the common currency, then silver, with gold having the most value.

"They'll give five hundred if the person who brings you in has to kill you to do it." Tagert concluded.

"So it doesn't matter if I've declared war on them or not, they've declared war on me, personally. This could get even worse if they can convince any of the nobles this is a personal fight." Roanne closed her eyes and concentrated for a moment. She too could hear the voices on the wind. Very faint, but they were there.

"Have you told the others?" She asked, "They might turn me in for that much money."

"I think that's the reason they made it so much," Tagert agreed. "I told Zen, and he's arranging sentries around the camp tonight. Five more men from this village will join us, that way we can send out more outriders."

Roanne saw the sense in all that, but if they had to face wizards, the men would not be enough. She went to Lonora, who seemed to be the logical choice.

"Lonora, you said I wasn't ready for this, yet," Roanne confronted the older woman.

"That was before I heard how you escaped from Calum," Lonora corrected her. "Now, I'm not sure."

"Well, what can you teach me that might help," Roanne knew there had to be something Lonora could teach her. "Have you heard what Tagert found out?"

"Yes, Zen told me," Lonora said. "But I'm not sure there is anything I could teach you."

"Can you communicate?" Fenicia, who was sitting nearby, asked Roanne. "Some women can."

"I can hear them if I concentrate," Roanne answered. "I haven't tried or been tested for that, though."

"If you can broadcast," Zen said, stepping up to the fire, "it would tell them we can hear everything they say. It would force them to shut down their lines of communication."

"Is it better to do that," Tagert got into it, "Or to simply listen, so we know what they know?"

"Would they be able to tell where I am if I did that?" Roanne asked. "Or worse, come find me and listen to what we're talking about through me?"

They debated it for some time, finally deciding it would be best to simply let Tagert monitor what he could of their communications.

In the meantime, while they camped, Roanne would practice with her new skills, refining them. Following the suggestions of Lonora and Fenicia, she began to experiment, to see just how much she could do. She did her best to try and challenge herself. She kept this up late into the night and all the next day while she rode in a wagon with Lonora. From the trunks came a few of the books, and she sought out even more challenging tasks, always watching for clues to the air magic Calum used as she read.

That day two more families dropped from the group as they passed a midday settlement with plush fields of crops. They were down to four remaining families of the fugitives from Mathia's estate, but were gathering more men, as three from that settlement came along. This allowed Tagert and Zen to increase the outriders even more, expanding the guarded areas to their flanks, as well as behind and ahead of them.

It was not until the next day the outriders paid off, when the lead riders came riding hard back to the wagons. "There are five riders coming this way," the first man back reported. Everyone seemed to spring into action. The wagons were pulled off to the side of the road. The men came together as the other outriders were called in, using animal calls that hunters used. Bows were pulled out and strung. The women and children were gathered back behind the wagons, including Roanne.

"If they don't know you're here, they won't have any reason to bother us," Tagert explained his reasoning. "They should just go on by."

The riders came into view over the next hill, and pulled up to observe them. Then slowly they approached, while the men at the wagons waited tensely.

As they drew nearer, Roanne recognized one of them as a wizard, a student who had once visited the estate. She recalled he was apprenticed to Pavlin, and that scared her. Wanting to know, she began to move out from behind the wagon, only to be stopped by Lonora.

"What's this?" The lead rider among them asked as he approached. "Since when do travelers dig in as if expecting a fight when greeting others?"

"Haven't you heard what's going on?" Tagert stepped forward.

"Tagert?" One of the others recognized him. "What are you doing here? Weren't you at Mathia's?"

Tagert looked nervous, he hadn't expected to be recognized. "Yes, I was there."

"Then why aren't you with Calum, helping him run down the bitch that killed Mathia?" the first man took over again.

"Because Mathia deserved what he got," Tagert said back. "Only his death should have been slower, and more painful."

"Nothing could justify what the bitch did to him," the other wizard argued.

"How about slavery, multiple rape, and torture?" Tagert stood his ground. "His niece was only defending herself."

"Are you trying to tell us Mathia raped his own niece?" Another of the wizards spoke out. "Do you expect us to believe that?"

"I was there," Tagert countered. "Are you telling me what I saw was wrong? It was Calum who did the raping. He was keeping two young women in cages, torturing them between rapes. Mathia not only knew of it, he had given his niece to Calum for the same treatment."

"He's telling the truth," the man furthest backed kicked his horse sending it forward.

Queen of the Spinners

"And how do you know? You were in Esconda," the first wizard tried to hold the man back, but he broke free and came across to align himself with Tagert.

"I'm a communicator, I can recognize the truth in a man's words, you idiot, and I don't need a truth spell to do it," the wizard stated the obvious.

"Then what the communicators from the college are saying must be the truth, too." The other countered.

Another man broke ranks from them and came over to Tagert. "Not if the truth was kept from them, which means the council is involved in all this treachery." He told everyone who could hear. "And I will not stand in support of slavery."

"Spence, we could use men like you on our side," the one in control hushed down the remaining three on his side.

Suddenly Tagert stiffened, and the first man to come over fell out of his saddle, landing stiffly on the ground.

The one called Spence wheeled around. "What's this? Attacking your own kind? So what this man said was the truth."

"So, what?" the leader laughed. "The bitches deserved it, and once we have them again, they'll get even more, along with every woman. Look around you Spence, pick one out, and if you join us you can have her."

Spence had dismounted, and was checking on his felled companion and Tagert. "What kind of spell is this? What did you do to them?"

"Calum gives his friends special training, Spence," the leader explained. "But then you and he never did get along. It's too bad, really."

Talia came running out from between the men behind Spence. Pulling a dagger from someone's belt, she launched it at one of the men still on horseback. The man was quick to react, placing a shield of air between himself and her. Roanne was even quicker. The dagger passed right through the flames that erupted where the shield had been, and plunged right into the man's chest.

"Who did that?" the leader was backing his horse away from the group.

"I did," Roanne stepped forward, and walked up to where Tagert stood rigid.

Suddenly her mouth filled and the air around her solidified to hold her in place. "The bitch herself. We're going to be rich. Too bad, Spence, you could have had a piece of the action, but now, I'm afraid if you're not with us you're against us."

Spence went to help Roanne. "Stay away from her!" Lonora warned from the wagons, and Spence froze where he was, not trapped, but seeking the voice, confused.

Roanne became engulfed in flames, which began to rise above her even as they had appeared. When she could be seen again, Roanne was standing with her hands planted on her hips. The fire above her head condensed into a ball, and she found she could feed it to keep it going from the surrounding air. She increased the heat as she condensed it further, making it white-hot. Then she sent it at the leader. The ball was so hot it burned a hole straight through his chest. Leaving his corpse to drop to the ground.

The other man was panicking. "You," Roanne pointed at him, "Come forward." Sweating heavily the man did as she commanded. "I want you to go on to Altea, and deliver a message to the council for me. You tell them the truth of Mathia's death, and what happened here. You attacked me. I was only defending myself. Further, warn them until the reward is withdrawn, no wizard will be safe. I have no desire to hurt anyone, but every wizard in Tularand will be dead before anyone puts a collar around my throat again. Do you understand that?"

The man was visibly shaking in his saddle. His shirt soaked with perspiration. "I suggest you get going before I change my mind," Roanne coldly eyed him. Kicking his horse, he got it moving, and continued to kick until he was beyond their range of vision.

Roanne turned back to the group to see the man they had called Spence staring at her. Ignoring him, she went about freeing Tagert from the air holding him, working much faster with her growing confidence. Next she freed the communicator. They each checked themselves for burns afterward, as did Lonora, but there were none. Like with Roanne, not even a hair had been singed.

Chapter 8

As they made camp for the night, the lead outriders came with word of another group approaching, this one displaying what appeared to be the royal banner. Rather than wait and endanger the families with them, this time Roanne rode out to meet the newcomers, with ten men, including Tagert and Spence, who claimed to know the royal family. Two more groups of ten fanned out along either side of the road to hit the flanks of this new group if necessary. Roanne instructed everyone to use their bows should there be any wizards bent on attacking them, and she would be sure to eliminate any shields the wizards tried to use to protect themselves.

The banner was for the royal family Spence was quick to point out as soon as the riders were within sight. Roanne, after the recent visit of Regus was familiar with the banner, and knew immediately that Spence was telling the truth. The small troop halted a respectful distance from Roanne's small force, gathering around a figure at their center while one man slowly made his way forward.

"If I may, I believe I know him," Spence offered.

"Go ahead," Roanne said, "But be careful, my friends here don't put much trust in wizards these days."

Spence looked around the group accompanying them, noting that Talia, who had been quick to attack the earlier wizards, had joined them. "It seems to me they have good cause," he answered. "I just hope I can change that. As with any group of people, there are always good and bad. Most of the time, luck, more than anything else decides those you meet."

He nudged the sides of his horse, sending it forward at a trot. As he separated from the group, there was a stirring among the guards remaining with the banner. A figure emerged from the center, and came forward to greet Spence himself, rather than leave it to his emissary.

"Your Highness," Roanne heard Spence say, but she did not recognize the other man. Regus did have a younger brother, though, and a younger sister as well, that Roanne had never met. "What brings you out this way?" Spence was finishing his greeting.

Roanne put her own horse in motion, slowly moving forward. "Stay here," she cautioned the others. As she drew nearer, she could make out the familial resemblance between this man and Regus. He and the guard who had come forward were eyeing her, and the other guards were inching their way closer, until the prince put up a hand to keep them back.

The three men waited until she was close enough to hear easily. "Your Highness, Prince Jerol," Spence made as formal a bow as one could from a saddle, "May I present the Lady Roanne of the province Altea, daughter of Kendal the Wizard …"

"I know who the Lady Roanne is," Prince Jerol raised a hand to stop Spence. "Greetings, Lady, from myself, and my family. I had not expected to find you within two days ride of Esconda. As it happens, we were on our way to see you." He bowed as elegantly as Spence.

"Greetings, Your Highness," Roanne returned the bow as best she could, then took a few seconds to calm herself. "Might I inquire as to the reason for your journey, since as you probably know, the estate had the recent honor of hosting your brother, Prince Regus, and his intended, Lady Letitia."

Jerol smiled. "Regus said you might be suspicious if I showed up with a small army. Let me assure you, my journey is in response to your letter to Letitia. Regus thought things might be moving much faster then he had anticipated, and that these men might serve to protect you from those he feared might do you harm. As you may or may not know, each member of the royal family has twenty guards at their disposal, as an escort for journeys."

Roanne suddenly recognized the guard who had first come forward. He had been with Regus during the prince's visit, always present, though usually in the background, a bodyguard.

"Even Letitia," Jerol continued, "With her new standing, has a small contingent. We felt it might be wise to make these men available to you. Here we have the contingents for Regus, Letitia, my sister, Sheilla, and myself. King Sallas was a bit put out because we had to draw men from the barracks to watch over those remaining in Esconda, but Regus convinced him this was necessary."

"The Lady already has an escort of her own," Spence announced, reminding Roanne of the men they had in the woods. "Which includes three wizards, and a few spinners, besides the Lady herself."

Reminded, Roanne turned back to her men. "If you'll excuse me, Your Highness," she apologized. "Zen, pull back to the camp, it's all right. These are friends." Jerol and his guards noted the rustling in the forest as the rest of her men slipped away in the dimness of the evening.

"Have you met unfriendly travelers along the way?" the prince politely inquired.

Spence cleared his throat. "It seems the Council of Wizards has placed a bounty on the Lady, Your Highness. Three of my own companions attacked her earlier. That is how I came to be in her company."

"Well, I'm glad you were there to help, Spence," Jerol showed his approval for Spence's implied actions.

"I'm afraid," Spence admitted, "I had no idea of the truth of the situation. It was the Lady took care of the three, and saved two wizards, and possibly myself, in the process. She killed two of the attackers, and sent the third running with a message for the council."

Jerol straightened in his saddle, and took a second, closer look at Roanne.

"It is getting late to be traveling, Your Highness," Roanne tried to divert the attention. "We would be honored if you and your men could join us. There is a sizable pasture a little ways back on the road. Perhaps there, I can take the time to explain, while your men get comfortable."

"Only if we can do away with all these formalities," Jerol smiled at Roanne. "Regus told me you weren't very comfortable with titles and such, and Letitia had some interesting things to say about the way you treat people."

Jerol introduced the four captains with his guards. They were Stergis, the commander of Regus' guard, Lathom, Jerol's captain, along with Smithe, and Duval.

He continued to relate some of what the royal couple had told him of their visit as they made their way to the camp. Roanne was pleased they must have really enjoyed their stay, and proud both Letitia and Regus viewed her as a friend. "I hope we can be friends as well," Jerol concluded as they were dismounting in front of the gathering of Roanne's companions.

Roanne presented the prince and his commanders to Lonora, Zen, Fenicia, and Tagert. Telin, the communicator, already seemed familiar with all of them.

"Telin and I were apprenticed to Pavlin, who stayed behind when the summons of the council was sent out, his duty to the crown taking precedence," Spence took the opportunity to finally explain his own presence to Roanne. "Carlon was also working with Pavlin. He's the one you sent on to Altea. Sethe and Maison, the two you killed, were apprentices to a wizard named Erron, who was out of Esconda when word came down. He's probably on his way to Altea by a different route. He's not a council member, and not one I would think you have to worry over."

"Why didn't you stay with Pavlin?" Jerol asked Spence.

"Well, the messages were all sufficiently vague we weren't sure what all this was about. Vague enough, in fact, to allow the communicators to essentially lie, as I've just recently learned. Pavlin wanted Telin, Carlon, and I to find out what was happening, and report back."

"Have you reported back, yet?" Jerol pressed.

"No, I haven't had the chance," Telin answered for himself, "And, quite frankly, I don't have all the facts, yet. Though I am convinced Roanne has done nothing to warrant the bounty the council has placed on her."

"I guess I should tell you everything," Roanne launched into her story, introducing Talia and Shiva. Talia confirmed her part for Jerol when Roanne reached that point in the narration. By the time they finished, the soldiers were set up for the night, and cooks from both groups were collaborating on dinner.

"Slavery? Rape?" Jerol was beside himself with anger. He rose from his seat and began pacing. "We were aware some of the nobles were getting out of hand, and were trying a couple of political strategies to reign them in, without much success. The king has been leery of openly slapping those lords, fearing it could lead to a civil war. The kingdom is currently not as stable as we would like, but this is over the line, way over. Do you realize what this means?"

He looked at Roanne, but it was Lonora who answered him. "War with the wizards, if they persist in this, and with those nobles willing to side with the wizards in hopes of taking advantage of the situation." Jerol turned toward her.

"Lonora, right?" And you're Zen," he made sure he had the two names correct. "What exactly brought the two of you, and all these men here?"

"I'm a spinner," Lonora went right to the point. "Roanne is our Queen, and if necessary, every spinner in this kingdom, and the neighboring kingdoms will join to fight the wizards over this."

"I see," Jerol did not seem surprised, "And would expect no less, we know of the tradition behind the Queen of the Spinners, and my family has always honored whoever held the seat."

"It seems everyone knew about this except me," Roanne muttered, producing smiles and a few laughs around the fire.

Zen looked to Roanne before he spoke his mind. "You can trust him," Roanne reassured the farmer.

"My men and I are part of an underground organization trying to help the people when the nobles become abusive," he began. "We help people flee if we think they're in serious danger. The spinners have been helping us, so we also try to protect them when we can. When Duke Aston found out a spinner had healed a man he had ordered flogged, he threatened to torture them both to death. We got them both out of his lands."

"Your Highness," Zen finished, holding up his hands when Jerol tried to object to the formality. "If the crown will take a stand against the wizards for this, and against the abusive lords, you will have our complete support. We have many more than just the men you see here. We're not trained, as Roanne has pointed out to us, but we're willing to learn, and you will need all the help you can get."

"How many are you?" Stergis asked, "You're right, we may need the help."

"About a thousand, it's hard to tell some times," Zen was unsure of the size of their organization, and did not realize he had just given away important information if the crown chose to oppose them.

Smithe whistled. "They match the number of trained guards of all the nobility, Jerol, and half the king's guard."

"And to whom are you loyalties?" Jerol asked.

"Right now, to Roanne," Zen was perfectly honest about it. "If the crown were to refuse to back her, and the spinners, against the wizards, she would still have us, and if I can be frank, if the crown is not with us in a situation like this, we have no choice but to figure you're against us. Slavery is not something you can be neutral about as far as we're concerned."

"Do you realize we have twice the number of men you have here, and ours are well trained?" Duval warned Zen.

"In this situation, sir," Zen countered with confidence, "I think it's important we all know exactly where the others stand. There is no room for politics in war."

"Duval," Spence advised the young captain, "All they would have to do is make sure you don't get to Roanne." They all noted how a small group had gathered at her back when the tension in the talks had risen, just as guards had been quietly gathering behind Jerol. Spence continued, "You wouldn't stand a chance. I think she could wipe out your men with little trouble, even if all three wizards here tried to stop her. I've seen her work."

"I don't think that will be necessary," Jerol tried to reestablish the good cheer they had shared when they had started, foregoing all sense of formality. He stepped around the fire, taking Zen's hand and shaking it. "I can't say I speak for the king, he will have to speak for himself, though I'm confident he would agree with me. I do speak for the rest of the family, though, who sent these men with me to help. We will not permit slavery in our land, and we have been trying to urge our father to move more decisively on the matter of the abuse." He paused, taking a breath, and swallowing. "It must end now. If Regus and I make a stand, the king may not openly help us, but he will not oppose us. If that happens, we may indeed need your help, Zen."

Jerol moved over next to Shiva, who was standing with her parents. He touched her cheek, looking into her blank expression. "By my father's own standards, the ones he taught his children," he went on, "any king who would stand for this has forfeited his right to rule. I will see to it he is reminded of those standards, and bring those responsible for this to justice." There was anger in his voice, and Roanne noticed he was struggling to control it. All through Talia's description of the way she and Shiva had been treated, Jerol had watched Shiva, the anger in him rising with every word.

The refugees had few provisions with them, having relied on the villages along the way to lend them aid. They offered what little they did have, but the guards were well provisioned, having expected to be traveling for several more days. When the meal was ready, they ate together. Jerol did his best to help serve Shiva, who had to be fed like a baby, now, her emotional state seeming to worsen with time. When everyone else had finished eating, Jerol had yet to begin his own meal. When Shiva's mother took her off to bed, Jerol angrily threw the half eaten plate they had been feeding Shiva into the fire, and stalked off toward the surrounding forest.

The soldiers just watched him go, even scrambling to get out of his way. Roanne removed the plate from the fire, using her power to avoid burning herself. After cleaning it in a nearby stream where others were doing the same, she searched out the cooking fires. She had to stop the cooks from clearing away the leftovers, catching them just before the meat was put away.

Jerol had gone farther into the woods than she had thought, or, she was beginning to think, she must have gone past him in the dark. She was just about to start backtracking when it was he that saw her.

"Who's there?" a voice out of the darkness asked.

"Roanne," she answered, "I brought you something to eat."

"I'm not very hungry," his voice had an even angrier edge to it, now.

"Neither was Shiva. She never seems to be anymore, but that doesn't mean we stop feeding her," Roanne countered, locating his darker shape against the shadows of the forest. She came toward him, offering the plate.

"I have a bit of a temper," he seemed to think he had to explain his behavior. "Sometimes it's better to walk away, before you blow up, and make a fool of yourself. I came awfully close to treason earlier, though I believe my father will back you." He took the plate, and at least began to nibble at what it had to offer.

"Some things deserve our anger," Roanne rationalized. "I don't think anyone will hold it against you if slavery angers you, but that's not all it is, is it?"

"No, that is not all of it," he admitted. "I'm angry at my father, at myself, at everything I am supposed to represent. We could have prevented this. If we had cracked down hard on the nobles who've been abusive, the wizards would have known they could not get away with this."

"I hate to point this out," Roanne hesitated a second, "But, so far they have gotten away with it."

"Two, no, three of them are dead, including a member of the council itself," Jerol reminded Roanne. "Calum is on the run. Once the wizards see what they've unleashed, they're going to regret it. Still, we could have put an end to this before it started, before anyone died, or anyone was raped."

"No you couldn't." Roanne contradicted him. "The wizards have been getting desperate about their self esteem, which has been sinking. Sooner or later, something was going to give. It might not have been the same kind of mistake, letting Calum into their ranks. It could have been worse."

"What could be worse than this?" Jerol argued.

"They may have tried experimenting with things they're not ready for," Roanne knew the answer. "We could have another Varden. I'm not excusing what they did. I had a collar around my throat, but I can think of much worse things that could have happened. Some things we would not be able to do anything about."

"That does not excuse our negligence in letting this happen," Jerol was adamant.

"No, but at least it's not too late to put a stop to it, before there are more like Shiva," Roanne concluded.

Jerol ate in silence for a few minutes, clearing the plate she had brought him. "Are you really as good as you think you are? There's a lot hanging on that. Some of the nobles are going to side with whoever they think will win," He watched her as she thought about her answer.

"I never thought I was as good as I am," Roanne carefully considered the best way to answer the question. "I always thought of myself as a simple spinner. The question is, am I as good as everyone else seems to think I am? I don't know. I'm still learning, and there is so much to learn, and so little time.

I'm working somewhat in the dark right now, doing some things almost purely by instinct, and that troubles me in some ways."

"How so?" Jerol had not gotten the answer he was hoping for.

"Take this afternoon," Roanne explained, "If I had known what I was doing, maybe I could have handled the situation without killing two men. I'm trying to figure out if I let my temper get the best of me. The way things are going, I can't afford to let that happen again. Just the thought of losing control, with what I'm learning I can do, is scary."

"Like you said, some things are worth getting angry over," Jerol tried to ease her conscience. "I think if you had lost control, you would have killed all three, but you did not. In your place, I would have. The fact your power scares you says a lot, also. Your conscience is still working, which is not something the members of the council, and some of the nobles, can say right now."

"It still doesn't answer your question," Roanne observed. "We don't know if I'm good enough to pull us all through this."

"Just the uncertainty might be enough. At least it is your limits we're unsure of, not your potential," Jerol thought aloud. "The wizards don't know, either. We may not be sure you can pull this off, but they don't know you cannot. If the nobles can't be certain who will win, they'll be more likely to make their decision for the right reasons. It's a shame we can't simply count on their morality and not have to worry about their politics."

"We don't know how good Calum is, either," Roanne pointed out. "Evidently, this use of air he is teaching to his supporters is not something the college normally teaches, and may be new to even the council for all we know. There are variables on both sides of the equation."

"We know you can counter the spell," Jerol kept thinking things through. "Calum may be able to do more, but we haven't seen any evidence of that, yet."

"He can teach others to do what he does," Roanne picked it up, "I can't. Evidently, what I do defies conventional thinking about magic. I don't understand it, which makes it difficult for me to teach others. We'll need to if we want to neutralize Calum, I can't fight them all by myself."

"Why don't you try teaching what you do," Jerol suggested. "In the process, you may come to understand it better. The essence of what you do, from what I heard, is to control heat and fire. Almost every wizard I've ever met can light a lamp. They should be able to do this."

"If they can control it," Roanne began to pace the small clearing. "The fire burns very hot, and they could end up doing as much, or more, damage than good if they can't control it."

"I would suggest starting with Spence," Jerol pushed. "He's a recent graduate, and very adept, if not an Adept. Of those wizards we have with us, he's probably the best." He stood up, the empty plate in his hand.

"Thank you for the food," he gestured with the plate, "But we had better get back to camp. We wouldn't want people to get the wrong idea, the two of us alone out here."

Roanne laughed lightly at the thought. That was the last thing on her mind after what she had been through, but admitted to herself for all her power, she could not control what others would think. Together they turned back toward the camp, picking their separate ways through the tangle of trees and underbrush.

Telin greeted them at the edge of the wood. "Your Highness, I've contacted Pavlin. His first suggestion was I make a general announcement of the truth of the matter. Before I do so, I wanted to check with you, and with the Lady Roanne, as to exactly what to say." He fell in step with the pair as they continued on toward the fire, where the captains and the leaders from Roanne's group were still gathered, already discussing the matter. It was quickly agreed to keep the message simple, announcing the accusation of slavery against Calum and the council, and urging all wizards who opposed such activity to gather in Esconda, as opposed to going to Altea. Hopefully, they would get some idea of the breakdown of the wizards' loyalties.

If they could draw a vast majority of them to Esconda, the situation might resolve itself much more easily. The council would know they could not stand alone.

Chapter 9

"How will we be sure the wizards who come to Esconda are on our side?" Zen asked as he rode along side Roanne the next day. "They could be spies for the council." They had been discussing everything they had gone over the previous night, wondering what, if anything, they had missed.

"I'll know if they are," Telin emphatically answered. All the wizards, the captains, and the prince were near enough to be sure to hear whatever was said. Telin moved off to one of the wagons, where he would ride while he worked. He periodically repeated the message he had sent out the night before, and would continue to do so for the next several days. Tagert went with him, to watch over the wizard while he was communicating with the their colleagues. Spence also started to follow his fellow wizards, but was held back by Jerol.

"I want you to try to learn what Roanne had been doing to counter Calum's spells," Jerol explained. "We need to find out if she can teach it."

Roanne made no comment when Spence turned to her. She was not ignoring them. She was simply not sure how to start.

"You've seen her work," Jerol picked up Roanne's hesitation, "Do you think you can handle what she does?"

"I've been thinking about that," Spence said, "But I'm not exactly sure what it is she's doing."

"It's a lot like lighting a fire," Roanne decided on the words she wanted. "Only you have to control the process, directing the heat where you want it to go. I was going to wait until we camp to try some things. It will be much safer to do this when we're not bouncing around on the back of a horse."

For the rest of the morning, Roanne and Spence talked about magic. Roanne picking up some ideas from Spence through his education at the college, and Spence learning, in theory, how Roanne dealt with Calum's spell. Together, they sought out Fenicia and Lonora, to get their opinions. It would have helped

Queen of the Spinners

if Pavlin could communicate with Telin, and answer some of the questions that came up, but their enemy might be able to eavesdrop on such a link, if it were possible.

There was no fire for lunch, and by the time they stopped for the night, they had made it to the town of Scala, where they camped at the edge of town. The leaders, though, were put up in the local inn, at the insistence of the town's people, who would not have it said a member of the royal family had to sleep on the ground when visiting them.

The inn served a fine dinner for the royal entourage, which now included the spinners, wizards, and captains, including Zen. At Stergis' suggestion, Jerol had taken a moment to recognize Zen's status among Roanne's people with an honorary rank of captain. Zen had agreed to go beyond that might actually damage his authority in the odd coalition he represented. The conversation was casual during their meal, covering everything from the weather, to a stone lodged in the hoof of someone's horse's hoof during the day's travels.

After the dinner Roanne pulled Spence aside, and all the spinners and wizards followed, aware of the discussions that had gone on all day. They gathered at a table in front of the unlit fireplace in the dining room of the inn. Roanne took a lamp down from the wall, and placed it on the hearth.

"If you want to learn to burn the spell Calum uses, you have to be able to light a lamp," Roanne began. "This is pretty simple, and most of us have done it so often, we do it without thinking. We have to start at the beginning though, so I want everyone to take a turn at lighting, and extinguishing the lamp."

While they were doing that, Roanne went to the innkeeper, asking for several items. When she returned, she had with her some lamp oil, and some mugs with water in them.

"Now I want you to describe to me what you did," Roanne requested when Fenicia, who was last, extinguished the flame in the lamp.

"I lit the lamp, and then put it out," Tagert answered, drawing chuckles from everyone in the group.

"More specifically," Roanne insisted.

"We used magical energy to heat the oil in the wick to the point it would burn," Spence offered. He had the advantage of his discussions with Roanne, who had needed to pound that point into him several times, and he had still resisted the idea. "I see what you were talking about earlier." He concentrated a moment, mumbling and making gestures with his hands. Lifting the lamp cover, he experimentally touched the wick inside, feeling the warm wick. A few of the others stepped forward and tested the wick for themselves, nodding as they caught the significance of what Spence had done. "I can also heat the wick with less energy than is required to make it burn. So while it doesn't burn, it does feel warm. Isn't that how you described what you did?"

"Very good," Roanne was impressed. "But you need more control than even that. Can you light the wick and then cool it so you can touch it?"

A few seconds later the lamp flared to life, burned a minute and then went out. Spence made a few more futile gestures with his hands, then threw them up. "I can't picture what I'm doing," he complained. "When I heat something, I can sort of picture the heat, I see as fire or light, the hotter it becomes, the brighter the light. I have no reference to picture cold by."

"Use the light," Roanne suggested. "Make your reference, or starting point a specific intensity. To heat, increase the intensity by feeding energy into the process. To cool, draw energy off, dimming the light."

Spence had to think about it for a moment, then turned his attention back to the lamp. Ordinarily he would simply snuff the flame, this time he drew the heat off more slowly, checking his progress by the size of the flame. When the flame went out, he kept going. Hands gesturing, and murmuring, he continued to force the light of the fire in his mind to dim, drawing off the energy and letting it go. Finally confident, he reached out and touched the wick.

"It would have cooled faster by itself," Roanne commented sarcastically, and everyone laughed. "Try it again, faster this time."

After he had done that, she set two glasses of water on the table near the fireplace, and gestured for him to join her. She concentrated a second, cooling the water, then turning the mug in front of her over, and dumped the ice onto the tabletop. "Try that. Instead of cooling a flame, you'll need to cool the water." Roanne omitted that this was the first time she had done this. It was one of the ideas that had occurred to her during the day, and she was pleased she was able to do it so easily. It took Spence somewhat longer, but in the end he managed to do the same.

The two of them spent the next hour helping the others in their attempts to copy them. Tagert had the most trouble, and even Telin struggled to get through it. To everyone's surprise, both the other experienced spinners, Fenicia and Lonora, had an easy time of it. Talia had to struggle simply to get the lamp lit, cursing the whole time in frustration. Lonora tried to assuage her anger, explaining it would take time, but eventually Talia would get there. Tagert always had a realistic view of his own abilities, but for Telin, being bettered by the spinners was an embarrassment. He had been near the top of his class the year he had graduated from the college. There had been times he and his fellow students had teased those with less talent about being spinners. To be bested by spinners was, for him, an insult.

"I suppose it didn't occur to you you're being taught by a spinner," Tagert tried to goad Telin.

"I don't know what she is," Telin gestured toward Roanne, "But she's no spinner."

Spence took it all in stride. "By the time this is over, I think we will all be redefining the boundaries of magic, and the relationship between wizards and spinners."

"You can rewrite the dictionary later," Roanne interrupted. In the fireplace, she poured out some lamp oil onto the stone hearth. After almost no thought at all, she lit the oil, and the flames covered the surface of the puddle. As everyone watched, she pushed the flames back across the circular area covered by the oil, so only half of the surface was burning. With a playful smile, she began to move the flames even more, making patterns and pictures. Finally gathering all the flame at the very center of the puddle, before snuffing it out.

Spence blinked at the puddle, where he had been staring in amazement. "Heating and cooling at the same time?" he asked. "You heated one part, then cooled another part of the surface."

"No," Roanne answered. "I controlled the heat, limiting it to only those parts of the surface I wanted to burn. Use the example of the light you talked about earlier. The light is the magical energy that is heat, since you can see it, in a way, you can control it, move it about. You might want to start with simply pushing it back away from one side of the oil, the way I did. Then practice developing finer control."

"Is all this really necessary?" Telin complained.

"When you were trapped in that wall of air, yesterday," Roanne explained, "I burned it away. In doing so, I had to control the heat of the fire, making sure it burned away the air surrounding you, but not you. If I had not been able to control the heat, you would have burned to death." Roanne supposed it was possible he might have only been badly, or even severely burned, but the thought of death put the emphasis Roanne wanted on the idea.

Telin still looked skeptically at the oil. Roanne realized he doubted not her reasoning, but after being beaten by spinners once, Telin was beginning to doubt himself. "Telin, take your time with this," she tried to unruffle his feathers. "As I understand magic, and you can probably correct me if I'm wrong, most people seem to have one area of exceptional ability, and few are lucky to be able to do well in more than one area. I seem to have a knack for burning things, but I can't communicate very well. You can communicate, so it's not surprising you might struggle with this at first. Once you practice I'm sure it will come more naturally, almost without a second thought." Telin's expression was still wary, Roanne had conveniently left out that

Lonora was a healer, a higher ranking skill at the college than communicating, and still caught on to these new ideas more easily than he did. Roanne risked a quick look at Lonora, who had a knowing smile on her face.

Spence, in the meantime, had relit the oil on the hearth, and accidentally snuffed it out in frustration, three times now.

"Keep trying," Roanne tried to sound encouraging, as she retreated from the area, letting the others gather around Spence to watch him work. She still needed to figure out the next step in this exercise. The obvious next step was to fashion a block of air or something using Calum's spell, and letting them practice on that. Nobody in the group was familiar with Calum's spell, though.

Taking Spence's advice, she tried to form a picture in her mind of what Calum was doing. It would have helped if she could see air, but she had no idea what air was. Even some symbolic form, like the light Spence used to visual the heat. Once again she searched her memory. When the wizards had confronted them, attacking Spence and Telin, Talia had thrown her dagger and Roanne had known there was a shield of air blocking the way. She could sense the magic because she had already been exposed to it, but how could she explain that?

"What's next?" Spence broke into her thoughts.

"To be perfectly honest, I don't know," Roanne admitted. "I was just thinking where to go from here. It would help to know what it is Calum does with the air. If we could duplicate it, we could practice with it, but I haven't figured it out, yet."

"Could it be like we did with the water?" Spence suggested. "By freezing the water we made a solid out of a liquid. If you heat water, it evaporates into the air. That would seem to suggest you could pull the water back out of the air, and freeze it to make a solid barrier."

"But water wouldn't burn," Roanne countered. "In fact, if he were using water in the air it would put out the fire."

"So, it's not water, but something else in the air," Spence agreed. "We could still see water, or steam, to visualize what he does. Even smoke might work. Anything to will help us understand what is happening. It's some place to start."

Roanne thought about that a moment then retrieved some of the ice that was melting on the table where they had left it. She placed the ice into a mug, and began to heat it. As the heated water evaporated into the air she kept control, tracking it by the temperature, then, working as quickly as she could, dropped the temperature. A collection of snowflakes fell to the ground where they melted again almost immediately. "So much for that idea," she commented, discouraged.

Spence had watched closely. "Not really, we can learn something from that. Maybe you need to move more gradually, collecting the water so it can form ice. You simply cooled it as was, so spread out in the air only flakes could form."

Roanne tried it again, but as the water formed from the gathered steam, it poured down to the floor with nothing to hold it up. More water was brought, and on the next try she froze the material faster once the water began collect from the steam, and was rewarded with a ball of ice that fell to the floor. She stared at it as the ball began to melt, her frustration evident on her face.

"You're making progress," Spence was far more enthusiastic. "Unless you can do kinetics, you would need to form the ice around something to support it to hold it up. When Telin was trapped, the air solidified around him. The shield you burned to let that dagger through was resting on the ground.

"Maybe," Roanne caught some of his enthusiasm. "But, I still don't know what is in the air for me to collect and make something solid out of it."

"Maybe that's what Calum does," Spence brightened even more. "Instead of using temperature, they use kinetics."

"Kinetics?" Roanne asked. "I've heard the word before, but I'm not sure I understand it."

"It means moving objects," Lonora interjected, glad of the opportunity to get into the conversation. "I know you've done it before, Salina reported it some years ago."

"I have?" Roanne was taken aback. "When? Wait a minute. You mean like using magic to help lift a cart to repair a wheel, or lifting a stain out of clothing. I guess I just never thought of it that way. It's called kinetics?"

"Oh, gods," Spence moaned. "You mean to tell me you've been doing all these things, and you never even knew what you were doing? One of these days we're going to have to sit and figure out exactly what it is you can or can't do."

"That still doesn't help," Roanne ignored his comments. "Those things I could see, even stains in fabric. I can't see air, so we're back to the same problem."

"Can you lift up water?" Tagert asked.

"No, I can only hold part of it at a time and the rest always slips away," Roanne asked.

"But you could hold up ice," Tagert picked up his line of thought. "If you hardened air, then you could move it around."

"But I still don't know specifically what is supposed to harden," Roanne repeated.

"What about smoke?" Fenicia suggested.

"I don't know," Roanne was getting confused, then she remembered the first gag Calum had used on her, the one with the grease and flour from the stains on his robe. She told them about how she had been able to pick it apart.

"It would seem foreign material, like smoke, weakens the spell," Spence observed.

"The grease is almost liquid getting in the way, and the flour was solid," Lonora pointed out. "They're not the same as smoke."

"Calum uses something that burns," Spence offered. "What was it you said before, when you described the ball of fire you threw at Sethe?"

"That was kinetics," Lonora jumped at the example. "You threw the fireball using kinetics."

"Not that," Spence was on his feet pacing. "You said usually when you burned away Calum's spells, they only burned long enough to consume whatever Calum was using, then the flames would go out. When you put the ball together, you said you fed it, to keep it burning. What did you feed it?"

"Air," Roanne realized the obvious. "I also knew when Maison and Sethe put up their shields, but I don't know how I knew it."

"The breeze?" Spence speculated. "Is there a breeze created when they start to manipulate air? Could you be sensing that somehow?"

"Maybe you just caught their hand movements," Lonora offered, "And used intuition."

"It's more than intuition," Roanne shook her head. "I had to know where the shield was to burn it." She continued to shake her head, and closed her eyes, rubbing at her temples in an effort to relieve the pressure building there.

"It's getting late," a new voice broke in. "Why don't you all get some rest, so we can get an early start in the morning? We should make Esconda tomorrow, maybe Pavlin will be able to help you think this out." Roanne had not even realized Prince Jerol had been watching them the whole evening, though she was grateful for the timing of his suggestion.

"That's not a bad suggestion," Spence agreed. "You've been on the road now a few days, and must be tired. I'm sure you'll appreciate a real bed for a change, and maybe you'll be able to sort things out better when you're more refreshed."

Roanne was not about to argue. When Talia and Lonora took her arms, she simply let them lead her to the room set aside for her. "You've been using an awful lot magic the past few days as well," Lonora warned. "The rest of us are tired just from the travel, you must be bushed."

"I'm not that tired," Roanne tried to insist, but was asleep even before Lonora could get her properly settled in the bed.

Chapter 10

They were late getting started the next morning, as Jerol decided to let Roanne sleep. When she finally woke, the sun was already high in the sky. She dressed in a hurry and rushed down from her room, only to find Jerol, Spence, and Lonora talking quietly in dining room.

"Relax," Jerol laughed. "We have plenty of time to reach Esconda, and we all agreed you needed the rest. I sent a few men ahead to let everyone know we would be arriving today, so you'll get a proper welcoming to the capital."

"A proper welcoming?" Roanne asked after catching her breath. "What does that mean?"

"You've never been to court, have you?" Jerol had a mischievous grin that put Roanne on edge for some reason. "It simply means all the nobles will be gathered to greet you, after all, you're traveling with a member of the royal family. We can hardly go skulking into town unannounced."

Roanne rolled her eyes. "Why me?" she asked no one in particular.

"Is there a problem?" Lonora seemed to be delighted with the plan.

"Just what am I to wear to greet the king?" Roanne complained. "A cotton blouse and breeches? The ladies at the court will be real impressed with that."

"We'll take care of it when the time comes," Jerol promised. "I believe Letitia and Sheilla will have something appropriate prepared. Remember, Letitia has been expecting you."

They rode out at midmorning, expecting they should be able to reach Esconda just about dark. The pleasant day was lost on Roanne, who suddenly had a multitude of things to consider, most of which she considered trivial, given the situation.

Roanne's first look at the capital came as they crested the hill just east of the city. A few of the palace towers had been visible for some time, but as the walls came into view, the size of the city became apparent. The east wall of the city filled the horizon from the south to the north. From atop the hill they could see over the wall, getting a hint of the regularly spaced streets forming a grid over the city. There were three walls, with each wall built further out from the center of the city, where the palace towered over everything.

"The city keeps growing," Jerol explained. "Every couple centuries a new wall has been built to encase the overflow from the previous wall. Naturally, it also adds to the security, since you would have to break through three walls to get to the palace. I dare say, it would be near impossible to take this city by force."

"Unless you had strong magic to back you up," Spence corrected the prince. "Though, even with magic, it would still require a monumental effort, and an equally monumental loss of life." He hastily amended when Jerol gave him a look.

"You're right," Jerol agreed, "Unless the defenders also have magic."

"In which case everyone dies," Roanne interjected. "More and more would die as each side escalated the danger, while countering the latest move of the enemy." Everyone was looking at her, wondering what had prompted the remark. "It was one of the theories my father had on the origin of the Varden Wastelands. Eventually the two sides simply ended up destroying everything."

"Is that something we should be concerned about?" Stergis inquired, recognizing they once again faced a conflict where magic would make the difference between defeat and victory.

Roanne did not answer, but her gaze dropped from the panoramic view to the ground beside her horse.

"Most of the magic used for warfare has long since been lost," Spence tried to sound optimistic.

"But we seem to be encountering new things, or old things we've forgotten," Roanne finally spoke. "I promise you Jerol, it will not be me who escalates things to that kind of level in this conflict."

"Personally, I think I would rather be dead than live in a world where men like Calum are in control," Jerol settled the subject, unresolved though it might be. He spurred his horse forward drawing the others with him in silence. Even if they did not talk about it, Roanne's comment would be cemented in all their thoughts from this point forward.

The city was still some ways off, though it dominated their view. There were still several smaller hills along the way, and each time they descended the valleys between, they would loose sight of the walls, only to repeat the experience of having them rise up before them each time they climbed the eastern slopes of the rolling terrain.

As they drew closer, one of the scouts came back to report there was a party coming from the city to meet them. The soldiers, who had been rather casual up until now, suddenly formed up around the prince and his guests. Roanne noted Zen and his men must have been taking lessons as they came together around her. When Jerol moved near her, the soldiers showed surprising respect for their momentary allies, resulting in an awkward arrangement. The soldiers held the ground to Jerol and Roanne's left. To their right the peasants lined up, with several guards scattered amongst them, providing suggestions to Zen, and organizing the less trained ranks of men. More guards moved out to the right beyond Zen's men, shoring up that flank.

"The scout reports it's a royal carriage, though since all the family's usual guards are with us, they can't be sure which member of the family it might be," Jerol informed Roanne as they continued to move on, though at a slightly slower pace.

They met the coach a short time later. The sole occupant was Jerol's sister, the Princess Sheilla, a stunning brunette, who surprised Roanne by emerging with a riding habit on, rather than some fancy gown.

Jerol found the whole scene amusing. "How did they get you to ride in the carriage, Sheilla?" he asked with a broad smile as he greeted her. "Sheilla loves to ride." He explained to Roanne and the others.

Sheilla ignored the question, searching the faces of their group. Roanne noted she seemed to have a special smile for Stergis when he rode in from the flank where his men had been helping Zen's. Finally she fixed her gaze on Roanne, who straightened unconsciously in her saddle as Sheilla took her measure.

"Forgive me," Jerol blushed, before making all the proper introductions, presenting Roanne last.

"Your Highness," Roanne did her best to bow in the saddle.

"It's Sheilla," the princess smiled briefly, before turning seriously to Jerol. "Letitia and Regus send their greetings, also. Jerol, there's been trouble in the city. Letitia was attacked by wizards this morning."

"Letitia?" Jerol was stunned. "Why would they attack her?"

"Because," Roanne knew immediately, "Calum saw the two of us together at the estate, and may suspect she was my closest ally in your family."

"That's what Regus thought," Sheilla confirmed.

"Is she all right?" Jerol's anger was barely under control. "What about her attackers?"

"The healer, Tezza, says she'll survive. Five guards were killed in the attack, and Letitia would have been, had not the people rose up against the wizards in numbers they could not deal with, but they did get away." Sheilla could not meet his eyes. "There's a problem with Letitia's leg, though. Tezza's trying her best. She even called in two other healers from the city to help. Tezza says the leg may be lost, and at best she'll be lame for the rest of her life. A man from the village has a similar problem with his arm. Tezza isn't sure what the problem is, or how to deal with it."

Lonora forced her way through to the front of the gathering. "Where are they?" she insisted, "I must get there as soon as possible." Jerol had introduced her simply as a spinner, not as a healer.

Queen of the Spinners

"Smithe," Jerol called the captain of Letitia's own guards, "I want you to take five men and Lonora on ahead, get her to the palace as soon as possible."

Roanne cleared her throat, and moved up next to Lonora.

"No," Jerol got her hint, "If they knew about Letitia, they might also know about your pending arrival, and may be waiting for us. They won't concern themselves with this smaller group, and Lonora doesn't look anything like you."

"Jerol's right," Lonora put a hand on Roanne's arm before she could object.

"You'll find them in Letitia's rooms at the palace," Sheilla informed Smithe. Then she turned to Lonora, tears threatening to run down her cheeks. "Do you think you can help?"

"She's the best healer there is," Roanne answered. Resigned to staying behind, she dismounted and placed a comforting hand on Sheilla's shoulder as the others rode away.

"We've got to be prepared for a possible ambush of some kind," Jerol was talking to the rest of the captains. "Sheilla, tell us everything you can about this attack."

"There were five wizards," Sheilla gathered her self-control. "Letitia was out preparing a few things for Roanne's arrival. She had insisted on walking, wanting to browse in some of the markets as she went. You have to understand even Letitia is unsure of what happened. They were in the market when one of the guards went down, then another. None of them saw anything. It was like holes had appeared in their chests by magic, spurting blood all over. Tensin kept his head enough to push Letitia behind some barrels of fruit, just before he went down with a hole in his back that went all the way through him. What ever it was cut Letitia's cheek badly. Something similar stuck Letitia in the leg, on the front of her thigh, and is causing all the problems. Tensin fell on top of Letitia, pinning her to the ground. Her head hit one of the barrels, knocking her unconscious. Some witnesses told the rest to us. All the guards were dead by then, and the wizards came out of their hiding places to check their work. A young man named Hazlet figured out who the attackers were, I guess his mother is a spinner, so he recognized it was magic being used in the attack. He and three men attacked one of the wizards, pulling him down and beating him. Seeing their success, others came forward to attack the wizards, but the rest of the wizards had seen the first one go down. They held off the crowd long enough to help the wizard Hazlet had attacked, killing both of Hazlet's friends. Hazlet is the man with the injured arm. Three other people were killed, before the crowd began to hesitate, giving the wizards the opportunity to escape."

"Hazlet's a good man," Zen commented. Jerol gave him a look, but said nothing.

"Who were the wizards," Jerol pushed for more information. "Didn't anyone recognize any of them? You must have at least gotten good descriptions."

Sheilla shook her head. "The only description we trust is the one Hazlet gave of the wounded one. You know how crowds can be. We got so many different descriptions of the others we can't sort them out."

"Which market did all this happen in?" Stergis spoke up, "Weren't there any other guards around?"

"It was in Plaza Square," Sheilla answered. "The five guards who normally patrol the market are all missing, probably dead, but nobody wants to admit that, yet."

"Zen," Jerol turned to face the honorary captain, "Can you take your men on ahead, one of my men will show you where the square is. Obviously you have contacts in the city, since you know Hazlet. You might be able to get more information than the regular guards could."

Zen thought a moment, then turned toward Roanne. "Go," Roanne told him. "I'll be fine."

"I'll guarantee that," Jerol assured him. "Come to the palace when you finish, I'll see to it there are accommodations available. There are always extra barracks for the guards of visiting nobility. One will be made available to you and your men."

Zen was still hesitant, but nodded to one of his men, who went off to gather the others. "That's what the carriage is for," Sheilla finally answered Jerol's initial question. "Roanne will be hidden from view if she's inside. Everyone will simply think I came out to meet Jerol on his return to the city."

"More likely they'll think you came out to meet Stergis," Jerol tried to tease his sister, but the humor was lacking. "It's a good plan. Let's get moving. We're sitting ducks out here like this."

The coachman held the door as Sheilla and Roanne climbed in. "At least I won't have to suffer in here alone," Sheilla commented. "You wouldn't believe how hot this thing can get out in the sun like this."

Roanne quickly learned the carriage was not much better than the wagons she was more acquainted with, even with the springs that were supposed to cushion the bumps along the way.

"What exactly was Letitia trying to arrange for me?" Roanne asked once they settled to a gentle rocking motion, after the jerky start.

"When word came back of what had happened, Letitia realized you must have had to flee the estate with nothing but the clothes on your back," Sheilla explained. "She wanted to arrange for a few simple dresses for you, and those other two, Shiva and Talia. Nothing really fancy, but at least presentable. Anything formal would require measurements, but she was also arranging for those once you arrived. Being the future queen, literally every dress maker in the city is at her beck and call."

"I doubt I have the money for such things," Roanne blushed. "And I know Talia and Shiva don't."

"The dresses were all taken care of," Sheilla acted as if she were insulted Roanne would think otherwise. "As for anything more fancy for yourself, what do you mean you can't afford it?"

"Well, I haven't much money with me, and I'm not sure how much my father set aside for me," Roanne shrugged. "He left some money for me in Pavlin's care, as well as what he gave to my uncle to look after me."

"Roanne, your parents didn't trust Mathia very much, which is perfectly justified considering the current situation," Sheilla was almost laughing. "What they left in Pavlin's care was a small fortune. Aside from that, you, not your uncle, own the estate where you've been living, and a ton of other little pieces of property throughout the kingdom. Legally, Mathia was your guardian after the disappearance of your parents, so Pavlin and others have had to do all they could to protect what you own from him. When you come of age, in six months if I'm not mistaken, about the time of Regus' wedding, you'll be as wealthy as I'll ever be."

"I ... I don't understand," Roanne stammered. "You're royalty, I couldn't have that much money."

"It's not all money," Sheilla tried to explain again. "Though there is more than enough money to go around. I don't know all the details. You'll have to check with Pavlin, who has all the deeds for your properties. From what I've heard, though, you own all the schools where spinners can go for at least basic training, two major trading houses, along with the estate, and a variety of other things. Some of the profits go to support the schools and a variety of other charities. You'll even be a partner with my father in some charities."

"Why do I keep finding everyone knows more about me than I do?" Roanne slumped back against the bench she was seated on, until she was nearly thrown off by a bump. "I still don't understand where it all came from. My father wasn't noble or anything like that."

"Your father was the son of a merchant, which is where one of the trading houses comes from," Sheilla was enjoying Roanne's reaction to all this. "Most if it comes from your mother, though. One way Spinners are legally recognized here in Tularand is that in spinner households the inheritance can pass through the daughters. You do know you're the Queen of the Spinners, don't you?"

"I always thought it was something people would tease me about," Roanne suddenly began to realize the seriousness of that title. "In that case, most of the property belongs to the spinners, not me. I can't go spending it. How do you know all this anyway?"

"Part of being royalty is knowing things, like who in the kingdom are important people, and why," Sheilla nonchalantly answered.

They made it to the walls of the city without incident. Inside, the walls, Roanne got a new perspective on just how big crowded and cinfusing the city was. There seemed to be people everywhere, with houses literally connected, as if they couldn't spare the room for space between them. The carriage was slowed by the need to avoid trampling anyone. Still, Roanne had not expected it to take another two hours to reach the palace from the gates. The heat inside the carriage got even worse once they were in the city, and Roanne could appreciate Sheilla's comment back when they first got on board. Once inside the second wall, the houses increased in size, and actually had yards, which also increased in size as they moved closer to the center of the city. Inside the third wall that trend continued, with houses nearly as large as the estate, her own estate, Roanne reminded herself, though still relatively crowded.

"You're lucky we came in through the residential side of the city. The other side is mostly warehouses and businesses," Sheilla served as tour guide along the way. "I'm almost ashamed to say, but as you get farther from the center of the city some of the areas are fairly poor. Workers don't get paid much in some of the smaller businesses in the city. Further in you find those with better paying jobs, the closer to the center of the city, the better paying the job. Skilled workers and owners of the smaller shops and businesses are usually found near the second wall, with the wealthier ones inside the wall. Then come the merchant traders, and some others, like the healers and other wizards and some of the better spinners, who provide services for people. Inside the original wall is almost all nobility, though a few merchants have amassed fortunes large enough they can afford the houses just inside the wall, and often fancy themselves as minor nobility."

"You have a house in this area, fairly close to the palace," Sheilla was not surprised Roanne had not known that. "Regus thought you might want to avoid it for right now. We can't guarantee your safety there. The place was checked out after the attack on Letitia, since Mathia hired all of the staff. Under the circumstances, I don't think we can trust them."

"That could be where the attackers are hiding out," Roanne hated the idea she could be harboring such men.

"When Letitia got your letter, she was concerned enough to have the place checked in case you had to come to Esconda," Sheilla told her. "Since the attack a more thorough search was done, but the wizards weren't found. It wasn't you we doubted."

"I know," Roanne smiled to show her appreciation.

At the palace there was no ceremony to their arrival. Any such plans had been set aside after the events earlier in the day. The palace guard was on alert, watching for any sign of danger.

Chapter 11

Everything was fine with Letitia and Hazlet by the time Roanne and the others arrived at the palace. Jerol went to report to his father and brother, while their guards went about taking care of all the equipment, and the animals. They also helped prepare for the arrival of Zen and his men.

Shiva and her family were taken to guest quarters to get settled in and cleaned up. They had been planning to stay with people they knew in the city, but Jerol had insisted they stay at the palace, explaining how Shiva was an important part of all this. Every resource the family had would be put to helping Shiva recover.

Roanne, with all the wizards and spinners, found Lonora catching a rest in the sunroom of the family wing, while Letitia rested from her ordeal. "We had to operate to remove the obstructions present in both the wounds," Lonora included Hazlet in her summary.

"Obstruction?" Roanne prompted.

"Yes," Lonora continued, "The weapons the wizards had used were lodged in the wounds. The healers couldn't see them, so had no idea they were there. That's what was interfering with the healing process."

"I knew I should have come," Roanne was angry with herself for being held back. "I could have taken care of this with no problem, you would not have needed to operate."

"It's just as well this way," Lonora was too tired to argue, but there was more to tell. "There won't be any scarring so in the end it doesn't make much difference."

"Doesn't make a difference?" Roanne was incredulous. "The last time I checked, it hurt when someone cut into someone else, whether surgically or in anger."

Lonora waved the objection away. "And this way, we have two samples of Calum's magic to study and learn from. You would have destroyed them in the process of removing them."

She held up a blood soaked, silk handkerchief wrapped around something.

That brought Roanne up short. "Really?" She took the kerchief, suddenly forgetting her previous objections. Moving to a nearby table, she carefully unwrapped the contents. Inside were two small spiked balls. If not for the blood covering them, she would not have been able to see them at all. The spikes around the surface were sharp enough to prick her finger when she tried to touch one of them.

"Whoever came up with those is one sadistic bastard," Talia commented, looking over Roanne's shoulder.

"By the gods," Spence had taken a seat at the opposite side of the table from Roanne. "If these are still here, what about the ones that might have missed their target? They could be laying in the square waiting for someone to step on them."

"I sent two healers out there to check around the area, and to let anyone who might accidentally encounter them know where to go for help," a new voice said. "They took several guards with them."

"I should have known you would have thought of that, Tezza," Spence stood to greet the new arrival. "Tezza, may I present the Lady Roanne ..."

"Just Roanne," Roanne cut him off. Introductions went all the way around the room.

"Pavlin will join us momentarily," Tezza took Roanne's offered hand. "He was in with the king and his other advisors when you arrived, otherwise he would have been outside waiting to greet you. I suspect they are all getting a full report from Jerol right now."

Sheilla appeared with refreshments before Roanne had even realized she was missing. "Rooms, with baths, are being made ready for everyone," she told her guests. "I thought you might want something to drink since it will be a few minutes."

"Since when do you serve drinks, Sheilla," Spence teased as she handed him a glass of wine.

"It's some odd notion Letitia came back with from her trip," Sheilla did not seem to mind when Talia quietly began to help her. "Something about not inconveniencing the ser ... I mean staff, unless it's absolutely necessary. Father says we all better get used to it, since Letitia will be running things around here soon."

Roanne could not help but giggle at the explanation. "She mentioned something about the way you ran the household at your estate," Sheilla glared at her. "For the most part it really doesn't matter to me, and the staff seems to like it, except when Letitia gets in the way in the kitchen. Some things are their jobs. We do pay the staff here. It's not like some places where they have to serve." She had to catch herself each time she used the word "staff."

"I think, maybe, Letitia is carrying it a bit too far," Roanne confessed.

"Tell her the first chance you get, will you, before she has me washing dishes," Sheilla widened her eyes in horror, but the smile she had showed she was only joking. "That's one chore I absolutely refuse to get involved in."

Roanne smiled back, and relaxed as she sipped her wine.

"I've never seen anything like this," Spence's voice drew Roanne's attention back to the artifacts from the attack on Letitia. "Has Pavlin gotten a chance to check these out?"

"He was in the room when I took them out," Lonora answered. "I was pretty busy at the time, but I seem to recall he cursed about something, I think he pricked his finger."

"That I did," came the older, familiar voice from the doorway, where Pavlin was entering with another older gentleman. Behind them came Regus and Jerol. "So, what do you think of them, Spence?" The old man waited patiently for Spence to think.

While he was thinking, Roanne crossed the room and embraced the man. "Pavlin, you don't know how good it is to see you."

"I've missed you, too," Pavlin returned the hug. "Let me introduce you. I believe you've already met the two princes, but this is King Arantin Sallas. You Majesty, may I present the Lady Roanne of Altea Province, daughter of Kendal and Ariele, Queen of the Spinners." Roanne blushed at the last part. She took the hand the king offered, curtsying as she kissed his ring. More introductions followed, Jerol making sure everyone in the room was acquainted.

"Well," Pavlin approached the table where Spence was still studying the objects. Roanne was reminded of the times Pavlin had visited the estate, and did the same thing to her, ask a question, then expect the answer after everyone in the room had forgotten he ever asked it.

"I don't know exactly," Spence started awkwardly, "I mean, I know what it is. It's like solid air, but I haven't a clue as to how it was made. We tried some experiments on the way here, but none of them compared with this. Frozen water is completely different."

"What do you think, Roanne?" Pavlin turned his attention to her.

"Actually it is like frozen water," Roanne shrugged an apology to Spence. "If I remember correctly, according to some of the books I've read, water is odd when it freezes, because it expands. Everything else shrinks in the cold. That's what makes this so confusing, maybe using water the other night in our experiments was the wrong choice."

"Very interesting," Pavlin rubbed his chin as he leaned over the table and took a closer look at the objects. "You might be right, Roanne. These are crystals, but not like any I've ever seen. I wish we had Kendal's books. I believe he has one about crystals."

"Crystals?" Telin asked, showing an interest in the conversation.

"Like diamonds, but using a different material to start from," Pavlin explained. "We had thought the use of crystals in magic had disappeared long ago. Wizards used to use them as a focus, more of a tool for centering your concentration, the way we use chants and gestures."

"Roanne doesn't do that," Talia spoke up, showing no sign of being intimidated by the company in the room.

"What do you mean?" Pavlin asked.

"I don't use gestures or chants anymore," Roanne answered. "I seem to be able to focus without them."

"Also," she went on before Pavlin could push more on the point, "I have as many of father's books as I could bring with me, particularly the older tomes, which is where the information on crystals must be. Maybe I have the one you mentioned."

"We'll check later," Pavlin refused to be distracted. "Explain what you mean about not needing gestures and chants."

"I can't really explain it," Roanne knew this would come sooner or later. "When Calum had me trapped, he fixed it so I couldn't speak, later Talia realized I wasn't using my hands either, yet I was working magic."

"First thing in the morning, I want you up in my labs," Pavlin waved a finger at Roanne, the way he always did when giving her instructions. "It's been far too long since I tested your abilities."

"Just what did the old tests tell?" Lonora asked.

"What?" Pavlin was caught off guard. "You know as much as I do, Lonora. Probably more, if you've seen her work recently."

"I've never tested her, though," Lonora insisted. "We need to know just how strong she is."

"And I intend to find out, tomorrow," Pavlin refused to give in, and nobody ever got the best of him when he was in one of his stubborn moods.

"I've just been told the rooms and baths are ready, for those of you who would like to freshen up before dinner," Sheilla interrupted before Lonora could press further.

"May I show you to your rooms," Jerol offered an arm to Roanne. He led her out to the hall, where he warned her of what was to come. "Representatives of all the noble families will be at the dinner. Once the dinner is over, they'll be expecting to hear from you, and from Talia, concerning Calum's activities. I told them Shiva was in no condition for that kind of interrogation, and insisted she be excused once the meal is done."

"Interrogation?" Roanne was suddenly wary.

"You didn't think they were going to take my word for what happened, did you?" Jerol did not seem concerned at all. "I wasn't even there. Perhaps 'interrogation' is the wrong word to use, but after what I just went through with some of the nobles, I'm sure it will seem that way to you. I'm just trying to warn you ahead of time. Regus will warn the others, he wanted another opportunity to thank Lonora for helping Letitia, so he'll be taking them to the guest wing."

"Aren't we going to the guest wing?" Roanne was getting concerned, and a bit confused, which did not help.

"Letitia wanted to see you," Jerol explained, leading Roanne in the opposite direction everyone else was headed. "I thought we could check to see if she's awake, before going to your rooms, which will be in the family wing."

"The family wing?" Roanne suddenly had something else to confuse her on top of everything else. For a panicked moment she sensed she was losing control of the situation. Calming herself, she kept her focus on one thing at a time.

"I believe that will be up to my father to explain," Jerol was being evasive. "He wants to speak with you after the dinner is over. I'm sure he'll explain everything."

Roanne could see by the set of his expression she would get nowhere down that line of questioning.

They came to a stairwell, which gave her a moment to gather her thoughts as she climbed. "About this 'interrogation' as you put it, it sounds as if there are those who don't believe me, and would side with the wizards."

"There are," Jerol was more candid on this subject. "A few families are simply afraid of facing off against the wizards. One or two, who usually see nothing but conspiracies, think you might be lying. They'll claim this is all a plot to usurp their authority over their peasants. They are the lords who have been abusing their people. When it comes down to it, though, their arguments are purely political. Father has already rejected them."

"So the crown will stand against the wizards in the dispute," Roanne hoped Jerol would confirm for her, "And demand Calum be turned over."

"Yes, father will be behind you all the way," Jerol's voice still hinted of a problem.

"What is it? You're not telling me everything," Roanne stopped, determined not to go any further until Jerol came clean.

"I think this is what Letitia wants to speak with you about," Jerol did not look Roanne in the eye. "If she's up to it. If not, I'll tell you, but I think she at least deserves the chance to say it first."

A door further down the hall opened, and Tezza slipped out. She hurried over to Jerol and Roanne the moment she saw them. "She's awake, but very tired. The wound in her leg bled a lot because of the trouble we had, and it will take a couple of days before she's fully recovered, despite the magic. Keep that in mind, normally I would forbid visitors right now, but she's rather insistent about this, and refuses to go to sleep until she speaks with you."

"We won't be long," Jerol assured Tezza. "Roanne still has to prepare for dinner."

They found Letitia lying in bed, looking pale enough to scare Roanne. "You really should be resting," Roanne tried to insist. "Whatever it is, it can wait until your feeling stronger."

"No," Letitia was adamant. "I want you to hear this from me, before you go to dinner. My father is not going to openly support you at the dinner." She looked away in shame.

"He's what?" Roanne had met Duke Bassel, and had liked the man. She had not expected this.

"He's worried about Timond," Letitia was obviously equally concerned. "Timond should have been at the college when

Calum reached there, and my father says he's concerned Timond could be held hostage, or killed outright."

Roanne had completely forgotten about Letitia's brother. "Can't Telin get word to him, or at least find out if he's safe?"

"He'll try when he gets the chance," Jerol answered. "Until then, though, Bassel doesn't have much choice. He won't openly oppose you, but he won't support you either, not until he knows Timond is safe."

"I'm not so sure," Letitia still avoided Roanne's eyes. "Timond was at the estate during the festival as you know. I supported his choice to become a wizard, and now I wonder if he knew about this the whole time. He's changed over the past year, and I thought it was just the pressure of the decision he had to make, now I wonder. My father told me on the way back to Esconda Timond had spent a lot of time with Calum."

"Surely he wouldn't support a man like Calum, he's your brother," Roanne pulled back a bit, but Letitia reached out for her hand.

"I don't want to believe it," Letitia finally met Roanne's eyes, "And I swear to you, Roanne, I'll support you. If my brother is involved in this he's wrong. This is not something where I can even give him the benefit of the doubt."

Roanne lightly wrapped Letitia in her arms. "I would never doubt you, and I have confidence in your father and brother. Remember, Timond had agreed to find out about Calum for us. Maybe that explains why he spent so much time with Calum. Now you get some sleep, I'm going to need a lot of help learning my way around here, and you'll be no help if you're in bed longer than you should be because you didn't rest when you should have."

"I'll be ready to help," Letitia hugged her back weakly, "I just wish I could see the faces on the other ladies when they see you tonight, and more importantly, the looks on the available men, and the recently married who missed out." She smiled as she lay back on her pillows, waving as Jerol escorted Roanne out. Roanne looked back through the closing doors, and saw Letitia was already asleep by the time her view was cut off.

Chapter 12

Evidently Letitia had not been attacked until the end of her errand, since Roanne found a simple, yet elegant gown of velvet, with a silk overlay for the skirt waiting for her in the rooms she had been given, just down the hall from Letitia's. She found each of the women in her entourage were similarly dressed when she got down to the dining hall. Even Zen had found a proper surcoat and breeches waiting for him.

The meal was nothing less than Roanne had expected. After days of eating on the run, the extravagant meal was a welcome distraction from Roanne's troubles. In her experience, only the feasts she had prepared for the festivals were comparable.

All the available spinners shared the table she had, while the king and his family sat at the head table. Across the way from her table, Roanne spared enough attention from the food to notice the empty chair at the table where Duke Bessal was seated with a number of other nobles. That would normally have been Letitia's chair, until the wedding. The noble families were spread throughout the hall, with those of greater influence, including those who served as advisors to the crown, seated closest to the main table.

At least the late hour of the meal did not seem to bother anyone, so hopefully they would not hold it against her. It was not her fault they got to the city in the late afternoon. Then again, she remembered Jerol had let her sleep in that morning. Several of the staff reassured her it was not uncommon to have such dinners to welcome new guests this late.

The festive mood of the meal, and the reaction of the other spinners, who had never experienced anything like this, was enough to keep Roanne's mind off what she knew was coming. For a while at least, she let herself enjoy the experience of life at court.

As the last remnants of the meal were cleared away, Roanne noticed when one of the captains from the table where Zen was

Queen of the Spinners

seated was called to the main table. It was a man Roanne was unfamiliar with, not being one of the captains who had accompanied Jerol. From the main table, he came toward Roanne, and she knew the time had come. "Would you please step forward, Lady Roanne? The nobles would hear your story now," the guard asked politely when he reached their table.

Nervously, Roanne rose to accompany him, the touches of encouragement she received from both Lonora and Fenicia, who sat to either side of her, helped. As she moved around the table, Talia stood, also, and began to follow her, a satchel in her hand reminding Roanne they had the collars as proof. Roanne had completely forgotten about them, which was just as well since she might have used them in her tests, and destroyed them in the process.

Each of them was asked if they had any objections to being truth read by Telin, and both agreed to allow it. They then offered their testimony freely, and it took some time for each of them to tell what they had been through, with Talia providing vivid and chilling details of the treatment Calum had given Shiva. Shiva's parents had taken her from the hall so she would not have to relive the telling. Spence came forward to tell of the attack he had witnessed, and included what he knew of the reward the council had offered for Roanne.

When they were finished, several witnesses, including Tezza and Lonora told what they knew of the attack on Letitia. Even Hazlet made an appearance, his pale complexion showing the same loss of blood affecting Letitia.

"I think we have a serious situation, here," King Sallas took control of the proceedings once everyone was finished with their statements. "The gravity of the accusations is such we have no choice but to move swiftly to right the wrongs that have been wrought by this attack upon citizens of this land. The evidence suggests complicity in this matter by the Council of Wizards, and possibly others. All must be brought to justice."

"Will we not be hearing from the other side in this dispute?" One of the dukes rose to complain. It was Duke Aston, which was no surprise to Roanne. Jerol had escorted her down to the hall, and made a point of identifying him to her. "Or do we now render justice on the word of individuals who could easily be involved in a plot to usurp the power of the nobility?"

"The Council of Wizards has been offered the opportunity to respond to the accusations. We were even willing to allow them to speak through Telin," the king informed them all. "Pavlin, has there been any response from the council?"

"There has been no word out of Altea since the offering of the reward for the capture of Roanne," Pavlin stated. "As for myself, as a member of the council, and those present who might otherwise have been represented by the council, we denounce the activities of this Calum, and fully support the crown's desire for justice." Pavlin was at the table nearest the dais. Every wizard in the hall rose to their feet, one at a time, to echo his sentiments. "The witnesses have all been truth read on this matter, which leaves no doubt." Pavlin concluded.

"We all know there are limits to truth reading," Aston pointed out. "Perhaps the real truth is, like other spinners, these two view any marriage arrangement to be a form of slavery. Are we all not familiar with the history of the spinners, who force inheritance through the daughter, not the son. They would probably like to have all our wives set free. Was not Mathia the guardian of Roanne, and thus responsible for arranging a suitable marriage for her? Telin, would not such a stretched truth in the mind of a fanatic be seen as truth by your spell?"

"Yes it would," Telin ducked his head at his admission.

"Further, what of the death of Mathia?" Aston pressed on. "By her own admission she attacked an unarmed, defenseless man from behind. We will all rue the day the crown countenances the cold blooded murder of a loving parent."

"Since when is any wizard, let alone a member of the council, defenseless?" Regus spoke up. "As to your other argument, if I ever learn you've fallen to keeping your wife in a cage, I will personally come to your lands, and set her free." He rose to his feet, slamming a fist on the table before him.

Jerol, seated on the other side of the king, rose, also. Sallas would have held them in their seats, but in trying to reach for one, lost his chance to stop the other. Around the room other nobles were rising to their feet, also. Sallas had to pound the table to reestablish order in the room.

"I will have no threats in this room from anyone," Sallas glared at his two sons, then realizing his daughter was also standing, and did not spare her.

"Thank you, Your Majesty," Aston had turned as pale as Hazlet, but kept his composure. "Finally, there is the question of her open alliance with rebels." An accusing finger found Zen at the back of the room. "Rebels plotting the overthrow of the nobility." That accusation carried weight with this particular audience.

Regus nearly stood again, but Sallas caught him in time. "Is that all you have to say Duke Aston?"

Aston took a broad stance in front of his seat, his arms across his chest. "Is that not enough? If justice is truly the goal of this gathering, then we must hear from all sides."

"Do you have a response?" Sallas turned his attention back to Roanne. "How would you answer Duke Aston?"

Roanne took the satchel Talia had been holding. She reached in, and came out with nothing, or so it seemed. Quickly realizing the problem, she searched the tables, finding a bowl of butter that had yet to be cleared away. Explaining as she went along, she smeared butter over the surface of the two collars, making them visible to all.

From a pocket, Regus produced the two objects removed from Hazlet's arm and Letitia's leg. The captain who originally came to Roanne's table to begin the proceedings and Stergis took all four objects around the room so everyone could get a closer look, particularly at the small weapons. Their significance was further explained, as the two guards did so.

"Perhaps we should check to see if this," Roanne held up one of the collars afterward, "Is the kind of ring Duke Aston gave his wife at their wedding. I believe his mistreatment of the people working for him is already well documented." She crossed the room to the duke's table and looking directly at the duke's wife, dropped the collar on the table.

"If it is," she addressed the woman, who was much younger than the duke, "All you need do is ask, and I will remove it."

Roanne remained by the table, standing right across from the duke. She had only a few minutes to think of what she was going to say, and the next words would be risky. Motioning with her hand, she called Stergis over near her. "Would you give the duke your sword, please, Captain Stergis?" She asked. Stergis hesitated until he caught a nod from Jerol, then drew his sword, offering it to the duke. When the duke refused it, Roanne took it by the blade and laid it on the table, the hilt toward Aston. "You claimed the unarmed Mathia was defenseless. Well, so am I, I have no weapon on me, and I'm a spinner," she put special emphasis on the last point. "Go ahead and attack me."

A hush passed through the assembly. This time the king began to rise, but was held by both his sons.

"I have no cause to attack you," Aston visibly shrank from the sword.

"You just said I was a rebel," Roanne countered, "Is it not your sworn duty to protect the kingdom from me. Well, now's your chance. Do your duty."

Stergis wiped at his nose to cover the smirk on his face, though others were not so circumspect. A few in the hall actually laughed out loud as Aston's hands began to shake. He had been paying more attention to some of the stories than Roanne had thought.

A commotion broke out at one of the other noble tables, drawing the attention in the room away from Roanne. Two guards began moving in that direction as a young woman was struggling with a man. When the guards grabbed the man, the woman was able to break free. She stumbled down the main isle toward Roanne, falling finally. Determined to get where she was going, the young woman crawled the rest of the way. At almost the same time another fight broke out.

"Lylla!" Stergis called out, snatching his sword from the table and heading toward the second disturbance.

Lylla, Stergis' sister, was struggling with the man seated next to her. A second man was helping the first, but stopped when he saw Stergis coming. Frantically he began making gestures, which ended with a throwing motion aimed at Stergis. Roanne concentrated, and the thrown object burned away just before reaching Stergis, who froze at the sight of the burst of flames just in front of his chest. The wizard was motioning again, but this time the fire caught while the object was still in his hand. He screamed in agony, before passing out from the pain.

The other man holding the woman turned white at the sight, which gave the woman the opportunity she needed, breaking free and making it around the table before she tripped and fell. Stergis, recovering quickly from his own shock, was there to catch her.

Something whirled through Roanne's line of vision. Without thinking she followed it's motion, ready to burn it before she realized she could see this object. The dagger planted itself hilt deep in the chest of the man seated next to Duke Aston, whose hand began bleeding as he clutched involuntarily at the invisible object it held. Another movement behind her caught her attention, but as she spun she noticed she was becoming disoriented and confused. She stopped herself from doing anything until she could figure out what was happening and who was who.

The man behind her was Jerol, now holding the tip of a sword at Aston's throat. Stergis left the girl on the floor and was advancing on the man she had been struggling with. It took five guards to stop Stergis from killing the man and the wizard with him. It was all happening too quickly for Roanne to keep track of. She checked back in the direction where the confusion first broke out. Several guards seemed to have that situation under control. Their biggest problem was keeping Talia and Sheilla away from the man.

Another scream of agony came from that area of the room. Roanne only caught sight of the tail end of the burst of flames, and wondered who had managed that. Then saw Spence standing on his table so he could see better through the panicked crowd.

Something caught Roanne in the shoulder, sending a bolt of pain through her, and buckling her knees. She could feel the object caught in the fabric of her dress. She burned it away in such a hurry she scorched the material. Fortunately, it was only a glancing blow, though the pain had shocked her for a moment. Searching the room, she tried to identify where the attack had come from. Two men were in the balcony overlooking the dining area, both busy making gestures and throwing. Following their movements, Roanne saw they were targeting the king. Two of the guards who had went to watch over him were already down. Realizing what was happening, the king upended the table, pulling both downed men behind it for shelter. Two objects flamed just before reaching the king's back, as he dove for cover, one trailing flames like a shooting star in the night. Spence and Telin came to stand in his defense. Telin's effort was not as efficient as Roanne or Spence's, but he may have just saved the king's life. The side door of the balcony burst open as Lathom and Duval went after the two wizards. One pulled a shield out of thin air to hold the captains off, leaving his companion free to continue the attack. Gesturing wildly, the second wizard prepared to strike, and Lathom and Duval would have been defenseless against such an attack. When Roanne burned away his weapon, the hall filled once more with screams of pain. When the shield burned away, Lathom's sword passed freely into the chest of the other, while Duval dispatched the injured wizard.

"That's four," Roanne climbed back to her feet, one hand clutching her shoulder, her eyes searching the room again.

"Five," Corrected Jerol indicating the man with the dagger in his chest. The tip of his sword was digging deeper into the Aston's throat, and was already drawing blood. Two guards were standing at either side of the prisoner, hesitating while Jerol tried to control his temper. Roanne put a hand over Jerol's grip on the sword, tempted to push it forward, but knowing she could not. Slowly, together, they eased the point back, giving the guards room to move in and secure the duke.

It wasn't until then Roanne remembered the first girl who started the struggle, she was still clutching at Roanne's skirts, fear and hope mingling the tears on her face.

"The Duchess Aston," she reminded Jerol. Taking any opportunity to vent his anger, Jerol slammed a fist into the table, smashing it, before crossing over the debris and picking up the duchess from where she cowered on the floor. Stergis finally made it back to Roanne then, clutching Lylla in his arms. Regus came with him, a fourth young woman carried in his arms.

Roanne looked around, and saw Lonora, Fenicia, and Tezza scrambling to check the wounded, and realized she should help. "Take them all ..." she was at a lost in the unfamiliar environment.

"We'll take them to your rooms, in the sitting room," Jerol suggested. "Are there any other women?"

"Not here," Regus said, "But Duke Cezar had two with him. We had better send some men out to check the residences of the three of them. There are probably more."

"Their provinces, too," Stergis pointed out.

"Let's deal with things here in Esconda, first," Jerol took control. "Stergis, get a couple of men and take these women to Roanne's suite. Lathom, don't sound an alarm, but gather enough men to take the three houses. These dukes have maybe twenty guards apiece here in the city? Perhaps thirty, considering what they were doing. I want at least twice that at each house, and be sure to do them all at the same time. I don't want warnings going from house to house."

"No!" Roanne had begun to check around her for injured, and found Zen, with a hole in his chest. He must have tried to get to her from the back of the room, where he had been seated for the dinner. "No!" She cried again, searching for any sign of life in his slack form.

Jerol pulled her back away from the body, wrapping her tightly in his arms. Lonora took Roanne's place checking over the body for only a moment, before reaching out and closing his eyes.

Lonora then checked on Roanne's shoulder. She fussed with Roanne's skirts, peeling them back to find the white petticoats. Tearing off a piece, she packed it against the small wound to stop the bleeding. "Hold that," she instructed Jerol before moving on. "There are others needing my attention. She'll be all right."

Others began to appear out of the confusion around the room, Talia and Sheilla, then Spence, with Tagert and Telin. Finally Pavlin and the king came forward, and all gathered around where Jerol held Roanne.

"I'll be fine," Roanne had managed to collect her wits. She wiped at the tears running freely down her cheeks, watching as Zen's body was removed to another part of the palace. Another figure appeared, dropping a bundle of bandages, and Jerol began to wrap Roanne's shoulder.

"So the war begins," Sallas commented sadly, looking around the room. "Lady Roanne, I checked those women as Stergis removed them. They are all bound somehow, their hands, their necks, even their feet are hobbled, which explains why they fell as they tried to run. It seems they are even gagged, not unlike they way you described earlier."

"Who's Lylla?" Roanne pulled the name from her confused memory of the events.

"Stergis' youngest sister," Jerol informed her. "Their father married her to Duke Markum's brother, who was here representing the duke. Duke Markum holds the neighboring province to Stergis' Lancarn, they were hoping the marriage would improve relations between the families. Stergis had opposed it from the beginning."

"I don't get it," Tagert spoke up, scratching his chin. "How could they be so stupid as to bring those women here? Did they actually think they would get away with it?"

"They probably would have if Roanne had not confronted Aston the way she did," Jerol looked dejected. "It would have been a major insult not to bring their wives to such a social event as the arrival of an honored guest to the palace, and if they had managed to slip out quietly after the discussion, no one would have known. How did you know?" Jerol looked to Roanne.

"I didn't," she admitted. "I was just searching for some way to counter the duke's arguments. It never occurred to me the duchess, let alone others, would take up the offer I made, or would actually be wearing collars."

Captain Duval came to address the king. "Your Majesty, we've secured the palace. There were five dead, seven injured in the fighting. Fifteen representatives of the three families, including their guards who were outside, have been taken. They have seven injured, another six dead. Of the five wizards, three are dead, and the other two are severely injured. The prisoners have all been taken to the wall where they can be kept safely in the cells there. Our men are doing their best to help the injured."

"Not healers?" Sallas questioned. "I want those wizards alive for questioning."

"The healers have agreed to help treat the prisoners, sire, but only after they have seen to the rest of the injured," Duval explained. "We've sent for more healers from the city, it shouldn't be long before they begin to arrive."

"How severe are our injured?" Jerol cut in.

"Three have the same problems Letitia went through, the weapons are imbedded in the wounds, and the healers are having trouble finding them since they can't be seen," Duval reported.

"Where are they?" Roanne struggled to her feet, with Jerol's help. "I can take care of that problem." She was glad there was something she could do to help, and to take her mind off other things.

"I understand you can also deal with whatever it is they used to bind those women," Sallas commented.

"That goes without saying, Your Majesty," Roanne answered, as Duval led the way to the wounded. Jerol came with her, staying right at her side. Spence also followed, explaining he wanted to observe her work.

As they left the hall, the crowd around the king had grown, as the remainder of the nobility gathered around their leader. The word "war" was a prominent feature of the new discussion.

They found the wounded in a make shift hospice just outside the hall. Roanne immediately began checking which had magical weapons still causing problems, until Lonora noticed her. "I've already removed one of them, and Tezza is working on another."

"I can deal with them much easier than you can," Roanne pointed out. "In addition, with my way, the healing process afterward will be much easier."

"Do you have the control you need to do something like this?" Lonora asked.

Roanne blinked. "What's that supposed to mean?"

Lonora said nothing, only touching the singed edges of the sleeve on Roanne's gown.

"That was in the middle of the fighting," Roanne brushed aside Lonora's concern. "I was confused, and in pain."

"And you're in no pain, now?" Lonora asked.

Roanne wondered why Lonora was being so hostile, and had to think a minute before she realized she was not in pain. Lonora, saw the surprise on Roanne's face, and began removing the bandage to check on the injury to Roanne's shoulder. While the bandage and the bodice of Roanne's gown were both thoroughly stained with blood, beneath the bandage there was no wound. The skin where the gash had been was as smooth and perfect as the day Roanne had been born.

"Well, that confirms what we talked about the other day," Lonora took a deep breath. "I apologize, I shouldn't have snapped at you the way I did. We've already lost one patient, and may loose the one who has one of those spiked balls embedded in his chest."

"No need," Roanne dismissed the apology, "Just show me where he is, and let's see if I can be of some use around here."

"Any idea how you did that?" Lonora indicated Roanne's shoulder again. "It could be most useful, now, and I fear, in the future."

"I hadn't even realized I had done it," Roanne could only shrug as Lonora took her hand and led the way to the patient needing Roanne the most.

Chapter 13

At the sight of the injured man, one of the guards King Sallas had hauled behind the table, if her memory was right, Roanne became sick. She had barely made it from the room, and collapsed just outside the door, in the hall. Vomit covered the floor around her. Jerol came with towels, so she could wipe herself.

"Oh, gods," Roanne groaned, "Look at the mess I've caused."

"Don't worry about it," Jerol's arm around her shoulder bolstered her, as she fed on his strength, then stood and returned to the bed where the patient waited.

Lonora, knife in hand was about to begin operating, when Roanne reappeared. The guard had two wounds, and Lonora, seeing the determination in Roanne's eyes, explained she thought both weapons were still there. They had not been able to stop the bleeding in either wound.

Roanne fought back the turning of her stomach this time, drawing more strength from Jerol, who had stayed with her. She took a moment to gather her concentration, and when Lonora peeled back the skin around the first wound she looked inside. It was the thought of this sight, inside the wound, that had sent Roanne running only moments ago, but this time she held fast.

"Would burning help stop the bleeding?" Roanne thought aloud, looking to Lonora for the answer.

"Don't get any fancy ideas," Lonora admonished her. "All you need to do is get rid of the thing in there. I can take care of the rest."

It took only seconds once Roanne located what she was looking for. The second wound was easier since she knew better how to find the object in the pool of blood filling the wound. Having done what she could for this man, Roanne went and helped Tezza with the other man. His wound was in the back, with the object lodged in the side of his kidney.

Finished with her part in the healing, Roanne excused herself. "I made a mess, and I think I should help clean up," she told Tezza.

"Someone is already taking care of it," Jerol assured her, so she stayed and watched Tezza as she began to work on repairing the injury.

Roanne could see Tezza was tiring, looking around, she saw Talia and Fenicia were working with the less seriously injured. Tezza and Lonora were the only two true healers there, and Roanne could see the work was even beginning to strain Lonora. Healers often had to feel the pain of their patients in order to heal it, which was why her ability to heal herself was so remarkable. The pain Tezza and Lonora had to absorb, particularly in a situation like this, was horrendous, and was obviously taking its toll.

"Where are those other healers?" she asked Jerol. "These two can't keep this up."

"They should have been here by now," Jerol agreed, taking his leave to see what was causing the delay.

Roanne watched Tezza work for a while, sensing the magic as Tezza manipulated the energy to feed the tissue that needed to grow, and renew itself. She could tell Tezza did not have much energy left, and the wound to the kidney was being difficult. Roanne had little understanding of the process of healing, but she knew well the energy Tezza needed to facilitate that process.

Tezza blinked and looked around the room in confusion, finally finding Roanne behind her. "Just use it," Roanne told her, and Tezza went back to work, moving much faster now. The wound was healed in as much time as it had taken Tezza to merely patch the kidney. Through the link Roanne had made with Tezza, Roanne saw more clearly what Tezza was doing, and even felt some of the pain through the link.

When Jerol returned, he had two women with him, who immediately went to work on the others Talia and Fenicia had been helping.

"Thank you, Roanne," she heard Tezza say, and realized she had finished with the patient before them. "I don't think I would have been able to make it if you hadn't done whatever you did."

"Rest a few minutes," Roanne told Tezza, guiding her to a chair. As Roanne suspected, the moment she stopped feeding energy to the healer, Tezza tired again, as if the help had never been there. Roanne searched her memory for the explanation of the spell in one of her father's older books. There was some danger to lending energy this way, even more so if you used the energy to replenish the borrower, since any later use of the energy would also affect the donor. Because her energy was used to do the healing, Roanne felt the pain Tezza would otherwise have had absorb, but Roanne also saw more closely exactly what Tezza did with the energy to perform the healing.

Looking across the room she noticed Spence was now doing the same thing for Lonora, evidently this was something they did still teach at the college.

"Jerol," she called out, "Help me get Tezza out of here. She needs to rest, and will need food, plenty of it. The same goes for Lonora."

They took Tezza to another room, moving toward the residential wing. It was the same sunroom where she had found Lonora the day before. Spence soon followed with Lonora on his arm.

"I had no idea I could do that with a spinner, or I would have helped much sooner," he remarked as he settled Lonora on a couch. "I wouldn't have even thought of it if Roanne had not done it."

Lonora smiled at Roanne, "Where did you learn that? Spence tells me they teach it at the college."

"Books," Roanne answered, collapsing in a chair. She had not realized how tired she was. She noticed the weak light in the windows of the sunroom, and knew dawn approaching. They had been up all night.

"I had better go take care of those other women," she said, trying to force herself to her feet, but Spence stopped her.

It was obvious Spence was even more tired than she was. "You need rest, too," All he could do to stop her was sit on the floor against her legs, but that was all it took. "I don't know what those books told you, but sharing energy is not very efficient, and can be twice as draining on the donor."

Lonora and Tezza were already curled up and sleeping on the couches, and even as Roanne watched, Spence leaned his head against her knee and went to sleep. Jerol came with the food then, and helped get Spence to a more comfortable position, even if it was on the floor. Roanne tried again to stand, but he stopped her this time.

"You haven't fully recovered from all the strain you went through on the way here, it tends to accumulate if you don't take time to recover," Tagert, who came in behind Jerol, carrying another tray of food, explained. "Personally, I have no idea how you keep going."

When Roanne woke later in the day, there were bodies scattered throughout the room, most of them sleeping. What had wakened her was the commotion caused by the arrival of Sallas, who was piling food onto a plate at the table in the center of the room. Roanne wiped her eyes, trying to clear the haze in her mind at the same time.

Seeing she was awake, Sallas gave up his plate to her. "Pavlin tells me you will all need to eat as soon as you are awake," he said. Returning to the table, he began filling another plate. Roanne did not need to be told twice.

Over the next half-hour Sallas served the others as they came to life, Tezza being the last of those Roanne knew. Among the others, sleeping on any available furniture, and the floor, Roanne recognized the two healers who arrived late with Jerol. There were twelve in all, now, including four wizards, and eight of them were sleeping. One of those awake explained they had not made it to the palace until most of the work was already done, but had been asked to stay. Roanne checked the windows, noticing it was dark again.

Jerol and Regus crept into the room, and began to grab plates. "We need to talk," Regus told Sallas.

Roanne paid them little attention, until she noticed Jerol was having trouble piling the food on his plate. Then she noticed the blood on his and Regus' shirts. She set her empty plate aside, and rushed over to check them both out. "Lonora," she called as she went.

"You're hurt," Roanne blurted as she came to the two men.

They looked at each other, then at themselves, seeming to just notice the blood. "We're fine," Jerol contradicted her, "That's not my blood. How about you Regus?"

"I'm fine," the other prince answered. "But you should let someone look at your hand, Duval told me you were fighting off handed at the last house."

"There are others coming soon who will need their attention more," Jerol dismissed the injury.

"Let me see it," Lonora was used to unruly patients. She took the hand gently then began poking at the area around the swelling. Leading Jerol by that hand, she took him over to a lamp so she could see the injury. "It's broken," she concluded.

Jerol rolled his eyes. "It's nothing."

"I thought I ordered the two of you to say out of the fighting," Sallas interrupted. "Not that I expected you to listen, but now you see what can happen. We cannot have either of you laid up with an injury right now."

"It didn't happen in the fighting," Jerol tried to excuse their disregard of the order. "I lost my temper and smashed a table last night."

"Last night?" Roanne was shocked, remembering how he had cleared his way to the Duchess Deallah, Aston's wife. "You should have had it taken care of then."

Regus laughed. "She sounds a lot like Letitia," he teased Roanne and Jerol.

"I think we had better take this elsewhere," Sallas broke in. "These healers need rest, and as you said, Regus, we need to talk, all of us," he included Roanne, Lonora, and Tezza.

"This would have been no problem last night," Lonora admonished Jerol. "The longer you put it off, though, the harder it gets."

Sallas led the way to another room, just down the hall. It took several minutes for Lonora to take care of Jerol's hand, in spite of his protests. Roanne could tell it wasn't easy for Lonora, but the healer flatly refused any help.

Sallas arranged to have drinks and more food brought to this room while they were waiting on Lonora.

"Oh, I've got something else I need to do. The women from the dinner are still bound in those things," Roanne suddenly remembered.

"That can wait, you need to hear this, if the preliminary reports I have heard are true," Sallas held her arm to keep her from rushing off.

"Regus?" Sallas turned to his oldest son.

"We've taken the three houses of the nobles involved in last night's attempt to kill Roanne and you," Regus reported, and Roanne reacted with shock, not having considered what had really caused all the fighting. "Those wizards were there for a reason, and it wasn't to welcome you here," Regus explained. "There are more injured, but we have some healers from the city helping at the scene, others will be coming back here, but it will be a while yet. Hopefully those other healers will have had a chance to rest, they weren't taxed near as much as you were." He looked at Tezza and Lonora then.

"I want the two of you to promise me you will make full use of the others before you push yourselves the way you did last night," Sallas demanded, and both healers agreed.

Pavlin had come into the room with the drinks, along with Spence, who had finally wakened. "And I want your assurance," Pavlin pointed a finger at Roanne, "There will be no more sharing. It's dangerous, and more draining than you think. It's only to be used in the direst circumstances. I can accept this morning, those men might have died otherwise, but we have more than enough healers, now."

Spence shrugged to show he had already received his lecture on the subject, and Roanne agreed, unless it was absolutely necessary.

"We don't have numbers on the injured or dead, yet," Regus picked up the report. He turned and looked right at Roanne. "There are more women with those things on, though. Close to fifty of them."

Roanne collapsed into a chair. This was far worse than she could have imagined.

"Apparently they were stocking up," Jerol put in. "They were planning to sell them, either in their own provinces, or in the other kingdoms. We know slavery is tolerated to some extent up in Curiland. This is probably only the beginning, when we get to their provinces, who knows how many we'll find, which makes it imperative we get moving."

"I had no idea it was this bad," Sallas hung his head in shame. "Where is Telin?" He turned to Pavlin. "I have a message for that council of yours."

"He'll be here momentarily," Pavlin said. "I would remind you that I believe most of the other wizards will be on your side. We will do all we can to help make those responsible for these atrocities pay."

Sallas visibly calmed himself. "Of course, forgive me my friend. This just angers me so much, mostly because I should have seen it coming."

"There's more," Regus spoke, again looking at Roanne and Lonora, who had moved to Roanne's side. "We've learned several spinners in the city were attacked. It looks as if the wizards were searching for a healer after the one was injured in the attack on Letitia. Several spinners said word of the attack on Letitia had spread, and many of the healers might not have wanted to treat the wizard unless he turned himself in to the guards. The wizards also would not want any spinner they went to for help, healer or not, to be able to identify them. So far, we've found nine spinners who were killed."

Lonora was turning red with rage and grief. She clutched at Roanne's hand, and Jerol came over to try and help comfort her. Roanne was also angry, but no more than she had been in the past several days. She wondered about that as she pulled Lonora close to her. It seemed to her the Queen of the Spinners should somehow have more of a reaction to this news, but it seemed somehow trivial, Roanne hated that thought, compared to what the women from the three provinces were suffering. Their suffering was the focus of her outrage, and her doubts.

"Is that all we know?" Sallas asked.

"For now," Regus replied. "At least until the final reports start to come in from the houses, and we get a more thorough search of the city going."

"Can't we get the people in the city to help?" Jerol suggested. "Zen had contacts there, it would save time and manpower."

"Zen's men are already helping," Regus said. "I believe Kerlon has stepped into the leadership. I'll speak with him."

"Tell him I said to do whatever you need," Roanne offered. "They'll have men available out in the provinces, also. You have three provinces, and the college to go after, which I suspect will leave you thin on men. You may want their help, even if they're not the best trained."

"Zen himself made the same offer," Jerol told his brother. "She's right, we're going to need them. What did Zen say they had, nearly a thousand men? They admit they're not well trained, but just their numbers make it a formidable force."

"Gather the nobles for a war council," Sallas instructed Regus. "We need to figure out exactly what we will need, invite this Kerlon, as well. We will meet first thing in the morning, by then we should have all the facts, and I hope, some concrete suggestions." He made that last an order, not a request. Roanne heard it in his tone, even if the words were different.

"I hope the rest of you can be there," Sallas concluded, "I would appreciate your support and advice. I will see you all then."

"Now," Sallas was completely in control of the room at this point. "There is a personal matter needs to be dealt with. The Lady Roanne, actually the title is a bit premature, is it not?" He looked meaningfully at Roanne. "You have a problem because you not of legal age yet, by the standards of the nobility or the spinners. There are a couple of possible remedies to this situation, I had reviewed them prior to last night's debacle, and have decided to make you my ward for the next six months. Just so you know, I also considered simply declaring you of age, and even favored the idea. However, it was pointed out to me such a precedent would probably result in severe headaches in the future. Hoping to spare my ancestors the pain of dealing with it, I hope you will accept this solution. It is only six months, and I have no intention of interfering with any of your holdings. I suspect you will be of age before we sort out the rest of this current crisis, so in the end it will not really matter. This action has a second purpose. It will make clear my stance on this issue, and my sincerity when I promised to see justice done."

Roanne was frozen in her seat, she had not really heard much beyond the first few sentences. The cold anger dominating her mood melted slightly. "I'm honored by your generous offer, Your Majesty." Lonora had recovered herself enough to embrace Roanne, giving her endorsement, and to Roanne's mind, the endorsement of all the spinners. Lonora moved aside to make room for Jerol and then Regus to embrace her, welcoming her to the family.

"Sheilla wanted to be here for this," Regus told her. "She's always wanted a sister, and though she and Letitia are great friends, a sister-by-marriage is not the same thing. To Letitia's frustration, and my relief, there are some things a sister simply can't tell her brother's wife, and I hope you remember that." He had a smile like the one she remembered from the festival, before all this started.

"Ahem," Sallas grabbed everyone's attention again. "One other thing. Word of this has already leaked out. I did not bother trying and contain it, since I had intended to inform everyone at the dinner last night, once this business had been put aside. Almost every family has already made at least one offer of a marriage proposal for you." He held up his hands to forestall Roanne's surprise, and concern. "Each offer has been answered that any such matters should be taken up with you, not me. I have made it clear with both my sons and my daughter. I will make every effort to accommodate their wishes. In your case, you will be of age shortly after Regus and Letitia's wedding, and no other arrangements will be made prior to then, so in effect, the only one who has any say in your marriage, is you."

"Thank you," Roanne could not hide her relief. After her experience with Calum, she thought it would be some time before she would be making any choices of that kind. The king bent over her and kissed her on the forehead, offering his own welcome to the family.

Chapter 14

Roanne found Sheilla in the rooms Roanne had been given. Sheilla and Talia were doing their best to help the four women they had found at the dinner.

"Did father tell you?" Sheilla asked at Roanne's appearance.

"Yes," Roanne was preoccupied with seeing the women again. The embrace from Sheilla caught her by surprise.

"Welcome to the family," Sheilla gave her a second hug, then held her at arm's length. "You don't look very happy about it."

"It's just," Roanne indicated the others in the room. "Under other circumstances I would probably appreciate it more. Right now, I'm a bit overwhelmed. They're finding a lot more women at the houses of those three nobles, and expecting perhaps hundreds by the time they get to the provinces. I can't handle that many."

"You'll think of something," Sheilla's smile did not diminish. "It's a family trait that fits you rather well from everything I've heard."

Roanne smiled. "How are they doing?" She gestured again toward the women.

"They need a healer as well as your services," Sheilla shook her head as Talia came over to join the two of them. "They're covered with bruises. It looks like they've been raped several times."

"All the others are probably in similar condition," Roanne saw a monumental task coming their way. "Have you told Lonora?"

"I left a note for her," Talia informed her, and as if on cue, there was a knock at the door. A maid, waiting for instructions on what to do next, answered for them, and let Lonora in. Talia brought her mother up to date.

"This is going to take a huge effort," Lonora spoke the words Roanne had not wanted to face. "We have a dozen healers at least. That's what, four to five patients per healer? The other women are already arriving, I saw the first wagons pulling in through the hall window."

"I can't handle this," Roanne sagged into the closest available chair. "I'm already tired, and there are over fifty who need to be helped. I'll burn out before I can do even ten."

"We'll simply have to pick up the learning curve," Lonora stated flatly. "Get all the available wizards, including Pavlin, we'll put them to work on the bindings with Roanne."

"I can do healing," Roanne contradicted her, "That's more important than the bonds. As long it's not anything real complicated, like a surgery."

"Since when?" Lonora demanded.

"Since last night, when I linked with Tezza," Roanne shrugged, maybe Spence can heal, too, since he linked with you."

"Wait a minute," Lonora slowed Roanne down. "Explain what you meant by since you linked. What happened in the link that you can heal all of a sudden?"

Roanne shrugged again. "When I linked with Tezza, she used my energy to do her work, since her energy was nearly depleted. Since it was my energy, I could tell what she did with it."

"Did someone go for the wizards, I think I need to speak with Spence?" Lonora became urgent. "If that works the way you said, maybe you could use links to show everyone how to control the burning of those damnable bonds on the women."

Lonora took Roanne by the arm and led her to the closest of the four women, who were quietly watching the exchange. She quickly examined the woman, then motioned for Roanne to move closer, showing Roanne a deep bruise on the woman's shoulder. "Go to work. I want to see if this is real or just that you think you can heal."

Roanne went to work, gathering energy first, then using her hands to gently feel the injury as she fed energy to the tissue, enabling it to heal itself at a faster rate. After a few minutes the bruise had faded.

"I hadn't even thought to try that," Spence was saying when Roanne freed her attention from the task. "It never occurred to me I could track the energy to see how it was used."

"Finished," Roanne announced, and looked across into the smiling face of the woman she had just healed, realizing it was Lylla, Stergis' sister.

Pavlin, who had arrived with Spence, and Lonora both came to check Roanne's work. "How did you do it?" Lonora asked, checking to see if Roanne really understood the process or was just working from mechanics.

"Mostly I let Lylla do the work," Roanne smiled back at the girl. "I just supplied the energy she needed to speed things up. There were a few things I shifted around, getting the blood clot in the bruise out of the way, but mostly it was Lylla."

Lonora seemed satisfied with her answer, so Roanne relaxed a moment. "Can you spot an infection?" Another question came at her.

"Uh, yes," Roanne answered. "It gets puffy and whitish." She didn't know the exact words to use.

"If you see an infection you leave it for one of the healers to deal with," Lonora instructed. "We could use the help on the minor things, though, so you'll be working with the healers, if you can teach Spence, Pavlin and the others to deal with the bonds."

"What's the difference?" Roanne asked. "With the infection, I mean."

"Infections are caused by things outside the body that get into the wound," Lonora explained. "It takes time to learn to distinguish the infection from the normal tissues, time we don't have right now. If you worked an infected area, you might accidentally give the energy to the infection, not the healing process. That could be a deadly mistake, so make sure you don't make it."

Roanne swallowed, and checked with her confidence level to be sure she thought she could manage what Lonora was suggesting. "Spence," she decided she could, "It's time you learned how to do this. You, too, Pavlin. Then the two of you can show the others."

"We have four more wizards available, including two adepts, who answered Telin's call," Spence informed them all.

"Are you sure about them?" Roanne was wondering whom she could and could not trust.

"Telin read them," Spence nodded, "They had no objections to it. They even volunteered after hearing what had happened last night."

"Did they bring any news?" Lonora asked. "Maybe they know something we don't."

"There hasn't been any communication with Altea since the reward notice, though they have heard from others," Spence passed on what he had been told. "It seems there are more wizards headed this way, instead of to Altea, but we don't know the numbers, yet."

"Well, link, and let's get this going," Roanne told Spence, "and pay attention this time. You'll have to teach the others."

"I still don't like all this linking," Pavlin warned. "There can be problems."

"We can keep it to a minimum. Everyone who learns the technique teaches two others," Spence suggested. "That way we spread the knowledge faster, and each person links only once, and gets linked to only twice. Everyone knows the linking spell."

"Not everyone," No one had seen Fenicia come into the room. "We have twenty spinners available who aren't healers. They'll do whatever they can to help, and are willing to learn."

"I can teach them the link," Pavlin offered, getting into it all for the first time that Roanne had noticed. But then, she had to admit to herself, he had spent most of his time with the king, while she was elsewhere.

Anthony Fredericks

"Great," Roanne pressed on, "Now if you only burn what you need to remove the bonds, I think you can save a lot of energy in the long run. This way we can also save the remaining samples of the bonds to have people practice with as they learn." She could feel it when Spence linked in with her. Slowly she heated the band of air around Lylla's neck, carefully directing the heat away from Lylla. She did the same with the bonds around Lylla's wrists and ankles, then flamed away the gag, the last remnant of Lylla's captivity."

"Did you catch all that?" Roanne turned to Spence. "More importantly, can you do it?"

"I see how you do it, now," Spence was amazed at how clear it was. "Except, I need to work out the gestures. You don't use any."

"Almost any gestures will do," Pavlin told the younger man. "All they really do is focus your concentration."

"Here," Roanne held something out to Spence, and when he put out his hand she placed one of the cuffs from Lylla's ankle in his palm. "Burn it." She told him.

"No, problem," Spence turned and set the object on a nearby table.

"No, no, no," Roanne snatched it up and put it back in his hand. "You don't work on any people until you burn this while it's in your hand. The healers have enough work to do, we don't need to add any burns."

Spence's eyes widened, but Pavlin laughed. "She should be teaching at the college," the older man managed between chuckles.

"You're next," Lonora reminded him, bringing instant quiet. "I wish I could have done something similar to test her healing, but I already knew she could heal herself, and I don't know how."

"Can't I practice first, with something on the table?" Spence asked. "If I burn myself, it would only add to the healers work as well."

"Come with me Pavlin," Roanne took the man's hand, leading him to the next woman, Aston's wife, Deallah.

As Roanne demonstrated for Pavlin, a healer went to work on Lylla's remaining bruises. By the time Roanne had freed the next woman, another healer she had yet to meet was ready to begin the healing process for her physical injuries. When Roanne looked into Deallah's eyes she was reminded of Shiva, and knew the mental scars would linger for a long time. She remembered two of these women had sat quietly until someone came for them after the fighting was over. A simple glance at the other two victims was enough to tell which was the fighter, and which had given in. The dull eyes were obvious when you knew what you were looking for. She worked quickly through the rest of the restraints on the women, setting the bonds aside for both Spence and Pavlin to practice with.

It was only a few moments before Pavlin came to where she sat, and holding something in his hand, burned it away completely, a smile on his face. "I don't want to hear any young hot shot out did me," he revealed the reason for the smile.

Spence came right behind him, repeating the trick. Neither of them suffered even redness to their hands. Thinking back, Roanne wished her first attempts had been as easy as theirs had been.

Lonora came and sat next to Roanne on the couch. A maid brought a thick broth for them all to drink as they worked, and both were grateful to whoever had suggested the idea to the kitchen. It was no accident there were virtually no fat spinners or wizards. The process of using magic consumed a lot of energy.

"Is there any way we can help their minds recover?" Roanne quietly asked Lonora. "That blank look, like the one Shiva has these days, is as scary to me as the bruises."

"I wish I knew some way," Lonora's voice betrayed her sympathy. "If I did, I certainly would have done something for Shiva long ago."

"Are you up to this?" Lonora took Roanne's hand. "I don't care how strong you think you are, you've done an awful lot of work in the past week. Promise me if you get tired, you'll take a break."

"Only if you promise the same to me," Roanne insisted. "You were close to burning yourself out yesterday. I'm surprised you can do anything at all today."

A squeeze of the hands they still held was their agreement. Finishing their drinks, they got back to their feet, each watching to see just how tired the other was, then laughing about it.

"What's so funny?" Tezza asked, having finished with her patient, Willa, the other woman who had fought. The two other healers were soon finished also, and were ready for the drinks. Neither of them was as strong as Lonora, nor Tezza, and had been significantly drained from their efforts.

"You all watch yourselves," Lonora gave the same warning. "And remember, there's no hurry. Do the worst ones first, leave the easy ones to either Roanne, or for another day. They'll all survive that better than a mistake by one of us."

Sheilla came back into the room, and Roanne realized she had again lost track of her comings and goings. "They're putting the girls from the houses in some of the guard's barracks," she told them all, but held up her hands before she let them all go. "I want to warn you, the men have all been getting sick over what they found. It's not a pretty sight. You all know Jerol, or at least his reputation, right now he's throwing up out by the stables. So, be prepared."

"Jerol's reputation?" Roanne pinned Spence with a look saying he had better answer.

"A fighter, tough guy, you know how men can be," Sheilla answered before Spence could even decide what to say. "Whenever there's trouble, and you need someone to fight your way out of a jam, he's the man you want. That's why Regus sent him after you instead of going himself."

"She doesn't know how men can be," Talia confided to Sheilla, causing Roanne to blush. "Her uncle kept her almost cloistered in that house."

Sheilla laughed, thinking Talia was kidding, then saw Roanne's blush. "My god, we are going to have to have a long talk, sister." She put an arm around the newest member of her family as they both moved toward the door. "And I thought having an older sister would mean she might be able to give me some tips on men."

"I can do that for you," Talia offered, teasing the two of them.

"Oh, no you don't!" Lonora playfully cuffed her daughter's ear, pushing her lightly away. "The king would have my head if his daughters took up after you."

Talia just stuck her tongue out, and moved quickly up ahead of them, putting a little extra sway in her skirts as she went past Spence and Pavlin. Spence's reaction was not lost on any of the women bringing up the rear. Lonora cuffed him the same way she had Talia. "That's my daughter you're staring after, young man." Spence colored with embarrassment, Roanne had noticed him watching Talia on other occasions, while Pavlin just laughed and gave him a pat on the back. "She's just jealous," the old man quipped, earning himself a similar cuffing.

The teasing banter kept up until they had nearly reached the barracks, when Lonora swore and broke ahead of the others. "By the gods," Lonora called out. "What are you doing here?"

On a bench outside the barracks was Letitia, getting sick. Lonora held her until the spasms subsided. "I thought you understood you were to remain in bed until further notice," Lonora continued to berate Letitia.

"I was feeling better today," Letitia wiped at her mouth. "At least until I went in there and saw them. Everyone's been so busy doing this or that. I wanted to help. It's a useless feeling laying in bed up in my room, knowing what is happening around here, and not being able to do anything to help."

"Roanne," Lonora grabbed her hand as Roanne was following the others into the impromptu infirmary. "This is your first charge. I want her back in bed, and tie her there if you have to, but make sure she stays there. She's not ready for this, though, I think she can begin to take her meals with everyone else. Just go slow, a little more each day, before you know it, you'll be back to normal."

Roanne helped Letitia to stand, then let Letitia lean against her as she led her back toward the residential wing of the palace. "I would have thought you were busy enough arranging my life for me," Roanne teased, guessing she was right from the grin Letitia returned.

"Well something had to be done," Letitia stated as if it were nothing. "The king and his advisors were discussing a lot of other options, none of which you would have liked. I thought this was far better, and really, kind of harmless."

"Unless the king decides to marry me off in next few months," Roanne countered. "I think that's the only concern on that front, and it's a rather minor concern compared to Calum."

"I heard some of what happened back at the estate," it was beginning to seem as though Letitia was supporting Roanne as much as Roanne was her. "It must have been a living nightmare. There are few people who would be able to hold it together the way you have."

"There are more than you think," Roanne thought of all the women who could be involved, and hoped she was right. "Look at Talia, who went through far worse than I did. Calum held her captive for nearly two weeks. Lylla was married for more than two months from what I heard, and the other woman who started the fighting last night, Willa, looks as though she's holding up."

"Maybe, but some are just fooling themselves right now," Letitia rested a moment as they climbed the stairs to her rooms. "They're still in trouble, especially Talia. I met her in your rooms this afternoon. Watch her Roanne, she's consumed with the thought of vengeance, which can be just as bad as the reactions of Deallah and Mina."

They made it to the rooms, where Roanne insisted on seeing Letitia all the way to her bed. "Lonora would have my head otherwise."

"I'll be good," Letitia pretended to pout, "But you better come get me for the meeting in the morning. I am not going to miss that. Lonora can't complain if I go down for breakfast and stick around."

"You don't know Lonora," Roanne laughed. "I'll come get you, and we can catch up with each other over breakfast."

Letitia gave Roanne a hug before letting her go back to her work. "I would welcome you to the family, but officially I'm not in it, yet."

Chapter 15

Back at the barracks, Roanne took several minutes to gather her will before stepping inside. No amount of preparation would have helped, though, and after looking around for a moment, she found herself back outside, right where they had found Letitia. Even there, the images of the bruised and battered women, some with burns and whip marks haunted her vision.

"Everyone has made this little trip," Fenicia came out to check on her.

"I'll be all right," Roanne was already trying to gather the courage to go in again. Fenicia entered with her this time, directing Roanne right to the area set aside for those not in need of serious healing. Using the concentration she needed to do the healing, she blocked out the worst of the scene around her. Her first patient was easy. The girl had a few bruises, which were quickly taken care of. That done, Roanne found herself unwilling to leave the bonds in place for one of the wizards to remove. They might not get to her until the next day.

A fire had been built in the fireplace for disposing of the bonds not needed for teaching others. "You'll tire yourself out quickly that way," Pavlin commented as Roanne tossed the offensive items into the flames and watched them flare.

"Don't count on it," Roanne was finding her anger was better at blocking out the queasiness of her stomach than the magic had been.

Her next patient had an infection where a whip had broken the skin in several places across her back. Roanne was tempted to try anyway, but remembered what Lonora had said about mistakes. Her anger was continuing to grow as she released the bonds holding the girl captive, before passing her on to a more experienced healer.

After that, she noticed almost all the patients she saw had already been freed physically, though most had the emotional scars in their eyes. Someone, Pavlin she suspected, was making sure to cut her workload by keeping anyone with bonds away from Roanne's area.

Before Roanne had finished two more patients, Lonora brought an older healer over to Roanne. "Roanne, this is Moran, she's getting too tired to do heavy work, so I've asked her to coach you a little. She's good, and I have every confidence the two of you, together, can handle almost anything." Lonora left as the two women shook hands.

"It's hard to imagine me teaching the queen anything," Moran said.

"I don't have a lot of experience at this," Roanne admitted. "Most things I've done with magic could be done with brute force. Only recently have I had to control the magic."

"From what I've seen and heard," Moran began to lead Roanne where the worse problems had been placed, "You're better than anyone I've ever met. Lonora says if you see something once, you have it mastered, just like that. I've never even heard of anything like that before."

The patient they came to was the same girl Roanne had passed on because of infections earlier. "Ill let you know how to distinguish the infection from the person," Moran began as Roanne gathered her concentration.

The rest of the night was a blur of torn, burned, and bruised skin. After three more patients, Moran moved on, ready to do more work herself. Roanne just kept going, not even stopping to think about how tired she was. She saw Lonora headed her way at one point, but Pavlin cut her off. They argued a moment, during which Roanne finished the patient she was working on, and moved off to another area, where it would take Lonora a few minutes to find her again.

"You're through for the night," Lonora announced when she did find Roanne again. "As it is, you'll probably sleep right through the meeting, and the king might take that the wrong way. I don't know what Pavlin and Moran were thinking."

Six patients, nine counting the easy ones, Roanne counted them up in her head. She felt satisfied she had carried her load, and was not feeling all that tired. The broth had replenished her energy even better than food. She remembered what she had told Jerol about anger, and smiled to herself, proud she had not let her anger drive events around her, but had used the anger to better purposes.

"You should have quit after four maybe five," Lonora was still lecturing Roanne. Roanne thought better of telling Lonora exactly how much she had done, including the bonds. "Every other healer has had two or three breaks by now. I just found out you haven't stopped all night. Are you trying to kill yourself?"

"I had all easy ones, really," Roanne suspected that was true. None of her patients had been in severe condition, compared to some of the others she had glimpsed around the room. "The broth helped a lot, and I made sure to pace myself while working." She was searching for any possible explanation to calm Lonora.

"Sheilla, take Roanne to her rooms and make sure she goes to bed," Lonora found Roanne's new sister near the door, where a few of the girls were being reunited with families from the city. All too many had no families in the city, being either runaways, or girls brought from the provinces. Lonora and Roanne watched, heartened by the smiles of one girl's parents, even if the blank look in the girl's eyes failed to answer their joy.

Sheilla finished with the family, and turned the next girl over to another waiting spinner who was helping to sort things out, having finished with the bonds the former captives had been brought in with.

"What seems to be the problem?" Sheilla asked, coming over closer to Lonora and Roanne.

"Your sister," Lonora emphasized the words, "Doesn't seem to want to recognize her limitations. She needed to be in bed an hour ago. Do you think you could handle this for me?"

"I knew she would fit right into this family," Sheilla smiled taking possession of Roanne's arm, and leading her out the door toward the residence.

"They're all but finished for the night anyway," Sheilla told Roanne as they went. They stopped at the kitchen on the first floor of the residence, where the broth was being made. "Pavlin is the one Lonora is really angry with," Sheilla went on. "I heard her ask him earlier to keep an eye on you because she was so busy. Later, I heard him and Spence talking while they watched you from near the door. Pavlin said something about finding out what your limits are. He was intending to let you keep working until you were too tired to do any more, which is what most of the healers did."

"I hope I didn't disappoint him," Roanne was beginning to feel tired now that her anger was draining away.

"Only in that I wasn't able to learn much," Pavlin had entered the kitchen behind them. "I don't think you were even close to your limit."

"You knew Lonora would be upset," Roanne raised an eyebrow suspiciously.

"Of course," Pavlin shrugged. "Circumstances kept us from testing you this morning, I just thought this was an opportunity to learn something. The nobles would like to be reassured you can stand up against the wizards."

"It's not as if she has to take them on all by herself," Sheilla commented. "More and more wizards are coming to our side, there are all the spinners, and the guards."

"True," Pavlin conceded, "But Roanne remains the central figure in this conflict. She will have to be there when we face down the council members, and this Calum. Everyone will be counting on her to lead the others in countering whatever the enemy comes up with."

"I don't know if I can do that," Roanne turned her back to the others, looking out the windows as another family left the courtyard with a daughter found among the slaves.

"You won't be alone," Sheilla put a supportive hand on Roanne's shoulder. "So don't go letting him convince you that you will be. There will be many others there to help." Taking Roanne's arm, Sheilla led her from the kitchen up to her new rooms. Where, hopefully, Roanne would get the peace and quiet she needed to get some rest. She had been at the palace for two days now, and this was the first time she actually slept in the bed she had been given.

"You get some sleep, I'll see to it someone comes to get you in plenty of time for the war conference," Sheilla assured Roanne as she sent her through the sitting room into the bedroom.

"Letitia, too," Roanne stopped and turned at the door to the bedroom. "Lonora says it's all right for her to start moving around, and she wants to be in the meeting."

"I'll see to that, also," Sheilla smiled, thinking if Roanne and Letitia had been around her entire life, it would have been a lot more fun, and interesting.

Roanne was tired the next morning, but not so tired she could not appreciate the deftness with which King Sallas handled the dukes. Before the meeting was over, he had the duikes handling the problem of the provinces, with the help of token units from the royal guard. Two of the troubled areas were neighboring provinces, Tusca and Rivard, and only Rivard had its duke, Markum, in residence. Aston and Tusca's Cezar were already in the palace dungeon. An army composed of the combined forces from twelve of the provinces would be sent in to secure these areas, and Golare, Aston's province. Spinners and wizards from among those at the palace now, who were learning how to free the slaves of those bindings, would also learn to defend themselves against magical attack by Calum's allies. Spence and Roanne were assigned to handle the training. Word had come that more wizards were on their way to Esconda, including a contingent from Altea. The group from Altea was led by Timond, which was a relief to Duke Bassel and Letitia. They were allies, not enemies, according to the advance notices they had received. Timond's arrival would bring the first real news they would have from Altea, and would help them decide how they would handle Calum. Tentatively, they planned for the bulk of the royal guard to go to there, with support from the remaining four provinces.

Queen of the Spinners

Timond was not due to arrive for another day, but from the reports he had nearly all the students from the college, and most of the teachers with him. There was no word on any members of the council, or of Calum.

The meeting broke up much sooner than Roanne would have thought. Sallas had simply laid out his ideas, and those he had received from his sons. Barring any better ideas, that was what would be done. Nobody had any better ideas.

Roanne caught a little more sleep that morning, then met with her new family for lunch, including Letitia. Jerol came in with Shiva and her family, he brought them over to introduce them to his siblings, and even grabbed the king when Sallas came in for a quick bite, and introduced him.

King Sallas studied the expression on Shiva's face. "I have seen that look all too often of late," he shook his head.

"I think Shiva's actually getting a bit better, Your Majesty," Shiva's mother smiled. "Thanks to your kindness. She actually ate by herself at dinner, yesterday." It was small improvement, Roanne noted, but it was something substantial, not a mother's desire to see improvement where there was none.

"It must be difficult," Letitia brushed a stray hair from Shiva's face.

"I just wish we could get some sign the things we're trying to tell her are getting through," Shiva's father had a healthy skepticism. He wasn't being a pessimist, just a realist. "I'll be happy when I hear her speak again, so she can talk about what she went through. Some of the healers say it's what she really needs."

"I've tried talking with her," Jerol contributed, "Her eyes will shift now and then, but it's hard to tell if that's a response or a random movement. I wish we could see into her mind. We could find what's troubling her, and reassure her."

"See into her mind?" Roanne repeated the words. They meant something to her, telepathy. "Communicators used telepathy. Where's Telin?" Roanne was on her feet without even realizing it.

"Probably up in Pavlin's area of the palace," Sheilla shrugged. "You might want to consider whether you want to go near there, Pavlin's likely to keep you there once he gets his hands on you."

"Eventually I have to go speak with Spence," Roanne accepted that possibility. "We're supposed to come up with a plan to teach the others how to fight Calum's magic."

"You have time to take a day off to rest," Regus told her. "Messengers to all the provinces won't be leaving until tomorrow, while father and some of his advisors work out the wording. Some of the dukes who are here in Esconda want to go and personally gather their troops. It will take Bassel two weeks to get to Bergain, three weeks if he has to go around Tusca and Rivard, where news of the other night is bound to reach ahead of him."

"War is a slow business," Jerol leaned over to whisper to Roanne, "It takes time to put together all the men and the supplies."

"Good, then I have time to check on this idea with Telin," Roanne stood from the table. "Where is Pavlin's study?"

"I'll show you the way," Letitia offered, "Lonora and Pavlin are feuding, so I figure I can avoid Lonora for a while if I go with you. "Maybe, as an added benefit, Pavlin won't try to monopolize you if I'm there."

"Don't go out of your way to thwart Lonora," Regus put an affectionate hand on Letitia's shoulder. "She does have your best interest in mind."

Letitia and Roanne made their way through the maze of corridors to the very rear of the palace, where they finally found Spence. He wasn't who they were looking for, but at least he could point them in the proper direction.

"It's about time you showed up for your test," Pavlin was on them immediately when they entered the study.

"Actually ..." Roanne tried, but Pavlin would not be diverted. He took her by the elbow and led her through the study, to a back corridor, then out of the palace altogether.

Queen of the Spinners

"Where are you going?" Letitia had managed to grab Telin as they passed through the study, and was dragging him along by the elbow.

"There's been something I've been wanting to try for years now," Pavlin answered. "I want to forge a sword, and I think Roanne, here, is just the one to do it."

"Whoa," Letitia grabbed Pavlin's elbow with her free hand, "That's no proper test. All it will do is waste her energy, and maybe incapacitate her for a day or two."

"What!" Pavlin was incredulous Letitia would suggest such a thing.

"She's right," Roanne pulled free of Pavlin, and headed back toward the study. "Thank you, Letitia. Telin, you and I need to speak."

"Just who do you two think is in charge here?" Pavlin was standing right where they had left him, his hands on his hips.

Letitia and Roanne looked at one another. "We are," they agreed, and continued to escort the helpless Telin, who could only shrug, back to the study.

"Can you communicate with nonmagical people, Letitia, here for example?" Roanne asked the confused wizard.

"Why in the world would he want to do that?" Pavlin had come back into the palace behind them.

Letitia whirled on him. "Are you implying there is no legitimate reason anyone would ever want to communicate with me?" Pavlin was too flustered by this time to answer.

"I've never tried," Telin at least took the question seriously.

"I'll make you a deal, Pavlin," Roanne cut him off before he could protest further. "Just cooperate with us, and tomorrow morning I'll do the sword trick for you. This is more important right now. In fact, if Telin can do this, I think you should declare him an adept. It would be worthy of the distinction even in my father's time."

"Do what?" both Pavlin and Telin asked, suddenly more interested.

"Help the women who were held captive to recover, psychologically," Roanne put her arms across her chest, and waited for their response.

They were both silent, either lost in thought, or confusion. "What do you mean?" Pavlin finally asked.

"Communicators use telepathy to speak with each other," Roanne thought it was obvious once she had it figured out. "Those with the biggest problems from their captivity seem withdrawn, like there is nobody there. You can see the lack of emotion or even life in their eyes. We can't seem to get through to them that it's all over now, that they're safe. A communicator might be able to get the message to them."

"Even if this works," Letitia had not been sure what Roanne intended, "How many communicators are there? We could be talking about hundreds of victims."

"There are only seven general communicators," Telin was shaking his head. "There's no way we could handle all that."

"What about the spinners?" Letitia asked. "Do they have any communicators?"

"I have no idea," Roanne admitted. "I don't think they test for this kind of talent, since they can't get the training they would need."

"Holbert," Pavlin pointed to one of the wizards who had recently arrived in Esconda, "Go find Lonora, and bring her here. This is worth pursuing."

Roanne and Letitia exchanged smiles.

"What are you waiting for, Telin?" Roanne pointed at Letitia, who straightened on the stool where she had seated herself. "Communicate!"

"Communicate what?" Telin was still somewhat confused.

"Anything," Roanne persisted, "Just do it."

"Not just anything," Letitia disagreed. "If it's anything improper Regus will have your head."

Telin blushed, then hesitated, and Roanne wondered just what he had been thinking to say. "Anything she normally would not know," Roanne instructed. "The names of everyone in your family for instance."

Telin nodded then concentrated. The silence in the room was exaggerated as they all waited expectantly. Letitia even closed her eyes as she concentrated, too.

The silence stretched on for a long time, until Roanne realized she was holding her breath, and let it out. Roanne's exhale distracted Letitia from her efforts.

"This isn't working," Letitia threw her hands up.

"Yes it is," Telin jumped up to put her back onto her seat. "Just give me a moment, I only just now sorted you out from everyone else around here." Pavlin's study was far larger than the one Roanne was used to at home, and there were nearly a dozen wizards in attendance at the moment, all watching their efforts.

"Wizards have kind of a unique energy about them, so do spinners," Telin explained. "Normally I don't even look for anything else, so it took me a while to pick you out, but I had just found you. Now I know what to look for, and I think I can do this. Let me try again." Telin's excitement was evident on his face.

"Try what?" Lonora came in with Holbert. "Pavlin, if you're experimenting with Roanne again, I swear ..."

Pavlin held up his hands in surrender. "Actually, she's the one doing the experimenting on Telin and Letitia."

"What?" Lonora turned to Roanne. "If Regus hears about this he's going to put all our heads in nooses."

"Just go ahead," Roanne said to Telin, while she took Lonora off to the side to explain exactly what they were doing.

"Interesting," Lonora scratched her chin. "This could be a huge breakthrough in mental disease if it works."

"What about the spinners, can they help?" Roanne asked. "The wizards would not be able to handle this on their own."

"We've never tested specifically for this talent," Lonora said, but she smiled. "However, of the talents we have tested for, virtually every talent commonly found among wizards has been found in the spinners."

"We did it!" Letitia jumped up from her stool. "Alea, right Telin?"

"That's my youngest sister," Telin confirmed.

"And Beraine?" Letitia went on. "Alea and Beraine are both spinners, and might have the same talent you have, since talents are inherited. That was the message."

"She got it," Telin was grinning from ear to ear. "My sisters both live in Tulard, maybe a day's ride from here."

"Wait a minute," Lonora put a damper on everyone's enthusiasm. "Come here, Telin." When Telin crossed the room, Lonora whispered something in his ear. Telin closed his eyes in concentration.

"Oh, that's even better," Letitia lit up again. "His sister's are actually here. They heard Telin's broadcast for the wizards. Gathering more spinners along the way, they came here to help, that's one of the reasons there are so many spinners around all of a sudden, including the healers."

Telin crossed the room and embraced Letitia. "Take me to Shiva," he knew exactly what it was Roanne had in mind.

Chapter 16

The next twenty-four hours were absolutely restful compared to the past few weeks, in spite of Pavlin's efforts to try and get Roanne to help make his sword. It was not that she was trying to get out of the commitment she had made, but she couldn't very well turn down an invitation from the king to go hunting the next morning.

The brisk morning ride had little to do with chasing animals. For her part, Roanne simply enjoyed the ride, and the sunshine. After the ride, the family gathered for lunch in the king's rooms, where they would be undisturbed. It would have all been thoroughly enjoyable, if Letitia had not been pouting over Lonora's refusal to allow her to ride.

Roanne was going to spend the afternoon working on their strategy for fighting Calum with Spence, but more news from Timond put any thought of that aside. In the group Timond was bringing, there were several wizards who had defected from Calum, once they learned what Calum was doing with the magic he had taught them. Information of the kind those wizards could provide was such that making any plans without them seemed superfluous.

The news of Timond might have dominated the talk at meal, if it were not for the other news. Shiva was talking, after several hours of working with Telin. It was progress beyond what anyone had hoped, and now that she was talking, conventional methods could be used to help maintain the improvement. Telin was already lining up other patients, and teaching his sisters to do the same thing.

Jerol had nixed the idea of sending out a summons for all the other communicators. "They're the link between the provinces, and we'll need them during the fighting," he explained. "You can train all the unassigned wizards and any spinners you can find, but not those assigned to provinces."

Telin and Roanne were disappointed at the setback, but also appreciated Jerol's position. He was the military leader of this campaign. All seven of the other general communicators had provincial assignments, including Telin at the court. It was unclear whether other communicators could do this work, possibly any sender might be able to reach some of the patients. All they had to do was get them talking.

At dinner, Roanne ate at the main table with the royal family for the first time, which drew plenty of looks from the rest of the nobility. The women were not pleased at all, Sheilla and Letitia were happy to note, and nearly all the eligible men were dressed as if for a formal dinner. After the dinner, Roanne swore she was introduced to each and every bachelor within the city. The rest of the family thought it was all very entertaining, since they had all been through this nightmare themselves.

"Roanne should relieve at least some of the pressure on you, Sheilla," one of the Duke Rambert's daughters, Genna, teased. Genna was young enough not to be concerned over the newest competition at court, yet aware enough of what it meant for the others. "I'll bet even Stergis' father would love to have Roanne in his family. She could double or triple their family's worth, particularly after the disaster of Lylla's wedding."

Sheilla refused to be baited, and was saved from having to respond by Stergis, who came and put an arm around her waist. "Not to worry, Genna, I know what it takes to stay alive, and sisters wouldn't cheat on each other."

"Tell that to Ritha and Nel," Genna moved on, looking for another target for her barbs.

"Duke Bellin's daughters," Letitia informed Roanne with a blush. "Rumor has it Ritha killed Nel because Nel was pregnant by Regus. I don't think a week goes by she doesn't try to get a rise out of me with that."

"I'm not biting either," Roanne smiled at Letitia, though she was dying to know if it was true or not.

"Regus was not even in the city during the time Nel had become pregnant," Letitia whispered. "He was in Bergain with me."

"Have you noticed even though every man in the room would give up an arm for a match with Roanne, none of them has said two words to her beyond the usual introductions." Sheilla was eyeing the room, noting pockets of men, who all tried to watch their table without being noticed.

"I think they're all scared of her after the way she handled Aston," Letitia watched as a few parents around the room tried to push their sons toward them, but they all seemed to find some excuse to head in some other direction. "This is no fun at all, they're supposed to bother you all night long."

"I have no complaints," Roanne leaned back in her chair and relaxed.

"That's just it," Sheilla threw her hands up. "They drove me nuts. They drove Letitia nuts. With Regus and Jerol it was the women."

"I still get some of the more persistent ones chasing me down," Regus confirmed.

Letitia just laughed, but when Stergis made the same comment, Sheilla demanded to know whom they were, while Letitia and Regus laughed.

"The hall doesn't seem very crowded," Stergis said trying to change the subject. "Where's Jerol? Most of the girls are probably out chasing him."

"He's over with Telin, at Shiva's table," Regus reported.

"I still don't understand it," Sheilla shook her head, "Why isn't he getting bothered, either?"

"Why aren't you getting bothered?" Roanne pointed out. "You're not married, yet, and I'm sure the men are probably just as rude as the women can be, still chasing Stergis and Regus."

"They don't want to fight Stergis," Sheilla dismissed the thought. "He's the best in the kingdom with a sword."

"I thought someone told me Jerol was," Roanne thought this might be safer ground.

"Jerol's the best fighter," Regus corrected her. "There's a difference. I wouldn't want to see the day he and Stergis went at it."

Stergis stayed silent on this subject.

"I suppose it's a good thing Stergis is involved with Sheilla," Roanne surmised. "There's no possible conflict there."

"Still," Letitia was eyeing Jerol, noticing the entire side of the hall where he was sitting was nearly vacant of women. "The last time I saw Jerol at one of these dinners there were always three or four girls vying for his attention at any one time. Something is wrong here."

"Finally," Sheilla nudged Roanne with an elbow. "Terren is making his way over here. He's the duke of Setille, the land you came through just east of here. His father died last year, so he inherited young. He's good looking, too. He's one you might want to get to know."

"Tovan saw him, and is coming, too," Letitia advised. The two women pointed out the two men as they snaked their way around other people, heading generally in their direction. "Tovan is a snake. I'm surprised he would try anything with you in front of either Sheilla or me. Feel free to put him in his place."

Both men suddenly switched directions, actually heading back to where they came from. Only Letitia caught the line of vision they were both watching just before changing their minds, and saw Jerol had stood from the table where he was sitting and was now headed toward the head table. Two girls, who, the last time Letitia saw them in the same room with Jerol, had been draped all over him, actually moved out of his way. Letitia got up from the table and headed him off well before he reached their table.

Jerol greeted Letitia with a smile, which she quickly erased. "What is going on?" she demanded. "Not one man in this room is willing to talk to Roanne, and the women are all but running from you."

"Haven't you heard the rumors?" Jerol laughed, leaving Letitia behind as he continued on his way to the table where Roanne was enjoying Letitia's frustration.

"What rumors?" Letitia asked when she caught up to him.

"Now how would it look if I, a member of the royal family, stooped to passing on rumors?" Jerol teased.

"We do it all the time," Sheilla and Letitia answered together. "Besides," Letitia went on, "I would already know if it weren't for Lonora locking me up in my rooms. If you don't tell us, we'll find out anyway."

"Why Letitia, you helped start the rumor, according to my sources," Jerol was not about to give in. "How could you not know what it is?"

"Jerol!" Sheilla was getting frustrated now.

"Roanne," Jerol ignored the others at the table, "Shiva's doing much better, but I think what she needs is to talk with another woman. Telin has managed to draw her out, but she shies away from men, as if she expects us to hurt her. She won't say more than two words to me."

The two of them went off toward Shiva, then, together with Shiva's family, they left the hall. Letitia grabbed the first staff member to come within reach, but Sheilla put a hand on her arm.

"No need," she nodded toward Elayne, one of the more ardent pursuers of Jerol, and the two watched as Elayne's eyes followed Roanne and Jerol to the door. Elayne was ignoring Terran, who had decided she was the next best option available in the hall. Once Jerol and Roanne had left, Elayne stomped from the room in a fit, leaving poor Terran lost in confusion. "I think that says more than any rumor," Sheilla concluded.

"Those rumors are about us, aren't they?" Roanne whispered to Jerol, taking his arm as they exited the hall.

"I knew you were a smart one," Jerol smiled. "If it bothers you, I think I can see to it they stop."

"If it means a chance for peace and quiet, I can live with it," Roanne really did not mind. "In fact, if it frustrates Sheilla and

Letitia's matchmaking attempts I'm all for it." They laughed together.

"Maybe I'm not the right person to talk to Shiva," Roanne changed the subject. "It might be better to get someone who has been through what she was. I escaped before Calum had a chance to rape me. Talia, or better yet, Lylla might be a better choice."

"Possibly," Jerol became thoughtful, "We can try at another time if this doesn't work. I thought of this because she seems to know you were the one who pulled her out of there."

When they reached the guest quarters where Shiva's family was staying, Telin stopped Roanne outside the rooms, and brought her up to date. "She's afraid of men, which is perfectly understandable. I think she might have talked to me out of fear I would punish her if she didn't, which is not what we really wanted. I haven't told her parents, but I thought you should know. Jerol and I will wait in the lounge across the way."

An hour later Roanne returned, holding up her hands to show she had no better luck than they had. "She grabbed onto me, and refused to let go. She thanked me over and over, and begged me to protect her." Roanne could not hold back her tears any longer. "I kept trying to tell her everything would be all right, that nobody was going to hurt her. When I told her about you two I could sense her fear rise at first, but I explained you would protect her, too. After a while she was less tense when I mentioned either of you. I'm not real sure if that is progress or not."

"Lonora says we have to either get her to talk about what she went through, or make her forget it," Telin paced the room in frustration. "We'll try Lylla and Talia, tomorrow. Maybe even more than that, get a whole group of them. I'll be the first one to admit I haven't a clue as to what it would be like to be raped."

"I'll have Stergis talk to his sister, Lylla," Jerol offered. "But I can't promise anything, she might not want to talk about it, either."

The next morning there was a group of ten victims getting together for breakfast. Letitia and Sheilla, who Roanne had spoken with before going to bed, had offered a room in the family wing for the gathering, a sewing room where the old queen would gather her friends for afternoon tea. They both made sure to attend also, hoping they might be able to reassure the women they were safe now.

Pavlin had cornered Roanne at breakfast about his sword, and before Roanne could think of any excuses she found herself in the smith's shop. Lonora showed up right on their heels, having been told by Letitia what was happening, and accusing Pavlin of being frivolous with Roanne's power. Roanne had just quieted Lonora, explaining the deal she had made, when Jerol showed up with the same objections.

"Actually, you're just the person to witness this," Roanne shut him up. "Pick out the best hilt in the shop for this sword, I want to give it to you when I finish. Then pick out the block of metal you want for the blade."

The smith had already been sorting through his supply with Pavlin. Jerol gave Roanne a skeptical look, but gave in to her insistence. Once the three of them had agreed on the metal, and the hilt, the smith began to clean the area around his anvil so they could get to work. Pavlin explained all he wanted was for Roanne to heat the metal until the smith could mold it, then do all the cooling, and eventual quenching.

"Oh, come now, Pavlin," Roanne lightly pushed him aside. "If I'm going to do this, I intend to do it right."

Jerol had picked out the hilt, and Roanne handed him the block of metal. She checked how the hilt would need to be attached to the blade, then told Jerol to hold the metal in place. It became warm to his touch at one point, but after a few minutes he let go, and the block of metal was set into the hilt.

"Now," Roanne took a seat on the only available stool in the smithy, "I want you to describe for me the perfect blade as we go along, start with length, width, that type of information."

As Jerol began to talk, the block of metal at the end of the hilt slowly began to glow, then to change shape. Expecting the heat to sear his hands, Jerol nearly dropped the hilt, his eyes shifting from it to Roanne and back, but he kept talking.

Outside the smithy a crowd had begun to gather to watch what was going on. There were always a few boys who wanted to watch Samus work, but today, as word spread, the crowd had guards, nobles, and even a few of the wizards and spinners. Regus came through the crowd into the smithy itself to watch when he heard. Sheilla and Letitia came, hoping Jerol and Regus had put a stop to this nonsense.

Jerol was sweating profusely just thinking about the heat his hands should be feeling, as he watched the blade form, felt the weight shift. As Roanne worked, he described the balance he liked in a sword. She would cool the metal, so he could swing it lightly, testing the blade as they went.

"Wait a minute, it's too thin," he objected as they neared the end.

"You said you wanted it sharp," Roanne complained. She was sweating from exertion, now, and getting testy at his criticism.

"The sharpness won't matter if the blade breaks," the smith, Samus, offered.

"Don't worry," Roanne insisted as she made the blade even thinner. "Explain the quenching to me, Samus."

Regus rolled his eyes toward Jerol who shrugged in response.

Roanne used no water in the quenching, doing it magically. During this part Lonora raised more concerns as Roanne swayed and nearly fell off the stool she was seated on.

Finally the blade was finished, and the men gathered around to inspect it, while Lonora caught the slumping Roanne. Regus and Jerol helped as soon as they noticed. Jerol took Roanne in his arms and began to carry her out.

"I knew this would happen," Lonora admonished everyone present.

Queen of the Spinners

The real folly of their experiment hit home as they reached the palace. Captain Duval met them at the doors. "Where have you been?" he snapped, obviously tense, "The king is looking for the three of you." Then he noticed Roanne, and his sword sprang from it's sheathe. "What happened, were you attacked?"

"No, no, nothing like that, she's just exhausted," Regus quickly put him at ease.

"Exhausted?" Spence pushed out from behind Duval. "No, you didn't have her do the sword, Pavlin. Tell me you didn't." Regus held up the blade he had been carrying for Jerol. "Damn it, she can't face Calum in that condition." Spence's words sank in to everyone.

"Calum?" Jerol's spine stiffened, and he nearly dropped Roanne. "What have you heard?"

"Calum?" Roanne came awake, her struggles forcing Jerol to set her down, though he had to hold her up or she would have collapsed. "Calum, what about him?"

"The king is waiting in his conference room," Duval informed them. "He's not going to be happy at all with this." He turned his back to them and retreated into the palace.

"I'll take Roanne to her rooms, then meet the rest of you in the conference room," Jerol turned to Regus with a guilty look that was shared by Regus and Pavlin.

"I warned you," Lonora moved past them all. "I even tried to stop that nonsense before she got too tired."

Jerol shifted his way through the door. When they came to the residential wing, and Jerol turned to go upstairs to Roanne's rooms, Pavlin tried to follow, but Regus caught his shoulder.

"If you think I'm facing my father alone with this, you're crazy," Regus said, pulling Pavlin along toward the conference room.

Jerol had gotten Roanne into her bed, and was leaving the rooms when everyone showed up in Roanne's rooms anyway.

"What is this all about?" Sallas demanded. "Is she going to be all right?"

"As I was trying to explain, Your Majesty," Pavlin said from behind the king, while Lonora, Sheilla and Letitia came through them all into Roanne's bedroom, with Talia taking up a position near the door to block anyone from following. "We needed to test her abilities to see just how strong she is."

"So you had her make a sword," Sallas turned on the wizard. "What kind of test is that?"

"Actually, it's a very significant test, if she succeeded," Spence came to the defense of his mentor. "The energy it takes to do the melting and quenching is tremendous. To do it right requires fantastic control. There are legends of blades quenched with magic, but nobody in recent history has been able to do it properly."

Jerol took the blade from Regus and checked it again.

"Jerol!" Sallas reprimanded him. "We have a problem here, and we needed her. What are we going to do now?"

"What's the problem?" Jerol put the blade aside, blushing.

"I got in late last night," Timond pushed his way through to Sallas' side. "Telin is still clearing the wizards who came with me. Essentially, Calum is running for the border to Curiland, and if he makes it, it will take a war with them to bring him to justice."

Chapter 17

"Why weren't we told this sooner?" Jerol found Telin in the crowded room. "The communicators should have passed this along, or those who brought word Timond was on his way."

"It wasn't like that," Telin objected to the accusation. "I passed the word they were on the way. I could tell how far they were when I communicated with them. But they don't have any communicators with them."

"Calum slaughtered all the communicators when Telin broadcast the counter accusations against him," Timond explained. "If I had any way of informing you I would have."

"So, what do we do?" Sallas repeated his original question.

"How many wizards does Calum have with him?" Jerol asked.

"About thirty, including seven of the council members. The entire council, excepting Pavlin had answered the summons to find out what was going on. The rest of the council was killed before Calum left Altea, including Werdel, who had come to Altea with me. We tried our best to put up a fight, but even with the wizards Calum trained, who came back to our side once they knew the truth of the situation, the best we could manage was a stalemate. Without anyone leading our side, we lost nearly a hundred wizards. I would have been here sooner, but we had fifty-some wounded with us, a shortage of healers, and some wounds resisting all their efforts until we figured out the weapons Calum used were still imbedded in the wounds." Timond raised his hands in a helpless gesture.

Jerol went over to him and put a hand on his shoulder. "I'm sorry. You did well just to get here, and you, to keep us as informed as you could, Telin." Everyone could tell Jerol was struggling to control his temper. He took a deep breath.

"Calum will need to reach the Border River, where it enters Luden's gulf to cross the border," Jerol began pacing as he thought, and the others watched him. There was not a better military mind in the kingdom.

"That's in Golare, Aston's province," Regus noted. "So we might have to fight Aston's guards as well. After what we captured at his house, he probably has about thirty left."

"Can any of the wizards help?" Spence spoke up. "I mean those who know Calum's form of magic."

"We know how to do it, not fight it," a new voice came from the back of the room.

"That's Olen," Timond introduced the man.

"I can fight it, and it will help if you can teach others to do it," Spence looked at Olen. "You can use it to defend yourself can't you?"

"We can do that much," Olen perked up, "And if you teach us, we'll fight. I swear, we had no idea what Calum was up to. Some of us are hurt pretty badly, but there are ten healthy wizards who know what Calum does, and we're ready to go any time. Calum has to be stopped."

"We know," Sallas dismissed the apology.

"One other thing," Olen offered. "Calum thinks he's invulnerable with his magic. He had no idea how Roanne escaped, because he burned the estate down in anger before investigating. He was gone from Altea by the time Carlon arrived with Roanne's message, and the news of how she had defeated Sethe and Maison. We had to kill Carlon to keep him from following Calum and warning him."

Letitia came out from the bedroom, and all eyes turned to her. "How is she?" Jerol pressed first.

"Tired, pretty much out of it," Letitia hung her head. "Lonora says it's hard to tell when someone's that tired. It will be a day at least, maybe two, before she could be ready to travel. More before she would be in any condition to fight Calum. The broth might help, but she's so out of it now we can't get any of it into her."

Sallas turned to Pavlin. "She went way beyond what I asked her to do," the old wizard backed away from the angry king. "As

Spence explained, all I wanted was for her to heat and quench the blade. Instead she did it all, even using magic to mold the blade, and I suspect to refine it."

"That sword could only be used ceremonially," Sallas waved at it, where Jerol had left it on a table. "The blade is too thin, it will snap the first time anyone used it to parry."

Jerol grabbed the sword again, and swung at the table, fully expecting the blade to shatter against the solid oak wood. It sliced right through the wood, leaving the table to collapse in half. Everyone stared in amazement, stunned to silence.

Lonora broke the silence, as she and Sheilla came out. "Pavlin, I will have your head for this," she advanced on the older man, who was still staring at the sword. His odd behavior caught her attention, and she turned to see the table and the sword.

"Spence," Regus finally spoke, "What was it you said about legendary swords?"

"That still does not solve our current problem," Sallas pulled himself out of his trance. "How many men do you need, Jerol?"

Jerol, inspecting the sword more closely, went to thumb the edge of the blade. "Are you sure you want to do that?" Regus caught Jerol's attention with a hand on Jerol's shoulder. Jerol closed his eyes a minute to collect his thoughts.

"Uh, five," he answered his father's question just as Sallas was about to repeat it. "Five men. Me, Stergis, Lathom, Spence, and the best of those wizards who know Calum's magic. Roanne, too, if she can somehow be ready in time."

"Five?" Regus stepped back. "Have you gone crazy? Just because you have a sword that will cut through a table does not enable you to take on thirty or more wizards and thirty guards."

"Think about this. If Calum is running to Curiland, he's there already," Jerol informed everyone. "He would have been there well before Timond got here. I can take the same men I took to get Roanne. While Duval, Smithe and the rest take Golare, I'll go into Curiland with only a small band, and I'll bring

Calum back, or kill him. That way, we might be able to avoid a full scale war between the kingdoms."

"I can be ready to go anytime," Olen volunteered right away, eager to make amends for the mistake he had made. Spence, Stergis and Lathom were also ready and willing.

"We can leave first thing in the morning, with or without Roanne," Jerol concluded. "We'll need healers and wizards to deal with the captives in Golare, but they can come a day behind, Roanne could come with them if she's not ready in the morning."

"Are you sure about this?" Sallas asked.

"Regus can lead the rest of the men to Rivard and Tusca," Jerol nodded. "Once you get everything here settled, which should take some weeks, start organizing for war, just in case. You'll need to recruit any man available, start with Zen's, or Karlon's men. Get them training now so they'll be at least somewhat prepared. If what we know is accurate, the Curilanders have a standing army of at most two thousand, but not much to recruit from beyond that."

"It's suicide," Sheilla shoved her father's hand off Jerol's shoulder, and spun him to face her. "You can't be serious about this. Five men, Jerol? And you think I'm going to let you take Stergis in that group?"

"Sheilla," Stergis stepped between her and Jerol. "He's right, it's the only way to avoid a war. We can't just walk into Curiland with an army. You take as few as you think you can get by with, and you make them the best you have."

"You want to help?" Jerol reached around Stergis to his sister. "Then, get Roanne back on her feet as soon as possible, but make sure she's ready before she comes after us. Send word through Telin when she will be coming, and maybe we'll be able to wait for her. She could be the difference."

As everyone dispersed to get organized for their individual tasks, the table caught Sheilla's attention once more. "That sword sliced through it like a knife through butter on a hot day," Letitia told her.

"Watch, Roanne," Sheilla's eyes lit up with an idea. "The smithy was covered with scraps from the forging, I want to catch Samus before he throws them out. Maybe he can make me some arrows with those scraps on the heads."

Letitia caught on immediately. "As long as I get some of them," she almost pushed Sheilla toward the door. "I can handle Roanne for a while. She'll probably sleep the day through, and I'm sure Lonora will be back before long."

The palace was filled with tension the rest of the day as preparations were made for Jerol's departure. Regus and the rest would be leaving the next day, which would keep everyone just as busy.

Roanne slept through most of it, but did wake for a few moments during the evening. Letitia and Sheilla got some broth into her then. Only half awake, Roanne still pestered them with questions, remembering something about Calum, some news, and wanting to know what it was.

"If she finds out Jerol is going after Calum without her, we won't be able to keep her from following right away," Letitia commented on the side to Sheilla. "Don't tell her a thing until she's ready."

The next morning, the two of them left Talia to watch over Roanne while they went to see the men off. Sheilla kissed Stergis good-bye, then turned on her brother. "If he has so much as a scratch on him when you come back I'll never forgive you," she threatened, then gave in to her emotions and embraced him. "And that goes for you, too."

Everyone noted Jerol was carrying his new sword. "His only sword, now," Stergis corrected. "We sparred last night to test the new blade, and it sliced right through mine. He gave me his old one to replace it, which, I have to admit, is an improvement for me."

Word had leaked out, and the streets to the northern gate of the walls were lined with people to see them off. Letitia put an arm around Regus. "They know you would rather be going with them," she said quietly to him.

"I'm just glad I have a brother who's willing to take the risks I can't for a throne he'll never inherit," he replied.

Sheilla heard that, and poked at him, "And you just be sure he never gets the chance to inherit. You stay clear of the fighting, you're going along to command, not fight. That's why Jerol does what he does. He's the fighter in the family, not you."

"I know what I'm doing," Regus insisted.

"We know," Letitia pushed on. "So, remember, you don't have anything to prove to anybody." She kissed him, then made room for Sheilla to get in on a three-way hug.

Sheilla and Letitia found themselves back in Roanne's sitting room, where their group, which now included Shiva, was gathering. The others had gone to the sewing room where they had first met, then found their way to Roanne's rooms by asking after Talia, Sheilla, and Letitia. Lonora showed up to check on Roanne, and watched over her while the others talked again.

They talked most of the morning, though Shiva did not say much. As the others were leaving, Shiva pulled at Sheilla's sleeve to draw attention to her. "Talia says Roanne's sick," Shiva said. "Can I help take care of her?"

Sheilla gave Shiva a hug, then took her back into Roanne's bedroom, where Roanne was still sleeping. "Can you watch her for us? If she wakes up, come get Letitia or I. We'll be right outside in the sitting room."

Shiva nodded, and Lonora gave up the chair near the bed so Shiva could sit. "We'll keep a close eye on them both," Sheilla told Lonora as they slipped out of the room. "Shouldn't you be getting ready to leave with Regus in the morning?"

"I'm pretty much ready," Lonora said. "It's not like I brought a whole lot with me." They met Letitia in the outer room.

"Can you do me a favor?" Letitia asked Lonora.

"Keep an eye on Regus?" Lonora knew what Letitia wanted. "I'll do my best, but he's awfully pigheaded, maybe as pigheaded as Roanne, and I wasn't much help stopping her."

For the rest of the day Sheilla and Letitia made sure one or the other of them was in the sitting room at all times. Every once in while, one or the other would slip out to stretch her legs, or run some errand. Roanne woke twice during the day, the second time she tried to get out of bed, demanding to know what was going on. It took both Letitia and Shiva to keep her in bed. When she settled down, and took the time to notice it was Shiva, the surprise was enough to give Letitia an opportunity to shove Roanne back into the bed.

"If you want to know what's happening, stay in bed. We'll have dinner brought up in a few hours, and you can join the rest of us then," Letitia told Roanne.

"Shiva," Roanne's attention was sufficiently diverted by her alone. "How are you doing?"

Shiva didn't answer, just took hold of Roanne's hand. "Please rest, everyone says you need to rest."

Letitia retreated from the room, knowing there was no way Roanne could argue with that.

Lonora approved of letting Roanne out of bed for dinner. She had to eat to recover Lonora pointed out. All the members of the royal family came to Roanne's room for dinner, along with Pavlin and Timond. Shiva was intimidated by all the men, so Roanne let her go eat with her family, getting someone from the palace staff to show Shiva the way to the dining hall.

"I really do apologize," Pavlin cornered Roanne, "But I had not expected you would carry it that far. It worked marvelously, though. That sword is going to go down in legend. I have a list the length of your arms from others who are willing to pay through the nose for a blade just like it."

"There won't be any more," Roanne brushed Pavlin aside and approached Regus.

"Where's Jerol?" Roanne demanded, and all of a sudden no one in the room would look at her.

"He went after Calum this morning," Sallas finally faced up to it.

It took several minutes to calm Roanne, and then to explain the plan. Most importantly, in terms of soothing Roanne's temper, they explained she could catch up with him along with the spinners and wizards heading for Golare the next morning.

"But only if you've fully recovered," Lonora warned, "So you better eat." Lonora pulled Roanne to a seat at the table.

The next morning, Roanne's mood had not improved at all, but she had the strength to be sure her horse was saddled, and be waiting in the courtyard even before the sun had come up.

"I slept all day," she shrugged when Lonora tried to lecture her. "I couldn't sleep anymore."

Lonora was about to order her to return her horse to the stable and go back to her rooms when Sheilla and Letitia showed up and put their weight squarely behind Roanne.

"Jerol and Stergis might not be coming back unless they have Roanne there to help," Sheilla backed Lonora off. "We're talking about my brother and the man I love. If Roanne says she's ready, then she's ready."

Aside to Roanne, both Letitia and Sheilla warned her to be careful. "Don't go if you're not ready," Sheilla seemingly contradicted herself. "If you're not, it would only mean we could loose you, too, and I wouldn't want that."

"Are you sure you are ready?" Sallas butted into the huddle of women.

"If one more person asks me that ..." Roanne threatened, and they all agreed she must be better.

They all went over to see Regus and his group off, which included Lonora. "Now I don't want to be hearing you overworked yourself," Roanne fussed with Lonora's saddlebags like a mother.

Lonora gave her a warning look, but then smiled, shaking her head. "You be careful, Roanne." She reached down and took Roanne's hand. "That sword is a work of wonder," she admitted, "But your timing could have been better. If anything should happen to you ..." Lonora couldn't finish the thought.

Sallas and Regus were nearby, and Roanne called out to them both. "If you wouldn't mind there's something I need to take care of," Sheilla and Letitia came near, where they could

Queen of the Spinners

hear. "If anything should happen to me, I want all my property to go to Lonora, until such a time as a new queen is found. I guess that would make Talia next in line. After Talia should be Fenicia."

"Nothing is going to happen to you," Sheilla insisted, tears forming in her eyes. She knew both Jerol and Stergis would have to be dead before they let anything happen to Roanne.

"Even if I'm captured and not killed," Roanne thought this through. "All my things must go to Lonora. If Calum has me, I don't want him to get even a copper of my property." She swallowed and knew in her heart it would never happen, because she would not be taken alive if she could help it. She still could not meet any of the other's eyes as she left them and went to mount her horse.

Letitia said her good byes to Regus, then came after Roanne. "What was that all about?"

"I had to designate an heir in case I don't make it. I have no family," Roanne shrugged.

"Not that, I understood that, the rest of it," Letitia pushed. Sheilla joined them now.

"There's a chance," Roanne had to swallow, and start over. "If things go really wrong, there is the possibility I could be brought back here with a leash around my throat. If that happens, I don't want whoever holds the leash to have any claim on my property. In fact, if that happens, I will already be broken. I want both of you to promise me, if it happens, you'll kill me. Put me out of my misery."

They began to back away. "Promise me!" Roanne demanded.

"All right, but if we can save you we will," Sheilla insisted, and Letitia agreed.

"If it gets that far something will have gone drastically wrong," Roanne insisted. "I'll already be dead for all practical purposes. I'm just asking you to make sure to finish it."

"If they do not, I will, I promise," Sallas came up behind Letitia and Sheilla.

"You just make sure it's not necessary," Sheilla left the courtyard before she began to cry, and Letitia went after her.

"You have a brave soul and a strong heart," Sallas took Roanne's hand. "I could not ask any more of you if you really were my daughter, nor have any more pride in the way you have handled yourself."

"Except for yesterday," Roanne winked at him. "It was a stupid thing to do."

"I am not so sure of that," Sallas smiled, "I saw what that sword could do, cutting an oak table in two with one swing. Somewhere down the line it just might save Jerol, or give him the ability to save you. In the legends, seemingly crazy events turn out to be the difference between victory and defeat. Maybe it was necessary for this legend that you make the sword. Who knows?" He shrugged and let her go, stepping back out of the way.

Chapter 18

That evening, Sheilla and Letitia were staring at each other across the empty chairs at their dinner table. Every once in a while, Sheilla's eyes would wander to where Stergis would normally be seated. The hall was nearly deserted, most people having left at the end of the meal.

"If all you two are going to do is pout, why not go to your rooms?" Sallas commented, moving from his seat at the center of the table to between the two young women. "Everyone in the room is catching your mood."

"I feel so useless," Sheilla twirled the wine in her glass. "There is this feeling we missed something, but I'm not sure if it's real, or just that I miss Stergis and Jerol. I even miss Roanne, and I've only known her less than a week."

"I have noticed she has that effect on people," Sallas nodded his agreement. "I feel the same way, but I guess I learned a long time ago, when your uncle went off to defend the Curiland border, I just was not fated to gain fame from heroics in battle. Your brother did not leave me enough men to lead an attack on a pub in the city."

"At least there is something for you two to do," Sallas kept going. "I have heard about what you are doing for the victims."

Letitia's attention slid to the table where Shiva's family normally ate. They were gone already. Earlier in the day, their session with the victims had not gone well. Neither she nor Sheilla was in the right mood for it. Talia might have held the group together, but she had gone with Roanne's group. Both Sheilla and Letitia knew Talia would find some way to wrangle her way all the way to Curiland.

"Me, all I can do is sit here and wait for reports from the communicators," Sallas was going on. "With the shortage of communicators, we do not even have one who could send messages, so I cannot even help them plan. Besides, once Jerol goes on to Curiland, he will not have a communicator with him."

He noticed his talk was not helping either of the ladies' moods. From the corner of his eye he saw a woman who looked like she wanted to approach their table, but was unsure. It was not a woman he recognized at first, but that was not surprising with all the strangers around. Letitia and Sheilla turned to see what he was looking at.

"Rysa?" Letitia stood up. "Is something wrong?"

"Who?" Sallas asked.

"It's Shiva," Rysa was wringing her hands nervously.

"It's all right," Sheilla stepped forward and took Rysa's hands in her own. "Have you met my father, King Sallas? Father, this Rysa, Shiva's mother."

"We met briefly the other day," Sallas remembered. "What happened with Shiva?"

"We told her Roanne had to go, and tried to explain why," Rysa was still hesitant. "When we told her Calum had run to Curiland to try and get away, she said something we thought was odd. She asked if Varden was in Curiland."

"Varden?" Sallas sat up straight. "Why would she ask that?"

"I have no idea," Rysa shrank from him, but Letitia placed a hand on her shoulder in support. "I mean, we tried to find out, to get more out of her, but we didn't get very much."

"Just relax," Sallas reached out a comforting hand, also, while Sheilla poured the woman a cup of wine. "Start from the beginning and tell us what you learned."

"Well," Rysa calmed visibly at Sallas' gesture. "When she first said it, I tried to think where she might have ever heard anything about Varden, but then, it was not an uncommon topic around the estate, given Kendal and Ariele's situation, and Roanne's belief that they must still be alive. But Shiva said one other thing, something about Calum saying he wished he was home in Varden, where the all the women were well trained. It didn't make sense to us, but we thought we should tell someone."

Sallas sat back in his chair, scratching his chin, while Letitia and Sheilla exchanged looks.

"We can't be sure if it means anything, really," Rysa concluded, "Not with the way she's been lately."

"But she spent a lot of time with Calum," Letitia pointed out, "And could have heard him say something like that."

"How could Calum be from Varden?" Sallas was not ready to accept it. "Tezza," he called out spotting the one healer who had been left to serve the palace, "I need to speak with Pavlin, do you know how to find him?" Tezza gave him a nod, and rushed off toward the rear of the palace. "Bring him to my conference room, along with any other wizard still at the palace." He gestured for one of the guards near the door of the room. "Summon the captains to the conference room," he commanded.

"I want to thank you, Rysa," Sallas stood before the woman. "This could be very important, you might just have saved Jerol and his group from a wild goose chase, and the embarrassment of possibly starting a war on bad information."

"You did the right thing by coming to us," Sheilla embraced Rysa, "And be sure to thank Shiva. We'll thank her again when we see her, but do so now also. I hope it will help her to realize she knows things we need to know to catch Calum."

"Can you bring Shiva to my conference room?" Sallas asked. "It might help if we can talk to her."

"I don't know," Rysa hesitated.

"Sheilla and I will go check," Letitia offered. "Shiva is afraid of men, bringing her into a room filled with them might not do us, or her any good." She took Rysa's arm, and Sheilla followed as they headed for the guest wing. "We'll bring her if we think it might help."

"Good," Sallas could understand why they were hesitant, and after their work with the girl, knew they would know best if anything else could be learned from the girl.

Everyone was gathered in the conference room when Letitia and Sheilla brought Shiva in. The room went quiet, and at a look from Sheilla, everyone got out of their way as they made their way to Sallas. Rysa slipped into the room behind them.

"King Sallas, this is Shiva from Altea," Letitia introduced the newcomer. "I believe you've already met once, but Shiva might not remember."

"We have met," Sallas smiled at Shiva. "I have heard your getting better, Shiva. Is that true?" Shiva looked to Sheilla, but nodded in response.

"Remember, Shiva," Sheilla told her, "Nobody here will hurt you. We won't let them. Roanne needs your help. She needs you to tell King Sallas everything you know about Calum. You need to help her, just like when you helped watch her while she was sleeping the other day."

"Calum said he lives in Varden," Shiva said quietly. "He wanted to go home there, because Talia and me weren't behaving right."

"Did Talia know this?" Sallas asked.

Shiva shrugged. "She wasn't there when he said it to me. She was in her cage."

"Did Calum mention Varden any other time?" Sallas put out an encouraging hand to Shiva, inviting her to sit next to him.

Shiva eyed the seat before sitting, then shook her head no to answer his question. "I don't remember. He was real mad because I wouldn't behave. I was hanging from the ceiling, while he got ready to punish me." She looked down at her hands in her lap. "That's all I know, I swear it."

Sallas leaned over and kissed her on the forehead. "Thank you, Shiva. Roanne will be glad to know this, it will help her catch Calum, so I can punish him for what he did to you." He waved to Rysa, who came forward, to take Shiva back to their rooms. "Rysa, I would like for you and Shiva and the rest of your family to dine with me tomorrow, to show how much I appreciate what Shiva has told me." Rysa nodded and thanked him as she took Shiva away.

"And to fill all those empty chairs at our table," Sheilla teased her father while they waited for the two to leave before starting.

"Pavlin, what do we know about Varden?" Sallas turned to the wizard when the door closed.

"To tell you the truth," Pavlin was embarrassed. "Roanne would be the one to ask. She's been studying her father's notes for years now. I know some things. Nothing grows in the region, and the few excursions to the edge of the wasteland have never even reported animal life out beyond the sands. Kendal did the deepest probe into the region, two years before he led the expedition into the area, intending to find the center, where the legends said there was a city, a port along the coast of the Whale's Sea. The entire region of the wasteland is inside the province of Bergain, which has gotten wealthy by trading the sands from the wasteland to make glass."

"Kendal must have learned something before he went on the excursion, was he not reporting to you as his advisor?" Sallas pressed Pavlin.

"Well he thought there were pockets of poisonous air or something floating through the region," Pavlin picked up the point. "As it passed over the sands, it killed any life form that might have tried to spread into the region from the forests surrounding the wastes. After his first try at probing just the edge of the region, he said he encountered the bad air, but thought there was something magical about it. That would confirm the theories about a magical war being responsible for the wasteland, not the gods. Ariele could sense the magic in the 'poison clouds,' and with her help, Kendal thought he could find the center of the wasteland, and the source of the magic maintaining the poison clouds, and thus stop the clouds. If he could do it, we could begin to reclaim the land. For anything more detailed than that, I would have to refer to Kendal's notes, and those books with what we would need to know were probably taken with him into the wasteland."

"Poison air?" Sheilla picked up that theme. "Could it be related to what Calum does with air?"

"I have no idea," Pavlin admitted.

"It makes sense," Letitia spoke up. "If there were people at the center of the wasteland, and they captured Kendal, they might have known who Roanne is. They would have to have some understanding of magic to maintain those clouds, and would now if Kendal and Ariele had a child, that child would be special."

"Those people would have sent an agent to do something about Roanne, before she came looking for her parents," Sheilla added. "That doesn't explain the dukes and the slavery all over the kingdom, though."

"It all sounds more like whoever is at the center might be getting ready to come out," spoke out Felder, one of the remaining captains, "and plans on taking over. They get a few dukes behind them, enticing them with the slaves, and corrupt the council with promises of renewed greatness. Then they try to take out the biggest threat to their chances of succeeding, Roanne."

"Aren't we getting a bit carried away here?" Tovan, who was there representing his home province for his father, spoke up. "We have no idea if there are people at the center of the wasteland. Further, we know there are people in Curiland, and some of them tolerate slavery."

"But in Curiland they have little tolerance for magic, which would seem to preclude someone like this Calum having much influence," Terran contradicted Tovan.

"I would tend to agree with Terran," Pavlin finally reentered the conversation.

"We have to get word of this to Roanne," Letitia interrupted their speculation.

"Unfortunately, we can't," Pavlin held up his hands. "There are no communicators left who can send. We have one man available for receiving messages, and that's it."

"Then I'm going," Sheilla stood up and headed for the door. At a signal from Sallas, two captains stepped in to block her path. She turned back to face her father, a furious look on her face.

"Going where?" Sallas asked. "After Roanne? I think not, we have guards who can do that."

"That she'll trust with information like this?" Sheilla countered. "I'm the best rider you have left in the palace, and you know it, damn it! Everyone else is gone."

"I'm going to tell Regus," Letitia stood and moved next to Sheilla. "He needs to know, since if Calum is running for Varden, he'll already be west of Golare, and Regus would be more likely to run into him. Further, it may come to a battle around Varden, in Bergain, I will not sit here in Esconda, while there is war in my home."

"Put these two in Sheilla's rooms, and post a guard. If they get out, I will have the guard's head," Sallas pointed toward one of the men blocking the way out of the room.

"Why don't you just put collars around our throats while you're at it?" Sheilla screamed back at her father, and the room went silent, her father's face turning white. "Or have you forgotten Letitia and I both have a stake in the outcome of this."

Sallas fell back into his chair, the tension in the room rising by the second. "Tell me what you both have in mind," Sallas finally conceded.

"I'll go warn Roanne about this," Sheilla jumped right in. "If I leave now and ride all night, I'll probably be able to catch them breaking camp in the morning."

"Beraine, Telin's sister, is with Roanne, she can send word on to Jerol through the wizards," Pavlin offered. Sallas was ready to wave away the suggestion, hoping to come up with a better counter argument to stop Sheilla from going, but Pavlin got it out before Sallas could react.

"Once Golare is secured by the men you sent with Jerol, he can take his strike force and move west instead of north, and meet up with Regus in either Rivard or Tusca, wherever Regus is. Telin is with Regus, so he and Beraine can help the two groups stay in touch."

"And just where will you be while all this is happening?" Sallas wanted to know.

"Well, I suppose my job will be done once I get the message to Roanne," Sheilla was trying to think of some reason she should go along.

"Which means you can come back here, right?" Sallas pressed.

"Something could come up where I could help," Sheilla tried, knowing it wasn't going to work.

"I want your word," her father was not going to give in on this, "You will turn right around and come back here."

Letitia could see Sheilla was trying to think of some way out of the promise. She started to speak up but was stopped when Sallas raised his hand. "You can go after Regus, there is nothing I can really do to stop you. You are not my daughter. Though I suspect neither your father, who will be joining Regus, nor Regus, will be happy to see you. They would both prefer you remained here, safe from the battle."

"If we loose this battle, there will be no place in this kingdom safe for me, or any other woman," Letitia said.

Sallas sat back in his chair, eyeing Letitia as he thought. After a moment his eyes began to wander, taking in the room around him. "You know," he paused, whether in thought, or for effect nobody could be sure, "You are absolutely right."

Letitia grabbed the nearest chair and let herself drop into it. She had not thought it would be this easy to get her way. She watched as Sallas' eyes finally came to rest on Sheilla, that thoughtful expression coming back to him.

"What are you waiting for," he said to Sheilla, "I thought you wanted to be on your way so you could catch Roanne by morning. You, too, Letitia, if you were thinking the same way. Can you handle an all night ride?"

Sheilla grabbed Letitia's arm and headed for the door, dragging Letitia behind. It was not until they were in the corridor before Letitia pulled free and halted.

"What are you waiting for?" Sheilla complained. "For him to change his mind?"

"He's not going to change his mind," Letitia planted her hands on her hips. "I think he has something completely different in mind. He's going to follow me in the morning, catching up with Regus, while Regus is straightening things out in Rivard and Tusca, just as I was planning to do."

Sheilla turned back to look at Letitia. "He wanted us out of the way because we're the only ones left who would argue about it," she was suddenly torn between running off with a chance of being with Stergis and Jerol, or staying and making sure her father was safe. "It really doesn't matter," she finally saw what drove him to that idea. "You were right, if this goes wrong it won't matter where he is, he won't be safe."

Sheilla was the first to reach the courtyard, where a groom had already saddled her horse, and Letitia's. Flinging her saddlebags over the horse's rump, she tied them in place, then ran back into the palace, through the guard's entrance. Letitia had the same idea, and Sheilla found her in the armory, picking out a crossbow. Most women in the nobility could use one. Festivals often featured archery contests for women, who might be expected the use a bow in battle, particularly defending the walls of a keep. They both had daggers, and knew how to use them to protect themselves. Sheilla grabbed a sword and began belting the scabbard around her waste. Letitia watched a moment, then copied her.

When they finally came back to the courtyard, Letitia carrying her saddlebags, Sallas laughed at the sight of the two swords. "Does either of you know how to use one of those?" He pointed to the belts around their wastes, and Letitia nearly tripped over the dangling sword. "You are more likely to cut yourselves as the enemy. I would suggest you stick with the crossbows."

Sheilla quickly said good-bye to her father, kissing him on the cheek, and mounted her horse. "I would rather stick myself with this sword than have somebody put one of those damned collars around my neck," she said looking down at her father.

"Let's make sure it does not come to that," Sallas hugged Letitia and watched her get onto her horse. They were both skilled riders he knew, and Sheilla had not been kidding when she said what it would take to stop them. "Maybe you can help keep Regus out of the fighting like I told him," he gave Letitia's hand one last squeeze before moving off toward Sheilla.

"And keep you out of the fighting," Sheilla pointedly let her father know she knew what he was planning. "You be careful, and I'll see you in Bergain, if not sooner."

Her father kissed her hand. "I would tell you to try and keep Jerol and Stergis out of trouble, Roanne, too, but I know it would be useless. You can stay out of trouble, though, and I expect you to be smart. I didn't raise any fools, except maybe Jerol." He smiled, and they both knew what he meant. Jerol would fight an army by himself if he thought it was necessary, but they all knew that was his job, since Regus was the heir.

The two women brought their horses together so they could at least take each other's hand and exchange an awkward hug. "Keep my father and brother out of trouble, Letitia," Sheilla said. Then pulled away and rode out through the northern gate of the courtyard. Letitia spun her horse around, and headed for the western gate.

Chapter 19

Jerol and his men had stopped to set up camp just before the border that would put them in Aston's province of Golare. As they had the night before, the wizards were gathering near the center of the camp to go over how they could defend against an attack using the kind of magic their enemy was likely to use. Spence had warned Jerol they only had seven wizards who could be of help when it came to an attack. The remainder were to be used only in defense. Few of their wizards were very strong, so Jerol had to have his men ready to pick out the wizards on the other side, and take them out as soon as possible. The other side was likely to have members of the council on their side, making it unlikely Spence's wizards could win a duel of magic.

The strategy for the archers was simple. Spence was beginning to appreciate the military genius of Jerol. Several wizards would build a defensive wall of flame for the archers to take cover behind, and fire back from, while the stronger wizards, particularly Spence would be seeking to find and destroy the defenses of the enemy wizards.

Beraine had sent word Roanne was on her way, having recovered enough by that morning. Jerol was fingering the hilt of his new sword, thinking whether to be happy about it. He knew he needed her skills, particularly once they went into Curiland, where they could find themselves facing up to thirty wizards. On the other hand, he wanted her to be safe, and thought the safest place was in Esconda, in spite of the recent attack on Letitia.

A tap on Jerol's shoulder interrupted the debate in his mind. "Remember what Olen was saying about Calum's arrogance," Spence said in Jerol's ear, pointing to the north. A line of men was forming out of the forest from that direction.

"Get your wizards and archers ready. I hope this strategy works," Jerol urged Spence, then moved quickly to his horse and mounted. Spence did the same, and Olen himself quickly joined them.

"They're too far to pick out any wizards," Olen commented as they came to the edge of the camp, where soldiers and wizards were taking up the positions they had planned.

Stergis rode up next to Jerol. "They have a lot more men than we thought," he was straining his eyes. "Maybe a hundred and fifty, almost two to one against us."

Jerol reached back in his saddlebags, feeling his way as he kept his eyes on the approaching enemy. "Here," he handed the spyglass, which had been a gift to him from Letitia, made from the sands of the wasteland in Bergian, to Olen. Olen recognized what it was immediately. "Use it to pick out the wizards."

Three men rode out ahead of the enemy, which was mostly on foot. "All three of them are wizards, and council members," Olen reported, moving the eyepiece along to the line of men. In spite of the jostling of horses around him, Jerol could hear the wizard counting under his breath. "I count only ten wizards," he said. "They're the ones on horses."

"Watch the flanks, and our rear," Stergis pulled his horse around and began directing men in all directions.

"We could have a problem," Olen did not want to report what he realized.

"Out with it!" Jerol commanded.

"The lead rider in the group coming forward is Duran," Olen looked away from Jerol. "When Calum left Altea, they had burned the bodies of the council members they killed, so we had no idea which of them had fled with Calum. We knew how many by the number of skulls."

"So, why is Duran a problem?" Jerol was beginning to get impatient.

"He's the council communicator," Olen ducked his head. "He could have been monitoring our communications."

"So they know Roanne is coming behind us, not with us," Jerol began cursing. His horse caught his mood and began to fidget. "Damn, that's where the rest of them are, including

Calum. All right, listen up, I want these wizards taken out fast. Spence, do they have shields up?"

"Yes," Spence answered.

"Don't burn the shields until the archers are ready and have already launched, then do it fast," Jerol was trying to think as he went along, and his horse was not cooperating, taking much of his attention to control it. "As soon as those wizards are down, I want our wizards to pull back and get mounted. Lathom, you'll have to handle this rabble with the wizards."

"Sir," Jerol turned to see who dared interrupt him. It was Karlon, the man who had replaced Zen, another man was using the spyglass Jerol had given to Olen, since Olen had finished picking out the wizards. "Those men over there," Karlon pressed on disregarding Jerol's expression. "A lot of them don't have uniforms, and we can pick out several we know will turn on them, if we give them the chance."

"Are you sure?" Jerol was suddenly not as angry at the interruption. Karlon nodded with confidence. "Stergis, get your men ready to go with the wizards. You move out as soon as those wizards are down, and head back to help Roanne. Lathom, you do the same once you take care of the army over there. Leave behind only what you need to guard any prisoners, none of them will be wizards. Karlon, let's hope you're right, pick some of your men they might recognize and get over there in a hurry to have those men either surrender or run. We know your men, because of the green, but in a fight we won't know who's who over there."

"Who's in charge there?" the riders from the enemy were now within easy calling distance.

Jerol let his horse move forward, ahead of their own line where it finally had room to prance about. The only limit Jerol imposed was keeping out of the line of sight of the archers flanked to either side. "I am, Prince Jerol."

"Well Prince Jerol," Duran answered. "If you surrender, we will spare you. By now you probably know we've destroyed the council of wizards. So, you know you can't stand against us."

Jerol simply drew his sword, and the archers took the signal and fired. Shields around each of the wizards burst into flame, and Duran's laughter turned to screams. Fighting broke out along the line of men behind the wizards, as those not in uniform turned on those in uniform. The wizards had been what held the peasants in line up until then.

Three wizards survived the first volley of arrows. Spooked by the flames, two of the wizard's horses bucked, throwing the wizards form their backs. One fallen wizard was attacked immediately by the peasants around him. With just as many archers, and only two remaining targets, the last surviving wizards became pincushions for arrows.

Lathom pulled up next to Jerol for only a second. "We'll be right behind you, now get going!" He urged Jerol before charging at the enemy.

Jerol swung his horse around letting the flow of men headed for the battle, if it could be called that, surge past him. "How could those wizards be so stupid?" he muttered to himself, as he searched for the communicator they had brought with them.

He found Estam as the wizards and Stergis' men surged out the back side of the formation, along the road back to where Roanne and the healers would be camping. "Estam," Jerol rode up alongside him as Stergis, at the front of the group set a pace the horses would be able to maintain for some time. It could take until morning before they would reach Roanne, and Jerol only hoped they would be in time. "Is there anyone else who might be able to intercept or eavesdrop on a message between you and the healers?"

"Duran was special," Estam took the time to consider before he answered further, "That's why he was on the council, he heard everything. I guess I refused to think he might be one who went over to Calum, I knew him, and trained under him. Sorry."

"Never mind, we all assumed they would be off in Curiland somewhere, not waiting to attack us," Jerol pushed, "He's dead, is there anyone else?"

Queen of the Spinners

"Not if I target the message," Estam suggested, "but I don't know the spinners well enough to target any of them."

"We'll have to take the risk, then" Jerol decided, "Warn anyone you can in Roanne's camp an attack might be imminent."

Roanne was sitting with a group of spinners who were practicing defense against the two wizards in their group who had been trained by Calum. In return, those wizards were learning to fight. Both wizards were near exhaustion from making air traps for the spinners to burn away. She had been learning to use Calum's spell for most of the afternoon, while riding in a wagon. At that moment she was considering whether to replace the two wizards before they completely exhausted themselves.

"Roanne?" Beraine interrupted Roanne's train of thought. "I just heard from Estam, the wizards just attacked them, and he says we should also expect an attack."

"Damn, I thought they were supposed to be off in Curiland," Roanne cursed. She began pacing, looking around at the place where they had camped. Because they were pushing for time, they were between the normal stops along this road. The few guards they had with them were organizing the camp for the night. "Fogart," she remembered the senior guard's name, "Come here."

Fogart swore expansively when he heard the news. "We have few weapons, and only a few guards," he threw up his hands.

"Then we had better find a place where we can hold them off until help arrives," Roanne suggested. "What about the farm a mile or so back up the road. It had stone walls around the house that would make a solid defensive line."

"Against magic?" Fogart asked, "I saw what those five wizards were using in the dining hall the other night."

"Then you know a stone wall will stop it, Sallas took cover behind a table," Roanne pointed out. "Get everyone moving, leave the wagons, but bring every weapon. Some of the spinners have crossbows."

The people around her were already moving. Within minutes they were mounting up. A lot of them had been traveling in the wagons, which also carried medical supplies, and food, trying to anticipate their needs once they got to Golare. Those who rode in wagons were doubling up with the riders.

A rider came barreling into camp from the north. He was one of the men Fogart had sent out to scout. "A group coming hard, with maybe twenty to thirty," the scout reported. At least the men coming would stop to investigate the wagons, buying Roanne's group a few precious minutes to make it to the farm. Roanne was one of the last to leave the camp, along with Fogart. They made it back to the tree line of the forest between the clearing where the camp would have been and the farm before the men came into view from the north.

"I went to the top of the hill back there," the scout explained how he spotted them so far away. "The road dips into a wide valley from there, and I could see them coming over the next hill. We still probably have a minute or two before they come over the top of the hill where they can see the camp."

From the tree line Roanne stopped to watch the hill and look back at the camp. They had not even gotten around to lighting the cooking fire for their dinner. On a whim she reached out with her concentration and lit it, just before the riders crested the hill. Upon seeing the fire, the riders came to halt. They waited a moment, then seven riders split off to each side, leaving seven behind. It was obvious they were hoping to surround the camp.

Roanne looked around her, and noticed all that remained of her people was the scout and Fogart. "Damn," she swore at herself, "It would have been nice to prepare a little surprise for one of those groups splitting off."

"We could still take a couple of them," the scout offered. "It would cut down their number a little, and if they're wizards everyone we can deal with helps."

"No," Fogart objected, "We retreat to the farmhouse and hold out for reinforcements."

"What reinforcements?" the scout asked.

"Jerol knows about this," Fogart explained, "He sent a message back, which means he must be sending men, too."

"They said they were under attack," Roanne corrected him, "Which means he probably doesn't have the men to spare. Fogart, leave me your crossbow, and go get them organized at the farm. We'll be along in a few minutes. What's your name, again?"

"Evin, Your Highness," the scout answered.

"Skip the titles," Roanne told him, taking Fogart's bow and brace of arrows.

Staying to the growing shadows along the tree line, she and Evin circled slowly, until they could see the men coming. There were four, now, and as they watched, one fell off and turned toward the camp. They both loaded crossbows, but Roanne handed hers to Evin. She pointed toward the approaching men. "We're going to try something I've used before against these wizards," she whispered. "When the first one goes down, take the one to the right first, then the one on the left. Reload fast, because the fourth one should come running, and the other will probably notice what I do."

Her plan worked as well this time as it did the first time she tried it on the road to Esconda. The moment the wizards saw her step out of the woods they tried to entrap her in walls of air. Just as before, she burned them away, making a fiery ball, and sent it right at the one in the middle. They were so shocked, neither of the other two had shields up when Evin fired the first bolt, taking out the one to the right. The other one got his shield up, but like Talia's dagger, the second bolt passed right through the burning shield. The fourth rider, as Roanne thought, saw the flames in the twilight, and she suspected others did as well. She retreated to the edge of the wood. Evin had both crossbows loaded and ready. Wary, the rider approached more slowly than the others, then saw the empty horses and stopped.

"Can you hit him from here?" Roanne asked Evin.

"Any hunter could," Evin answered.

"I'll flame the first bolt to take out his shields, fire the second right after it," Roanne instructed.

It worked perfectly. Alerted by the other horses, the wizard had his shields up, until the first arrow hit, and set the shield on fire. The second bolt made it through to the wizard.

Across the clearing they could see several of the wizards were headed for them, now. "Time to retreat," Evin suggested, though he reloaded the crossbows, and returned one to Roanne. "We can slip back through this wood, and cross the fields to the farm instead of using the road."

Hoof beats back the way they had come drew their attention. Charging along the edge of the wood was the wizard who had probably circled all the way around from the other side. He was getting close enough to see them. Roanne searched for and found his shield and lit it from where she was, that last trick used less energy than this, but she had no time. Evin was paying enough attention to fire at the same time Roanne did, which Roanne thanked the gods for when the horse reared in response to the flames, and her bolt missed the wizard. Evin's bolt did not miss. Even as the wizard went down, they were threading their way through the trees, the fields they needed to reach only a hint of lighter shadows in the distant moonlight. Roanne's heart was pounding as they cleared the woods. There was no sound of pursuit behind them, like the trampling of leaves and snapping of branches accompanying their passing.

"Well, we cut them down from twenty-one to sixteen," Evin seemed proud of their efforts.

"But we may have also tipped them off to something they didn't know," Roanne warned as she mounted. "I don't think they had any idea we had a way to fight them. Well, they know now."

They raced across the field arriving at the farm well before any pursuit materialized along the road. "They're regrouping," Roanne surmised, as two of the spinners took the horses and headed for the barn to hide them.

"How many?" Was all Fogart asked as he came up to them.

"We got five, leaving sixteen," Evin reported.

"They must be rethinking their strategy," Roanne said. "Otherwise they would have been right behind us."

Low on the ground behind the stone wall surrounding the house were several spinners and all the guards they had available.

"Why don't you get inside and rest?" Fogart suggested. "I don't want them to see any obvious activity as they approach the farm. If we can hit them by surprise, maybe we can take down a few more before we have to retreat to the farmhouse itself."

"How do you plan to cover the retreat?" Roanne asked.

"Ideally, I would like to have a wall of fire between them and us," Fogart said. "The spinners inside are going to see if they can manage it. Our two wizards are going to see if they can back that up with a shield of our own at the wall."

"I think I can help the wizards, and that should do us," Roanne nodded her approval. "We should have the spinners save their strength. This could turn out to be a siege."

An older woman came out of the house as they approached. "Your Highness," she seemed undecided between a bow and a curtsy. "Welcome to my home. I don't recall anyone in the area having the chance to host a member of the royal family in years. I'm Luanna."

"Thank you, Luanna," Roanne was equally unsure how to handle the situation. "I just wish the circumstances could be better, you know we're expecting to get attacked by wizards, don't you?" Roanne looked to Fogart to be sure.

"The spinners explained it all, they're brewing some broth they said you might want when you arrive," the woman held the door open for the rest of them. "I think you know Hazlet," she added, closing the door, "He stopped by yesterday with all those soldiers to warn me there could be trouble."

Roanne was comfortably settled in a chair with a mug of broth when someone at the front windows sighted the riders emerging from the forest. The wizards had waited longer than Roanne had thought they would. The moon was past its zenith and on its way down. Roanne came to the window so she could see for herself. The men had stopped at the edge of the forest, checking out the farm from a distance before moving closer. Instead of moving in, or splitting up, the way they had for the camp, several of them dismounted. It was hard to see what they were up to, but after several minutes, they sat on the ground, and the rest of them dismounted as well.

"What are they doing?" Roanne was frustrated at not being able to see clearly.

"Waiting for the moon to set, maybe," Fogart shrugged. "Not that it will matter, the spinners can feel the magic, they don't need to see it, right?"

"You can't see it, even in full daylight," Roanne answered.

"And flames from the burning will guide the archers," Fogart finished his original thought. "If they want to wait, it's fine by me."

The wizards did wait several hours for the moon to set. In the farmhouse they had been sleeping in shifts. Always keeping plenty of eyes in the windows on every side of the house. When the wizards did make their move, though, they stayed together this time, advancing slowly toward the house.

Quiet animal calls were used to alert the spinners and guards at the walls, and Fogart slipped out, taking advantage of the darkness, to direct the movements of people. From the side and back walls guards and spinners came scurrying along the ground, being sure to stay out of sight, to the front wall where the wizards were approaching. Their defense had anticipated the wizards would try to surround them again.

In the dark of the night, the sense of magic being used, which Roanne had used to find and burn shields several times, now, was more than obvious. She could track the movements of the wizards that way, and was hoping the other spinners were doing the same.

"Beraine," Roanne turned away from the window a moment, finding the girl back near the hearth where the broth was cooking, "Have you heard anything else from Estam?"

"Not yet," Beraine answered.

"Can you, or anyone else here, contact him?" Roanne asked.

"I've been practicing since I arrived in Esconda," Beraine smiled, glad to be of some use rather than simply hiding in the corner.

"Tell him where we are and there are sixteen wizards against us," Roanne ordered, "And see if you can get any word on where they are, and how their battle went."

When Roanne turned back to the window, the wizards were much closer. As she sorted the feel of each wizard's magic, finding the distinctions so she could track them, she suddenly came upon one that made her stomach clench. She backed away from the window, trying to get control of the fear suddenly attacking her mind, nearly causing her to panic. "And Beraine," she added, "Tell Estam Calum is here."

Roanne forced herself back to the window, telling herself she could fight him. She knew more, and was much stronger than the last time they had seen each other.

The sixteen riders were spreading out across the front of the farm, now, with Calum at the center. "Roanne," he yelled out. "Yes, I know it's you." Roanne's stomach tightened even more, but then she started to get angry with herself, and as she had done before, let the anger grow, transferring it to Calum, which allowed it to grow much faster and stronger. "If you give yourself up," Calum continued to call, "I might let all these others go."

"I wish they would come a little closer," Fogart, who had returned to the house, muttered, "We can't afford any misses."

"I'll bring them in," Roanne opened the door and stepped out before anyone including her own fear could stop her. She continued out to the center of the yard.

"Now that's better," Calum called, as all the wizards moved a bit closer. "You did pretty well back there, catching a few of my men by surprise with your little light tricks and illusions. We're ready for you now, though, and you know you can't fight me." Walls of air tightened around Roanne's sides and back pushing her toward the walls of the yard. The dreaded gag reappeared in her mouth also. She let it happen, but not without fighting, drawing them in some more. She had to fight back panic as much as she fought the walls, convincing herself she was the one in control this time, he just didn't know it, yet.

Finally, as she neared the gate of the wall, she lit the air around her, spitting the gag as it burned, and sending it toward the wizard next to Calum. As the wizard's shield lit, the archers sat up behind the wall, and shields all along the wizard's line burst into flame as well.

Calum's horse reared, taking the crossbow bolt in the chest for him. As the horse went down, Calum took cover behind its body. Unable to see Calum behind the horse, she sent the rest of the burning air that had trapped her a moment before to harass the wizards who survived the attack, giving their archers time to reload. Most of them managed a second shot, even as the wizards turned and ran. Calum scrambled to a horse with an empty saddle, and in the darkness and other confusion, managed to mount and follow his fleeing allies. In the light of the stars, Roanne thought she saw five men ride away, but when she came storming through the fence it was toward the horse Calum had been riding. When she found he was gone, she screamed her frustration. "I'm the one hunting you, now, Calum!" She yelled after the retreating riders.

"We got twelve," Fogart came out of the darkness to report, but Roanne was hardly paying attention.

"Roanne!" Beraine came running out of the house, "Where are you?"

"Over here," Roanne answered, gathering her wits, and letting her anger drain away.

"Roanne, those riders are going to run right into Jerol," Beraine could hardly control her enthusiasm.

"What?" Roanne couldn't believe her ears, but her attention snapped to the break in the tree line where the road passed into it. The last fleeing rider, who she did not realize was Calum, was just entering the cover of the trees.

"Jerol and our wizards are right up the road there," Beraine tried to make it clear to Roanne. "Those wizards are going to run right into them."

Roanne was running for the nearest horse. Before anyone could grab her, she was mounted and on her way.

Jerol caught glimpses of the approaching riders in the starlight, but it was the word passed up from Estam that got him to draw his sword. "The wizards are running right at us!" Man after man repeated so everyone got the word. Jerol saw the wagons and fire off to one side to the road, but ignored them, heading straight at the oncoming riders.

The riders pulled up when the saw Jerol coming, gesturing frantically with their hands, Jerol ignored it all as he plowed in among them swinging with his sword.

"Damn, they got their shields up," he heard someone behind him curse, but that did not seem to matter as one then another wizard went down when their shields failed to stop his sword. After taking down a third, Jerol found he had went right through the small group of wizards. Before he could even think to turn back another rider came through the trees at the end of the clearing. Hearing the battle, this lone rider turned to run back the other way. Jerol kept going after him, trusting the others to find a way to deal with the wizards behind him. When lights flared behind him, he knew they had found a way.

The last rider to enter the woods came back out within a few seconds, turning to cross the fields rather than take the road leading back toward the farmhouse. Roanne saw him come back, and pulled up to try and think what he was doing, remembering the road turned slightly as it crossed the farm, and the wizard must be cutting diagonally across the field to where the road reentered the woods at the opposite side of the farm.

Another rider came sprinting out on the road from the woods, coming right at Roanne. Roanne stopped to think what she should do. She could not sense any magic coming from the rider, and when she glimpsed the reflection of the stars off his sword she realized this was not a wizard. "It's me, Roanne," she called as the rider barreled down on her.

The rider did not slow, but did pull back his sword. "Roanne?" Jerol was just as surprised as she was. "Were you the one who came through the woods?" He pulled his horse around once he was past her, making sure to avoid a collision.

"He went across the fields," she gathered air in her hands the way Calum taught the wizards, forming a solid ball. Gathering her concentration, she sent it off into the air above the fields then lit it, feeding more air into the ball, she turned up the heat, making the ball of fire brighter.

"I see him," Jerol told her.

Roanne heard Jerol take off in pursuit, then once she felt confident she could maintain what she had started, she opened her eyes. The ball of fire lit the entire field, putting the fleeing wizard in plain site. He was watching her, and in the light of the fire, Roanne could see it was Calum.

"It's Calum," she called after Jerol, "Be careful!"

Nearly across the field, Calum pulled up and began to gesture.

"He's attacking, Jerol!" Roanne screamed. She tried to sense the magic he was forming, but was so tied up in her own spell she was finding it difficult. Time seemed to slow as she saw Calum begin the last part of the spell, the throwing motion she had seen the wizards from the dining hall use. Roanne tried to untangle her power from her spell, desperate to protect Jerol, who she knew was counting on her. He wasn't backing off his charge at all. Calum launched the spell at Jerol, and Roanne was unable to track it. Her heart sank, knowing Jerol was about to die.

Suddenly the weapon Calum had used flared as it neared Jerol, burning away before it found its target. Turning, Roanne found Spence sitting on his horse a short distance behind her.

Calum never got the chance to launch a second attempt, though he did try. Before he could get to the final motion, he suddenly straightened in the saddled, then slumped forward along the neck of the horse, and then to the ground.

Jerol pulled up in confusion, unsure of what had just happened. From behind Calum, another rider came out of the shadows of the forest, a crossbow resting against one thigh.

Roanne and Spence were moving across the field, and were just close enough to hear Jerol's words. "Sheilla, what are you doing here?"

Chapter 20

They all returned to the original camp, where the fire Roanne had lit was barely alive, reduced to a mass of glowing coals sunk within the hole dug out just for that purpose. Their combined groups spread around the fire. The soldiers who came with Jerol were exhausted, as were their horses. The same was true of Lathom's men when they came riding in not long after they had begun to organize themselves. Those who had held up in the farmhouse were by far the freshest individuals, so it fell to them to maintain a watch while the others rested. The healers had checked the wizards to be sure, and declared they all were dead. A small detachment was organized to dig a mass grave for wizards across the road from the camp, near where they found the bodies of the first wizards Roanne and Evin had killed.

All the main players in the battle were exhausted. Even the broth that seemed to almost magically restore wizards and spinners was not much help to Roanne. The burning light she used to light the field where Calum had died had nearly grown beyond her control as she watched. She had to struggle to control it after that, and finally managed to extinguish it, plunging the area back into darkness. The effort had not cost her as much as the sword had, but she had the feeling if she had not regained control in time, the spell would have drawn even the life energy from her body, and it scared her. The moment she was back at the camp and on the ground, she fell asleep, a fitful sleep, haunted by nightmares in which Spence had not been in time to save Jerol, or she had not managed to control the spell.

Jerol, Sheilla, and the others also got what rest they could, having ridden all night. Nobody, not even Stergis, had the energy to question Sheilla's sudden appearance out of nowhere. There would be time later for them all to catch up on the news. Even Sheilla's news could wait considering the events of that night.

As night waned into morning more of their men, the ones who had to drop back for fear of running their horse into the ground came straggling into the camp, and were welcomed with a warm meal and places to rest themselves and their weary animals. As the sun came up so did temporary shelters to provide shade for those trying to recover from their efforts.

It was not until well after noon that individuals came back to life. Stergis and Jerol were the first, and immediately went about checking to see everything was in order. Lathom awoke, and went to check the few injuries some of his men had taken in the first fight the day before, and heard from a messenger from the troops he had left behind. When Sheilla woke, she almost regretted it, as Stergis immediately abandoned what he was doing, and marched toward her. She was expecting to get raked over for being there, but instead was taken up and swung around in a hug. Jerol was coming over by the time Stergis put her down, and the look on his face was not as welcoming.

"I thought you might need that before your brother gets a hold of you," Stergis said as he let her go.

Jerol's hand came up, pointing at her as he approached, and Sheilla ducked behind Stergis for cover.

"I think he should be thanking her for saving his life," Roanne was just sitting up, her hair a mess, and her face streaked with dirt, that only got worse as she wiped at her eyes with even dirtier hands.

"She shouldn't even be here," Jerol spun toward Roanne.

"Roanne's right," Spence was nearby getting a mug of broth he then gave to Roanne, pouring another for himself before sitting down. "I'm not sure I could have stopped Calum the next time."

"You?" Jerol stepped back. "I thought it was Roanne did that."

"I was too entangled in the spell that lit the area," Roanne took a sip of the broth, then made a face, setting the mug aside. "I've had so much of this stuff lately, if I drink any more of it, I think I'll be sick."

Sheilla jumped out from behind Stergis, seeing her chance. "That's right," she said as if she had known it all along. "And what about you, you fool. Where did you learn to go charging headlong at a wizard with his kind of skill? Are you trying to get yourself killed?"

Once the laughter died down, they settled around the fire pit to go over everyone's account of the events. All the appropriate people joined in the group to provide their own accounting.

"I left Karlon and Hazlet in charge of the other battle site once we had everything under control," Lathom summed up the first battle. "They had about twenty prisoners who surrendered when the wizards went down. We hardly had to do any fighting. Most of our injuries came trying to stop the peasants from slaughtering Aston's remaining guards. I'll head back in the morning, along with the wizards and spinners, and we can move on into Golare and start setting things right."

Jerol gave his accounting of how things happened next. "The only thing I regret is not really getting the chance to test this sword," he admitted at the end.

"Just what did you do with that blade?" Stergis turned to Roanne. "It cuts right through the wizard's shields."

"It should cut just about anything," Roanne shrugged. "I don't know what Pavlin originally had in mind. But that was the way one of my father's old books described using magic to make swords. I said I wanted to do it right if I were going to do it at all. The edges are as sharp as I could make them, which is far sharper than any hammer was going to do. If I had the chance I would have told you," she turned toward Jerol. "It's a powerful weapon, but I have confidence you'll use it well, or I wouldn't have given it to you."

Finally everyone turned to Sheilla with an expectant look on their faces. She looked away at first, but realized it was time. "Well, I came through the woods on the other side of the farm just before the fighting started. Not sure of what to do, I just held back, retreating to the trees. Once I figured out what was happening I wanted to help, but by then the wizards were on the run. When Calum came back, I nearly panicked, because I didn't know who it was. Then the light appeared and it nearly blinded me, it took a moment for my eyes to adjust. I heard Roanne yell something, but all I could make out was Calum's name. The next thing I realized, he had stopped, and turned away from me to attack Jerol. I just did the only thing that came to mind, I'm a pretty good hunter, but I've never shot at a man before. I thought I was going to be sick afterward."

"What I want to know," Jerol was pointing at her again, "Is what you were doing here in the first place. You should be back in Esconda."

"You're just mad because you didn't get to kill Calum," Roanne scooted across the ground over next to Sheilla, and gave her a hug. "Thank you for saving his life, even if he'll never admit it."

"I did admit it," Jerol straightened his spine, and realized he had not thanked her. He moved closer to his sister and kissed her on the forehead. "Thank you for saving my life."

"Now ..." he tried to get back to where he had left off, but Roanne cut him off again.

"Now we can sit back and relax for one night, and celebrate that this is all over," she pronounced. "Calum is dead, and all that remains is to put all the pieces back together."

"That's not as easy as you make it sound," Stergis pointed out the obvious.

"It's not true, either," Sheilla ducked her head as everyone turned their attention back to her.

"What do you mean?" There was a dangerous edge in Roanne's voice. Jerol put a hand on her arm to keep her from exploding.

"Calum is dead," he repeated for his sister. "What else is there?"

"I'm not sure, but I know it's not over," Sheilla looked directly at Roanne. "I'm sorry to have to tell you this, but it's the reason I'm here. We found out Calum was not running to Curiland, and though we didn't know exactly where he was, we knew he was still in Tularand. I came to stop you from going to Curiland."

"Then where was he going?" Jerol had the dangerous edge in his voice, now.

"Shiva is beginning to talk more, and she said Calum had mentioned where his home was once during a fit of anger," Sheilla looked again right at Roanne. "Calum said he was from Varden."

"Letitia went to warn Regus," Sheilla kept going in the stunned silence. "We thought Regus might run into Calum as Calum worked his way across the kingdom. Father will have left this morning to join Regus, and to go on to Bergain. They'll be looking for any sign of Calum, so we should let them know what happened."

"Estam," Jerol searched around, only to find Beraine right behind him, listening to all this.

"I'll get to it as soon as we finish in case there is anything else you might want to add," Beraine offered Jerol.

"Nobody in Esconda had a good idea of what it might mean," Sheilla went on. "Pavlin said Roanne was the best expert on the wasteland, having been studying her father's notes. He told us what Kendal had thought was the reason for the wasteland, and what Kendal was hoping to do." Sheilla went on to repeat as much of what was said by Pavlin, and everyone else at the king's meeting.

"Shiva is a very sick young woman," Fenicia, who was leading this contingent of spinners as Lonora was leading the group with Regus, spoke up. "Can we be sure of what she said? I don't mean to insult her, but her mind might not be healed all the way. It could be memory from a nightmare while she was held by Calum, or the result of delirium."

"I believe her," Sheilla went on to give the exact context of how this all came out, trying to remember as best she could the exact words Shiva had used.

Roanne reacted strongly to that.

"It implies there are others in the wasteland," she was on her feet before Jerol could grab her. "My parents could still be alive." Jerol finally got hold of her, and pulled her back to the ground. "I knew it. All these years everyone kept saying they were dead, but I knew they were alive." She turned to Jerol. "I can go get them, I know I can. They must be prisoners or something."

"Or something," Jerol repeated the words slowly for Roanne, and the excitement in her eye went out, even as they grew bigger and sprouted tears at the corners.

"No," Roanne shook her head, then tried to shake free of Jerol's grasp. Jerol hung on, drawing her closer, wrapping his arms around her. Sheilla did the same from behind her. "No!" Roanne yelled, but then broke down and cried. "I would have known it if they were dead. I know they're alive." Roanne managed to say between the tears.

"I don't …" Hobert the wizard healer began, but Stergis cut him off with simply a look.

"You've seen for yourself the way women are treated, think about the words Calum told to Shiva," Fenicia tried to explain to Hobert. "Something about all the women at home are well trained, Ariele has been there for eighteen years, and you've seen what only a few weeks, or even months can do to a woman."

Hobert thought about that. "But Ariele and Kendal were both very powerful," he said, wary his next words would not go over well. "We have to consider the possibility …"

Fenicia lashed out at him, while Jerol and Sheilla struggled to control Roanne who looked ready to kill Hobert. "I knew them both, I even helped to train Ariele," Fenicia declared, when she let up on her assault. "Neither of them would ever be a party to this atrocity. Is there anyone else thinks that way?" She turned slowly around, taking in each face around the fire.

At a nod from Jerol, Lathom grabbed Hobert, and moved him away from the area.

"Bring him back here, I'll …" Roanne was still struggling to break free.

"Roanne!" Sheilla grabbed Roanne's chin and made Roanne look directly into her face. "Nobody who knew your parents, or really knows you, will think such a thing." Roanne closed her eyes and gave up then, and the tears returned, while Sheilla continued to do her best to try and comfort her.

Jerol rose and went after Lathom, with Stergis scrambling to his feet to follow, not liking the look in Jerol's eyes. They found Hobart saddling a horse while Lathom looked on. Jerol had to stop and pace a moment, trying to master his anger, which made Stergis breathe a lot easier.

"Hobert," Jerol finally said, "I can understand, why someone who did not know any of them might need to ask that. Right now, though, I want you to know for your own safety I am going to insist you leave here." Hobart was giving no argument, as he scrambled into the saddle without even checking his the saddle to be sure it was on right.

"I'm not going to argue," Hobart managed to keep his voice almost calm, even though his shirt was soaked with the smell of fear. He rode off without a look back.

"Roanne will come to understand," Stergis placed a hand on Jerol's shoulder. "I don't think she would seriously hurt him."

"I wasn't worried about her," Jerol turned and headed back toward the fire. Stergis and Lathom exchanged looks, neither one of them was surprised at Jerol's admission.

"I think he's learning to control his temper," Lathom smiled to ease the tension. "When I first saw him coming after us, I thought we were going to have to bury Hobert."

Sheilla, with a lot of help from Jerol managed to calm Roanne by the end of dinner. Roanne was in such a mood most of the camp gave their area a wide berth during the meal, with only those who knew Roanne willing to sit near them.

"I contacted Telin in Regus' group," Beraine reported, "Letitia caught up with them early this morning, and explained the new information from Shiva. They'll be moving into Rivard tomorrow, but so far there's no sign of resistance. Regus was happy to hear Calum is out of the way, and everyone was safe.

There has been no sign of King Sallas, yet. Finally, he agrees this news about Varden changes everything, and will be expecting to meet you in Bergain, if not sooner."

"All right," Jerol set his mind to the planning mode they had all seen in operation recently. "Stergis, I want you to have your lieutenant, Durelle, take over here. All the captains will be coming with me, so advise each of your lieutenants accordingly. Instruct them, once Golare is under control, to move on toward Bergain. It wouldn't hurt for any spinners or wizards who care to volunteer to join them. Be sure Golare is secure, and has enough people to do what needs to be done. They'll have Estam who can contact us if anything goes wrong."

"The rest of us, the captains, Roanne, Beraine, Spence and Olen will leave for Rivard first thing in the morning," Jerol checked on Roanne from the corner of his eye, trying to reassure himself she would be ready. "We should be able to meet up with Regus there, then on to Bergain."

"I'm going with you," Sheilla objected, from where she sat with Roanne.

Jerol wanted to argue the point, but right now, Roanne seemed to need Sheilla's support. He was hoping his support would be enough, but realized Sheilla could give to Roanne something he could not, right now, her full attention. He hoped Roanne would understand the reasons for that.

Chapter 21

Everyone was grateful for the one day of rest Jerol had allowed them afterwhat he put them through the next three days. Sheilla was one of those people who simply loved to ride, and much to her father's chagrin, took advantage of every chance to do so. After three days of hard riding, as Jerol seemed intent on pushing them all right to their limit, even she was beginning to see this ride as Jerol's punishment for her being there.

Talia had inserted herself into the group, literally, by simply following them on their first day out. "I wouldn't be much help as a healer, yet," she explained to Roanne at the camp that night. "And, as I told you before, I intended to be there when you brought all this to an end, and I meant it." Jerol was angry about it, but could hardly argue. Either he let her join them, or she would simply continue to follow along behind.

When they finally saw the lights of Regus' camp outside the city of Rivard, Roanne considered magically launching fireworks in celebration, but she was too tired. They had pressed so hard conversation along the way had been all but impossible. Each night when they stopped, everyone was so tired, it was all they could do to get some semblance of a meal together, and collapse onto blankets spread on the ground. The only talking came when it was your turn to stand watch, when you had to keep talking just to stay awake.

The third night, Jerol had insisted they were close enough to Rivard to keep going, so it was in the light of the moon they first saw the camp. They were met by sentries at the edge of the camp, who let them pass the moment they recognized who they were. Sallas and Regus had set up headquarters in the home of the previous duke they were told, and all the remnants of the activity there had already been removed.

"Remnants?" Roanne asked.

"The duke had cages for women in his bedroom, and in the cellars," the guard, whom she didn't know, explained.

Another guard had been sent ahead to announce their arrival. They might have enjoyed the easy pace at which Jerol led them into the city were it not for the soreness they all felt after the past few days' ride.

"I can't wait to dive into a tub of hot water and soak until all my skin wrinkles right off my bones," Sheilla admitted for Roanne's ears only. They had agreed the first time Jerol had put them on watch together he would not hear one peep of complaint from either one of them and had kept their word.

Everyone came out to greet them in the courtyard, and to congratulate them on their success. Roanne was surprised at finding Letitia in breeches and shirt, since she had always seen her in fine gowns or riding habits. Sheilla fit the more casual image much more easily, actually feeling more comfortable in utilitarian clothes. Roanne thought that was an odd contrast when you considered Sheilla's complaints about the way Letitia was running the palace back in Esconda. As she watched the two of them exchange greetings, Roanne decided they both were equally good at either of the images.

Regus had them taken directly to their rooms, where baths were being prepared. All the rooms were in one wing, and they were shown a lounge where food would be brought for them.

It was not until the next morning everyone gathered to compare notes on the status of their campaign to clean up the kingdom. They tried to tell it quickly, sticking to simply the facts, but as Jerol and Lathom related what had happened in the fight at the border of Golare there were so many questions from Regus, Sallas, or Pavlin it took nearly an hour. Olen contributed a few things as well, mostly concerning the arrogance of the wizards, and how that turned the battle to a route.

Once Roanne began her part of the story, Lonora came back with as many questions as the others. They all seemed particularly interested in her role in Calum's death. Pavlin noted she had finally found a limitation to her power in the light she had made.

"Not really," Roanne hung her head at what she was about to admit. "I was not as tired afterward as I was with the sword. The problem was in my control. When I lost control over the spell, I found myself trapped in the spell for a moment. If I had kept control, I don't think there would have been a problem. The spell could have helped even, because, after thinking back, I probably could have just used it to kill Calum."

"What made you loose control?" both Pavlin and Lonora wanted to know.

Roanne knew the answer to that, and so did Sheilla after their conversation on watch, but even Sheilla agreed she might not want anyone else to know the answer. It was not just the personal nature of the problem, but it could possibly be used against her at some time in the future. For several minutes, Roanne appeared to be debating the answer, when she was actually debating if to answer at all.

"I was scared," she tried to shrug off the answer. It was the truth, if not the whole truth.

"Scared?" Lonora seemed surprised, just as surprised as everyone else in the room was.

"Yes, it happens sometimes, you know," the response her admission had received angered Roanne. What did they expect from her? Did they think she didn't have feelings anymore? She stood and walked out the back of the room, keeping her back to them all so they could not see how upset she was. Sheilla, aware of exactly what had scared her, followed, and the two of them found chairs in the corridor where they could talk quietly.

"Why does it shock them so much that I might be afraid of something?" Roanne asked. "It's like they don't think I'm human anymore. Well, I am, and I can be just as afraid as anyone else!"

"I know," Sheilla put an arm around her shoulder, and wiped away Roanne's tears with her other hand.

Letitia whispered to the king from her chair next to Sallas, then came and sat on the other side of Roanne, taking one of her hands to provide what support she could. "What were you afraid of Roanne?" she asked.

"I've been afraid of a lot of things since this all started," Roanne remembered how she explained it to Sheilla. "I was afraid of Calum. I was afraid of what I might be becoming, and the damage I could do with just that kind of spell. That night I panicked, I tried to move too quickly to protect Jerol who was charging at Calum, counting on me to be there." She turned to look at Letitia, the tracks of tears on her cheeks. "I was afraid because I knew I was going to fail him, he was going to die because he counted on me, and I failed him." She buried her face back against Sheilla's shoulder.

"A self fulfilling fear," Letitia squeezed Roanne's hand, and put her other hand on Roanne's shoulder. "You were afraid your fear would bungle things, and it almost did. It happens to everyone at some time in his or life. Do you know what I would do if I were you? I would talk to Jerol about it when you get the chance. Tell him everything, and I mean everything."

The mention of Jerol brought the three's attention back to the room, where Sallas could be heard berating Jerol for charging at a wizard, using many of the same words Sheilla had used several days earlier.

Next came Regus, who gave a report on what they had found in Rivard, and later in Tusca. The three women returned to the room to hear what he had to say. There was practically no fighting involved, as most of the guards either surrendered, or fled. Those who surrendered generally claimed they were waiting for someone to come and set them free. So far they had found another hundred women who had been held captive, and they were still searching the countryside, to be sure there were no more. Fifteen were being held in the house where they were now staying, held in cages in the basement. The cages in Duke Cezar's bedroom were empty, probably because he was not there. In Duke Markum's home, two girls were being held in his bedroom, with ten others held elsewhere in the house, including two in his son's rooms. The presence of Duke Markum had inspired most of his men to put up a token resistance, which resulted in arrow wounds for three of the guards fighting with Regus. A few of the guards actually turned on their duke and his son, killing them before the men from Esconda could secure the house.

Lonora reported a few of the girls they found were severely injured. Markum had been branding them like cattle, to show whom their owner was. Most of the healing was done with, though, and they were all freed of their restraints.

Pavlin reported on the two wizards who had been killed. Each had been caught completely by surprise. While they had put up shields to try and protect themselves, the men had overwhelmed them with numbers, just as the crowd had in the attack on Letitia. Lonora added that only two men had wounds from the attacks on the wizards, and both were fine, now.

"So what do we do from here?" Sallas was searching for suggestions. "Everything in the provinces should be wrapped up fairly quickly. I was hoping this would be the end of it. However, what we have since learned about Calum, and the possible involvement of Varden means we need to think this through again. Roanne, you know more about the wasteland than any one. Pavlin brought with him the notes and some of the books from your father, so you can double-check them if you like. I want to talk again this evening after dinner, right here in this room, to get your and anyone else's first thoughts. We have time to try and think this through. Keep in mind, Kendal thought this through for years before he went. I will talk with you all later."

Everyone recognized when they were being dismissed, and still distraught from the earlier exchange, Roanne was the first one out of the room. Sheilla tried to follow, but Letitia put a hand on her arm to hold her back. The king was right behind them, and Letitia pointed out the direction Roanne had taken.

King Sallas arrived at the door to Roanne's room, but hesitated a moment. He had played a large role in the development of Jerol as the warrior he was now. In addition, he had raised Sheilla, who he thought had turned out to be a fairly well balance young lady, even if she were a bit impetuous. From everything he had heard, Roanne had no one during much of her life who offered the training and advice she needed to help her through this situation. He knocked on the door, and waited for an answer. Knocking again, he began to wonder if she were in there, or had gone on to find some other refuge. A noise inside the room told him she had not, and finally the door opened, before he had to knock again. Roanne simply left it open, retreating to one of the chairs in the room.

Sallas closed the door behind him, confident Letitia would see to it they were not interrupted. It was one of the things he loved about his future daughter-by-marriage, she had a very good sense about things like this, and always seemed to know just what to do. He just hoped he could live up to that standard in this situation.

"I wanted to say I was sorry for the way I reacted when you admitted you were afraid," he stepped into the center of the room. "In the short time I've known you, you've shown amazing courage. Having been around Jerol for so long it is easy to become accustomed to such behavior. There is not much that he's afraid of. We sometimes dehumanize people when we are ignorant of the things they might be feeling, and it is wrong. It is not the first time I have been guilty of that, and unfortunately I doubt it will not be the last. I am lucky to have someone like Letitia around to point out when I have done it. She at least gives me a chance to apologize, or even make amends where necessary."

"Somehow I can't picture Jerol panicking about anything," Roanne was grateful for the king's efforts.

"Most people think courage is a lack of fear," Sallas moved a second chair in the room a bit closer to Roanne and sat down. "Real courage is being able to handle your fear, turn it to something more positive."

"I've heard the same thing said about anger," Roanne commented. "It was a lesson Salina, the spinner who raised me, made sure to impress on me. Probably because I've always had a bad temper."

"If you can do it with your anger, then handling fear should be no harder than that," Sallas picked up the point. "I am betting you have not had much to be afraid of in your life. Your uncle kept you very sheltered out there at the estate. There are a lot of scary things in life that have passed you by, but a lot of good, also. Like the peasants who have risen to fight this with us, or the mother who struggles in poverty to raise her children, and is rewarded with a son whose success in life allows her to live out her years in comfort. The world is full of good and bad, and what you have seen is only the tiniest piece of all that is out there. It just happens to be a particularly ugly piece. Those peasants will forever be grateful for what you have done for them the past few days. I think if Salina were here today, she would be extremely proud of the way you have handled yourself. Your anger is something you have learned to deal with over the years, to use constructively. As for your fear, that is still new to you. You have not had time to adjust to it."

"Does it go away?" Roanne did not think so.

"No, what you must do is learn to understand the fear," Sallas stood up sensing it was time to make an exit. "Once you understand it, it might still be there, but it is not nearly as scary. Just keep that in mind while you figure out how we can deal with this other problem."

"And what if I can't figure out my fears in time, and Spence isn't there to cover for me next time?" Roanne asked, making Sallas halt at the door. "What happens when someone is counting on me to be there, and dies because I fail?"

"That depends," Sallas thought for a moment, "On whether the expectations of those counting on you are realistic. I think Jerol put you in a bad position by rushing his attack on Calum. He knows it, I think, which is why he gets angry every time someone brings it up."

As the door closed behind Sallas, Roanne wondered how much of the truth he had guessed, or if he was simply generalizing. He might not understand, but Letitia obviously did. Roanne knew Letitia had figured it all out long ago. As Sallas had hinted, she did seem to have a talent for such things. At the moment Roanne was very grateful for that, and resolved to be sure and thank Letitia when the opportunity presented itself.

Roanne was left alone for some time, thinking over her fears, and trying to understand them. It was not an easy task, particularly since it demanded she be completely honest with herself, and with those depending on her. She never did like facing up to her own shortcomings.

She finally decided she had better go and find Pavlin. Her father's notes were waiting for her. She knew them well enough, she thought, but it would be good to have them handy, and organized so she could refer to them if necessary.

Roanne and Pavlin drafted any help they could get to organize the notes and books, then began moving the ones of most interest to the conference room. They had just arranged them all on one end of the table when the rest of the leadership began to slowly filter into the room, each of them noting the array of books.

The books left little room at the main table for people, who retreated to other chairs and smaller tables in the room. Dinner for all of them was delivered to the room. When the meal was finally cleared away they all converged on the larger table, arranging themselves so those who had some idea what was in the stack of books, primarily Roanne and Pavlin, had easy access to whatever they might need. Sheilla and Letitia stayed near, as did Spence in case they could help in any way, the three having spent their entire afternoon lugging and sorting books.

"So, is there anything you can tell us about the wasteland that might give us an idea of how to approach this problem, Roanne?" Sallas opened the discussion.

"Well," Roanne had organized her thoughts around the things they already knew, or thought they knew, "To begin with, I think I would like to do away with one myth I've heard. These 'poison clouds' are not really poison, and not really clouds. My father was able to observe several, and reported they were not unlike the sandstorms that are well known in other desert areas, like those in Barsted, the kingdom to our south. Basically, the winds pick up sand from the surface of the ground. This windblown sand is capable of scouring the flesh from your bones if you happen to be caught out in such a storm. In the wastelands the storms tend to be far more frequent than is known of other deserts, and the winds are stronger, making them more dangerous. The curious thing was both my father and mother could sense magic of some kind associated with the storms. Which was why he felt someone or something was creating those storms."

"Could that magic be related to the spells Calum was using?" Regus spoke up when Roanne paused.

"They could be," Pavlin answered. "They both involve manipulating air, holding it still in one case, and forcing it to move in the other."

"So, that would seem to support the idea Calum came from there," Regus concluded. "We don't know of any other examples of magic using air."

"Not unless you go far back in history," Pavlin pointed out. "We've always known magic is a form of energy certain people have the ability to manipulate. Long ago there were few restrictions on how we used that energy. In Tulurand, the first time there were restrictions was after the wasteland came to be. Before then, magic was used to control weather at times, which is another related use."

"That would seem to suggest such magic created the wasteland," Sallas commented into the quiet as everyone digested what Pavlin had said.

"That's what Kendal concluded," Sheilla agreed, showing she had been paying attention, and even doing a little reading, during the day's work.

"Can the spells Calum was using protect us from a sandstorm if we went into the wasteland?" Jerol jumped in.

Queen of the Spinners

"You are getting ahead of us, Jerol," Sallas reigned his son in. "We have not yet decided if we should go in."

"The answer is simple, though. We don't know, but we do know how to find out, if we do decide to go." Spence handled the diplomacy of the situation extremely well, satisfying both Jerol and Sallas.

"I wish I knew how my parents planned to get around the storms." That was the most important thing her parents might have provided for them, and the one thing Roanne had searched the hardest for since she first delved into her father's library. "They must have taken the information with them."

"He had this plan to take a portable shelter he was going to put up if a storm came," Lonora informed them. "I thought it was ridiculous, which is why I objected to your mother going, Roanne."

"What else should we know?" Sallas asked.

"There is one book with several maps of the region," Roanne searched for a moment before Letitia handed her one of the books from the stack in front of Letitia. "It compares ancient maps to newer ones. It's interesting how none of the old maps mentions a city name Varden. Although, several do have a small village called Lindor in the area, near the coast."

"How big is the region?" Regus re-entered the discussion.

Roanne opened the book to two pages with similar maps drawn on them, and passed it around. One map was older, with no wasteland on it, and one newer with the wasteland clearly delineated. "According to everything my father could find out, the size of the area seems to stay constant. It's not expanding, and the forest around it does not seem to be able to penetrate it. You might call it a standoff between the magic of the wasteland and nature. The scale is hard to tell, but I think it would be no more than six hours' ride to cross from almost anywhere along the edge, to the coast of the ocean at the center."

"Kendal figured about the same, but intended to make the trip at night, because of the heat out on those sands during the day," Pavlin said

"Are the legends about the seas in the area real?" asked Stergis who was taking his turn with the maps.

"We don't know," Pavlin said. "I remember how mad Kendal got about that. He was no sailor, and he could not find one sailor to take him into the waters in the region. He even tried to go up into Curiland to hire a ship, and was chased out of two ports."

"The same storms the legends say sink any ship venturing into the area could be related to the sandstorm," Roanne went a little further. "High winds that make sandstorms also make for rough sailing at sea."

"It's odd," Lathom traced a line with his finger on one of the maps. "The region is almost a perfect circle, with its center right where the village was."

"Another indication this is not a natural phenomenon," Pavlin agreed.

"This is much better than what we had the last time we discussed this," Sallas complimented them all. "What else do we have? Is there any indication of what Kendal expected to find at the site of the village?"

"Not that we were able to find," Roanne shrugged.

"It's hard to believe people are living out there, and we haven't had any sign of them in over five hundred years," Jerol was frustrated, since this was the information he needed to make any plans. He had visited where Roanne and the others were working during the afternoon to press on this point.

"How about old wives tales?" Letitia hesitantly offered.

"Old wives' tales?" Olen scoffed, but found himself the object of more than a few reproachful looks.

"Letitia, anything might help," Roanne encouraged her.

Letitia still hesitated, eyeing Olen from the corner of her eye. "Ignore him," Sheilla pushed. "Even the most absurd legends are built around a kernel of truth."

"Well, I didn't think of it when Varden first came up in all this, until I saw something in Ariele's notes," Letitia began slowly. "There's an old wives' tale in our area of the kingdom that says if you don't behave, demons will come in the night and take you away. Ariele investigated three such disappearances while Kendal was doing his work to prepare for their journey. She concluded the individuals might have wandered out into the waste and been killed by sandstorms. It happens in Bergain more than we like, and the wives tales are only told in the western region. I checked with the staff of this house, but only one from a village at the western edge of Rivard knew the tale."

"So what," Olen felt vindicated. "You would expect people might get lost in the desert from time to time."

"Most of the tales, the disappearances Ariele checked out, and most of the disappearances I can remember being brought to my father's attention involve girls." Letitia gained confidence from the reactions of several others in the room who had sat up as she had talked, including Sallas, and most importantly from her perspective, Regus. "It could be raids from people in the wasteland, looking for slaves."

"We have plenty of tales in the east to scare children," Lonora spoke, even as everyone else in the room was trying to remember the tales they had heard. "None involve being taken away, though some have the children being eaten. None of them are just girls or just boys, but always children in general."

"Letitia's right," Timond finally came to his sister's aid. "I wish father had not insisted on going on ahead to Bergain, he would know much better than I. There were a lot of disappearances years ago, and until a few years ago, about the time Calum showed up in the kingdom coincidentally, we always had more than runaways would account for, particularly among girls. My father once told me grandfather thought of putting a wall around the wasteland so people couldn't wander out there."

"Why would the stoppage and Calum be connected?" Regus asked.

"I'll bet the first slow down occurred about the time Kendal and Ariele disappeared," Jerol broke in. "They decided they were drawing too much attention to themselves, so slowed it down. Now, they could be thinking of attacking. Calum was certainly interested in establishing a power base within the kingdom that would have made such an attack much easier. Until now they would have caught us completely by surprise. Why gamble on getting caught on a slave raid, and giving away that advantage?"

"You are making a lot assumptions in your theory," Sallas pointed out.

"The more I think about it the more it makes sense," Timond disagreed.

"I agree. There is more than enough reason, with Calum, and all this, to at least warrant further investigation, including going into the wasteland," Regus gave his opinion.

"At least a small scouting party, to find out what is out there," Jerol agreed.

"Like the one Kendal took with him?" Lonora objected. "I know you're expecting Roanne to go, and the spinners have already lost one queen to such foolishness."

"I think we can all take the rest of the night to consider what our options are," Sallas announced an end to the meeting, sensing an impending clash of wills. "Tomorrow, we will discuss those options, so I expect you to have ideas ready."

Chapter 22

Roanne figured the next day would not be as busy for her, not being a strategist of any repute. She hoped she could take the day to relax. At breakfast Roanne was joined by Letitia and Sheilla. They started the meal with nothing but small talk. Sheilla joked she was still sore from their ride across the kingdom, but she had checked her horse, and at least he seemed to have fully recovered.

After eating a light meal, Roanne got up, intending to go gather the books they left in yesterday's conference room. The others offered to help, and trailed along with Roanne. In the conference room, they found Jerol going over a few of the books, particularly the one with the maps. Suddenly all the other women remembered something else needing their immediate attention. Letitia was the first to excuse herself, though she promised to be back in about an hour. Sheilla recalled she needed to check on her horse's recovery from their arduous journey.

Roanne almost followed them, but Letitia closed the door, leaving Roanne and Jerol alone in the room. Behind her, at the table, she heard Jerol's light laughter.

"I think Letitia wants us to talk," Jerol rose from his seat, moving to a table at the back of the room where there was a tray with a pitcher and several mugs. He gestured to one of the chairs near the table. "Which might not be such a bad idea."

"Sheilla and Sallas think so, as well," Roanne agreed, walking around the table, and taking the offered seat.

Jerol poured two mugs from the pitcher, which was filled with taze, and passed one of them to Roanne. "Yes, those two have said a few things to me." He took the chair at the opposite side of the table.

"I'm not very good at this," Jerol jumped in before Roanne could get started. "But they are right. I do owe you several apologies. That stunt with Calum was rather foolish, if I had waited for you, we probably could have figured a better way to get him."

"I don't know," Roanne honestly appraised her memory of the events. "He had a significant head start, and might have gotten away. If he found Sheilla, he could have hurt her. As it was, she was able to surprise him."

"He was not going to get away," Jerol was back on his feet pacing back and forth in front of Roanne. "That at least I am sure about. I saw we might be able to end this whole thing right there, and I was determined to do so." He stopped pacing right in front of her, looking down into her face. "I wanted this to be over for you, so you could put it all behind you and get on with your life."

Roanne bowed her head, unsure how one should answer a statement like that.

Jerol knelt, taking her hand in his. "You said you were afraid of something. If I had my way, you would never be afraid again."

"I don't think that's possible," Roanne told him. "Some fears are simply too closely related. But I think you could help me deal with my fears, Sallas says you're good at that. Using your fear instead of letting it use you."

"I'll do whatever I can," Jerol squeezed her hand to emphasize the point. "What was it that upset you so much, yesterday?"

Roanne told him what she had told Letitia and Sallas, without telling him the whole truth. "There's no shame in being afraid when you are facing a threat like Calum. Only a fool goes into battle without fear," Jerol tried to reassure her. "What was it scared you about Calum? The slavery? Rape? I would not have let anything like that happen to you."

"I wasn't afraid for me," Roanne shook her head at his suggestions. "By then I was getting fairly confident I could handle Calum if I had to, he would not have been able to hurt me. I was afraid for you, and I panicked when I realized I wasn't ready to defend you if he attacked." It was her turn to rise, turning from him, not wanting him to see the tears threatening to stain her cheeks again. She fled to the large table with the books, but he was right behind her.

"So, I did rush off after him too fast," he put a hand on her shoulder and turned her back toward him. "The reason I made that mistake was for you. I would say that makes us about even." He wiped away a tear from the corner of her eye before it had a chance to leave its trail along her cheek.

"Even if I accepted your reasoning for your mistake," Roanne brushed his hand away from her face. "Your mistake would not have killed me. You might have died because of my mistake, or worse yet, could die if I make another mistake like that."

Jerol put his hand back under her chin raising her face so she had to look him in the eye. "You and I are in a rather select group of people, because every day we make decisions that will affect the lives of others. All the nobles, the wizards and the spinners are in a similar position. None of us are perfect, but we do the best we can."

"And when our best isn't good enough?" Roanne asked.

"It never is," Jerol answered. "People die every day because of choices others make. A healer goes to a neighboring village to check the people there, and isn't home when a mother from her home village comes looking for her with a sick child. Do we blame the healer for the death of the child? Almost every death comes with at least a dozen decisions that if made differently, might have prevented that death. The mother may have let the child wander, allowing the child to encounter whatever made it sick in the first place. The child, for whatever reason, chose to wander."

"So I should just go on with my life, and if people die, so be it?" Roanne could not accept that option.

"No, you learn to deal with your fears, so the next time, you are ready," Jerol had anticipated her reaction. "And," he turned her to the table where the book with the maps was laid open just as he had left it before she interrupted him, "You and I, and whoever else we need, have to plan this trip as carefully as we can, trying to anticipate what we might encounter."

"We can't anticipate everything, though," Roanne felt better now, and his arm around her waist gave her a comfortable, safe feeling. "I'm sure my father tried to do the same."

"One thing you have to remember," Jerol nodded his agreement, "Everyone who goes on this trip knows the risks, and accepts the possibility they might not come back. I won't force anyone into going."

"And you also won't stop me from going, and neither will Lonora," Roanne made her point on that subject.

"Just as you can't stop me from going," Jerol agreed.

"You're the expert planner, so what do you suggest?" Roanne took the chair by the table that Jerol offered, and then he went to retrieve the mugs they had left behind.

Following dinner that evening, the same group was again gathered in the conference room. "After much thought," Sallas opened the meeting, "I think it is incumbent on us to investigate the wasteland to see what we can find in there. It is our best lead right now to the origins of Calum. While we do that, though, I want Regus to select a dozen men to go into both of our neighboring kingdoms, Barsted and Curiland, just see what is going on in those places. See if there is any evidence of conditions like those we are finding in the provices. Have each man go alone into differing areas of each kingdom. It is time we start paying more attention to our neighbors."

"I'll get them moving first thing in the morning," Regus agreed.

"Good," Sallas went on, "Now for the wasteland. Telin, did you manage to contact Duke Bassel?"

"He confirms what Letitia and Timond told us about the disappearances," Telin answered, nodding toward Letitia in acknowledgment. "He could confirm three missing women in the past year, which is low, but, as yet unexplained. There was too much information gathered over the years to pass along. He and Andres are going to try and organize what is known so it makes some sense by the time we get there."

"Roanne and I were going to suggest we send some men on ahead, as early as tomorrow, to check out the rumors." Jerol had taken a seat beside Roanne at the end of the table for this meeting, which had not gone unnoticed by the others as they straggled into the room. "We could send ten men, and they could do a survey of the villages to see if there were any incidents not reported, and help in checking the three cases Telin mentioned. Timond could be put in charge, and Telin should go along to keep the rest of us up to date on what they find."

"That sounds good to me," Sallas nodded toward Timond. "Can you be ready to go by morning? Regus can see to it you get the men you need."

Timond's chest swelled with pride. "I'll be ready. I know of two of the cases Telin mentioned. The third must be more recent, though, and might have the freshest trail."

"I have some of the information on who and where," Telin offered, "We can talk about it along the way."

Roanne noticed while Timond was excited at such a role in all this, Letitia seemed a bit let down. She took Letitia's hand under the table, and winked at her when Letitia looked up.

"Lonora," Roanne spoke up, "We thought it might be good to send spinners in with the men on this. Can you pick out ten, one to accompany each man? You would know better than I who might be best suited for this kind of work."

"I can think of ten right now I think would be willing," Lonora smiled, glad Roanne seemed to be keeping the spinners as major players in this afair.

Regus made a mental note to be sure to pick men for this who would work well with the spinners. Some of the men did not care for them or wizards.

"You two," Sallas was eyeing Roanne and Jerol with approval, "Seem to have given this all a lot of thought. What else have you come up with?"

"Spence mentioned yesterday he thought the shields Calum used might be useful for protection against the sandstorms in the wasteland," Roanne spoke up this time. "We think we should send him ahead tomorrow to check that out, along with Olen and a few others to help." Throughout the day they had called several people to the conference room, using Sheilla, Letitia, and Talia as messengers. Spence had been one of them, so this suggestion was nothing new to him.

"I'll travel along with Timond if he'll have me," Spence accepted the assignment. "I imagine at least one of the villages he'll need to check must be along the border of the wasteland."

"How do you plan on testing it?" Regus asked.

"I'll take some potted plants out there," Spence was ready for the question. "With Calum's magic, I'll put a small dome over the top of them, with some added shelter for shade from the heat, and leave them in the path of one of the storms. It may take a few days to locate a storm that can be used. I checked with Kendal's notes on how he observed them. They seem to follow a regular pattern, which is odd. I'll need to confirm the pattern is still the same, or if a new pattern might have emerged."

"That odd pattern is another indication these storms are not natural," Pavlin noted.

"What else?" Sallas looked back to Roanne and Jerol.

"Telin, what's the latest from Golare?" Jerol turned to the wizard, another of their guests that afternoon.

"The guards and the bulk of the wizards and spinners should be ready to leave there tomorrow," Telin reported. "Beraine says they expect it to take ten or eleven days for them to reach Bergain."

"Mother is going to have a fit with all these people coming," Letitia muttered under her breath. Roanne remembered when she had first met the duke, he had commented on how the duchess generally hated preparing for festivals, and smiled.

"That would simply be as a precaution," Jerol noted. "I want to be sure we have backup if we need it. By then, I hope to have scouted the wasteland, using Spence's idea, so we'll know exactly what we're up against. If there is trouble, we have the forces we brought this way originally to try and contain it, until those others can arrive. I've been checking with the sources Lonora provided, and have been assured the people will give their full support as well."

"What exactly are you expecting the people to do?" Sallas was a bit uneasy about that.

"First of all, they are going to be ready to evacuate the women and children from Bergain and anywhere else it might become necessary," Jerol smiled at Roanne, who had suggested this, as he spoke. Roanne had felt it was important to involve the people, not treat them like pawns in a game. "Those men who can fight will back up the guards, but the guards will do their best to handle as much of the fighting as they can, if there is any."

Sallas nodded, seeing the point in all this once he figured out it must have been Roanne's idea. He was well aware it of Roanne's influence in the way Letitia treated the palace staff back Esconda.

"Initially, we'll have to spread ourselves pretty thin to cover the entire border of the wasteland," Jerol went on. "Which means the people can play an important part, particularly those who know the area. They can do things like provide guides in some of the more forested areas, and help with lines of communication along the border. We need to spot anyone coming from or going into the wasteland, and capture them for questioning."

"If Calum had any allies out here, they might decide to make a run for it," Roanne explained. "If he's from Varden, that may be where they run. On the other hand, if people from Varden are sneaking out to kidnap women, we might catch them. It would be a lot better to get answers from someone who knows them, than to speculate, which is the only thing we can do right now."

"That all sounds reasonable," Sallas complimented them. "Now, exactly how are you planning to get into the wasteland?"

"Well," Jerol hesitated, not knowing what to expect, and thus, how to plan. "We have several contingency plans, depending on what we find."

"And just who are 'we'?" Lonora interrupted.

"Jerol and I," Roanne gave Lonora a look saying there would be no argument on that, "And six volunteers, who have already come forward."

"Lathom, Stergis, Duval, Spence, Talia, and Sheilla," Jerol finished the list, bringing Sallas out of his seat.

"Why Sheilla?" he objected, "She's not a fighter, and has no magic."

"Talia does not have enough magic to be considered for something like this," Lonora joined the protest from a different perspective.

"I tested Talia," Roanne disagreed, "She has more than average power, and in the next two days, she has to learn to use it, to both defend herself and fight. I will see to that."

"Of the women I know, Sheilla is more than an adequate fighter," Jerol tackled his father's concerns. "Her crossbow accuracy is as good as most men. She handles those daggers she carries like a street thug. Further, she is more than adequate as a messenger, as you so aptly demonstrated not long ago. If we need help, I can't think of anyone I would rather have going to get it."

"Why not another spinner, or a wizard?" Sallas pressed them.

"Lonora, perhaps?" Roanne countered. "I have a lot of respect for Lonora, but if we have to move fast she could be a liability, and she not only can't handle a weapon, but as a healer, would refuse."

"With all due respect," Jerol bowed to Lonora, "The others we considered all had greater liabilities than Sheilla. Another consideration is we did not have to ask any of those who were included. They all came to us to volunteer."

"Were you planning to take anyone who volunteered?" It was going to take something else to sway Sallas.

"No, we refused three people," Roanne said. "Smithe, Regus, and Letitia."

"At least you have some sense," Sallas reseated himself. "Find someone other than Sheilla."

"No!" Sheilla came to her feet now. "I'm going. The people of this kingdom pay to feed me. They pay for my clothes. They house me. What do they get in return? They get my willingness to do something like this when it's necessary. You taught me that," She pointed an accusing finger at her father, "And now you want me to ignore it, well I won't do it. I am just as capable of assessing, and accepting the risks of this as Jerol. I don't see you questioning his going."

"This meeting is over, and I have made my decision," Sallas slammed his hand on the table. "I want everyone out of here, except you." His finger pointed right at Sheilla.

All individuals involved in the planning stayed in support of Sheilla. Everyone else all but ran from the room.

"I feel I should remain," Jerol spoke up as the door closed behind the last of the others. "If it is your intention to take Sheilla to task for this plan, you have to remember the plan was mine."

"And mine," Roanne stood next to him.

"The rest of us supported it," Regus stood his ground, with Letitia next to him.

Stergis was standing firm just behind Sheilla. Lathom, Smithe, and Duval were all nearby. Spence moved from his original seat, and was now standing with Talia.

"Get out!" was all Sallas had to say, daring them with his eyes to defy him.

Sheilla whispered something to Stergis, who passed on a look to Jerol and Regus. Slowly they withdrew, drawing the rest with them. Jerol had to pull Roanne out of the room. In the hall outside, they all waited.

"Why don't the rest of you go wait in Regus' rooms," Letitia suggested. "I'll bring Sheilla there when it's over."

Beyond the closed door, where three guards stood at attention, Sallas could be heard yelling, though his words could not be made out.

"I'll wait here with you," Roanne took Letitia's arm.

In the background, they could hear Sheilla doing plenty of yelling of her own.

"I'll see what kind of refreshments I can scare up around here," Jerol offered, herding everyone but Letitia and Roanne on down the hall. He and Regus were smiling and shaking their heads.

Chapter 23

The tension from the argument carried over to the next morning. Glances and whispers followed all the members of the royal family as they went about their early morning routine. Regus had offered his rooms for breakfast so they could discuss the situation, and decide what, if anything, they could do. Regus and Jerol tried to pass it off to others as one of several ongoing arguments Sallas had with his daughter, joking they would both still be at it if they had not gotten horse from yelling. At least until they heard some of what had gone on.

Sallas' anger focused more on the fact this was the second time in about a week Sheilla had openly challenged his authority in public. The shouting back and forth had gone on for nearly an hour, before Sheilla had fled the room in tears. She had gone right to her room, telling Roanne and Letitia she wanted to be alone. Roanne went to Regus' rooms to let the others know, before joining Letitia in trying to calm Sheilla.

She found Letitia trying to stop Sheilla from packing saddlebags. It took most of the night to get Sheilla to tell them what had been said.

"Either way I have to pack," Sheilla insisted. "If I don't get out of here now, he's going to send me back to Esconda under heavy guard come morning." Sheilla had tried the argument that had won him over concerning her role as a messenger to Jerol, asking whether he intended to put a collar and leash on her, too. Sallas ended up getting angry enough to threaten to make new wedding arrangements for Sheilla if she did not start getting some cooperation out of her. That was when Sheilla had stormed out of the room.

Roanne and Letitia had managed to convince Sheilla to talk it all over with her brothers before she did anything rash. They finally got Sheilla to agree, on the condition Stergis could not find out about the marriage threat.

With everyone gathered in Regus' rooms, Sheilla began to tell what had happened. She had intended to stop short of bringing Stergis into the tale, but never got the chance. Regus and Jerol were on their feet and headed for the door long before she could have gotten to that part. Letitia went after them, catching them in the hall. She made them wait until she went back and got Sheilla. The four of them slipped into Jerol's room for only a few minutes before Jerol came back to Regus' rooms.

"Roanne, can you teach Talia what she needs to know while we travel? We won't be pushing it, so we'll be stopping early to make camp, leaving a lot of time in the evenings." Jerol asked. Roanne knew they would be leaving that morning instead of waiting until Talia and she had more time. "It will take us about five days to get to Bergain, and then a couple of days for Spence to test the shields."

"That's plenty of time, but I need some of my father's notebooks," Roanne knew exactly which she wanted. The one with the maps, and two others, then mentally added the notebook from her mother. "I'll go get them, and get the few other things I need."

Everyone scrambled to get the things they needed. Spence, already packed for his departure, went to the stables to have their horses saddled. Jerol told him to include Regus' and Letitia's. To show his solidarity with their strategy, Smithe was now coming with them.

Roanne thought she would be the last one to the stables. Lonora and Pavlin were waiting for her in the conference room, to try and talk her out of this mission, and tried to keep her from taking the books she needed. Even with the delay, she was still at the stables ahead of Regus and Jerol, who had gone to inform Sallas they were moving on to Bergain. Sheilla had not gone with her brothers, since not even Regus could be sure Sallas would not have Sheilla taken under guard.

Duke Cezar's home was surrounded by a wall. The group waited at the gate, saddled up and ready to go. Spence even stayed to travel with them instead of leaving with Timond, who departed just after Jerol had made the decision to change plans. Those guards heading for the other kingdoms were only just now getting ready to leave. Spence told the others Sallas had been out to see the others off. Regus and Jerol had joined him, and then the three of them had gone back inside, with Sallas looking very unhappy.

They were all caught off guard when the portcullis to the gate came clamoring down, blocking their exit. "Pavlin," Spence sensed the magic that had done this at the same time Roanne did.

Sallas came out of the house, accompanied by Lonora and Pavlin, and closely followed by twenty guards surrounding Regus and Jerol.

"Oh, brother, I was hoping it wouldn't come to this," Duval muttered.

"Just keep in mind, the oath you took as a guard was to the kingdom, and we are acting in its best interest," Lathom reminded him.

"I'm not backing down from the commitment I gave," Duval hastily amended. "But I would still prefer not to have to face this."

Sallas came close enough to talk without shouting, though the redness in his face suggested he might have liked to shout. "I would appreciate it if you would hand over my daughter, and Letitia," Sallas said, barely controlling his temper. "We can do this the hard way, or the easy way." The captains all formed up around Sheilla and Letitia.

Roanne moved over to Spence's side. "Ready to get some practice putting up walls," she whispered. "Get behind the others, then put up a corridor between Jerol and Regus and the guards, so they can both get to us."

When she moved, Pavlin had stepped up next to Sallas. "Don't bother Spence, I won't let you burn down the portcullis."

"Thank you, Pavlin" Roanne said to herself, as she moved forward to face the king. "Just what are you doing?"

"On the advice of Pavlin and Lonora, I have decided there will be no expedition into the wasteland," Sallas crossed his arms over his chest. "We will watch the borders carefully of course, but any threat from the wasteland is safely contained at the moment. Pavlin believes we can keep it that way."

"And what if there is nothing in the wasteland?" Roanne countered. "What if the threat is actually from elsewhere?"

"The scouts we are sending to the other kingdoms will tell us that," Sallas was not about to back down.

Roanne could only shake her head. "The biggest threat from the wasteland is the uncertainty it will represent. How long do you think the western dukes will remain loyal if the throne does nothing to alleviate the threat? How long will the people remain loyal if the kidnappings in those provinces continues, and they think we've discovered the source of the problem, and done nothing about it?"

"I will deal with it," Sallas gave a nonanswer that, the look in his eyes told Roanne, did not even satisfy himself.

While Roanne talked with Sallas, she noted both Regus and Jerol had their hands tied. When she felt Spence's walls go up, she burned the strand of leather around their wrists. The guards near them immediately moved to secure them again, only to come up against Spence's wall. Smiling, Jerol strolled forward to Roanne, with Regus moving on past to their horses.

Roanne saw both Lonora and Pavlin begin to gesture, but too late. She felt Spence take down the walls, before they had a chance to ignite them. The two older teachers Roanne had looked up to had been caught completely off guard.

"Pavlin," she said. "I am going out the portcullis, now. Spence, warn anyone on the other side to stand clear."

"There are archers targeting you at this moment," Pavlin warned, gesturing to the top of the walls.

"Sallas," Roanne looked the king right in the eye, "I don't think you can give the order. You came out here to stop us because of your fears we might not come back. Killing us would hardly accomplish what you want." Sallas had turned from angry red to a shocked white.

Sheilla moved up next to Roanne on one side, "He could think killing you might stop the rest of us. He would be wrong, though." As Stergis took the reigns to Sheilla's horse, Sheilla climbed across to the back of Roanne's saddle. "Let's get out of here, now."

Roanne turned her horse noting both Lonora and Pavlin had been gesturing for some time, probably bolstering their defense of the portcullis, to keep it from burning. Instead of burning it, though, Roanne lifted the gate. It took enough of her concentration she was glad to have Sheilla ready to take the reigns, and lead their horse out. Once they were all clear, she let the gate drop back into place, turning to look over her shoulder through the bars, at the surprise on both her mentors' faces.

"That was smart thinking," Spence dropped back in the group to their side. "You probably could have burned it, though, the two of them are no match for you. I doubt you would have even needed my help."

"True," Roanne admitted, "But it might have taken longer, and this way they have to take the time to deal with it, if they decide to chase us."

Jerol, riding close enough to hear, laughed. "She's as quick at the study of tactics as she is at magic," he said to anyone within hearing range.

There was no pursuit that they noticed, and as Jerol promised Roanne, they kept to a comfortable pace. They still caught up to Timond, who, unaware they would be coming, already occupied the inn where they would otherwise have stopped for the night. Rather than causing more trouble, and confusion, Jerol led them on to a clearing in the woods beyond the town, where they made a camp.

The first night's camp was their time for airing out all of their second thoughts and doubts about what they had done. In the process Stergis had learned of the threat Sallas had made concerning him and Sheilla, which erased any of his doubts. Sheilla herself justified their actions, noticing that with the arrival of Roanne, and the rise in prominence of the spinners, no woman could be taken for granted any more. Her father did not want to admit it, in fact resisted it, but times were changing. Women would no longer sit by and observe the changes without comment, particulary when women were affected by those changes.

The irony of the whole situation was the special role that nobody but Sheilla could have played in their plan, which would now have the extra credibility of Regus and Letitia. They had to face the possibility of finding an entire community of wizards in the middle of the wasteland. If they could not sneak in, or worse, if they were caught, Stergis and Spence were going to take on the role of slave traders, pretending to know Calum. Jerol was going to take on the role of the traitor. Being the second son, he would say he was looking for the opportunity to move up, with the leader of the wizard community at his side. As a token of friendship, he would hand over his sister, the only daughter of the king, along with other slaves Stergis had collected. Now, they would have to decide if adding Regus and Letitia to the scenario would make it more believable. The other debate involved whether to tell the truth of whom Roanne was, or to hide her identity, making her a servant of the princess, so their enemy might not take any precautions about restraining her. Roanne shuddered at the thought of having a collar put around her throat, but if Talia were willing, in order to help in the ruse, how could she refuse?

Any second thoughts at defying Sallas were washed away when Jerol reminded everyone of how they had become involved in this in the first place. In the process he repeated the promise he had made to Roanne the first night he had met her. She would have his full support in ending the problem of slavery and abuse in the kingdom. The others all joined in the promise.

If their enemy had any spies still watching, the family dispute would only help the ruse.

The discussion dominated so much of their first night Roanne had no opportunity to begin teaching Talia. The second night was better, and even Spence helped, so they could use the sharing of energy in small amounts to speed up the process. Spence was also helpful because Talia needed the gestures and chants he provided to focus her energy.

On the third night they came to the city of Tomen, where they spent a day as guests of Duke Lamond. They were grateful Sallas had not sent word ahead to try and stop them, or Duke Lamond had chosen not to obey after Regus explained their mission. It was not as if the duke was in any position to stop them anyway, since nearly every man he had was busy in Tusca, helping to settle things there.

The reason for the day lay over was to give Letitia time to do what she did best, go shopping. The captains needed to lose the uniforms they were wearing, and if it became necessary to rely on their ruse, the women would need something to wear besides breeches, particularly Sheilla. The enemy was not likely to believe she was the king's daughter unless she was properly dressed. Never mind the fact that seeing Sheilla in breeches never surprised anyone who knew her.

Roanne and Spence made good use of the time. Though Talia was dead tired by the time they let her go off to bed that night, she had made drastic improvements in her ability to focus her concentration. She could now do both Calum's spell and the burning to destroy it. She could even do minor healing, though everyone hoped it would not come to that. With practice she would be more than good enough for what they needed from her.

There was some news on their second night in Tomen. Word came in by way of a messenger from Duke Lamond's men. Things were pretty much under control in Tusca, and his men would be returning sometime that day, unless the duke had anything else for them to do. Royal guards would be staying to watch over Tusca until a new duke was appointed for the province, as would be the case in the other affected provinces. The bad news was Bassel had recalled all of his men, and nobody was sure what that might mean. It could be interpreted as Bassel getting ready to try and stop them, or with as much as he had at stake in this situation, he might be preparing to support them.

"I wish we had some way of knowing," Regus was saying as they sat around the lounge in the area of the house Lamond had set aside for them. Regus knew Bassel would be as upset at Letitia's involvement in this as his father had been at Sheilla's. Though Bassel's views might be tempered since this problem lay right in his province.

"Know what?" Asked a familiar voice from the door to the room.

"Telin?" Roanne turned to see the wizard leaning against the door jam. "What are you doing here?"

"I thought I would come see what I could do to help," Telin shrugged. "I've gotten pretty good with all the spells needed for this kind of work, and you could probably use my communication skills. Maybe I can find out whatever it is you were just wondering."

"Telin," Jerol was standing, "Who's helping Timond with communication if you are here?"

"He picked up a spinner who can communicate," Telin explained. "Timond and I had both noticed your group lacked a communicator when you caught us the first day out of Rivard. After we left Tomen this morning, he and I talked it over and decided you could probably use my services, so I came back. If I had known what you were planning, I would have volunteered from the beginning, but I had no idea since I was spending so much time communicating with Bessal and Beraine. It hurt to watch you all leave and not be able to help. So, here I am."

"Can you contact my father?" Letitia immediately jumped on the opportunity. "We need to know why he pulled his men from Tusca. Is he going to try and stop us?"

"Is that what you were talking about?" Telin found himself a seat. "He won't try to stop you, though he will probably take a shot at talking all the women out of going, including Roanne, offering all his men if necessary to replace you on this mission. I've been in touch with him from time to time as he got out the information on disappearances in Bergain. He had heard through other communicators in Rivard how King Sallas and Pavlin had tried to stop you, but Bassel wouldn't go that far, he knows this will be his problem forever if King Sallas gets his way."

Chapter 24

Bessal was there to meet them when they arrived at the border between Tomen and Bergain two days later. Timond came through the day before, gaining a day while Letitia did her shopping, and letting his father know the others would be along. There was a small village at the border where a bridge crossed the Eagle River. When they went to the inn to get rooms for the night, Bessal was waiting, alone, in the dining room.

"Welcome to Bergian," he stood to greet them. "I've taken the liberty of providing for your dinner, a deer I caught while hunting earlier in the day." The duke was all smiles, which made Letitia wary. Her father did not have the temper Sallas often displayed, depending, rather, on political guile to achieve his goals.

"Bessal," Regus smiled at is future father-by-marriage, "It is good to see you. Did you happen to catch Timond on his way through?" When it came time for Regus to rule, everyone figured he would be much more like Bessal than his father.

"Yes, I did," Bessal took a moment to give Letitia a big hug, and a kiss on the forehead. "We talked nearly the whole night about the missing people, and I sent my men with him to help comb the countryside."

With an arm around each of the future royal couple, he led them to an area where he had gathered a few tables to make one large one. "Mathia, our guests have arrived," he shouted out and a portly man in an apron came from the back of the inn to pass out mugs of ale for those who wanted it, and wine for the others. "Merely his name," Bessal noticed Roanne's reaction. "I hope you won't hold it against him. He's a fine man, and sets the best table this side of Esconda."

"I won't," Roanne could not help but respond to Bessal's jovial mood with a smile. "It is a common name. I would be hard pressed to hold a grudge against them all."

Queen of the Spinners

"So, you are all intending to go into the wasteland," Bessal broached the subject they were all expecting once they were settled around the table. "I think I would go with you, but I'm afraid I might represent more of a handicap than an asset. I'm no longer in the trim fighting form I had in my youth."

Letitia knew right away where his statement would eventually lead. "Sheilla and I had much the same thought," she jumped in, "Wanting to do something to help support the effort, without causing as many problems as we might be able to solve."

"Of course when it comes time for fighting," Sheilla pounced on Letitia's theme. "There isn't a whole lot we can do. Sure, we're both pretty good with a crossbow, and can handle daggers, but we both know when it comes to a sword fight, we would only be in the way."

"Did you know it was Sheilla who killed Calum?" Roanne chipped in. "It's kind of ironic how with all the soldiers, wizards, and spinners who were hunting him, it was Sheilla who did it." Bessal sat up at that, obviously he had not known.

"Anyway," Letitia continued, while her father was still caught off guard by that bit of news, "At first Roanne was the only woman who was going to go into the wasteland, until they realized they might need other women. It was actually Talia's idea." Letitia pointed out Talia, who the duke had never met before.

"Jerol pointed out that it could not be just any women. They would have to be able to do a variety of things to contribute," Sheilla picked up where Letitia had left off. "Aside from the magic, which Talia does have, we fit the needs. It's not like we could go out and order other women to go in our place. We know what the risks are."

"I'm not going to be able to talk you out of this am I?" Bessal threw up his hands. "What about you Regus? Isn't this a bit of a risk for the heir to be taking, particularly with the rest of the family involved? If, like Kendal and Ariele, you don't come back, where does that leave the throne?"

"If we don't come back, I don't think it will matter," Regus answered. "This has to be stopped here and now. Otherwise, there might not be much left of the kingdom to rule. This is what the people pay us for, Bessal. We all lead pretty good lives, luxurious by most standards. In return, we are supposed to take the risks for our people. Otherwise they have no need of us."

"We do more than just fight wars," Bessal pointed out. "You're forgetting the next in line, should something happen to both you and Jerol, is Duke Alverne, then his son Tovan. I for one don't relish that possibility. If Letitia weren't my daughter I would even consider advising you to get her with child before you go, and leaving her behind. Then again, if she were pregnant, maybe she would reconsider all this."

"Father!" Letitia was scandalized by such an idea.

"If you were not my daughter," Bessal hurriedly emphasized. The men around the table laughed until a few well-placed elbows from the women restored order.

Mathia and two young girls served the dinner then, delaying any further argument until their stomachs were full. The meal was delicious and filling, leaving everyone in a more relaxed mood.

"Have you considered how you are going to deal with Sallas once this is all over?" Bessal asked as the last of the plates was cleared away. "I can't ever recall seeing him this angry, and from what I was told of your departure from Rivard, it could easily be interpreted as treason." He leaned back in his chair, waiting for a response.

"We feel this is in the best interest of the kingdom," Lathom said. "That is all we need, or would you prefer we do as Sallas suggested just before we left, and leave the wasteland alone. He thinks we can simply control whatever is in there."

"It seems to me, all he's doing is dropping it all in your lap, Bessal," Spence observed. "Do you want us to turn back?"

"No," that was the last thing Bessal wanted.

Queen of the Spinners

The next day, they made it to the border of the wasteland just as the sun set over the sandy dunes. Roanne was reminded of the only other time she had ever seen this place. She stood staring at the scene until the sun had disappeared. Jerol had to come and take her back to the camp, which, even with a fire, was far enough back in the woods to be hidden from prying eyes.

Bessal had managed to accomplish what he wanted in the end. He came with them, and was intending to stay until their return. His reminder about Alverne and Tovan had slowly worked its way through to Regus' conscience. Letitia was caught in this problem, also. If Regus dropped out, it became more difficult for her to justify her addition.

"Jerol," Regus called as he and Letitia intercepted Roanne and Jerol as they came back to the camp. "I hate to admit this, but Bassel does raise a point about the lineage. He's got me feeling guilty."

"The problem is you feel just as guilty about not going with us," Jerol filled in what was left out. "Don't worry about it, to tell you the truth, I would feel much better if we stuck to the original group, with the exception of Telin and Smithe. I was happy to have them join us. Bessal's communicator is with Timond, who will be joining you here. With Telin we can always be in touch."

"If everybody goes in," Roanne summed it all up simply, "Then who would be here to communicate with?"

Letitia laughed. "You're getting as bad as Jerol at being blunt," she said.

"We all do what we can," Jerol shrugged. "Bessal and his communicator are both limited in what they could do to help. They can provide a rallying point, with you available to lead our back up. If anything goes wrong, we'll be counting on you to use whatever information we can send you in order to make sure this goes no further than here."

After discussing various options with Bessal, they estimated there could be over one hundred men, thirty spinners, and twenty wizards available within a day if needed. It seemed as though

Bessal had been gathering his resources even before their arrival, particularly making a point of getting the spinners and wizards within his province and from just across the borders in neighboring provinces organized.

Everyone seemed more at ease with the idea of Regus and Letitia staying behind. "You two have done more than your share in this conflict," Stergis told the two of them, "and in ways nobody could have predicted, or most people will ever realize. If you hadn't come this far, we might have had even more trouble getting out of Rivard, so don't get the idea you got yourselves into all this trouble for nothing."

"I don't think anything would have kept Roanne in Rivard," Regus shook his head. "As far as the trouble we're in, it was worth it if the only thing to come out of it is for everyone to know I ..." Letitia poked him with her elbow, " ... we support Roanne and every one of you all the way."

They settled in for the night with a comfortable fire, and stories of all the times any of the royal children had gotten into trouble. Sheilla had a lot of stories about her brothers, most involving Jerol's famous temper. The brothers then felt obliged to retaliate. Bassel even contributed a few stories about Letitia, to her embarrassment, and the surprise of Regus. Roanne was almost happy nobody there had any tales to tell about her. Though she found she was enjoying the stories of Jerol's misspent youth.

When the sun rose, Spence was already awake and checking the storms against the timetable in Kendal's notebook. They all waited anxiously while he, Duval, and Telin rode out into the desert. They tried to busy themselves by cutting down a tree to make potting buckets for the plants when Spence was ready for the test. Those going into the desert never stayed there long, timing their forays according to Kendal's table to be able to see what they needed and then retreat before the heat could begin to affect them.

The storms were still on the same schedule Kendal had timed out. "Kendal doesn't say so," Spence was looking over the maps of the area and the schedule just before they would loose the sun for the day, "But I would bet this is just one storm, which circles constantly around the region." His finger traced a circle around and around the area of the wasteland on the map. "It makes a complete circle about once every two hours. Anyone attempting to cross would get caught in the storm at some time. Kendal did note the storm keeps a similar schedule during the night. It lasts fifteen minutes each time, which, with those high winds, is plenty long enough to strip the flesh from a man's bones."

"That is definitely a form of defense against intruders," Jerol concluded right away.

"It could simply be a remnant of the spell that caused the wasteland in the first place," Telin disagreed for a moment, then shook his head, "But I doubt it. You could feel the magic behind the storm when we were out there."

They had managed to carve out five crude buckets with tops to shade the plants from the daytime heat. The next morning plants were put into them, and they were taken out and left right in the path of the storm. Spence formed a shield over the top of them before leaving them. Two hours later, Spence and Stergis retrieved the plants, which looked a little dried out, but otherwise intact. The sandstorm had not gotten to the plants. The only problem was how the sand had covered over the shield, burying them. If not for Spence's ability to track down his own magic they may never have found the plants. It was not something to overly concern them though, as the shelter for all of them would be large enough not to get buried.

"We need to go out and stay through the storm tonight," Stergis said. "Plants are one thing, but I'm wondering what it will be like for the horses in the shield, they might go crazy."

"I also want to know how fast things cool down out there once the sun goes down," Jerol added. "So we can leave as early in the night as possible. No matter what, we'll have the cover of darkness once we reach whatever is at the center. If we're really lucky, we might be able to get in and out in one night."

Anthony Fredericks

Roanne and Jerol insisted on going along and staying in the second test of the shields. They and Spence stayed, while Stergis, Lathom, and Duval returned to the camp with the horses. As evenings go, it was not anyone's idea of a good time, but they felt the horses would be fine. Sound did not penetrate the shield very well, and at night there was literally nothing to see during the storm, since the sand completely blocked out any light from the moon and stars. When the three captains returned with the horses, they found the three of them easily, as the sand had only piled against one side of the shelter, never fully covering it.

"Interesting," Jerol stuck his hand into the pile. "We should pass the word to watch for this type of phenomenon around the edges of the wasteland, and watch for them whenever we move around out here. Everything else is relatively flat. This would be a definite sign someone had put up a shelter of some kind."

"It may not last beyond the next storm," Roanne pointed out. "The wind is likely to pick the entire pile up and carry it away again."

Back at the camp they found something they would never have expected to find. Sallas had come after them after all. He and Regus were off to one side of the camp with everyone else, including the ten guards who had come with Sallas, keeping as far from them as they could get.

Everyone's attention swung to those returning from the desert as they came through the woods. Immediately upon recognizing his father, Jerol and Stergis looked around for Sheilla, who was sitting with Letitia and Bessal under the temporary shelter they had put up. The two of them dismounted quickly, Stergis going right to Sheilla, and Jerol going to join Regus and Sallas. Roanne decided to be bold, and went after Jerol, while the others kind of split the difference, going to the fire where a pot a taze was being kept warm. Roanne noticed the actions of Spence and the captains, and suddenly understood more clearly why it was Jerol had welcomed each of them so enthusiastically when they had volunteered for this duty.

Turning her attention to the smaller gathering of father and sons, she approached slowly, giving any one of them the chance to give some sign whether she would be welcome or not. There were no signs at all, even though Regus and Sallas were looking right at her. Jerol had his back to her as he greeted his father with a handshake and a hug.

A twig snapped behind Roanne, and she caught movement in the shadows cast by the fire. Coming quickly behind her were Letitia and Sheilla, with Stergis right behind Sheilla. Sallas' eyes went straight over Roanne's left shoulder to Sheilla and stayed there.

"I think I should apologize for the threat that was made against you, Roanne," Sallas started. "I need you to believe I had nothing to do with the archers on the walls in Rivard. I want all of you to know that. Pavlin was the one who had arranged it."

"It was Pavlin who made the threat, not you," Roanne acknowledged that, remembering how scared Sallas had become when Pavlin had made it. "What have you done about it?"

"He's dead," another familiar voice said from back near the fire. Roanne spun around to find Lonora there. "I thought you should hear it from me, because I was the one who killed him."

"Lonora?" Roanne was ready to cry. She had always looked up to Pavlin. He was the one man she thought she could trust when she was growing up. The one wizard who had thought her skills could amount to something. "Why?"

"He was going to try to kill you when you turned your back after dropping the portcullis behind you," Lonora explained. "I saw him start the gestures. The same ones those wizards had used during the attack in the dining hall, and very similar to the spells of the wizards you fought on the road to Esconda."

"Here," Sallas held out a cloth bundle toward Roanne. "We found it in his hand after Lonora grabbed a dagger from one of the guards and stabbed him with it."

Roanne found a weapon similar to those used by Calum's allies. Her knees gave out and she sank to the ground. "I don't understand this, why would he ... He was my friend, and my father's friend."

Letitia and Sheilla were right there, but they moved away to let Jerol move in and put his arms around Roanne, who could not stop the tears no matter how hard she tried. They were tears of grief, but grief at what, she was uncertain. Tears for a lost friend, or tears born out of the betrayal threatening to rip her apart from the inside out, she was not even sure of the difference between the two any more. The others slowly moved away toward the fire, leaving her and Jerol alone.

With Lonora's help, Sallas was able to patch together his family that night. He did not apologize to Sheilla for his anger at her. The two knew each other well enough Sheilla would have seen right through that. Instead, he explained his anger was out of concern for her. He had learned to live with the risks Jerol was always taking in his name, and in honor of his family. He admitted having trouble dealing with the idea that Sheilla was now at risk. Fresh out of the fight he had with Sheilla over her public berating of him, Sallas had been left open for Pavlin's manipulation. Lonora, similarly smarting over Roanne's rejection of her advice, was similarly vulnerable. They both let Pavlin lead them down the wrong path.

Lonora had drawn Sheilla away from the camp to a spot where Sallas was waiting by a small stream that could be heard better than it could be seen with the light of the moon blocked out by the leaves of the forest.

"I wish I had the patience Bessal has," Sallas admitted, "But I am not Bessal."

"At least with you I know where I stand," Sheilla felt the need to tell him. "With Bessal as a father, Letitia must have spent half her life figuring out the hidden meaning in his words, maybe that's why she's so good at reading people."

"It seems everyone in the family, except Regus, has the same temper," Sheilla shrugged. "My own temper was no help, and perhaps I should have met with you in private, so you wouldn't be caught by surprise by what we were planning."

"I heard Bessal managed to convince Letitia and Regus to stay behind," Sallas still hoped he could do the same with Sheilla.

"Don't even think it," Sheilla warned. "The part I have in this is not something anyone else can do. If we have to, Jerol is going to try and play the traitor, and I'm the bait to make that believable. If we get caught, it will be up to me to buy enough time for the others to be able to do something."

"I know. Jerol told me the morning you left Rivard," Sallas held out a hand to Sheilla. "Are you sure you are up to this? You have seen what some of those women had been through."

"You knew?" Sheilla was caught off guard this time.

"I had been getting suspicious of Pavlin," Sallas revealed. "In my position you learn a few things over the years, like wizards cannot easily spy on other's communications. They had to be expecting them, which suggested there must be a spy somewhere in our group. I wanted the split in the family to be made really obvious, and it worked. It drew Pavlin out. Pavlin did not want this expedition to take place, and he tried to use me and Lonora to stop it."

"That does not mean I am not angry over your behavior," Sallas quickly added, "But I do want to take back what I said about your marriage. I want there to be two weddings within the next year, if you and Stergis feel you are ready."

They made their way back to the camp, this issue not settled, but as usually happened with Sheilla and her father, a temporary truce had been declared. "Actually I am looking forward to the day Stergis will have to deal with your temper instead of me," Sallas teased. They were close enough to the camp when Sallas said it that Sheilla could see the smile he gave her in the light of the fire.

"Oh, really," she teased back, "And are you ready for a third wedding this summer?" As they cleared the woods she pointed out where Roanne lay in Jerol's arms, having finally cried herself to sleep.

"I do not even want to think about that right now," Sallas knew the trouble that situation could cause. "There are three provinces to be given away. One would usually have gone to you and Stergis, but he already stands to inherit a province. Normally, one of the others would go to Jerol, but as Timond has so recently reminded us, wizards are not allowed to hold a province. A match between Jerol and Roanne would mean I could not give any of my children a province. That would be very disappointing."

"She's not a wizard," Sheilla pointed out.

"If only she were a wizard, this whole discussion would not even be necessary," Sallas countered, getting a smile from Sheilla. "A spinner is even worse, and so close to the crown. What if Regus and Letitia had no sons, the crown would pass to Jerol's family where, due to Roanne, the daughter's would inherit. The nobility would love that."

"In that case," Sheilla had a mischievous glint in her eye as they joined Regus, Letitia and the others on the side of the fire away from where Jerol and Roanne were, "Regus just better be sure Letitia has a lot of sons."

"What?" Letitia suddenly sat up from where she had been leaning comfortably against Regus' shoulder, with his arm around her.

Duke Bessal laughed picking up immediately on the real topic of the conversation. He had caught Sheilla's gesture toward Roanne and Jerol. "I'm not sure all the sons in the world would satisfy some of the people who would not be happy with such a match." He quietly said, glancing across the fire to be sure Jerol did not hear him.

Chapter 25

Those going into the wasteland took the watches, staying up most of the night. They had all the next day to rest before using the next night to enter the waste under the cover of darkness. Those not on watch were gathered around the fire.

Jerol noted Roanne's disinterest in talking, and said nothing when she moved off to the edge of the camp. He let her alone for some time before quietly following. "Is something wrong?" he asked sitting next to her on a fallen tree that seemed to hold the surrounding forest back from the clearing.

"It just seems like everyone I've ever trusted has either betrayed me, or is dead," Roanne tried to explain the empty feeling she had after hearing the news about Pavlin.

"You trust me, don't you?" Jerol teased her, drawing a smile.

"Yes, and the others, too," Roanne took his hand and held it between her own, "And I'm scared they might not live through this."

"Then use your fear," Jerol quietly told her. "You've learned to use your anger well. You don't let it control you. You control it. Do that with your fear, use it to make sure what you fear never comes true."

"Jerol," Stergis called from where he and Sheilla were talking together. Stergis waited until Roanne and Jerol rejoined them before going on. "If Pavlin was on the other side, it could mean these people will know more about us than we think. They may even be expecting us, and have an idea of just who you would pick for such a mission and what we're capable of doing. Anything Pavlin might have known, they could know."

Roanne wanted to protest Pavlin would not do such a thing, but knew better than that now. "Not even Pavlin had much of an idea what I can do. Spence and Talia are way beyond anything Pavlin could have reported."

"Pavlin may not have had a chance to report anything, he died just as we left Rivard," Lathom suggested, "Up until then he thought he might be able to stop us."

"Still, we'll have to keep this in mind," Jerol looked up into the sky, as if looking for answers there. "It doesn't change our need to go, though it raises the stakes. Calum and the others seemed to have no idea we could fight them, which means they were not in very close touch with Pavlin, or refused to believe him. If they were in contact at all I would have thought Pavlin would warn them of Roanne's abilities."

"Unless he thought they already knew," Lathom pointed out. "Remember, we all thought Carlon had made it to Altea, but Calum had left before Carlon arrived. Pavlin might have assumed the same thing."

"We're guessing," Jerol interrupted the discussion. "Let's just go in the way we originally planned. We can't plan for the unknown and trying will only drive us crazy. We go in with our eyes and ears peeled back. That's why we're awake now, and will rest all day. Beyond that, we'll see when we get there."

They sat in silence for a long time, listening to the sounds of the forest around them. When the sun began to peek through the trees to the east those planning on going into the wasteland gathered and went into the shelter. They spent the day getting what rest they could, so they would be fresh come evening. The next night was likely to be as long as the past one, and much busier.

Sallas woke them in the afternoon. Someone had brought down a deer while hunting, and Letitia had run off to the nearest village. The result of all this was a literal feast that had been prepared for those departing. The leftovers were even packed away, to provide a quick meal that could be had on the run if necessary.

"I might not be able to fit into the dress Letitia bought after this meal," Sheilla joked when she set aside her plate. "I guess I had better go and change."

"That won't be necessary," Jerol told her.

Queen of the Spinners

"If you think ..." Sheilla began to protest, but Jerol held up his hand.

"In view of what has happened with Pavlin, I don't think we need bother with the dress," Jerol explained. "If Pavlin was in touch with these people at all, they're just as likely not believe you're the princess if we bring you in wearing a dress." Several people laughed at that, while Sheilla seemed unsure whether to be embarrassed or laugh along with them.

"I want to wish you all the best, and may the gods bring you all back to us," Sallas said, raising a mug of taze in salute.

Their horses were already saddled and ready to go except for distributing the food to everyone's saddlebags.

They went slowly to the edge of the wasteland, from where they could observe the passing of the storm in the last light of the sun. By the time the storm went on its way, the sun had gone down below the horizon. Spence observed that the passing of the storm cooled the air a lot, especially as the sun was going down.

All the good byes and well wishing, except that last from the king, had been done during the meal. Jerol wanted to move out quickly, to see how far they could get before the next storm. Taking just the few seconds he needed to plot the stars in his mind for keeping track of their direction, he gave his horse a kick, and led the way out onto the sand, the others following closely behind.

Roanne could not help but glance back from time to time, watching the forest shrink to nothingness behind them. If anyone remained to watch them go, which she was sure they had, they kept to the tree line, out of sight. She had gone this far the other night, when they tested the shield, but this time was different. There were tears on her cheeks, which she supposed she could blame on the wind, but she knew better. She might never see those they left behind again.

In the dark of night, it was also harder to see the approaching storms, so all the wizards and spinners opened themselves up to sensing the magic bringing the storm, which would give them enough warning to set up their shelter.

The ride was rather monotonous. All there was to see was sand and after a while, it almost seemed as if they were running and running, but getting nowhere. The moon was already well into the sky at the setting of the sun. It and the stars offered the only means to gauge the time, but moved so slowly, even that became deceiving. Before long, Roanne, who wished she had paid more attention to Tagert's project, lost all sense of time.

"I have a question," Jerol surprised Roanne who was staring at the sand as it passed below her in the dim moonlight. Looking up she saw he and Spence were flanking her. "Would it be possible to move the shelter within the storm?"

"Why would we want to do that?" Roanne had to wake herself up. She had nearly fallen asleep in the saddle. She checked quickly, but could not sense any magic in the area. For a second she thought they might have been caught off guard by a storm, because she had forgotten to keep watch.

"Depending on what we find, it could be useful," Jerol shrugged, but it was hard to distinguish from the rocking of his horse. "Maybe we could use the storm for cover. It could hide our movements."

"I think it should be no problem," Spence offered. "But I need my hands to do it, which means I can't ride at the same time."

"No problem," Roanne agreed. "I can move it, but I'm not sure how fast. That storm we rode out in the shelter was pretty strong. If the wind got under the shell it could blow away."

"Just something to keep in mind," Jerol said. "I like it as a possibility, though."

"How long has it been?" Roanne asked, catching Jerol checking on the stars and the moon.

"You might want to start watching for a storm," he answered. "When you sense something just raise your hand, everyone should know what it means."

Several minutes later, Roanne's hand shot up, quickly followed by Spence's. The group pulled up as quickly as they could without hurting the horses. Some accidentally moved on ahead a few strides, but quickly swung back as Spence was beginning the chant and gestures that would protect them from the ravages of the oncoming storm. Using their sense of magic to locate the storm proved its value, since the storm was nearly on top of them before they actually saw anything.

The horses were restless, and everyone dismounted to try and keep their mounts calm while the winds whipped by. The noise was worse in the center of the storm than it had been closer to the edge, where Spence had done all his testing. Before it ended, Roanne tested how easy it would be to move the shelter, and found it to be harder than either she or Spence thought it would be. Searching for the reason, she discovered Spence, without realizing, had anchored the shelter well into the sandy surface of the ground. To move the shelter, she would have to move a foot deep of sand along as well.

"All right, that's not an option then," Jerol said when she told him.

"Maybe Spence could change the spell," Roanne suggested.

"No, chances are he has anchored the shell every time he made a shield, even if he doesn't realize it," Jerol shook his head. "An unanchored shield is untested, and might blow away for all we know. Don't say a word to him about this, because he may unconsciously alter the spell. This is no time to experiment."

"I see what you mean," Roanne nodded after he explained.

In the end there was no need to discuss the observation with Spence. He had noticed the same thing himself, since he was thinking about it. Once the storm had passed, and they were moving once again, he came over to tell Roanne what he had realized.

"I know," Roanne told him. "Don't worry about it. Jerol and I discussed it during the storm, but we didn't want to disturb you. He figures we're better off not trying to change anything at this point, and I agree."

"So do I," Spence smiled, glad she was not disappointed. "I just wanted to make sure you knew." As he moved away to ride alongside Talia, Roanne noticed Jerol watching the exchange between her and Spence. She gave him a nod to let him know everything was all right.

Their next stop was called by Jerol, who raised his hand and pulled his horse to a halt. Roanne had not been slacking in her storm watch, and was surprised when it happened. Though it had to be getting close to that time again, if her sense of timing had any accuracy at all.

The captains quickly surrounded Jerol, while the others gathered close enough to hear what was said. "Does anyone else see what I see?" Jerol asked pointing out ahead of them.

"The stars seem different," Lathom suggested, "Or it could be lights, from windows. We're still too far to tell for sure."

"How long before the next storm?" Sheilla asked, and Roanne admired her sense of timing, as she felt the storm coming.

While Spence held their shelter together, the others discussed their options. "All right, this is what we'll do, Telin, I want you and Smithe to go on ahead, the rest of us will keep back a little. If you find anything, one of you can double back and tell the rest of us, while the other keeps an eye out." He pointed right at Telin to emphasize his next point. "In an emergency, which Smithe will decide for right now, because of his experience in these things, you can contact us by magic, but only in an emergency. We are probably dealing with wizards, and we don't know their capability. The shelters are necessary, and covered by the magic of the storms. Anything else might just give us away if they sense what you're doing."

When the storm cleared, Telin and Smithe were already in the saddle and ready to go. The rest led their horses on foot, watching as the two of them disappeared into the night. It was not long before Telin was back startling some of them as he suddenly appeared before them out of the dark.

"There's a forest out there," Telin informed them. "The lights we've been seeing are within the woods, and above it."

"The tower of Lindor," Roanne remembered. "It's said in some of the older books, there was a keep at Lindor, with a tower looking out over the coast on the point. It was a light house to warn sailors away from the rocky coast in the area."

The others were mounting up, and Roanne quickly followed their example. They rode slowly, but much faster than walking. Smithe was waiting not far ahead, keeping his eyes ahead, watching the thickening of the darkness along the ground ahead of them.

"I haven't seen anything," Smithe reported. "Telin and I were a lot closer before we realized what we were seeing. That was when I decided to send him back."

The captains all gathered around, as Jerol issued orders. They all moved out then, the captains all going ahead to scout the area. The setting moon was low enough to outline the tops of the trees as they moved closer. It also revealed the outline of the tower further on, with the lighted windows dotting its surface.

Jerol called a halt at the edge of the forest, where they waited for the captains to meet back up with them. Stergis appeared from out of the woods, and Roanne marveled at the way he could move about in silence in that environment. The others were equally as good, as one by one they appeared from the north or south of where they waited.

"The forest ends some ways in, but could be useful as cover if we wanted to try and observe anything without being seen," Duval reported. "Beyond it is what looks like plowed fields. I might have thought it was just open ground but the plants are growing with too much order."

"It is a farm, and quite a big one," Stergis agreed. "I agree we should use the cover of the forest to keep a watch. Even if it takes a day, we'll have a much better idea of what we're up against."

"We can scout routes further in much better in the daylight," Lathom suggested, "Especially now that the moon is down. There's a spot not far from here would make a good camp."

Jerol simply nodded his agreement, and Lathom led the way. The forest was eerily very much like the one they had left behind on the other side of the wasteland. It was as if the sandstorms had simply carved a path around this area, cutting it off from the rest of the world.

The captains moved off to their flanks a little, while the women and wizards stayed with Jerol. Everyone was a bit edgy, jumping whenever twigs snapped, or small animals scurried away in the darkness. Roanne half-expected demons to rise out of the darkness and attack at any moment, and wondered what childhood stories could be haunting the others.

As they settled in, Jerol and Telin worked out a very short message for Telin to send back. Duval went back to the desert, with Telin and Spence, so they could use the cover of a storm to send it. They kept the message simple, letting Sallas and the others know they were safe, had found a village, and that it had taken time enough for two storms to pass for them to cross the waste.

In the first light of dawn, the same birds they were all familiar with greeted them. The leftovers of the previous day's feast were passed around as they discussed how to proceed. Lathom would be going south, and Smithe north in order to get an idea of the extent of the forest. Spence and Stergis would check out the farm, taking shifts at the monotonous task since they were all weary after being awake all night.

The day was mostly uneventful for those remaining at the camp. Their imaginations were left to run wild about what the men might be finding in their search. Roanne welcomed the distraction of tending to the horses, which were left behind by the men since it was easier to move through the woods on foot. Still, the hairs at the back of her neck rose every time a storm went by out in the desert, and the work took hardly any time considering the number of people available, and looking for something to occupy their time.

Lathom returned at about noon, with the welcome distraction of news. "The forest goes right up to the coast where the cliffs drop off to a small beach," he told everyone. "I think we might be able to move in by that route, but I wouldn't want to do it once the moon went down. We would also have to leave the horses. They could never make it down the cliffs to the beach."

Spence came back in time to hear the last of that. "There are men and women working the field out there," he reported. "Along with an overseer, who we think must be a wizard." He looked down, swallowing before he went on. "I think the workers are slaves. The wizard is surrounded by magic, as if for protection. Out in the fields, we've noticed how the people seem to react like puppets, responding to tugs on strings reaching back to the wizard."

"Collars and tethers," Talia immediately recognized the description. "The wizard can probably strangle them by their tethers if they were to act up in any way."

"Those people won't be acting up," Spence shook his head. "They move around like they have no minds of their own. Stergis wants to try and follow them when they leave, to see where they go."

"No," Jerol cut off that line of thinking immediately. "In fact, go tell Stergis to come back to the camp. Lathom has found a way to get closer to the keep, which is where we need to go. That is where we'll find the leaders of this village, and the answers we need. I want to be ready to move out as soon as Smithe returns. Duval, you, Smithe, and Telin will stay with the horses. You can continue to scout the outlying areas. Just make sure you don't get caught. Telin, can you get back to the other side if need be?"

"Yes, sir" Telin snapped the answer as if he were in the guard.

"Good," Jerol clapped him on the shoulder. "If you don't hear from the rest of us by the third night, get out of here. Take what you know to Sallas and Regus. They'll know what to do." He was not so sure they would, but did not care to admit it.

Smithe did not return until late in the afternoon, reporting as far as he traveled there was no end to the forest, though there were several paths leading from the desert to the interior of the forest. There were more farms, and pastures with cattle and horses. It almost seemed like any other village you might encounter in the rest of the kingdom.

"Except for the slaves," Stergis corrected that notion, and the others explained what they had found to Smithe.

"It looks like we've found the enemy," Smithe summed up what they had all been thinking. "Now we just have to figure out what we're going to do about it."

"We need to check out the keep," Jerol agreed, and went on to explain the plan to Smithe.

Chapter 26

Where the forest met the coast their party descended to the beach and began to make its way toward the keep. As a precaution, Jerol had decided to wait for the cover of night. Lathom's description of the cliff included a path they hoped would be easy enough to climb by the light of the moon. Jerol led the way, while Stergis brought up the rear, with the others ranging in between. Roanne wished she had the time to savor the view of the sun setting over the Whale's Sea, of even just the sight of the sea itself. She had been raised within miles of the coast of the Serpent's Ocean, and yet, had never gone to see it. Instead of taking in the sights, all her concentration was centered on expanding her senses to detect any use of magic in the area. Talia was doing the same, as was Spence. It was up to them to be sure their element of surprise was not lost.

What they could see of the keep did not tell them much. The outer wall was high enough to hide whatever lay beyond, except the tower, whose light they had seen all the way from the desert. Evidently, there were rooms in the wall, where lights came on as the sun was setting.

They kept as close to the cliff as possible, often climbing over strewn boulders rather than venture out where they might be seen. As they neared the keep, the beach thinned, eventually ending as the cliffs rose to the keep itself. Trails wound their way up from the shoreline, which, while providing a way in for them, suggested the inhabitants of the keep might sometimes use the path. The ledge never made it to the top, however, ending abruptly at the entrance to a cave.

Jerol peered around the edge of the mouth to the cave, and ducked back quickly. His actions startled the others, until a flock of gulls, surprised by Jerol's appearance came flying from within the dark entry. Jerol made a second quick check, then slipped around the corner. Roanne followed with the others right behind her.

"I hope nobody noticed those gulls," Stergis whispered as the group gathered just inside the cave.

Jerol eyed Stergis guiltily, but only shrugged before moving on. Spence and Lathom fanned out to the sides of the cavern. Stergis lingered to the rear.

"I sense power being used," Spence informed everyone after only a few steps. All the others stopped, Jerol in mid step. "It seems more general, not directed at any of us," Spence quickly tried to ease the sudden tension in the cave. "There's probably enough to mask if we made a light for ourselves."

Jerol looked to Roanne, who had been aware of the magic. "All right," Jerol said when she nodded her agreement with Spence. Spence worked slowly, drawing only enough power to do what was needed.

The light revealed a stair leading up at the back of the cave. Empty sconces on the walls seemed in odd contrast to the clean swept path. Roanne followed Jerol's gaze as he noted these things. "Wizards wouldn't need torches," she pointed out, gesturing to Spence's globe of light floating just above them.

"This is too easy," Stergis' whispered back near the entrance.

"I don't know about that," Spence grabbed Jerol's arm as Jerol began to move forward. Picking up a small stone, he tossed toward the opening to the stair. The stone bounced back toward them.

Roanne was taken aback, she should have been watching for something like this, and had not been. A quick probe of the archway confirmed the spell blocking the way was the same magic Calum had brought into the kingdom. She nodded her appreciation toward Spence, as Jerol pulled the group back toward the entrance to the cave.

"All right, Sheilla, time for you to do your job," Jerol seemed almost relieved to say this. Sheilla had been uncharacteristically silent since the start of this mission, almost as if she thought Jerol might forget she was there. "I think we can safely agree this is what we came looking for. Time to let

Regus and father know what we've found. Take Stergis with you back along the shore. Telin can get you across the waste."

"Send Talia with her," Stergis suggested. "She can get them both across the waste. Sending Telin cuts off our communications."

"I know you don't want to go," Jerol took in both Stergis and Sheilla with his look. "Talia is stronger than Telin if it comes to a fight, and neither of you will be much help in that kind of fighting."

"It is almost morning," Jerol went back to the opening of the cave. "Stergis, if you leave at sunset, we should be able to give you two a couple of hours head start before we go through the barrier. I expect you can be back on the other side of the waste by morning. Lathom, you go with them as far as the camp on this side, then bring Duval and Smithe back to this cave, and wait here. Talia, Spence, Roanne, and I will scout the keep, and meet you back here before morning. Then we can figure out where to go from there."

Stergis and Sheilla both wanted to object, it was clear in their faces, but held their tongues for the moment. Throughout the day Stergis would approach Jerol from time to time, speaking briefly, before moving away again.

This evening, Roanne had the time to watch as sun slowly sank below the rising tide of the ocean. Only briefly was her view interrupted, as the storm protecting the keep from the outside world swept its way across her view on its way back toward the desert. She followed the storm with her senses as well as her eyes, tracing the lines of energy feeding the storm back over their heads to the walls above them on the cliff. Calling Spence and Talia to her, she confirmed they too could sense those lines of power, distinct lines of power, ten of them.

They quickly got Jerol's attention, and explained what they had found. "So? What does it mean, and how can we use it?" Jerol asked.

"It means the storm is not self sustaining," Spence began to explain. "They need to maintain it, which means we can stop them, and end the storm for good."

"It appears to need ten people, working in concert," Roanne picked up the discussion. "They probably need to be where they can see what they are doing at all times, which means the top of the tower where we first saw the light from the desert."

"Talia and Spence, you go for the tower and see what you can find out. Check the remainder of the outer walls while you're at it." Jerol was relieved to have some solid information on which to plan. "Roanne and I will take the keep itself."

Sheilla, Stergis and Lathom were ready to go, despite their objections. They were given this new information as everyone exchanged farewells, and Jerol ran over everything one more time. As the trio slowly made their way down the cliff to the beach, those remaining settled in to wait. If their entry into the keep set off any wards, they wanted to be sure Sheilla and Stergis were well clear of the area, and even on their way back across the waste if they could move fast enough.

Roanne watched until the others were out of sight around a turn in the beach before she turned her attention back to the ocean. Now she could not put off what she had to do. Somewhere above her in the keep were her parents. She knew as certainly as she knew the sun would rise again the next morning. She reached out with the same sense she had used to identify the lines of power to the storm, her sense of magic. For some time she searched the area around her, slowly, gently expanding the range of her probe. There was magic all around, but none she could recognize, if she were still able to recognize the work of her parents, it had been so long. She found the tower, where Talia and Spence would be going, and shared what she found with them. That concentration of power had drawn her probe like a bee to honey. It took a willful effort to divert the probe. There were almost thirty other sources of magic she could readily distinguish, but she could not identify any of them. That meant at least forty wizards or spinners at work, and only the three of them and Jerol's sword to face them. One source outshone all the others outside the tower, and in that source Roanne thought she could sense something familiar, then dismissed it as wishful thinking. Either her parents were not part of anything being done at this time, or she was not able to recognize them.

Roanne shook herself back to awareness of her immediate surroundings. "You didn't find them, did you?" Jerol's voice showed concern, and Roanne realized she was crying.

"That doesn't mean anything," Roanne tried to convince herself. "They're prisoners. If they could use their power, we wouldn't be here. They would have ended this a long time ago."

"There are at least forty sources of magic up there," Roanne went on to inform him. "That could be anything from forty individuals, or long lingering spells."

"If you think of this as an academy, where whoever's in charge is teaching what he knows, figure not even half of the wizards will be practicing at any one time," Spence offered from a few feet away, where he sat with his arm around Talia. "That would make at least eighty wizards."

"Where did they come from?" Talia asked. "Could they have been here since the War and the forming of the Wasteland?"

"One of the sources is extremely powerful," Roanne shrugged. "Who knows what such power can accomplish? They could be recruiting the same way the academy did, or after five hundred years they could simply be the descendants of Varden and his followers. Does it really matter?"

"No, but it would be interesting to find out," Spence answered her. "So you think the legends about Varden are true?"

"My father did," Roanne explained for Talia's sake, and to run it through her own mind again to see if she were missing some clue that might help them.

"It seems your father was right on almost all accounts," Jerol arms circled her waist from behind. "The only thing he was wrong about was when they got here, it was only the two of them, he and your mother, against who knows how many. They didn't stand a chance."

He felt the shiver run through her when he said that. "If they're still alive we'll find them, Roanne. I promise, but we are not going to repeat their mistake. Stergis is going to bring reinforcements. Regus will have been gathering wizards and spinners. Remember, this is a scouting mission, we have only three individuals with not much more talent than what Kendal and Ariele had. Remember they were the best of their time, and as good as the three of you think you are, we're still vastly outnumbered, and probably outpowered if Roanne is right about that one strong source she sensed. We get in and out tonight, Lathom and the others will be here to meet us by morning. We can plan better from there. By the time Stergis and the reinforcements arrive, I want a viable strategy for bringing this place down."

On the far side of the waste, Regus and Sallas were seated around the fire, once more going over the plans they had put together to cover nearly any possible situation coming out of the waste. Men had been arriving daily from all over the kingdom to lend support since Calum and the worst of the lords had been dealt with. They had been spreading the men out along the border of the waste in groups of ten, at least one wizard or spinner to each group. Anyone capable of wielding the slightest amount of power was being pressed into service learning to build the shelters Jerol and his group had used to cross the waste. So far two hundred men and women had been dispatched. In their camp were twenty-five newly arrived wizards and spinners, who would double the allotment per group once they were properly trained.

"Each group is putting a torch along the edge of the waste," Regus explained to his father. "That will be the signal to move out if or when the time comes."

Suddenly every wizard and spinner in the camp was on their feet, facing out toward the waste. Lonora, who had been seated across the fire from Regus, turned white as a ghost.

"Telin's dead," she informed them, lowering her head. "He was trying to call for help, but the message was cut off in mid word."

"How do you know he is dead?" Sallas asked. "There could be any number of explanations for the interruption."

"He's dead," Lonora shook her head. "It was the way the message was interrupted. It grew weak, to the point there were no words coming across, just his fear. Look around at anyone with power, they all know it. That was probably the strongest message Telin had sent in his life."

"His last message said they were splitting into two groups," Regus jumped in. "His message must have gotten to the others as well."

"Not necessarily," Lonora corrected him. "Telin has been targeting his messages in this direction, to avoid being overheard by those they found at the center of the waste. If the group without Telin was in the keep they said they found, then he might have left them out of the message. Not that it matters, they're all in trouble now."

Sallas and Regus exchanged only a brief glance before Regus made his decision. "Mount up," he shouted into the silence of the camp. "We ride into the waste. Light the torch to let the others know."

Everything was already in place, the horses had been kept saddled, all they needed was to gather weapons, which were close at hand, and to make sure all the latest comers were properly arranged in groups with enough protection from wizards or spinners to make it across.

Letitia mounted up on the horse next to Regus, and he was about to make his usual objections to her coming, until he saw the determination in her eyes. Neither Sallas, nor Bessal had been able to dissuade her. With Lonora mounted on his other side, and Fenicia providing protection for the group of men just north of their camp he could hardly argue. Roanne, Talia, and Sheilla were already in the waste. Then there was the package from Samus, the smith in Esconda, which had arrived with several men the morning after Jerol's group had left. It was a package of arrows for Sheilla's crossbow. Letitia had grabbed a crossbow and tested one of the arrows, which had split two trees before imbedding itself deep in the trunk of a third. As she mounted her horse, she had two quivers, each with twenty arrows. She intended to pass at least some to Sheilla if the opportunity presented itself. Truth be told, she wished Sheilla had them all at this moment, if they might help keep her and the others alive.

Having already traversed the ground once, Stergis, Lathom and Sheilla made much better time on their return to their camp, where they expected to find the others waiting. Stergis, leading the way, was the first to get sight of the camp, and froze in his tracks for an instant at what he saw. In the next instant he motioned the others to get low under cover as he did the same. Slowly, keeping low to the ground, Stergis continued to weave his way through the underbrush until he was virtually at the edge of the clearing where the camp had been.

Finally satisfied they were safe, Stergis stood and motioned the others forward. The camp was a mess of bodies. Most were obviously slaves from the keep, though two robed figures stood out amongst the tangle of naked limbs. What else stood out were Telin and Smithe, both of who were dead. Sheilla turned back toward the woods to vomit at what she saw.

"I count two strange wizards," Stergis announce quietly as he made his way to Telin.

Lathom went to Smithe, but both of them knew what they would find. "I don't see Duval, he could have been taken," Lathom was quickly checking the surrounding area. "The horses are gone, too."

Sheilla having left what little she had eaten in the woods came back to the edge of the camp. "The others will be walking right into a trap. We have to warn them."

"There is no way to, now," Stergis shook his head, "And without Telin, we can't go for reinforcements."

"They still don't know how many or where we were," Lathom tried to be encouraging. "It's possible the others won't be expected."

Sheilla simply gave him a look, with her hands planted on her hips. Stergis recognized the stance but had more important matters on his mind. "Sheilla, call Winter. If I know that horse of yours, he's still out here, maybe some of the others are still with him."

"Three wizards," Lathom returned from where the animals had been picketed, "It looks as though one of the horses kicked in his head."

"That would be Winter," Stergis looked expectantly at Sheilla, waiting.

"If there is anyone else around, they may hear, also," Sheilla cautioned. "If Winter is loose, though, she might be able to make it across to father."

"Without a wizard?" Lathom did not want to think about it. "If you don't make it ... " As if summoned by the thought, they heard the sandstorm approaching out on the waste, not far away.

"I know, but I think Winter can do it," Sheilla insisted, "Have you got any better ideas?" She put two fingers to her lips, and let out three shrill notes.

After a few moments of quiet, Sheilla was ready to try again when a crashing sound came through the forest from the direction of the keep. All three moved to the edge of the camp, inside the rim of the forest around the clearing. Winter came crashing into the clearing with three of the other horses close behind, but so were the shouts of men.

Sheilla was mounted on Winter's back before the horse even came to a stop. Stergis grabbed her hand, "You be careful, the storm has not gone completely past yet."

"You stay alive. I'll be back," Sheilla leaned down and kissed him. "And see what you can do to keep my brother and the others that way, too."

A light touch from her heels was all it took to get the horse moving again. Stergis would have stood and watched as she went, but Lathom brought over two of the other horses. One was Summer, his horse, and a brother to Winter. The horse Lathom mounted was Jerol's.

"We can use the edge of the storm as cover, move inland," Lathom suggested, "Then double back to the coast out in the desert. It should at least take them a while to figure it out."

They followed Sheilla back toward the edge of the forest, though Winter was outdistancing them even over that short span. Stergis saw Winter balk momentarily at the storm, then disappear along with Sheilla into the trailing edge of the blowing sands. During their crossing he had noted the trailing edge was not near as severe as the front of the storm. Sheilla would do fine for now, the question was whether she could clear the waste before the storm returned.

"She's the best rider I know," Lathom pulled up next to Stergis. "And that horse will run himself dead for her. If any horse and rider can make it, it would be those two."

"I don't intend to let it come to that," Stergis had to fight Summer to get him to chase the storm, but once he did, Lathom had an easier time getting his horse to follow.

"What's that supposed to mean?" Lathom yelled over the wind as his horse pulled even with Stregis'.

"It means we have less than two hours to take out the tower," Stergis answered. "Remember what they were saying back at the cave, no tower, no more storm."

Chapter 27

Jerol watched the stars to see how long it had been since the others had left, and judged it was time to make their move. The others all knew it was time when he unsheathed his sword.

"Allow me," Roanne held Jerol back as she approached the opening to the stairway. Her outstretched hand found the barrier, and then she fed the heat she produced with her magic through her fingers into the wall. "Now," she announced after a few minutes of concentration. "You can walk right through it."

Jerol hesitated only a second before doing as instructed, closely followed by the others, then finally Roanne herself. "That was weird," Spence commented on the other side, "It was like walking through a liquid wall."

"I'm hoping we won't set off any wards wound into the barrier," Roanne explained. "If we simply destroyed the thing, whoever put it there might notice."

"All right, we know what we have to do, so let's go do it and get out as soon as we can," Jerol gestured for Spence to lead the way up the stairs, since Spence would sense any more magical traps in their way. Jerol brought up the rear, sword in hand.

Moving up the stairs Roanne watched as Talia took stock of her weapons. There were four daggers, and the small crossbow with a quiver of about a dozen arrows. Roanne wished she had something similar to fall back on, but then Talia was more comfortable with those mundane things than with the power she only recently learned to use. Spence had a sword, which he kept sheathed at his side, having been trained to have more confidence in his power than in his sword arm. For him, having to draw the blade would represent failure. Roanne examined her own motives, and found for her success and failure were less complicated, being as definable as survival or death. The only thing complicating the dividing line was deciding whose death or survival mattered most. She almost wished Jerol had gone back with Sheilla, or better yet she could face this alone, but this was not something one person could handle, and she knew it.

There were no more barriers along the stairs, excepting the door at the top, which they found was not even locked. After putting out his light, and giving his eyes some time to adjust to the dark, Spence opened it just enough to see where they were, then they retreated down several stairs to consult.

"The door opens on the courtyard," Spence reported. "The tower is at the far side, so I guess Talia and I can check the perimeter walls as we make our way around. The keep must be off to the left, where I could not see. It's dark out there, so I couldn't really tell if anyone was about.

"Let's move out then," Jerol ordered, keep to the shadows, if anyone spots you, kill them before they sound an alarm if possible, otherwise get out as best you can. Each group is on its own from here on out. Being this outnumbered means the best we can do is make sure those coming later have the benefit of anything we can learn now. They learn nothing if none of us makes it out."

Talia and Spence went out first, slipping off to the right of the doorway. Jerol led the way for Roanne. They slipped around the door, then moved quickly to a dark corner where the wall of the keep proper met the outer wall. Both walls were solid stone. This was not a simple farm community, but rather a fortress. The wall was at least fifteen feet in height, and would be difficult to bring down if you had to attack this place.

Jerol scaled the wall rather easily, while Roanne watched the yard for any sign of movement. Jerol had to hiss to get her attention again as he held out his belt for her to grab onto and pull herself up. Once atop the wall they found the parapet went around the keep, which for them was fortunate. They were on the ocean side of the keep, where several of the overhead windows were lit. Those not lit presented them with several opportunities to get into the main building without being seen. Slowly they made their way along the wall, ducking twice under lit windows before coming to the first darkened room. Jerol left

Queen of the Spinners

Roanne there as he went on to briefly check each of the windows along that wall. Returning to where he left Roanne, Jerol peeked around the edge of the window to check the room before pulling a dagger of his own, which he used to pry the windows open.

"One could get the idea you've had experience at being a thief," Roanne teased in a whisper as Jerol handed her down over the windowsill into the room.

"I don't think you want to know," was his only reply as he closed the window behind them.

Out at the far end of the courtyard, Talia and Spence were doing similarly well, if for opposite reasons. For them, it was Talia who scaled the wall, and then had to help Spence climb up. Spence was almost over the edge when he began to slip, and the first thing he grabbed hold of to stop himself had been Talia's hair. The look she gave him when he was finally safe atop the wall suggested he might be safer if she had screamed out and the enemy had found them. She had squawked, but whatever noises they had made were covered by the sudden commotion over at the gate.

Keeping below the short rail to the inside of the parapet, they moved closer to the gate to investigate. Ten wizards were coming through with a troop of slaves.

"I'm sorry about your hair," Spence was whispering for the tenth time when Talia's hand clamped over his mouth. Her other hand was pointed down toward the gate.

"Those are our horses, at least some of them," Talia pointed out. "The others must have been caught, or gotten away, but either way our surprise is gone."

"You have six horses and only one prisoner, I assume the others are all dead," a voice rose from the courtyard.

One of the arriving wizards dismounted in front of the speaker, another wizard. "We killed two others we found at the camp. Four other horses, and three riders fled out into the waste, the storm will take care of them. We left several to watch in case they should try and return before the storm comes again. In all, there were four riders unaccounted for."

"The lord will not be pleased," the first wizard snapped. "Bring the prisoner, you can report to Lord Varden yourself on your failure to capture the others."

"I can't capture what is not there to capture," the second protested with a shaky voice.

"Explain that to him," the first turned and headed back toward the keep. The arriving wizard gestured to the others with him and they dragged a figure down from one of the horses and dragged it after their apparent leader.

"Did you make out who it was?" Spence asked. "I thought it was Smithe, but I could be wrong."

"I thought it was Duval," Talia disagreed. "Have you sensed anything from Telin since we left him? I haven't, but then I never really learned to communicate."

"Nothing, and that worries me," Spence sat with his back to the short wall to puzzle things out. "It suggests Telin was one of the two they killed, which means the others are trying to cross the waste without a wizard. If Telin were alive I can't see why he wouldn't have warned us."

"Sheilla is not among the dead, otherwise they would have mentioned one was a woman," Talia seated herself beside him. "So what should we do? Jerol and Roanne need to know about this."

"If we knew where they were," Spence began to shrug, then sat bolt upright, spinning in his place to peek back over the wall. "The tower."

"The tower?" Talia pulled him back down out of sight.

"We have to take out the tower so the others can safely cross the waste," Spence explained. "It's our only chance. On foot it would probably take two days for us to cross the waste, and we would never survive out there during the daytime. We have to make sure Sheilla can make it, and the only way to do that, is to stop the storm."

"I agree," Talia commented, "But Jerol said to get out if anything went wrong. I think it just did."

"Jerol said to use our own judgement," Spence countered. "Things have not simply gone wrong, they've blown up in our face." He needed to convince himself this was the right decision more than he needed to convince Talia, from the look in her eye.

"First we hit the tower, then we see what, if anything we can do for Duval or Smithe, whichever it was," Talia pitched in. "If we run across the others along the way, all the better." She grabbed his arm and began pulling him along the wall toward the tower.

Along the walkway near the gate were two guards in robes, which meant wizards most likely from what they had observed so far. They moved in quickly, with Talia lending a dagger to Spence. The two guards were taken out quickly, and surprisingly quietly. Further along the wall, once clear of the gates, they dumped the bodies over the outer wall of the battlements.

Before they could move on, two more wizards emerged on the stair leading down to the courtyard. "Krezin told us to double the guards on all the walls until the four outlanders are accounted for," One of them was saying.

Spence quickly put a trip wire across the last of the stairs, using Calum's brand of magic. The first wizard tripped grabbing at his throat even as he fell and Spence tied off the choker he had put on the man. The second man, surprised at what was happening was totally unprepared for the crossbow bolt that slammed into his chest, toppling him back on the stairs. Talia raced after him, stopping the body before it fell all the way to the courtyard where it surely would have been noticed.

A second pair of bodies followed the first, minus their robes, which Talia suggested they might be able to use.

"Someone is going to notice there are no guards at the gate," Spence said crouching in the shadow of the gate itself. He was studying the keep, noting each window where a light was visible on this side of the main keep. "I'm surprised we haven't been seen already."

"Damn that was close, too close," Talia joined him in the shadows. "We could prop the robes on something to make it look like there are guards here."

"But we only saved two robes, there should be four guards," Spence pointed out. "I was thinking we could put them on. We might be able to move around more freely that way. But, I guess that won't work too well, the robes have hoods, but I haven't seen anyone with the hood raised, and you would most definitely not pass for a wizard."

"Thanks, I think," Talia slumped until she was sitting with her back to the wall. "We've been lucky so far. Those guards were about as alert as a passed out drunk. It won't be as easy now that word of intruders is getting around, and there will more guards at the tower."

"We need to work together more, and to coordinate our use of weapons and magic," Spence agreed. "Have you been practicing this air magic they use? Do you think you could use it to gag someone, or choke them the way I did?"

"That was nice and quiet, the way you did it," Talia thought for a moment. She made a few quick gestures and Spence felt something tighten around his throat. "How was that?"

Spence reached for his neck instinctively before he realized what she was doing. "You're a quicker study than you or the others give you credit for."

"He made a series of gestures, then took the cloaks they still had, and draped them over the figures he had put together just outside the shadows at either side of the gate. "Hopefully anyone who looks out either may not realize the guards are supposed to be doubled, or will think the other guards are simply not in sight."

"It will have to do," Keeping low, Talia began to make her way toward the tower, which was at the next corner of the wall.

Jerol and Roanne had just missed all the excitement in the courtyard when they had entered the keep. The room they entered appeared to be quarters for one person, which seemed to confirm what Jerol had seen in the windows of other rooms.

Their good fortune in finding a way into the keep did not last. Since then, they had largely wasted their time, roaming through halls used primarily as residences. Counting the rooms, Roanne estimated there was room to house over one hundred wizards. Aside from that, though, they had been able to learn little, and Jerol was beginning to get frustrated.

"He must have a library somewhere in the building," Roanne insisted. "How could he be teaching the others without some record of the techniques and their history?"

"A library would only do us any good if we had several years to go through it," Jerol argued. "We need information now. We only have a few hours."

They were in a storage closet where they had needed to hide to avoid a passing wizard. Several times they had needed to hide, once even finding themselves in the communal bathroom. Each time they took the opportunity to try and make a strategy for how to proceed. Jerol had a tendency to want to proceed on military terms. Roanne viewed their situation through the eyes of a student with the opportunity to explore new areas.

After checking to be sure the way was clear, the pair moved on, rounding the next corner into a new hallway. The sound of running feet gave them ample warning of their next encounter with one of the residents. Unfortunately, the nearest door was locked and the next doors too far to be reached. Jerol hauled Roanne into an alcove at one of the windows, depending on the shadows to hide them this time. The wizard ran right passed them, an expression near panic on his face. At the next doors down the hall he skidded to a halt, then took a moment to catch his breath, before knocking. If there was an answer, the two intruders did not hear it, but after short wait, the wizard entered the rooms beyond the door.

Jerol moved slowly toward the door, keeping himself pinned against the wall. The door had not closed completely, and a shaft of light from within the room illuminated a good portion of the otherwise dim hall. Roanne made to follow, until Jerol gestured for her to wait.

"We thought you should be informed immediately of the situation, Lord Varden. The prisoner is being brought to the audience room," a voice Jerol thought must be the wizard who had just passed them was saying.

"Very good, Jekke," a second voice answered. "I shall accompany you there, and we shall see just what this intruder has to say of himself. Perhaps, at last, we can get some word of Calum's activities. It has been far too long since we've heard from him. He should have returned long ago."

Jerol came back past the window at a light run, knowing if the occupants of the room were to return the way the runner had come, it would lead them directly to him and Roanne. He snagged Roanne's arm as he passed, and they barely made the last turn before they heard the doors behind them closing. Back in the storage room they had just left, Jerol left the door slightly ajar, and was doing his best to get a peek at the men as they went past them.

The younger of the two men who strolled past his view was wearing the same black robe they had observed the other wizards wearing. The man was slight of build, with dark hair, but beyond that, the dimness of the hall that had saved them moments before, now worked against them. The second man was far older, though not as old as Jerol expected, if he could imagine how a five hundred and some odd year old man should look. His hair was white, and his shoulders bent, but the gate of his stride belied his appearance. The one thing distinguishing him was the white robe he wore.

Roanne was plastered to Jerol's back as she peered over his shoulder through the slight crack between door and jam. "That was close," she whispered once the two men had gone.

Jerol shushed her, then checked the hall for any others who might happen to be passing. When he headed the same direction as the men, Roanne knew they had finally found something significant. Following was not easy since they had to wait until their quarry had made the end of the corridor before they could follow without being seen. Finally, as Jerol peeked around the corner from one hall to the next, the men turned through a large pair of double doors where three more wizards stood guard. Jerol quickly retreated, searching for another room where he could tell Roanne what he had heard, and they could figure out what to do next. The room they found turned out to be the kitchens. Across the room, two slaves were cleaning up the remains of the evening's meal. They did not pay the newcomers even the slightest attention, not even glancing their way. Jerol and Roanne moved to the corner of the room where shelves of pots and pans separated them from the slaves.

"The old man was Varden," Jerol stated flatly, and was unsurprised when Roanne drew in a deep breath and held it.

"Not ..." was all she could say when she finally let the air out of her lungs. "I checked as we followed, he is the large source of power they I sensed from down in the cave. Could he still be alive?"

"Who knows? He could be a descendant, or maybe they use the name like a title, bestowing it on whoever's in charge," Jerol shrugged and gave Roanne a second to digest the information before telling her the rest. "The other man, Jekke, told Varden they have a prisoner. We have to get into that room and see whom it is. This could be a disaster."

Roanne tried to think. With three wizards at the door, it was going to be difficult to enter without being seen. She knew, between the two of them, they could handle the guards, but doing it without alerting whoever might be in the room was a problem. Any spell she tried could be detected, and a fight would surely draw attention.

"Jekke called it the 'audience room'," Jerol suddenly remembered. "There has to be another way in."

"I'll bet the slaves don't use the same entrance as the wizards," Roanne suggested. "Most courts have a separate entrance for staff needed during audiences."

They found the entrance they needed by backtracking along outside of the wall to the audience chamber. It was hidden at the back of a small passage they might have overlooked had not the agonized screams of some person led them to it. People in power wanted their servants to come and go with as little fuss, and as little notice, as possible, which served Roanne and Jerol well. The back wall of the audience hall, where the small corridor led them, was covered with tapestries, convenient for hiding once they were in the room. At first, the dais hid their view of the room, but as they moved toward the corner of the room the tableau unveiled for them was chilling.

Both Roanne and Jerol had to check their reactions. Duval knelt before Varden, his face a grotesque composition of anguish. "I will ask you again," Varden's smile suggested he was enjoying this. He let go of Duval's left hand, and the arm flopped uselessly to the man's side. Duval would have collapsed, but another wizard grabbed him by the hair to hold him up. Reaching down, Varden took hold of Duval's right hand. "Who else is with you?" Varden demanded. "And where are they?" The arm just above Duval's right hand began to twist like a wet rag being wrung out. As far as the corner where they hid, Roanne and Jerol could hear the bones within the arm being ground to dust.

Roanne's stomach turned along with the arm. Even with her limited training in the healing arts she could tell what was happening before her was the corruption of all the healers stood for. Varden was reversing the healing process to tear apart muscle and crush bone. She could not bear to watch this, and without realizing, gathered as much power as she could and stepped out from the curtain. She had to be able to touch Duval in order to stop Varden.

Jerol had lost Roanne in the folds of the tapestries. The scene being acted out in the room had caused him to gag, and he was worried how Roanne might react. Of all his worries, though, her revealing herself had not even occurred to him. Drawing his sword, he stepped out beside her. "What are you doing?" he asked her under his breath as he took a position between her and several wizards to one side of the room.

"What's this?" Varden seemed genuinely surprised. "A witch and a fool who think a sword will somehow protect them?"

Roanne kept moving toward Varden, only vaguely aware of Jerol until she came up against a barrier someone had put between them and Duval.

"Don't," Jerol stopped her from destroying the barrier. "Think, about it, they don't know you can handle their spells. Let's keep them ignorant unless we really need it."

"They don't know about your sword, either," Roanne reminded him.

"Are you a healer, witch?" Varden interrupted them. He let Duval's other arm fall limp at his other side, and waved away the wizard holding Duval up. "Let her try to heal that. In the meantime, Jekke, get some extra men up to the tower, increase the power and the speed of the storm. I want to be sure those who fled into the desert do not make it back to the other side."

Varden watched and got the reaction he wanted, at least from Jerol. The moment the barrier came down Roanne was at Duval's side, her attention completely on the task before her. Varden backed away as she came to Duval, seating himself on a throne at the center of the dais to watch.

"Can you help him?" Jerol pushed Varden's threat to Sheilla to the back of his mind, taking up the best position he could to protect them from the wizards in the room. The four who left the room with Jekke, who he recognized from the hall, made the odds only slightly better. There were still ten wizards in the room, and Varden.

"I'm not a healer," Roanne was uncertain. It took much more strength to build, or rebuild in this case, than it did to destroy something the way Varden had destroyed Duval's arms. "He's unconscious now. They must have been forcing him to remain awake the whole time. If I don't do something, he's going to die."

"Don't kill yourself trying if you can't," Jerol advised, wishing Roanne would conserve her strength, but suspecting she was about to put everything she had into the healing if needed. "Duval knew the risks when we came here."

Roanne was already into the spell, cradling Duval's crushed left arm in her lap. Beads of sweat dotted her brow. Jerol realized he had never her seen her strain like this before, except in the making of the sword. If she were as drained when she finished as she was then, they would be in trouble. He was torn between hope she might actually heal Duval, and the need to conserve, and conceal wherever possible, their strengths.

Chapter 28

Sheilla's heart raced in cadence to the pounding of Winter's hoofs on the scorched ground of the wasteland. Literally lying out along the neck of her horse, she had stayed there since the beginning of her race against the storm. It was not until Winter unexpectedly pulled up, nearly dislodging her from the saddle in the process, that she had any real sense of the area around them. They were no more then half way through the waste, and the storm should be out over the ocean somewhere. Sheilla was left in confusion as the horse rose on its hindquarters, spinning in place like a top.

Then she heard the thunder. Could the wizards have sped up the storm? The spin left her disoriented for a moment, and she had to check the stars to get her bearing before searching the horizon to her south for any sign of the storm. She was on the edge of panic when she realized the sound was not thunder, but hoof beats. Turning toward the direction she had come from, she tried to see if she were being pursed. Maybe Spence and Stergis were trying to follow her, but she would have left them far behind by now. She knew Summer, Stergis' horse, could not hope to keep up with Winter.

Several horses let out a cry to go with the thunder then, but the sound was behind her she realized, from the direction she had been going. Her heart leaped. Help was on the way, which meant Telin must have gotten off a message before he had died.

Scanning this third horizon she could now make out the cloud of dust being raised by a number of horses, far more than she could have hoped for. Black shapes soon emerged from the cloud, which soon became recognizable as riders in the bright moonlight. The riders pulled up as well, as soon as they realized there was someone blocking their way. They milled about uncertainly for a moment before one rider moved forward. "Who goes there?" Timond's voice called out.

"Sheilla," she answered.

"What?" Timond seemed excited, agitated, and afraid all at the same time. "Where are the others? No, wait a minute. Someone give me the torch. You may as well tell your brother, he'll need to know one way or the other." A flame came to life as he used his power to light the torch. The thunder to the north and south of them suddenly changed as the various groups crossing the waste halted at Timond's signal.

"We can't just sit here and wait for the storm," Sheilla reminded Timond.

"Sure we can, there are several groups north and south of us, and each has its own protection," Timond had moved close enough for the torchlight to allow him to confirm Sheilla's identity. "Are you all right? Telin got off a partial message before he died, so we knew there was trouble."

Horses approached from the south, and a moment later Regus and his group entered the circle of light provided by the torch. "Settle everyone for the storm," Regus ordered as soon as he saw the reason for the delay. "Sheilla, bring us up to date. What's happened?"

Sheilla gave a full accounting of what she knew, between gulps of water Letitia thought to offer along with her extra quiver, which put a light into Sheilla's eyes when Letitia mentioned Samus had sent them. As she spoke, Lonora and Timond were arranging to shelter them against the inevitable arrival of the storm.

"So you have no idea if Telin's message included Roanne, Spence, or Talia. They may still be unaware of the situation," Regus summed up.

"Or Stergis and Lathom could have gone back to warn them," Sheilla's voice cracked just a notch at the mention of Stergis, but nobody mentioned it. They could see she was doing her best not to dwell on that.

"Who's commanding Timond's group?" Regus called out.

"I am, Your Highness," Karlon stepped out from the crowd around them.

"As soon as the storm passes I want your group to split up, send them up and down the line. As soon as the storm passes each group can move forward until they can see this forest, then wait. We can't be sure what surprises they may have waiting for us. Those with talent can shield each group from attack the same way they are shielding us from the storm. If things get hostile, we'll try to draw the opposition out into the desert. When the storm comes and they try to shield themselves, we'll burn their shields down in the storm."

"Make sure you wait until they are in the storm," Lonora suggested. "If we're lucky, the storm will cover what we're doing. They won't send everyone they have after us, and if we can avoid tipping off how much we know to those left behind, it will be to our advantage."

"Good thinking," Regus nodded toward Karlon.

It was then the storm came. The group watched as the wall of sand engulfed the group to their south. Everyone was on edge as it moved closer and closer to their position. Only a few of them had actually waited out a storm in a shelter before this, and those without talent searched the air around them for some hint to confirm the shield would protect them. One man picked up a handful of sand and tossed it to the side. Everyone near him visibly relaxed a little as the tossed sand met up with a barrier and slid back to the ground.

Spence and Talia tensed for the attack. If they could just take out the two guards to this side of the tower, they would be able to enter and see what they could do to destroy it. This was the second time they had gotten this far. The first time, they had to withdraw when five wizards had emerged from the keep to come join the tower. Shortly after, Spence had sensed an increase in the power being fed to the storm. The wizards were obviously trying to deal with the threat they were most aware of, those who had fled into the wasteland. The guards had been very alert for a time after, but they had waited as long as they could. They had to stop the storm now. Tracking the power being fed to the storm, Spence could tell it would not be long before it did what the wizards were hoping. Sheilla and the others had no way of knowing the storm was moving faster, now, and without Telin, had no chance of surviving it.

The tower had three entrances they could see, two from the palisades on either side, and one at ground level. There was no way to approach it on the palisade without being seen, so the pair had descended to the ground where they had used the shadows of the wall to get to the stairs on their side of the tower. The guards they wanted to take out were on the palisade, right above the stair. They were a few steps from the top of the stair, where the shadow of the inner rail of palisade still provided some cover.

Spence held up one finger before Talia's eyes. Then a second finger joined the first. They were going to try and coordinate their attack as best they could, going on three. As Spence unbent the third finger they both moved, and nearly spitted themselves on the pair of swords swinging in their direction. Both guards were down already and two looming figures were just getting over the outer edge of the rail, their swords ready for unforeseen circumstances like two people charging at them out of the dark.

"Lathom?" Talia squeaked just in time to halt the blade pressed against her abdomen. Spence managed to back away from the blade menacing him, but would have tripped back down the stairs if Stergis did not reach out and grab his collar.

"Get their robes on so it looks as though there are still guards up here," Stergis pointed to the two dead guards as he and Lathom ducked behind the inner rail.

"Where did you come from?" Spence dared to ask. "We heard them say three people went into the waste, and thought you went with Sheilla."

"We doubled back to take out this tower like Roanne suggested, to make sure Sheilla makes it," Lathom answered quietly.

"Any ideas how to do that?" Stergis watched the courtyard until the Spence and Talia had the robes on, then relaxed just a little.

Queen of the Spinners

"There are fifteen wizards inside," Talia told the newcomers to their effort. "With four other guards at the entrances. Even if I were as good as Roanne those are not good odds."

"We were planning to get the lay of the tower, then decide what to do," Spence added. "I have an idea, but I need to check inside first." He edged his way to the open doorway as he spoke. Feeling his way he found the shield he knew would be protecting the entrance, then quickly, before anyone else could say anything, he repeated the little trick Roanne had worked on the barrier they encountered in the cave. A few seconds was all he needed, then he was back outside, thinking quickly how to answer the questions on the three faces of his companions. "Ever boil water for tea?" he asked innocently.

Talia glared at him, and the two soldiers were not expecting that question. "When we burn shields, its like boiling water," Spence hurried to explain. "If you've ever made tea in one of those kettles, you know how the steam bursts out through the top when the pressure inside the kettle gets to be too much. I want to do the same thing here. If we seal up the bottom of this tower with a shield, and then burn it, it should blow the top right off the tower, and everyone up there with it. The only problem is, it will take a while for Talia and me to build up enough of a shield in the bottom here to be able to do the job."

"Won't they sense what we're doing?" Talia looked doubtful. "And," she hesitated, "I'm not sure I'm good enough to be much help."

"You're just not well practiced, but you're strong," Spence was also concerned about it, since they would need to control the burning so the pressure did not simply leak out the entrances at the base of the tower. "Just lend me your strength. As for the wizards, this tower is radiating so much energy now I doubt they would notice what we're doing."

"Then you had better get to work," Stergis suggested, "We and Sheilla don't have much time."

Lathom had slipped away from the small group during the explanation, and retrieved the ropes he and Stergis had used to scale the wall. As Spence and Talia went to work filling the tower, Lathom put the ropes over the wall there, providing them a way out when they were ready.

Spence leaned against the wall of the tower near the entrance, his hand resting lightly on the shield in the entrance. He used the shield as his starting point, expanding it out into the tower itself. The process was tiring. After about ten minutes Talia, who held his other hand to allow him to draw power through her, began to sag until Lathom slipped in behind her for support.

"I'm almost ready," Spence announced then. "Get her out of here." He had not even finished the sentence when he felt the withdrawal of her power from him, leaving him on his own. Talia did not even protest as Lathom slipped over the rail and down to the ground outside with her over his shoulder. Finished, Spence prepared himself to light the fire and destroy the tower. He had conserved his own strength, to try and control the fire. Picking a spot at the center of the tower on the top of the barrier he had built, he set the initial flame. Below that, just above the level of the two palisade entrances, he set a barrier of cold, so all the pressure had to rise within the tower.

The result was much more spectacular than anything he had imagined. A deafening roar sounded as the top of the tower literally exploded, sending the stones flying in every direction. Flames shot up into the sky, and the shock wave literally rocked the palisade on which Spence and Stergis still stood. The distraction of all this, and the drain on Spence's power caused him to loose control of the flames.

Stergis caught the surprised expression on Spence's face and knew this was much more than the wizard had expected. Grabbing Spence much the way Lathom had handled Talia, Stergis scrambled over the wall just as flames erupted from all three of the lower entrances to the tower. He had made nearly half the way down before the rope was burned, and the two of them fell the rest of the way. He tried to roll with the landing, but Spence's added weight made things awkward, and he jarred his leg. The wall of the fortress began to groan, and a huge crack formed in the outer wall of the tower. Spence's gut had been over Stergis' shoulder during the landing and the wind had been knocked out of him. When he did finally manage to get air into his lungs, it seemed to help clear his thinking. It did not take a healer to see Stergis' leg was broken.

When the tumultuous landing ended, Spence lay on the ground next to the wounded Stergis. Slipping his should under Stergis' left arm he helped the larger man to his feet, and they began to struggle their way toward the woods some two hundred yards away. After only thirty yards, the wall behind then came crashing to the ground where they had lain only moments before. The impact staggered them, dropping Spence momentarily to his knees before he could recover his balance. Stergis let out a yell as he tried to catch his balance on his damaged leg. At fifty yards, Spence tripped and fell, toppling Stergis along with him. Looking back, Spence saw the object he had tripped over was the body of a wizard, its robes darkened from burning. He scrambled back to his feet, dragging Stergis with him. There were more bodies, but Spence could not take the time to count. Finally, from ahead of him, three horses exploded from the underbrush marking the edge of the woods. Lathom rode the lead horse. Right behind him came another, with no rider, and then came Talia, who Spence was relieved was well enough to ride on her own. Lathom dismounted when he reached them, helping Spence to get Stergis into the saddle of one horse. Talia then offered a hand to Spence, and pulled him up behind her on her horse, while Lathom regained his own saddle. They turned then, veering slightly left where a break in the woods led out toward the farmlands, and the wasteland beyond.

They had just cleared the farmland when a patrol of wizards left to watch the border came barreling down the road from the opposite direction. Spence had power left, since he had let the burning get out of control. He launched two burning missiles at the five wizards before they could react to the trio riding down on them. Shields went up between them and the wizards, but when two erupted in flame from Spence's missiles, the others came right back down. The confused wizards did not stand a chance as Lathom led the charge right into their midst, taking three of the wizards down before the rest could think to run. Denied the use of a shield by Spence's move, another wizard fell to Stergis who was swinging wildly with his sword, barely able to sit in his saddle let alone fight well. The wizards could not fight at all using conventional weapons, though. When one wizard tried again to put up a shield, Spence burned it away even as Stergis' sword passed through the flames to open the man's chest. The final wizard had turned to run, but took a dagger in the back from Talia. They all watched as the man's horse kept running even after its rider fell out of the saddle on its back. The whole battle lasted only seconds.

"Let's get out of here," Lathom said as the riderless horses around them scattered into the woods.

"Wait," Talia looked wearily over her shoulder to Spence. "Can you lend me some power? I am a healer after all, I think with a little power I can take care of Stergis, once we get the bone set. If we wait, the damage will only get worse. Healing has its limits, that was the first thing I learned from my mother when I was younger."

"How long?" Lathom asked.

"Not long if you can help me set it straight," Talia answered. "If we don't, he's not going to be able to even stay in his saddle for long, let alone across the waste."

Setting a bone was something Lathom understood, if not the healing power to come after. "Keep a watch," he ordered Spence as he dismounted and then helped Stergis to the ground.

The windows at the far end of the audience hall came crashing in as the walls and floor shook. The thunder made Jerol think the wizards had lost control of the storm, and it was hitting the keep. He covered his ears, and did his best to cover both Duval and Roanne. Wizards throughout the hall were diving for cover. When the shaking floor finally subsided, he tried to pull Roanne to her feet, the resulting confusion was as good a cover for their escape as any they were likely to get. Roanne was limp, though, completely exhausted from her efforts to heal Duval. He thought she was unconscious, but when he turned her around to face him, tears were streaking her cheeks below an exhausted pair of eyes.

"He's still dying," Roanne cried, and slipped through Jerol's grasp to sit on the floor next to Duval. "I failed him, and I've exhausted myself so much I've failed you, too." She started to fall over, but Jerol caught her. Reaching around her, he checked Duval. The arms were healed as best he could tell, but the beat of Duval's heart at the throat was barely detectable.

"He's still alive," he tried to buoy Roanne's confidence.

"I don't have the strength to finish," Roanne shook her head. "There was too much pain to chase away. There was pain in the healing on top of the pain he had already suffered. He's hiding from the pain, and I don't have the strength to bring him back."

Jerol knew they had to get out now. If Roanne could not help Duval then it was time to run for it. He could carry Roanne if he had to. When he tried to stand, though, something pushed him back down on top of her. Then pushed even more, pinning him there. His hands groped for his sword, finding it on the floor beneath them both, trapped by their combined weight. Their chance to flee was gone.

"Roanne," Jerol searched for any scrap of an idea. "Use my strength."

"You don't have the power to draw on," Roanne sounded ready to pass out.

"Not power, strength," Jerol tried to explain. "There is power all around for you to draw on, what you need is the strength to do so. You use magic to provide energy in the healing process, energy you could draw on. Find energy in me and draw on it."

"I don't think ... ouch," Jerol interrupted Roanne by pinching her arm.

"Don't think about it, just do it, now!" he demanded.

Roanne did not think, she was too tired to think.

"Use the sword if you have to," Jerol insisted. "It's on the floor beneath you. It links the two of us, and it has power."

The sword? Power in the sword, Roanne reached for it, and found it. It filled her, giving her new life, new energy. Beyond that, she found more energy and strength and drew upon it. She needed the strength, it would heal Duval, and she would not fail. She could beat Varden. Healing Duval would defy him, conquer him. She drew more strength as she needed it, letting it flow through her now, to Duval who was beside her. It was not until she could feel Duval's chest rise and fall as he breathed, could feel the beat of his heart in his chest that she even considered where the strength was coming from. "Jerol! No! What did I do?"

"What you needed to do," Jerol's voice was close to her, and stronger than she thought it would be. "I'll be fine."

"Varden?" Roanne suddenly remembered where they were, as if she had been elsewhere during the healing. "What's going on?"

"There was some kind of eruption out in the courtyard," Jerol explained it all as best he could. "Everyone rushed out to investigate, but we're pinned here. Someone put a small bubble over the top of us."

"A very small bubble," Roanne corrected him. "How long ago was that?"

"They'll probably be back any time," Jerol answered. "I could see flames through the windows earlier, but it's been some time since they went out. It must have been a couple of hours since we entered the keep."

"I need more time," Roanne shook with anger. "I'm in no condition to fight him. I think I can defend us from his attacks. All I need to do is put up a shield. But I'm not sure I could fight back."

Chapter 29

In the desert the storm had suddenly winked out of existence before it could engulf the shelter where Shiella, Regus, and the others waited. I love you, Stergis, and we're coming, so just hang in there," Sheilla whispered her thanks. Noticing the confused looks surrounding her, she explained. "Someone must have taken out the tower, ending the storm. We had better get moving, I don't suppose the wizards will be very happy about this." Their shelter came down, leaving them open to the last gusts, as the sand came down from the sky like rain. After only a few minutes the moon and stars were once more visible, along with the burning tower pointing out their destination to the west.

"Mount up!" Regus commanded, realizing his friends were probably in a battle for their lives at that very moment.

The burning tower had been extinguished before the forest in came into sight, and Regus called a halt to consult with the others on a plan of attack. Archers, watching the tree line from each group, nearly shot at the three riders rushing out of the woods in their direction. "It's Stergis," Sheilla knocked aside the bow of the archer nearest her, then kicked Winter out to the front to meet Stergis and the others, with Regus and Letitia quickly following. Behind Stergis a number of riders were emerging from the forest, forming up in a line between the invaders and the woodland boundary to their oasis. They stayed there, though, not advancing out into the waste.

"Jerol and Roanne were still inside the keep, and Duval was prisoner," Lathom summed up their report to Regus a few moments later. They had retreated to their own line, and both sides had put up shields for protection. For now it seemed to be a standoff.

"We'll have to assume the worst, then. You said one of the wizards mentioned the name Lord Varden?" Regus waited a moment for Spence to nod. "As unlikely as it may seem, he might still be alive, which suggests a lot of power, and then there is his little army of wizards." He gestured toward the line opposite them. "Any suggestions, anyone? From what you've said, they are not very well organized, could we use that against them?"

"We could just flame their shields and ride right through them," Spence suggested. "When I used flames against one of the guards he panicked, became confused. After I had burned his work once the others would not try it again, except for one."

"It's our best weapon, Spence," Regus shook his head. "I would prefer to hold it back a while. Someone over there is going to be bright enough to figure out they could do the same to our shields. Is there any other way we can attack them?"

"I could attack their shields without flaming them, so they might not detect what's happening," Spence shrugged. "Roanne showed me the spell at the keep, but I'm a bit weak, and nobody else has tried it."

"We need to take out the two riders at the rear of their line," Stergis was studying the opposition. "That's their command. None of them have any fighting experience, they'll break and run if we show them we can kill their best."

Letitia whispered something to Sheilla, who nodded agreement before they both cleared their throats. "We can take them out," Sheilla announced, while Letitia went to get their crossbows.

The others all raised their eyebrows at such an announcement. "The arrows the smith made for me," Sheilla took the weapon Letitia handed to her. "They're made from the steel chips leftover from Jerol's sword. At Galore, his sword cut through the shields, which means the arrows might do the same. They certainly go through trees with ease, Letitia tested one of them."

"So that's what's so special about those things," Regus commented thoughtfully. "I wondered what prompted Samus to send them."

"It would certainly send them into panic," Lathom agreed. "They might think all of our weapons can penetrate the shields."

Queen of the Spinners

He swallowed deep before adding, "But should we pick other archers to use the arrows. You're both fine marksmen," he hurriedly added at the sight of Letitia and Sheilla's reactions, "but we can't afford any misses."

"We won't miss," Letitia almost hissed. "Those two behind their line are as good as dead. I suggest the rest of you get ready to run down the rest of them before they make it to the keep."

Regus held onto any objections he might have had. "What do you think, Spence, Stergis?"

"I'm not going to argue with the lady," Spence was very conscious of Talia standing next to him. Even tired as she was, he would not want her looking at him the way Sheilla had looked at Lathom. "It was no easy shot when Sheilla killed Calum, I saw it. I've never seen Letitia use a bow before."

"I know Sheilla can do it, I've been hunting with her," Stergis watched his own words. "Letitia is good at hitting targets. You would know better than I, Regus."

Regus moved closer to Letitia, "It's not like shooting targets, or even a deer," he warned her quietly. "Are you sure you're up to this?"

"I know," Letitia closed her eyes, "If it were me in there, Roanne would not be sitting here debating. I can do this. I came because I can use a crossbow, and you needed archers. If I could not do this, I would have stayed behind."

"Lathom is only doing his job," Regus took her hand and squeezed it in support. "And if we had Roanne with us, instead of in there, you're right, there would be no debate. The fact she is not, is in itself cause for debate."

"Let me do this Regus," Letitia asked in a steady voice. Regus saw a confidence in her he had not seen before, and he liked it.

"Pass the word, start moving forward slowly, but stay behind our lead group. We'll charge when the commanders go down," Regus ordered the others. "Use flames if they don't panic, but not until we're close enough not to give them time to realize they could use the same tactic. Once we break their line, every third

293

group along our line will fall back to clean up any stragglers, all the other groups are to head directly for the keep. Form up again in the order we have here surrounding the keep. It looks as if most of what they have has been sent to meet us here, but I don't want any suicide charges at the keep until we have some idea what they might have held back." Karlon and his men disappeared into the night.

Regus gave Karlon's men time to move to the edges of their forces. "All right, you two take the lead," he ordered his sister and future wife. "Let each other know who has which target. How close do you need to be?"

"Just a little closer," Letitia said, getting agreement from Sheilla. They were more than a hundred yards from the enemy.

"Fine, but wait until we get really close, like from fifty yards," Stergis suggested. "The men have to be able to close the distance between us and them quickly once the commanders go down. Also, given the way these people think, they won't see women as a threat to them."

"You two," Regus singled out Talia and Spence, "Stay to the rear, you're both exhausted from what you've already done. You need more time to recover. I don't want any arguments, besides I want the two of you to be sure to protect Letitia and Sheilla once the fighting starts," he confided so the women he mentioned would not hear.

Everyone was mounting up as Regus spoke. They formed a line directly behind Letitia and Sheilla who moved forward at a leisurely stroll, walking their horses. At fifty yards Letitia glanced back over her shoulder at Regus, who waved them further on, holding the rest of the line back slightly. "Lonora, you are shielding them aren't you?" He asked to the older woman next to him.

"I'll open a gap for the arrows when the time comes," Lonora told him. ""I would not trust anyone else for this."

The wizards were pointing to the two women leading their enemy forward. A few were laughing at the notion women were leading the attack against them. The two commanders had positioned themselves directly opposite from the Sheilla and Letitia.

"Close enough," Regus called just loud enough for Letitia to hear. Their line was at fifty yards from the enemy. Sheilla and Letitia were only forty yards. "If either of you misses from here, your gender will not suffice as an excuse."

Sheilla glared back at her brother. Then knelt in the sand. Both women had already notched the bolts they would use. Quietly, they had discussed what they were about to do. "Ready," announced Sheilla once she was sighted on her target.

More laughter floated across the space between the two small armies. The wizards obviously saw no threat in two women with crossbows.

"Ready," Letitia announced she had her aim. They both waited two heartbeats, then together said, "Go." Both of the targets went down, knocked completely out of their saddles at such close range. Sheilla was up and in her saddle even as the dust was rising from the hooves of all the horses around them and the charge was on. Letitia did not rise immediately. Her mind replayed what she had just done several times before hands grabbed onto her arms. Talia and Spence all but dragged her away from the battle about to be waged.

"Damn Sheilla, Regus will have our heads," Spence said as Sheilla's horse caught up to the rest of the charge. Talia wrapped Letitia in her arms, unsure whether her future queen was about to become sick.

In truth it was not much of a battle. As with their previous fight with the wizards of their own kingdom, when the confidence of the wizards, which bordered on contempt for their opponents, was shattered by their initial attack, panic set in quickly. As the two sides came together, flames sprouted only here and there as spinners and Tularand wizards attacked the few remaining shields. Virtually all the enemies close enough to see their commanders go down had turned to flee. Those farther from the center of the action saw the panic of their brethren, and became confused. Few managed to stand their ground, and when their shields went up in flames, what little composure remained melted in the heat of the flames. Several wizards tried to form weapons, which burned in their hands as quickly as they were made.

Seeing the panic in the enemy, Regus charged right through the enemy line, cutting down two wizards as he went. They had the wizards outnumbered with magic effectively neutralized. He noted how sparse the flames were, indicating how much of a route the fight had become. He almost pitied the enemy, until he recalled the vacant look in Shiva's eyes when he had first met her. He was through the line now, taking down another wizard who was trying to flee. He let the anger at what was done to Shiva, and all the other victims of Calum's teaching, drive him on beyond the edge of the forest. Stergis and Lathom were right with him, and from the corner of his eye he caught sight of Sheilla, who let go another bolt from her crossbow that drove a wizard back against a tree, then passed through the wizard and the tree. The sight gave him pause, and he looked around to find Letitia, nearly panicking himself when she was nowhere to be found.

"What's the matter?" Lathom pulled up along with him. Stergis went on ahead, trying to keep up with Sheilla, whose horse's speed was beginning to show when she came upon a clear path through the woods.

"Talia and Spence have her," Lonora rode up to Regus, knowing what he was looking for.

Regus surveyed the area, one final time, then whirled his horse back after Stergis and Sheilla. "To the keep," he called out, and heard the order echoed throughout the woods to either side of him.

"I want you to meet some other guests who have been with me for some time," Varden's voice intruded on the silence that had settled on the audience hall. The weight holding Jerol down was lifted, but when he sprang to his feet, snatching up his sword, he found the shield still intact, only moved back to allow them some room. Varden stepped onto the dais in front of them, a woman following at his heels. When he seated himself on his throne, the woman sat at his feet. "But then I believe you already know of Ariele, I understand she was well known in your land before she came here," Varden's eyes soaked up the pain in Roanne's expression, only Jerol's hand on her shoulder restrained her from striking out with whatever she had left. Unlike the other slaves they had seen, the collar and leash on Ariele were plainly visible.

"You know it pains me to see us come to battle," Varden went on. "My men have detected a line of shields around the waste. Evidently Calum was not very circumspect about with whom he shared our knowledge. I take it he is dead, as will be those seeking to attack my little oasis."

"We uncovered your plans to conquer our kingdom," Jerol answered him. "Did you think we would not resist?"

"Is that the royal 'we'?" Varden laughed. "I had no such plans, though I am beginning to suspect Calum did. Yes, I think he even meant to betray me, his father. If you had not killed him, I think I would do it myself."

"If not to invade, what was Calum doing in Tularand?" Jerol challenged Varden's assertion.

"He was sent to retrieve something for me," Varden seemed unconcerned. "I am getting older, magic can only do so much to replenish a tired and worn body. Before I die, however, I intend to have a son, a special son, in which I intend to transfer my consciousness. That was why I kept Ariele, to bear that son for me. Unfortunately, all she bore were eleven daughters and only three sons. The daughters were destroyed, of course. Of the sons, Calum was the strongest, but not strong enough for my purposes. Ariele once told of something, though. Of a daughter from her and her pesky husband, I think Kendal is his name."

The tapestry behind Varden pulled back at his gesture. Behind it was a large crystal in which was contained the shadow of a man. "I used to allow him some pleasure now and then," as Varden looked back, the crystal began to glow showing the man within it clearly, a man in utter agony. "That was before Ariele succumbed completely to the new leash I developed. Since then, I found no need to pleasure my toy, and I do so enjoy his pain. What has it been, now, fifteen years of pure agony? I imagine he has gone completely mad by now. Oh yes, he is still alive after all this time, alive and suffering."

"Anyway, I digress," Varden returned his attention to the trio before him. "Calum was simply to retrieve Ariele's daughter for me. He seems to have failed in that little endeavor. All is not lost, though, as you seem to have brought yourself to me, Roanne. There could be no other from Tularand with the power you have. If the power I sense in you is real, you may finally succeed where your mother has failed me all these years, if you bear me a son powerful enough for my purposes."

Roanne was on her feet, making it difficult for Jerol to hold her back. "Not, yet," he urged her. She shook his hand from her shoulder, but somehow held herself in check.

Varden made two quick gestures with his hands. A collar and leash snapped into place around Roanne's throat, and Jerol found he was walled off from her. "That is a very special collar, my dear. It gives me control of your power. In time it will give me control of your mind, as well as your body. Ariele is incapable of thinking any thought I do not provide for her, are you my pet?" He toyed with the hair at the back of Ariele's head.

"No, master," the woman on the dais replied.

Varden stood now, approaching Jerol, holding the other end of Roanne's leash. From the fear in Roanne's eyes, Jerol knew Varden was not bluffing.

"I know who she is, but who do we have here?" Varden gestured to Jerol and the still unconscious Duval. "Ah, Prince Jerol of Tularand, and Duval, Captain of the Royal Guard. Thank you, Roanne, the leash is working already. Duval I have little need for, though I suppose he would work well in the fields. The Prince, however, I think I can use." Varden circled Jerol, who realized he was surrounded by shields. Roanne's fingers were working frantically at her throat, trying to free herself. "It seems she has very strong feelings for you, your Highness.

Perhaps I will replace Kendal with you. The cage you are in will grow smaller with time, only when it reaches you it will grow into you, becoming part of you. It will keep you alive, but like her father, I will be able to control what you feel, pleasure or pain. You will help keep her in line just as her father aided me in controlling her mother."

Varden retreated to his throne on the dais, where he tugged at Roanne's leash, "Come and join your mother my pet," he laughed. "I could hardly have hoped she would even come close to the beauty of her mother. I think I shall enjoy the coming years. You have provided a new pet to please me, and a new toy to torture."

Roanne resisted the tug on the leash held by Varden. He tugged again, harder this time, causing her to stumble against the front edge of the dais. In her initial panic she failed to notice everything the collar was doing to her. Varden seemed to invade her mind, but her frantic thoughts made it nearly impossible for him to pick out any one thought he might be able to use against her. That he had picked up Jerol's name was the result of her fear for him. When he ordered her to join him, an impulse to obey went through her, but she was fighting as best she could. Unnoticed in all this was the renewal of her strength. The tether was not a one-way link, though Varden held the dominant end of the relationship. She had needed to fill the void of power, and the collar was doing so, without her even realizing what it was doing, using Varden as the source of the power. Varden either did not notice, or did not care. Whether he held the power on his own, or she, he evidently had control of it. Try as she might, there was nothing she seemed able to do on her own.

Jerol could not stand what was happening. They had bought as much time as possible, now was the time to do something. He whirled around in a move that would have drawn attention on any ballroom floor, dragging his sword across the inner surface of his invisible cage. The walls of the cage shattered around him. From the corner of his eye he watched Varden, who was shocked at Jerol's ability to free himself. Varden was gesturing wildly, and Jerol knew he had only moments before Varden countered him. With Varden out of reach, Jerol went to next available target, slicing through the tether from Roanne's collar.

Roanne saw when Jerol broke free of his prison, and prayed he would free her next, giving her the chance to do something. The instant the sword severed the link between her and Varden she was ready. Varden's surprise at Jerol's success was compounded by what happened then. The collar holding Roanne erupted in flame. Also lit was the end of the tether, which went nearly unnoticed until the flames reached Varden's hand.

Varden was thoroughly confused, he did not understand how Jerol had freed himself, and then came what he thought was an attempt at suicide by Roanne. This had all begun as a result of his need of her services, and rather than attack, Varden's first thought was to try to regain control. A new collar was his first impulse, but it burned in his hand along with the previous tether. Not in half a century had he experienced any pain, let alone the agony running through his arm. His screams echoed from the walls of the chamber.

Jerol moved quickly, picking up Duval to carry him out of harm's way. He grabbed for Roanne's arm, but she shook him off.

Up on the dais, Roanne had freed her mother from the collar, but her mother still only sat at the feet of the man who had imprisoned her for so long. Roanne was trying to free her father, but Varden had been right about the crystal, it had become a part of him, and she had no way to separate them. To her horror, her father had simply fallen limply to the floor. She was not even paying attention when Varden's scream of pain, turned into a roar of anger. It was Jerol, staggering under Duval's weight, who positioned himself between her and the wizard.

Jerol had no idea of what to expect. Roanne or another wizard might have been able to sense the magic Varden turned lose in their direction. All he had was the sword, which he waved about aimlessly, searching for something to strike against. It met with something, shattering Varden's spell. All that reached the intended victims was a breeze as the battering ram Varden launched at them dissolved before the power of the sword.

Varden was enraged. Using his one good hand, he lifted Ariele by the hair and all but threw her at them. "Destroy them!" he ordered. The otherwise placid expression Ariele had shown all this time turned suddenly savage as she launched herself at them.

Jerol backed away, uncertain what to do. Kendal soon joined the attack. Roanne had freed his body from the crystal, but the crystal remained inside him, and Varden was taking advantage of that.

Roanne put up a shield between them and her parents, which Ariele charged headlong into, momentarily dazing her with its impact. "Jerol, what do I do?" It was the first words she had said to him since the battle began, and the desperation in her voice tore at his heart. When Kendal came to the shield it suddenly flared up and was gone, Varden had turned the table on their best weapon against him. Unfortunately, the part of the crystal remaining in Kendal also caught fire. The body that came through the shield simply collapsed, a charred shell of what it had been only seconds before. "No!" Roanne screamed, while Jerol continued to pull her back away from Ariele, who was quickly recovering from her encounter with the shield.

Ariele scrambled over the corpse of her husband as if it were not there. Behind her on the dais, Varden was pressing his advantage. Roanne's senses warned of another ram being sent at them, and having no other choice, put up a shield. Varden tried to light the shield, but she fought him for control of the temperature, cooling as quickly as he heated. The ram presented another problem though, and Ariele was caught between them. The crunch of bones as the ram trapped Ariele against the shield shocked even Jerol. When Roanne brought down the shield, Ariele's limp form was flung at them by the force of the ram Varden was still pushing at them. Jerol realized they had backed themselves into a corner of the room, and expected whatever had crushed Ariele would now get them. Nothing happened, however. In that moment he got a look at Varden, who had a look triumph on his face.

Roanne was pinned against the wall by her mother's body, growing more hysterical by the second. Another collar had been put around her throat in the moment she had let her guard down in a vain attempt to protect her mother. She was cut off from her ability to use the power they needed to defeat Varden. Jerol saw what had happened and moved to sever the tether again, but collapsed in agony next to Roanne. Roanne scrambled from under the weight of her mother to where Jerol lay, but could see no sign of what was causing the pain. Without her power, she did not know what she could do for him had she been able to locate the problem.

A shadow engulfed the corner where they had tried to make their stand. Looking up, Roanne saw Varden had come down from the dais, and was standing over them, his madness gleaming in his eyes.

"I put the crystal inside him this time," Varden laughed, "In his lungs where it will grow until it swallows him. It may take days of agony, but it will not kill him, because the crystal will feed on his life, on his agony." He tugged on the leash, dragging Roanne away from Jerol. "And I will do the same to you if you do not please me. Kiss the hand the controls your life from this point on." He held out the hand she had burned at the start of the battle, the battle she had lost. An impulse from the collar was trying to force her to do as he ordered. She began to reach forward to take the hand in hers.

The doors to the room slammed open then, causing Varden to turn and see what had interrupted his moment of triumph. A lone woman stood there in the door, a crossbow aimed at the wizard. Behind her, several men were coming down the corridor from the main entrance to the keep. Varden checked quickly, but could sense no power in any of these new attackers. His laughter echoed through the room even as he shielded himself from such a pitiful attempt to stop him. These people were full of surprises, though, and when the bolt from the crossbow hit his chest, his barely had time to register the shock. The bolt tore its way completely through him. Splattering blood all over the kneeling Roanne, and prone Jerol. His laughter was still echoing around the room as his body fell first to its knees, then toppled backward. The bolt ended up buried nearly the length of the shaft in the wall above Roanne's head.

Chapter 30

Roanne awoke in a bed, confused and afraid. Her body did not seem to want to listen to her. She tried to feel her neck, but her hands would not move from her sides. Across the room she could see Jerol's body lying in another bed. Were they both dead? That must be it, there was no other explanation.

Letitia came into view. She looked down on Jerol, before turning toward Roanne. "Lonora," Letitia called, "Roanne's awake again." Letitia sat on the edge of the bed next to Roanne who just stared at her blankly. "Are you all right? How do you feel?" Letitia asked.

"I'm dead," Roanne's voice cracked from disuse. "I'm just waiting for you to bury me."

Letitia smiled. "You're not dead, Roanne."

"How is she?" Lonora came up behind Letitia. Concern written over her features.

Roanne just blinked several times. "I failed Lonora. Failed everyone, Jerol, you, Letitia, Regus and Sallas. I failed my parents." Roanne closed her eyes, turning away from the two women looking down on her.

"How did you fail?" Letitia put a hand under Roanne's chin and made her look at them.

Roanne's eyes looked past them then, to the bed across the room. "He's dead, isn't he? That's how I failed. My parents are dead."

"No, no, he'll be fine," Letitia assured her. "He's just sleeping, it's two hours until dawn after all."

"I can't move," Roanne pointed out. "Why can't I move? I must be dead. I would rather be dead than have a collar around my throat. Why can't I move?"

"Whoa," Letitia reached out to hold down Roanne's shoulders. Roanne fought for several minutes before settling back down. This was more like what they had seen from her the

Queen of the Spinners

past three days. "You can move, Roanne. There is no collar. It's over, and there will never be another collar."

"Why can't I move then, it was the collar that stopped me before," Roanne insisted, her eyes shut tight.

"Look at me," Letitia actually slapped Roanne to get her to open her eyes again. "We've been through this before, there is no collar. We had to restrain you. You kept trying to claw at your throat. You almost killed yourself the last time."

"Before?" Roanne did open her eyes at least. "What did you mean?"

"It's been five days since the fight, Roanne," Lonora explained. "You've been out of it. Whenever you seemed to come around you clawed at your throat. We've had to have someone watching every minute to keep you from hurting yourself."

"Release me," Roanne demanded, even as Letitia began to loosen the straps holding Roanne's left arm down. Roanne's hand went right for her throat, but Letitia grabbed her wrist and pull it away. "I need to know," Roanne pleaded.

"Let her go," Jerol rose up from the other bed and crossed the room, around to the other side of Roanne's bed. He loomed there, ready to stop her if she tried anything.

Roanne's hand searched her throat all the way around to the back. When she fell back into the bedding, she did not know how to react. Jerol freed her other hand, and she had to check again to believe it was real. "What happened? My memories are all scrambled," she shook her head in an effort to clear them. "The last thing I remember was Jerol down, me with a collar around my throat. Somebody else came in, but Varden was ready for them. I think he used me to put up a shield."

"It was Sheilla," Jerol told her. "Varden was not ready for her."

"Sheilla?" Roanne could not believe it. "The blood? There was blood all over."

"Varden's blood," Jerol said. "Sheilla killed him. She's got quite the reputation as a wizard killer now, Calum and then Varden."

"But how?" Roanne could not figure it out. "Varden had shields."

"She had special bolts made for her crossbow," Letitia picked up explanation. She went to table near the door, and came back with one of the bolts. "The tip is made from the chips left over when you made Jerol's sword. When she fired, the bolt went right through Varden's shield."

Slowly Roanne figured it out. She remembered the bolt, buried deep in the wall. The blood was not hers, not Jerol's. Who else was there? "Duval? How is Duval?"

"He's fine," Lonora took her hand. Jerol told me what had been done to him. "I'm not sure I could have done what you did."

Regus and Sheilla came in then, Regus stepping up to the bed behind Letitia, his hand going around her waist. "I hope this is a positive sign. The last time ..."

It took several hours for everyone to tell their individual stories of what had transpired that day. Over the next several days Roanne tried to make sense of it all. Some of it made no sense, like Letitia feeling guilty she was unable to charge forward into the battle after killing the commander of Varden's army of wizards. Other parts were confusing. Such as how Stergis and Lathom had worked their way back to the keep without being caught. Finally there was her own role in all this, parts of which were still fuzzy in her memory. She had the time sort out the details of each story, though, since Lonora refused to let her out of bed for two more days.

Somewhere in all the talking Roanne learned they were staying at Bessal's estate in Bergian. Lonora had left strict orders Roanne was never to be left alone. So even when she found her way out into the gardens, which surpassed even Letitia's fervent description, there was Talia only a few paces behind.

"I need some time alone," Roanne turned on the other woman.

"Lonora would have my head," Talia leaned back against a tree. "She says you are not to be left alone, no matter what."

"In that case," Jerol came out the door behind Talia, "Allow me the pleasure of watching her."

"Why?" Roanne demanded. For answer, Jerol took her by the arm, leading her farther into the garden.

"Lonora is still afraid you'll hurt yourself," Jerol settled on a bench along the path, stretching out his legs. "Some of the girls we've freed since this began have committed suicide, and frankly, you gave us all several scares with the way you almost clawed yourself to death over the past days."

"I was delirious," she tried to explain what was still unclear to even her. She refused a seat, pacing nervously along the path. "I had to free myself from the damn collar."

"The collar was not there," Jerol pointed out. "There's something else I don't think Lonora has told anyone. I think she is not sure about it."

"What?" Roanne turned on him.

"You still haven't used your power," Jerol took hold of Roanne's wrist and turned it over, revealing the bruises still evident from when they had bound her in bed. "Not when you were delirious, and not since you finally woke up. These should have healed by now. Are you waiting for some special occasion? Bessal was afraid you would bring the estate down around all our ears when you were delirious, but Lonora never caught even a hint of power in you. Is it gone?"

"Does it matter?"

"Not to me, but someone has to take up the leadership of the Spinners and the wizards. The nobles need reassurance you will support those who supported you, and that you're capable of giving the support. The family wants to be sure you are still the same person who went into the keep, or to know what they can do to help, if you are not."

"How can I be the same after what happened in there? My parents are dead, and I can't even seem to mourn them. I lost the battle with Varden. He had crushed me, and I was about to give in when Sheilla came along. I let you down again. That's twice Sheilla has had to cover my mistakes."

"What mistakes?"

"You know damn well," Roanne stopped her pacing directly in front of Jerol, glaring down at him. "You tried to warn me. I almost sacrificed us both because I was not thinking about what I should have been doing."

"Try telling Duval that."

"It wasn't just that. I had a chance to get Varden, after the leash burned his hand. He was confused, and angry. He had let his guard down. I should have ended it right there. Instead I tried to free my parents. The result was you were nearly killed. You were counting on me."

"I think we covered this ground once already, and it has nothing to do with the reason you won't use your power. You think you should have single handedly went in there and simply ended the whole thing. You forget I was also counting on the rest of my family, my friends, and my people. You're still seeing this as your fight, when in reality it was all our fight. No one person could have gone into the wasteland and done what we did together, all of us."

Roanne seated herself at the opposite end of the bench from Jerol. "There hasn't been any need to use my power," she shrugged, getting back to the original subject. "If I thought I was still collared when I was delirious, I would have thought I couldn't use my power."

"You don't sound very sure," Jerol took up the pacing. "Are you trying to convince me, or yourself?"

"Maybe I'm just not ready," Roanne jumped to her feet and began walking further down to trail, stopping after only a few steps.

"Ah, now I think we're getting somewhere," Jerol put an arm around her waist, and they continued to walk together. "The power is there, you're simply not using it."

Roanne rubbed at the bruises Jerol had exposed only moments before. "It is said that healers cannot heal themselves, and Lonora was never able to explain how I was doing it. Well, I don't think it was my power. I think it was my mother's magic doing the healing, but I don't understand how. If I did, I could make sure nothing ever happened to you, or the others. It was that presence of my mother's power that told me they were still alive after all this time. Now that they are dead …"

Roanne leaned against his shoulder as they walked. They came to a flowerbed, where the stem of one of the flowers was broken. Roanne stooped a moment and healed the flower before they went on their way.

About the Author

Mice with eyes that glow in the dark, and frothing cauldrons growing strange life forms are not from Anthony Fredericks' imagination, but his reality as a research scientist. Is it any wonder his imagination tends to run wild every once in a while? He survived his undergraduate education on the classes where grades were based on papers rather than tests. In addition to his science, he has read more science fiction and fantasy than is probably considered healthy, and supplemented that with doses of renaissance festivals whenever the opportunity arises. Mix all this with the right combination of nucleic acids and amino acids and what do you get? Hopefully a scientist with enough imagination to see what is not always obvious, and while he sits at his bench pipeting away, the primordial soup of his imagination may germinate a story or two.

You can visit Anthony, or David Plieth as he is known in his other life, at anthonyfredericks.com. The web sight features excerpts from his fiction, photos from renaissance festivals, and some natural photography. There are knights jousting, fairies and gypsies dancing, and hawks and falcons flying. See the beauty of the world of birds, and the striking colors most people never take the time to notice in the dragonflies. You can even let Anthony/Dave know what you think of it all.

So, what do you get when you cross a mouse and a jellyfish?

The Story...

There is a new wizard, Calum, from outside the kingdom, who, though young, brings an older form of magic with him. The Council of Wizards, anxious to regain lost prestige, is willing to sell out the kingdom to gain this magic, and Mathia, a member of the council, is willing betray his own niece to be at the center of it all. Roanne, Mathia's niece, is the child of an unusual marriage between the Queen of the Spinners and a wizard. Untrained in the use of power, she unwittingly escapes Calum, discovering by accident the secret to defeating Calum's magic. With the support of the Spinners, untrained women with the power of magic, Roanne allies herself with Regus, Jerol, and Sheilla, the sons and daughter of King Sallas. Together they face Calum and his wizard allies to prevent them from enslaving the kingdom. But is Calum their real enemy, or just the emissary of a far greater enemy? The secret to that answer might lie in the Varden Wasteland, the very place where Roanne's parents had disappeared when she was just a child.